THE MAGPIE WINTER

The Magpie Winter

A Ghost Story

One for Sorrow
Two for Joy
Three for a Girl
Four for a Boy

Renira Barclay

First published in Great Britain in 2020 by R. Barclay

Copyright © Renira Barclay 2020

Renira Barclay has asserted her right under the Copyright, Designs and Patents Act 1988 to be identified as the author of this work.

Jacket illustrations by Renira Barclay.

Edited, designed and produced by Tandem Publishing
http://tandempublishing.yolasite.com/

ISBN: 978-1-5272-7712-0

10 9 8 7 6 5 4 3 2 1

A CIP catalogue record for this book is available from the British Library.

Printed and bound in Great Britain by CPI Group (UK) Ltd, Croydon CR0 4YY.

For my brother, Shane

PART I

_____

CAMELLIA

November 1962

What's the matter with Finn? Why don't his legs work properly on a walk? I don't like this weather and I don't like that tree up ahead in the fog. My pram wheels are getting very muddy and the tree scares me.

'Nanny Jan,' I say. 'What are those things hanging in that tree?' I am pleased Nanny Jan is listening.

'Those are ash keys, Camellia. That's an ash tree.' Another sort of tree for my list.

'WAIT FOR ME!' It is Finn. We've been walking along the lane for half an hour. Nanny Jan says it's good for our constitution. I turn my head and my duffle coat hood goes over my eye. Now I'm like Finn with his eye patch. I think his eye patch is stopping his legs from working. Poor old Finn.

Nanny Jan and I wait for him to catch up and we talk about ash keys. I spend so much time waiting for Finn to catch up. It makes me sad. My legs are six and a half years old and quite long, but Finn's are four and a half years old and quite short. I suppose he can't help it.

'Who do those keys belong to?' asks Finn, pointing.

'Witches.' Nanny Jan's reply is automatic. Finn's eye is very round, and I bet the one behind the patch is round too.

Nanny Jan is walking on. I check Baby in the pram. She's still asleep and her eyelashes are beautiful and black. This is Dorothy Baby and she's my favourite. Out of all my dolls she enjoys walks the best.

'Why do witches need keys?' Finn's voice is low.

Nanny Jan is way ahead. I sigh, patting Dorothy Baby's

blanket. My feet are cold in my new furry boots. Finn will need an answer otherwise he will whine.

'Why do witches need keys?' Here we go.

'They don't,' I say. 'Nanny Jan's just being silly.'

Finn pushes his eye patch. He does a lot of pushing his eye patch these days. Poor Finn. It's for his own good, Nanny Jan says, and so does Mummy. So, it must be true.

'I saw something behind,' he says. Nobody notices what he says. Well I do, but I am not going to say anything to *that*! Finn catches me up.

'Are the witches like Gretel's witch?'

I look at him. I know exactly what he means. He goes *on* about that fairy tale. I check Dorothy Baby again and march on. Finn's getting left behind again, and I can't see him very well through the fog. It's getting dark. Why can't Nanny Jan notice properly that Finn's legs are tired? Why does it always have to be me?

'Something behind me,' says Finn. He turns towards home.

'It's probably one of the dogs,' I say. I know how to calm him.

I wonder if he has noticed both dogs are behind Nanny Jan who's ahead of us. Banger's little white legs are brown with mud, just like my pram wheels. Bramble's black tail goes wag-wag.

Finn hasn't moved.

'I saw it.' I sigh. The dogs lie hasn't worked.

'Nanny Jan!' I shout. 'STOP!' I see her shoulders are annoyed. I push my pram up to Finn.

'Where is it now?' Finn pushes the patch off his eye and points down the lane. Into the fog.

'Perhaps you were seeing things?' I know I'm sounding like Mummy. Finn's mouth is pressed into a line.

'It was there!' Nanny Jan walks back to us.

'Does your eye hurt?' she offers.

'No.' Finn sits down in the road. He's gone on strike. He does this.

'I saw it.' His voice is very quiet.

It's getting dark. A duck flies over our heads, home to her

pond I should think, and a blackbird is calling goodnight in the hedge. Nanny Jan bends down to Finn, replacing the patch on to his eye. Then she lifts him to his feet.

'Home James.' Her voice is kind. She takes Finn's hand and tells him to march. The dogs run ahead. They know it's nearly dinner time. Daddy gives them their dinner and I like to help.

My pram wheels are squeaking now. It's very cold, and all around is more and more fog. The leaves on the lane are slimy and crushed. I steer my pram through them, avoiding a big bit of earth.

Finn is chatting now to Nanny Jan. His legs always work better when we're going home. He knows we're having crumpets for tea. So do I, and so does Dorothy Baby.

The light is going.

CAMELLIA
8ᵗʰ December 1962 – the Hunt

When I look out of my bedroom window it's dark. My watch says half past seven and it's meant to be morning.

Today is a hunting day and I dread it. I dread it for all sorts of reasons. Eight reasons actually. It's just a question of getting through to the other end when I can sit in my bath with the taps steaming, knowing I'll have boiled eggs with toast and butter for my tea.

I hate hunting because:

Daddy is always cross.

Mummy is always scared.

I never know what my pony Robin is going to do next.

My horrible grey jodhpurs are itchy. My string gloves are useless. I can't feel the reins properly in them.

It's always cold.

I don't know anybody apart from Mummy and Daddy.

Mummy never knows where we are going.

I feel sorry for the fox. I don't think Daddy would like to be chased and chased. And then killed.

So, it's a day that has to be got through. Finn's too little to go hunting so he will stay with Nanny Jan and watch. He sat on Robin two days ago and his legs didn't reach anywhere much.

Today the Hunt is meeting right here at home. And, because our house is new, everyone is excited. Everyone except me.

Finn and I are having our breakfast in the nursery. Nanny Jan peers out the window.

'Foggy again,' she says. 'But at least it isn't raining, Camellia. That's a mercy.' Nanny Jan loves saying 'that's a mercy.'

Nanny Jan knows I hate it when my string gloves get wet. Then they are even more useless. I'm in my itchy jodhpurs already and have to move about on my chair.

Finn spoons the porridge around in his bowl. 'What's a mercy, Nanny Jan?'

I sigh. This is a boring conversation. I have finished my porridge which Nanny Jan says will stick to my ribs for the morning at least. I ask to get down and Nanny Jan nods. I'm not sure I can cope with Finn's questions on a *morning such as this*. I close the nursery door behind me, because I wasn't born in a barn.

But suddenly all is commotion! I hear Nanny Jan scream from behind the door. She is screaming and screaming at the top of her voice.

I rush back into the nursery to see a bird flying about, black and white with a very long tail. Nanny Jan runs around flapping her arms like the bird, while Finn sits at the table, spoon in hand, his mouth open.

The magpie dashes itself against the French windows, getting itself in a tantrum. Nanny Jan backs up against the bookcase and flaps a magazine in front of her. She points towards the bird.

Why is no one coming from the kitchen? Can't they hear the commotion?

I'm not scared of birds, so I make my way towards the key of the door. The magpie is perched, beak panting, upon the curtain rail. I circle the key in the lock and push open the door. The hunting day fog waits outside, white and cold.

Nanny Jan crouches down with the magazine over her eyes. 'Get it out Camellia! Get it *OUT*!'

I look at the magpie and the magpie looks at me. I do a *'get out please'* sign with my arm. Finn steps down from his chair and stands beside Nanny Jan.

'The way is clear, magpie,' I say.

And the magpie is gone.

Nanny Jan's knees lose power. She slumps to the floor and Finn pats her head kindly.

'Poor Nanny Jan,' he says. 'All better now.'

I stand and stare out into the fog. The magpie is free, unlike me who has to go hunting.

'Bird all gone.' More kindness from Finn. Nanny Jan's red skirt has rumpled up. She gets her handkerchief out from her sleeve and blows her nose. I think she's been crying. *A grown-up crying about a bird*? Even my dolls aren't scared of birds.

'So sorry, children,' Nanny Jan's voice is croaky, and she gives a big sigh. 'All better now, Finn and thank you, Camellia.'

'Well, magpie has flown away now,' I say, locking the door.

'That's a mercy,' says Finn. Nanny Jan smiles at that and says 'Yes, it is.'

Suddenly Mummy is in the room, very smart in her smooth, cream jodhpurs with her hair in a net. Her eyebrows are in a line and her lipstick is pale pink. She takes in Nanny Jan on the floor and the nursery breakfast half-eaten.

'What on earth happened?' Mummy's face is stern. She says she heard the commotion all the way from her bathroom. Nanny Jan opens her mouth to explain, as does Finn but I get in there first. I'm proud I was so useful.

'Goodness,' says Mummy, 'And what sort of bird was it?'

Mummy does a funny thing when I tell her. She salutes and says 'Good morning, Mr Magpie.' She then does a nervous laugh. I know that laugh isn't real. It's not funny *ha-ha*. It's funny *peculiar*.

And now Mrs Betts is in the room too and, when she hears the bird was a magpie, she throws down her polish and does the sign of the cross. She offers to get Nanny Jan a hot cup of tea for shock because Mummy has already gone through to find Daddy. I hope she tells him how useful I was.

Finn walks round the nursery, flapping his arms and saying 'That's a mercy, Mr Magpie.' The big question the grown-ups are asking is *how on earth did it get in*? Mrs Betts rolls her eyes over Nanny Jan, muttering under her breath. One of the words is *unlucky*, but I can't quite catch the other one.

I go upstairs for a bit of peace and quiet. I tell my dolls about the magpie, and I know they can hear. They always listen, unlike the grown-ups who only sometimes listen. I find my *Little Book of Birds* and look up the magpie. Why are the grown-ups so scared of him? To me he's a fine-looking bird and the book says his black wings shine green and purple in the sun.

Perhaps I'll see Mr Magpie again out hunting. For Mummy's sake I hope she doesn't.

ANGELA
As if I haven't got enough to do today of all days. I cannot *believe* the noise going on downstairs. The screaming makes me feel quite sick. What on *earth* is happening? It's loud enough to wake the devil quite frankly. I simply haven't got *time* for all this. God knows I haven't got time for anything with all the organising and comings and goings and which and what. I shout for Gerald, just in case he's still in his dressing room, but I know he'll be downstairs or outside making ready for the bloody Hunt Meet.

Oh, for heaven's *sake*! As if I haven't got a million and one things to do, and it's another day's hunting and I won't know where to go again and Camellia will give me that look of hers.

I run down the back stairs, wondering what the hell will greet me. I'm late already and any minute Gerald will start chivvying me up. I simply can't bear that as it makes me feel even more of a fool.

'What on EARTH happened?'

Nanny Jan is collapsed on the floor with Finn patting her

head, and Camellia's standing beside the French windows. I'm glad to see she's already in her jodhpurs.

Camellia is the first to tell me and, as if a bird flying round the nursery isn't bad enough on this morning of all mornings, I'm appalled when she tells me it was a magpie.

At once the words *sorrow sorrow* circle around my head, followed by *death death* and, when I salute the magpie, I see Camellia's puzzled stare. I feel completely hopeless in this situation. I should be brisk and matter of fact, but I simply can't bear it. A magpie is quite, quite dreadful.

Both children are gawping now, so I laugh gaily, hoping to reassure them. Where's the bloody bird now? How the hell did it get in? How *do* magpies get in? Down the chimney? The nursery hasn't even got a chimney! As if I hadn't got enough to do.

I must keep calm but, when Mrs Betts comes in and throws down her polish, I know I have to get out of the room. I feel a mad laugh rising, as if I'm a lunatic, and I go running through to the hall, clenching my fists. I mustn't think about what a magpie means. I don't even know what it means, but I know it isn't good. As if I hadn't got enough to do.

'GERALD!!' He isn't through here. He's busy, always busy, making sure all is in order for this morning's Great Hunt Gathering and I'm *forever* worried about letting him down. Quite honestly, I *never* feel good enough and now we've had a blasted magpie *in the house.*

I rush back upstairs to the lavatory because now my fear has let me down. Please let this not happen out hunting because that is the very worst. Why can't I be like everyone else with well-behaved bowels?

I sit for a moment feeling desperate. Outside there's fog and more fog, as if we haven't had weeks of the bloody stuff. This will make it more difficult for Camellia and me to find our way, avoiding the jumps but, on the other hand, not so many people will see us.

Putting on my lipstick again, I notice my hand is shaking. I wonder how many people will think I'm not up to the mark today.

'Oh, FLAMING HELL!'

That helps and, tucking one of Gerald's red spotted handkerchiefs into my pocket for luck, I take a deep breath and run down the front stairs.

CAMELLIA

I walk as slowly as I can up to the stables. The fog seeps into my jacket. I take a deep breath and blow out even more fog, like a dragon. I push my riding hat back in case I see a magpie, and I swish my riding crop like a scythe, not that the grass is very long. It's a very pale green, all crisp and wintry. If the grass were really frozen, then we wouldn't be allowed to hunt. This is because it hurts the horses' feet.

But it isn't frozen today. I can see the stables now, looming out of the fog. All will be a bustle up there with Henry making the horses ready.

My tummy feels like a roundabout. I stop scything for a moment so I can take a deep breath. Daddy says I need to be calm and collected out hunting, but it isn't easy. Mummy tries to be calm and collected but I know she isn't. She does a lot of smoking when we are standing around. I am too young to smoke. I have to rely on my little collection of boiled sweets in my top pocket.

I say hello to Robin. He stands in his box, not looking like the usual Robin. The usual Robin is a mud ball. His mane is tightly plaited and he's tacked up, his saddle and bridle gleaming. He shows me the white of his blue and brown eye.

'Please be good today, Robin,' I whisper. 'Please.'

Henry comes clattering across the yard with a bucket. I like Henry. He is young for a grown-up and he listens and makes me laugh.

'Good morning, young Camellia. Robin is ready for you, but I could do with a bit of help cleaning Mr Gerald's martingale.'

I beam. There is nothing I like better than to be useful. We spend a happy ten minutes brushing and soaping tack. I tell Henry about the magpie and he laughs. He says he would have given anything to hear Nanny Jan shout her head off over the magpie. He says he doesn't salute magpies himself but knows people who do.

'Why do they do it?'

Henry shrugs, rubbing his hands together to get warm. 'I dare say it's superstition.' I've heard of this.

'Magic?'

'Sort of. Depends if you believe in it or not.' Henry's voice is low. 'It also depends … if you believe there's a GREAT BIG GOBLIN behind that muck cart!' He rolls his eyes as if he's in a pantomime.

'Ha-ha!' I cry. 'No such thing!' I'm glad Finn isn't here. Henry gives me a big smile and shows his friendly teeth. They are whiter than Robin's but still a bit horsey.

He asks me to bring Robin out, offering to hold him while I climb onto the mounting block. Usually I get up on Robin from the ground, but on hunting days I'm always allowed to use the block. Robin's shoes go clip, clop, clip across the yard and I see his hooves are black and shiny. They soon won't be.

Henry attaches the leading rein onto Robin's bridle and then loops it across his withers. I collect it with my reins as best I can with my useless string gloves, and we begin walking.

'A young miss such as you don't need the leading rein to walk down to the house,' Henry says in his pantomime voice. 'I shall accompany you by walking by your side.'

Henry is funny.

We walk down towards the house and occasionally Henry goes off the road in search of goblins. Goblins are harder to see in the fog he says. As we turn into the big driveway in front of the house, I hear a chattering sound from one of the oak trees.

I am on my own now.

CAMELLIA

The meet

There are horse boxes parked on the edges of the drive, with some riders already on their horses, prancing about. Daddy would say *on their toes*. Luckily for me Robin isn't on his toes. Yet. I hold the reins as best I can through my useless string gloves and look around.

Daddy is walking about in his pink coat, all blue eyes and laughing mouth under his moustache. He loves this, making sure he says hello to everyone and welcoming them to his new stone house. He wants everyone to enjoy what he enjoys. It's a pity Mummy and I don't enjoy hunting, but we can't tell him. We just can't.

Mummy comes out of the kitchen door. She's in her bowler hat, smiling at the people who hand out fruit cake and little glasses of port. The servers hold the trays up high for the riders to reach them, but the horses do a lot of prancing. This makes it difficult for everyone. A server can easily get kicked. I know I have to be careful of any horse with a red bow. They probably know that too. I long for a piece of fruit cake but my hands are too cold to take my gloves off. I'm not allowed port.

There's Finn with his eye patch, bundled up in his duffle coat but hood down, holding on tight to Nanny Jan's hand. They walk very carefully through the horses and the hounds. Finn doesn't like the hounds much because their tails smack him in the face. Now they are beside me.

Nanny Jan lifts Finn up to my level so he can pat Robin's woolly neck. I feel like crying but that wouldn't do.

'Good luck Camellia and Robin,' Nanny Jan says. Her voice is kind. 'Soon be over, and then you can tell us all about it.'

'I'll wait for you,' says Finn. Now my eyes are prickling. I sniff hard and blink. Then I ask Nanny Jan to feel into my pocket for one of my boiled sweets.

'You must finish it before you start trotting, Camellia,' she warns, unwrapping the orange sweet. 'You know that.'

I nod as she pops the sweet into my mouth. I must crunch

the sweet if we suddenly set off. I have to be brave for Finn and Nanny Jan, and especially brave for Mummy. I am shivering, my feet already numb. We have four hours to go until we can come home.

It's nearly time. Mummy is riding her dear horse Amber. Amber is a liver chestnut mare and she always behaves. Mummy should try riding Robin. Daddy should try riding Robin! When I think of Daddy riding Robin I smile, and Nanny Jan thinks I've cheered up.

'There now, you're feeling better already, Camellia!'

But I'm not feeling better at all. I know we are seconds away from moving off. Mummy needs to collect me on the leading rein but she's busy talking to other people. She's *always* busy talking to other people. Any minute Robin is going to start prancing. As soon as he hears the hunting horn, he starts prancing. He *always* does. I close my eyes and hang on tight. I feel sick. But it's no good. I've got to make Mummy stop talking and come over. Come *on*, Mummy! She's as pretty as a picture on Amber and she's doing her best at pretending she isn't frightened. She doesn't cover it up so well later. I always know.

HORN! Where is Mummy? The other horses are clattering and spinning round. The hounds have left, following the huntsman. More horn. It means we're off. Everyone knows what to do and where to go, but I don't. Robin dances on his toes, tossing his head and pulling. He wants to join the others, but I have to be on the leading rein.

'MUMMY!' I shout, pulling on the reins.

She's beside me now thank goodness, her mouth in a firm, pink line. I pass the leading rein up to her and know in that moment that we are going to have an accident.

My heart speeds up as we trot off. What a relief I finished my sweet, so no chance of choking. I have to kick Robin on to keep up with Amber. She's 15.2 after all. We're at the back as usual, our favourite place. The accident feeling is fading, nearly all gone. Only four hours to go and we shall be home.

All around is the fog and the sound of the horn.

CAMELLIA

The ghost

We are lost. This is what always happens. I push my glove down to look at my watch. It's twenty past one and Nanny Jan and Finn will have had their lunch by now. My tummy lurches and rumbles and I wonder if I should have my last sweet now, or should I save it?

Mummy and I have stopped by a huge fence and I lean over to see how churned up the mud is. When fences are this big it's good because there's absolutely no chance of jumping. But we wonder if we are on the trail of the rest of the Field. There's always a feeling of missing out and being left behind, and I know Mummy gets cross with herself because she should know her way round better.

'Where are we?'

Mummy doesn't answer. I don't dare tell her I'm hungry. I notice that Amber is jumpy, her ears back. Robin's ears are furry and sideways most of the time. He puts his head down to eat some winter grass. I tug on the reins to stop him, but he puts his head down again.

I listen hard for sounds of anyone else about. It helps if I tilt my head, but the fog makes everything quiet.

'Oh, for heaven's *sake*,' Mummy says. 'This really is the END!' She turns Amber round and Robin's head is yanked up from the grass.

'Let's go on to the next field and then take a guess.' Mummy always likes to go forwards, never turning round. She collects up her reins, kicking Amber on along a narrow strip of ground.

We make our way along what seems like a tunnel, with the wood on one side and a steep bank on the other. The branches over the tunnel are like witch's fingers stretching into the fog. Robin is being slow as usual, and the leading rein stretches tight between us. As I glance sideways, I see a hound running through the wood beside us.

'Look Mummy! There's a hound!' But Mummy isn't listening. She concentrates on steering Amber through the tunnel and fog.

It's because I'm looking at the hound that I don't see the woman quickly enough. She appears in front of Robin and he jumps back, flattening his ears.

I try and shout 'Mummy!' but I can't. The woman stands between us, staring at me with big eyes. She wears a long dress with a necklace! No coat in the fog!

This is too much for Robin who backs up sharply. The leading rein stretches tighter and tighter, and to my horror Mummy's arm is pulled right back, making her fall off into the mud. Amber wedges herself into the trees, stirrups free now of Mummy's boots.

I stare at this calamity through the woman's dress. How is this possible? There's a voice in my head, saying *please help me.* As soon as I hear it, the woman disappears. I can now see Mummy clearly and she has landed on her hand. Her bowler hat has come off so it's lucky she didn't land on her head!

'Mummy! Mummy!' I have a voice now. 'Are you all right?'

'No! I am NOT!' Mummy sounds hurt.

I feel very bad for Mummy who is not all right. So, I jump down off Robin who is snorting like mad with his ears back. I know I mustn't let go of the reins because he might take off, dragging poor Mummy with him. They are both attached to the leading rein after all. I bring the reins over Robin's head and loop them through my arm.

'My finger!' cries Mummy. I help push Mummy off her hand and then, pulling off my string gloves, unwrap the leading rein. It's difficult because my hands are freezing, but I know Mummy shouldn't have looped the leading rein like that. Henry says it's dangerous.

But this is not the time to tell Mummy about the leading rein. I know this is the sort of thing that annoys her, and I don't want to get into even more trouble.

'OW OW!' cries Mummy. 'I think I've broken my little finger!'

Very gently I pull Mummy's glove off and we both agree her little finger looks broken.

'Oh Mummy,' I say, suddenly tearful. 'I'm so sorry. But it was the woman!'

Mummy is stuck on the ground, shocked and dazed, holding her left hand out. Her beautiful coat is covered in mud and her jodhpurs look like mine! They are certainly not cream-coloured any more.

'Why did you pull me back?' Mummy's voice is sharp with pain. Do I tell her *again* about the woman? I feel Robin's breath in my ear.

'It wasn't my fault honestly, Mummy. It was the woman! She made Robin scared. She didn't have a coat on!'

Mummy looks as if she doesn't believe me.

'And she had a necklace!'

All at once there's a voice behind us and it's Mrs Martinswood. She's very old, wearing a top hat with a black veil, riding side-saddle as usual. We sometimes go the long way round with her. I give her a little wave.

'What have we here?' Her horse bows its head, rubbing its front leg. Mrs Martinswood lets the reins drop.

'Can you help us, please?' I look up, trying to see her eyes through the veil. 'We've had an accident! Poor Mummy has broken her finger.'

Mrs Martinswood's mouth purses. She's very sorry to hear that. She will go and put the word out to find Daddy, and then he can come and rescue us.

Luckily Mrs Martinswood knows exactly where we are, which is more than we do. She suggests I unhook the leading rein, get Mummy to her feet and is Mummy all right to lead her horse back through the tunnel into the open? Mummy says just about, and we follow Mrs Martinswood to where Daddy will find us.

Mummy's face is pinched with pain and I know I will get the blame. I watch Mrs Martinswood ride off into the fog and offer Mummy my last sweet. She says I'm a very kind girl, but she would never take my last sweet. She would prefer a cigarette and I watch her make a good job of lighting it, even with a broken finger. Mummy's always happy when she's smoking. She says it calms her nerves. Luckily the cigarettes didn't get squashed in her silver case.

We sit and wait while Mummy smokes and Robin munches grass. I decide not to talk about the woman with no coat. I know it isn't the time.

Soon Daddy comes to rescue us. He helps Mummy back up on to Amber and then he puts Mummy on the leading rein! I am to be all grown up, riding by myself behind them because my little finger isn't broken. Of course, Robin walks on nicely. He knows we're going home and there will be nuts in his manger.

The fog is lifting now with a cold breeze. As we make our way home, I think about what happened. How did I know we were going to have an accident? I know I mustn't share this with anyone, certainly not Mummy and Daddy.

Was it my fault? If I hadn't been looking at the hound, I could have stopped Robin going backwards and then Mummy wouldn't have fallen off. I watch Daddy and Mummy ahead, feeling sorry for myself.

They haven't noticed there's a magpie in the branches high above. He's watching all of us, especially me.

I refuse to salute!

ANGELA

My little finger is extremely sore. Dr Byng put it in a splint at teatime, saying there is nothing more that can be done. It has to mend by itself. I'm now lying in the bath, Badedas bubbles three inches high, with my hand hanging over the side. Still I suppose it could be worse. At least it's my left hand.

What a day that was! Alas, it will be remembered for all the wrong reasons, and I had wanted it to go as smoothly as possible. Gerald likes things to go perfectly, and this wasn't perfect by any standards. However, it's not as if I did it on purpose. What a bit of luck Mrs Martinswood found us. I must write her a letter on Monday. Quite frankly I didn't give a hoot having to be put on the leading rein. My finger was hurting so much by then that I just wanted to get home.

Camellia insisted that she saw a 'woman' and that the 'woman' made Robin go into reverse. I have to say it took me completely by surprise and who likes to be pulled off backwards? What a relief that bit of ground was soft. If it hadn't been, I might have broken my arm! It will take a long time to brush the mud out of my coat, and it will probably have to go to the dry cleaners. As if I hadn't got enough to do.

I think the Meet went well, everything considered. However, I'm looking forward to my glass of whisky this evening. I think I've earned it. I often think Gerald's pretty insensitive not to realise how bloody terrified I am out hunting. He seems to have totally forgotten how I broke my back falling onto the road, thanks to that mad horse. How was I to know it would rear up? I know there are people who say horses can feel your fear, even when you're trying to put on a good show. Amber's a dear, mind you, and I haven't fallen off her before. Not until today and that wasn't exactly her fault.

I am conveniently forgetting I wound the leading rein around my left hand. I'm pretty sure Camellia clocked this, as nothing gets past her green eyes. Like a cat she sees everything, but I really can't face being told off by Gerald for not holding the leading rein correctly. Honestly, I can't.

I wonder, if Gerald and I had been able to have children of our own, what they would have been like? Camellia is a very different bird from me, a South African bird at that, quite unlike our British birds. And thinking of British birds, how the hell did that magpie get in? If the magpie hadn't got in and frightened the life out of us, then maybe I wouldn't have fallen off. So, we can blame the magpie and Robin when people ask me this evening.

Returning to Camellia, I never, ever know how she's going to be or how she will react. She's so terribly serious half the time, well most of the time, and I wish she wouldn't frown so. When I tell her to mind her expression, the wind might change etc, all she does is look hurt. Finn is *so* much easier! He has charm plus an irresistible smile, and he's being so brave with his patch. Thinking of that, I must ring Mr Dyle on Monday to arrange Finn's next appointment.

Thank heavens Nanny Jan is here to see to Camellia, but perhaps I ought to have a chat with her before bedtime. She did look rather tucked up, walking back from the stables, her shoulders hunched over. If only I could understand her better!

Well I must be out of this bath now and see what needs to be done. I can hear Gerald whistling in his dressing room, God knows what tune, and I suppose I'd better have a think about what I'm wearing for tonight. We are eight for dinner and I hope Cook's up to it. Her boeuf bourguignon was decidedly below par last time with nowhere near enough shallots, or wine come to that. However, not being a cook myself, I have no idea how to put that right. Life is such a worry!!

I wonder if I should take an aspirin for this finger?

CAMELLIA

Crumpets for tea

I'm having my tea in the nursery with Nanny Jan and Finn. Instead of boiled eggs I decide to have crumpets. There are four of them, sitting on a plate in front of me. They are piping hot, the butter melting. They are my absolute favourite and, as I bite into the first one, I feel my tummy relax.

I munch happily while Finn looks at me. Both eyes are on show as Nanny Jan says he's been a good boy, wearing his patch for eight hours today, non-stop.

'What a day!' I say, copying Mummy. 'Luckily I didn't fall off as well.'

Finn eats a quarter of his crumpet carefully. He likes his cut up into quarters. I'm a big girl and have mine cut in half.

'Then what happened, Melia?' Finn asks. I've already told him the story, but he can't get enough of it. I haven't actually said *why* Robin pulled Mummy off because it might scare him. But, once I finish my second crumpet, I decide to tell them both everything. I just have to!

'Well it was this woman, you see. She just appeared.' Nanny Jan looks up from buttering her crumpet.

'Just appeared, Camellia?'

'Yes,' I say. 'She was there right in front of Robin and she was wearing a dress, a long dress and a necklace.' Nanny Jan raises her eyebrows.

'That's peculiar,' she says.

'Very,' I say. I'm enjoying the fact that I have an audience, but a little voice inside says be careful what you tell Finn, because you will pay for it later.

'Perhaps she was out shopping?' suggests Finn. We both stare at him and Nanny Jan laughs.

'In the fog, Finn?' I ask. 'Without a basket. Or coat? And where are the shops in the woods?' I am crowing I know.

Finn looks puzzled. Nanny Jan gives me the eye. Her eye says take care.

'Perhaps you imagined it, Camellia?' Nanny Jan has said what grown-ups always say, but I'm not going to let her get away with it.

'Did we *all* imagine the magpie this morning?' I say crossly. 'No, we did not.' Nanny Jan agrees we did *not* imagine the magpie this morning.

'Was she a witch looking for her keys and she didn't have a basket, just great big pockets?' This is a long sentence for Finn, and I'm impressed with his train of thought.

'Well she was quite pretty with big eyes,' I tell him. 'As much as I could tell, *and* she had a necklace on, and I don't think witches have necklaces.'

'And that made Mummy fall off?' Finn's eye looks a bit sore.

'Robin went backwards, Finn, and that pulled Mummy off. She fell off Amber and sat on her little finger.'

'And it *broke*!' Finn's mouth has gone down.

'But it wasn't my fault.' I need to get this across. Now onto my fourth crumpet I ask Nanny Jan a question. 'How can anyone disappear just like that?'

Nanny Jan doesn't know as she wasn't there.

I wiggle my toes in my furry slippers, much more comfortable than riding boots. The woman must have been dreadfully cold out in the fog, wearing only a dress. The thought of it makes me shiver.

'I shall draw her for you,' I declare. 'I know I only saw her for a second, but I can remember.' Finn likes the sound of this as he likes drawing too, even though his pictures are a bit wild. Nanny Jan says we can do some drawing after tea, but first we have to finish our crumpets.

After we get down, I find my coloured pencils in the cupboard, as well as my drawing pad. Next a pencil which I sharpen, and a rubber just in case, and then I settle down at the little table in front of the sofa. Finn has found his colouring book and I generously allow him to use my colours. I need to keep him happy while I draw the woman as best I can.

I draw her eyes big and her hair up in a bun. I make her mouth sad. Then her dress with a waist, no colour because it was the same as the fog but, now I remember, there was a green sash. Then I draw the necklace which was like big pebbles on a string.

Now she has brown hair which makes her look younger. I give her blue eyes, remembering them as big and dark and staring. I colour the sash a deep forest green. I'm not sure what to put around her. It doesn't seem right to draw Mummy falling off Amber.

Finn peers at my picture. Nanny Jan comes back from taking the tea things out and I call her over.

'Well, well,' she says. 'That's your woman.'

'What shall we call her?' asks Finn 'Not just *woman*?'

I'm not sure. I haven't thought about a name.

'What about Mercy?' suggests Finn. Nanny Jan says he's been saying this word a lot today.

Mercy. I repeat the name a few times. It will do.

'Mercy she is for the moment.' I spell the word *Mercy* and

write her name on the picture. She hovers in mid-air, so I draw a sun above her with a tree to keep her company. Then I sign my picture *Camellia*.

Nanny Jan switches her wireless on. It's playing 'Bobby's Girl' which I love.

'Come on, Finn! Let's have a dance!' Finn is delighted, and we jump around on the nursery carpet, shouting Bobby's Girl in time with the music. Nanny Jan smiles and says 'you two!'

The curtains are drawn and we are safe, warm and happy. Nanny Jan says tomorrow we shall make our paper-chains for Christmas. We can start them after church which luckily only goes on for an hour.

I go upstairs to check my dolls, leaving Finn to dance with Nanny Jan. My dolls have been all alone while I've been hunting. They get lonely, I know. I take my picture of Mercy with me.

CAMELLIA
Sunday, December 9th

I wake and check my little watch on my bedside table. It's nearly eight o'clock and everything is slower on a Sunday. I give a great big yawn and think about yesterday. What a day! I wonder how Mummy's finger is this morning and whether Daddy and Mummy will be in a good mood for church at ten o'clock. They had some people for dinner last night. I heard them parking their cars outside my window, scrunching on the gravel with lots of laughter from Daddy as he said hello at the front door.

I wish Mummy had stayed a bit longer saying goodnight to me. She sat on the end of my bed looking beautiful in a dark blue dress with pearls round her neck, but I knew she wanted to hurry off downstairs to get ready for the people. She didn't notice my picture of Mercy, but then I didn't feel like showing it to her. I had tucked it beside my nightlight as I thought Mercy would like that. My nightlight is a china house full of happy little china mice.

All Mummy did was ask if I was all right, so I asked if her finger hurt very much. I wanted to say I was sorry again but found I couldn't, because it wasn't my fault. As Mummy bent to give me a kiss goodnight, I breathed in her most delicious scent, her favourite and I asked for the name, even though I knew it.

'*Arpege* darling. Now you tuck up and sleep tight.' And that was it. Perhaps I'm not trying enough with Mummy.

But now it's Sunday and I did sleep tight. I can't hear Finn moving about next door, so he's probably still asleep. The light creeping round the curtains is very bright. It could be the sun, but it could also be more white fog. I pull back my curtains.

It's sun! And it's a sparkling day! Just the right sort of day to make paper-chains and think about Christmas. I bend down to check on Dorothy Baby fast sleep in her cot. Then I say good morning to my other dolls who are sitting on the shelf.

I say good morning to Mercy in my picture and I thank the little mice for taking care of her.

I search in my cupboard for a Sunday-best dress for church, choosing my red check one with a white collar. It's a bit itchy because it's made of wool, but my vest should protect me. I will wear my new dark blue coat over it. Mummy likes us to look well dressed for church, but luckily we always get changed once we get back.

I get dressed quickly and have another look out the window. There is a Mr Magpie doing big hops across the lawn, and he looks so funny! Every now and then he flicks his tail up. How can the grown-ups think he's bad? He's so smart he could come to church with us. But of course, Mummy wouldn't like that.

I hear Finn call my name next door and I wonder if I dare unbolt his door or whether Nanny Jan will be cross. But it's past eight o'clock and surely time for breakfast.

I reach up to unbolt the chicken wire gate and there is Finn, smiling at me.

CAMELLIA

We are on our way to church in the car. Finn and I sit in the back with a scratchy rug over our knees to keep us warm. Finn's legs stick straight out under the rug and we laugh about that. He's wearing his patch this morning because the sun's very bright but, if he's good, he can take it off at teatime.

Mummy's wearing her fur hat, looking as if she's got a beaver on her head! Mummy always says hats don't suit her, but she doesn't mind this one. Her coat is dark red and very thick wool.

Daddy is very smart in a tweed suit. Finn says he wishes he had a suit like Daddy's instead of his duffle coat, which Nanny Jan brushed this morning. Mummy tells him they don't make suits for four-year-olds. Finn puts his head down, so I pat his hand.

When we step into the church, I feel the cold immediately. There are no flowers because it's Advent. We are given our hymn books and prayer books, and Finn takes these even though he can't read properly. Lots of people are here already and they stare at us as we walk to our pew. I wish they wouldn't do that.

We are seated behind our grandparents, Gran and Grandpop, and they are Daddy's parents. Gran leans round, dressed from top to bottom in fur and says good morning. She is wearing dark pink lipstick and there is a little bit on her front tooth. Gran and Grandpop always sit in front of us.

I go to the far end of the pew with Finn beside me, and then Mummy and Daddy. Mummy likes to be next to Finn so she can remind him to be good. I don't need reminding. I always behave in church, even though I find it quite boring.

It doesn't feel like Christmas is coming at *all* in here. It feels old and cold and no fun at all. I check on what hymns we are singing from the numbers on the board in front. Only one has a good tune. Poor Finn has to go '*la-la-la*' to all of them. That sometimes gives me the giggles, and even Mummy finds that funny.

Dear Finn. He's such a love.

While we wait for the vicar to come in, I look around the church. The morning sun is flooding through the window opposite. How beautiful it is! Mary has a pretty, kind face, with Jesus standing on her knee, and there are angels surrounding them, every one of them with a lovely face. Not all Mary and Jesus pictures are as beautiful as this one. They are both looking straight at me, and suddenly out of nowhere I want to cry.

The first hymn starts and Finn does his usual 'la-la-las'. It's a very dull hymn luckily and it stops me from crying. Mummy's voice is high and round and she sounds rather grand, trying to reach the top notes, but anyone can tell this isn't her favourite either.

While Daddy reads the lesson, I look across at the window again, wondering if I will feel the same. If I make sure I look at the words underneath, and not Mary and Jesus, then I will be safe. It says the window is *Dedicated to Alathea Mary Philippa Goodridge who died on Christmas Eve 1896.*

It's as if I know her! It's like a sudden thud in my heart that hurts. I hear the word *sorrow* in my ear, and I know sorrow means a big sadness. Who is Alathea Mary Philippa Goodridge? And how awful to die on Christmas Eve which is the happiest and most exciting of nights! She wouldn't have been able to open her stocking!

Daddy finishes the lesson and I concentrate hard on what comes next. Quite a few things come next including the sermon, but that is usually quite interesting because of the vicar. He's quite young for a grown-up with very blue eyes. He's talking about getting ready for Christmas and how his cat likes the decorations on his Christmas tree. He always starts his sermon with something funny and finishes it with something to do with Jesus. Mummy gives Finn a sweet to keep him quiet.

During Communion Finn and I stay in our pew, and I watch the people who go up to the altar and back down again. They all look miserable! So serious and solemn, and now Mummy is wearing her after-communion face too. She kneels down to pray, but soon gets back up again.

I shall save my question about Alathea Mary Philippa who died on Christmas Eve until we get home. The after-church conversation in the car is often boring, usually about who we saw in church, as well as *wasn't it a lovely service?*

We say good morning to the vicar as we leave and then we're out into the bright December sunshine. We talk for a minute to Gran and Grandpop, and Gran says she likes my coat. The lipstick on her tooth has gone.

Mummy doesn't notice the magpie hiding behind the grave-stone on the way down the path. Finn sees it, but I put my finger up to my mouth and whisper '*no*'.

We're going home to make paper-chains and, because it's a Sunday, Nanny Jan will give us a big glass of Ribena and two digestive biscuits.

The sadness has lifted and I'm happy again.

CAMELLIA

Finn and I are busy making our paper-chains. I have a little pile of coloured rectangles beside me and a long chain of joined up paper-chain. I'm very quick at making them.

Finn, on the other hand, is slow. He has a big pile of paper rectangles on one side and a very short paper-chain on the other. He either soaks the end of the rectangle with the sponge or doesn't put enough water on.

'This is hard work!' he says. I look at his paper-chain and agree that it *is* hard for him, especially with his patch. I show him how to do blue, red, yellow, green because it looks more jolly. He takes no notice. Finn prefers to do blue, blue, blue, red, yellow or whatever takes his fancy.

Soon I have enough to ask Nanny Jan to loop my chain from one light to another. We use sellotape for sticking, knowing it will unstick in a few days and the paper-chain will come sailing down.

Now my paper-chain is up, I'm able to admire our first proper

Christmas decoration. This definitely means Christmas is coming! I know we have to wait another week for our tree, but there's a good reason for this. Mummy says, if we get the tree too early, then it will be bald by Christmas Day.

Mummy's new tree for the drawing room will never go bald. This is because it's made of the prettiest silver tinsel and plastic. It arrived in a big cardboard box last week, and Mummy unpacked it there and then to check it was all right. It's now waiting in the cellar, ready for Christmas. Mummy has bought some beautiful pale pink and blue angels for the the tree, and she says there are some white lights as well. I know it will be *magical*.

I settle down for some more sticking together and notice that Finn is making the most awful mess with his water. Now he has soaked his pile of rectangles.

'I'm fed up,' he announces, getting down from the table. Nanny Jan comes over to him, offering to put up his paper-chain.

Finn's not that bothered but it doesn't stop Nanny Jan sticking Finn's paper-chain to the light. It hangs down, all eleven pieces and just about touches the pile of books on the side.

'There,' Nanny Jan says. 'Doesn't that look splendid?!'

It doesn't but I say it does.

By lunchtime and thanks to my hard work our paper-chains are finished, the nursery looking as Christmassy as can be. Now all it needs is for Mummy to come in and say well done.

'Shall I go and find her?' Finn asks.

We're not allowed to go through to the drawing room because Mummy and Daddy have guests. Now they are coming into the dining room next door. We have our Sunday lunch here in the nursery.

'Best not, Finn. After lunch. Perhaps once we are back from our walk. Mummy will come in at teatime.'

I sigh. We *always* have to do the walk. I think I will take one of my other dolls out in the pram today. Dorothy Baby can sit in the nursery and admire my paper-chains.

Finn is staring out the window at something.

FINN

There's that thing!! It's moving. It's coming up the steps.

Maybe my good eye's gone funny?

I can see a face.

I can't see a face.

NO FACE!!

MELIA!!!!!!!

NANNY JAN

Finn got himself into a right old state before lunch. The poor boy was having ever such a lot of trouble with his paper-chains and he's a bit young to be doing them, if I am honest. However, he does so love to do whatever Camellia's doing. The trouble is Camellia is rather good at whatever she turns her hand to, and this makes it more difficult for Finn. Not only is she two years older, but anyone can tell she's an extremely talented child. That dear little boy is always playing catch-up.

It was as I was fetching lunch that Finn started to shout for Camellia. By the time I was back in the nursery, Camellia was already out on the terrace, leaving Finn standing there, rubbing his good eye.

'I didn't like it,' he shouted. 'It wasn't Mercy! Or Mr Magpie.' He paused, shaking his head and then he wailed.

I rushed over to scoop him up. His little hands clutched onto my apron and I did so feel for him in that moment.

Camellia came back in, bringing the winter air with her.

'Nothing there, Finn,' she said. 'Not now anyway.'

I gave the little boy a great big hug.

'All better now.' I wasn't sure it was actually. Finn's face came around to look at his sister. He took an exaggerated deep breath, opening his mouth wide.

'It wasn't Mercy. It wasn't Mr Magpie. I didn't like it. I DIDN'T LIKE IT!'

'Whatever it was, Finn. I promise you it has gone.'

I didn't think Finn believed her. It wasn't enough.

'Cross my heart and hope to die.'

What of course I didn't realise at the time was that this was the start of a very difficult time for the children. The house would become unfriendly and events would prove to be unpredictable and turbulent. This was just the beginning.

'It's just hiding,' Finn muttered.

'Then I will protect you,' said Camellia. 'I'm very brave.'

After her announcement I decided to take charge of the situation, suggesting we should settle down to lunch and talk about something else. I switched the wireless on, and we listened to 'The Clitheroe Kid' as a treat. Soon the children were laughing their heads off. I must say Jimmy Clitheroe is very funny.

CAMELLIA
The evening star

Charlotte Baby is in the pram for the walk. She's been looking a little peaky so I thought the fresh air would do her good. Finn is holding on to Nanny Jan's hand in case he sees the *Thing*. Mind you, we have the dogs with us, and they will keep us safe.

He told me after lunch it's the same *Thing* he saw on the long walk. He says it's mainly black and shadowy, that it sometimes has a face and sometimes it doesn't. I wonder if his *Thing* actually *is* a shadow, or whether it has something to do with his patch.

But it's important to believe in Finn and for him to know that I'll protect him. Whatever the *Thing* is, it's making poor Finn frightened and he's not his usual, funny self.

We laughed and laughed at 'The Clitheroe Kid'. I know what I am laughing at, but I'm not sure Finn does. He copies me. It was all right while the wireless was on but now Finn's gone quiet.

We are doing the short walk today which means down to the farm and back, not even as far as the letter box. The drive is nice and clear of leaves so my pram goes along like a dream. The sun has nearly gone down and we are walking in the half-dark. Nanny Jan says she hates the early winter evenings, having to draw the curtains at four o'clock.

Where is Mercy? Maybe she and Finn's *Thing* are together. I push my pram faster, trying to send this thought out of my head. When we reach the farm, we get a clear view of the west and I see a great big star.

'Look Finn!' I say. 'Over there! That's the Evening Star!' I know it's Venus from my *Observer's Book of Astronomy*.

Finn looks into the sky. He says his good eye is all swimmy and right now he can't see Venus that well. It could be because there is a cold wind blowing, but more likely poor Finn is crying. Nanny Jan gives him a handkerchief for his swimmy eye and calls him her brave soldier.

We turn around at the farm and make our way back up the hill. Nanny Jan carries Finn all the way and he wraps his arms round her neck. She huffs and puffs as we get near the house, but I know she's putting it on to make Finn laugh.

As we walk around the cattle grid, I stop with my pram. Something tells me to look towards the lost pond. We are told never to go too near its banks. This is because ponds are dangerous. Anyone knows that.

I don't know why I feel pulled to look. I screw up my eyes with the effort of staring into the shadows, but there is nothing there at all.

I push my pram up the last bit of hill, reaching the house at last. The windows are lit up and welcoming. I hope Mummy likes my paper-chains.

CAMELLIA

Nanny Jan is taking me to school in the car. Finn is too young for school so he stays at home, following Mrs Betts around with her duster and polish. I hope he doesn't see his *Thing* again because I won't be there to protect him.

Nanny Jan will be back soon of course, but she doesn't really understand about the *Thing*, not like me. Mummy's always extra busy on a Monday morning with hundreds of people to ring up. She says she's a martyr (whatever that means) to the telephone on her desk every Monday morning.

This Monday is cloudy and cold, but no fog. Mrs Betts said she thought the sky had a promise of snow, but Mrs Betts's eyesight isn't that good. I'm bursting with excitement to tell my friends about Mercy and the *Thing*, even if it's just a shadow. I have my picture in my satchel and I will have a chance to share my news at break-time.

Nanny Jan parks and walks me carefully across the road. She leaves me at the door, saying she will be there at half past twelve for pick-up as usual. Our classroom has a very high ceiling, dark wooden walls and big tall windows which face the road. I'm glad I'm wearing a thick cardigan because it's freezing, and I see my friend Annabel is wearing her big blue and white jersey which comes down to her knees. We wave at each other.

Miss Wiggins is already in her teaching chair, setting her books out and we know we have to get our stuff out as quickly as we can, settle down and face the front. There's no talking at this stage. Miss Wiggins has a cane which sits behind her on the shelf, and she uses it if she thinks you've been naughty. She is strict but she can also be quite kind. I think she's about seventy-five which is quite old to be a teacher.

It's a handwriting lesson first and I love this. I can practise my Gs and Ys, making the letters smooth and curved under the line, with a beautiful loop. Miss Wiggins walks between us and admires my work particularly. I wish she would admire Sarah's work more because Sarah tries so hard with her handwriting. Sarah is my friend because she's like a fairy and very kind. She has lovely, long fair hair and green eyes and she makes me laugh. If I ever tell her anything exciting, she opens her eyes very wide and says '*no*?!'

She's going to love my Mercy story, that's for sure. I can't wait for the lesson to be over because then it will be break.

But first Miss Wiggins is asking us to write sentences with words that have Gs and Ys. I write: *I went hunting on Saturday and Mummy broke her finger.*

At last it's break-time and everyone has milk and a biscuit, everyone except Sarah who's allowed orange juice because milk makes her tummy hurt.

I have my audience around me and we sit at the far end of the big hall. The other children run around, playing. We can play afterwards, but right now I must share my news. My three friends are Annabel, not in her jersey any more because she couldn't move her arms, Sarah and Melanie-Anne. Melanie-Anne is a scream, always saying funny things. She has a pony like me and sometimes goes hunting, but she has an even worse time because her mother actually *likes* jumping fences. We don't go outside to play at break because our school is on the road.

I tell them the Mercy story, leaving nothing out.

'*No*?!' Sarah says, and I laugh heartily.

'YES!' I say.

'Your poor Mummy with her broken finger,' Melanie-Anne says. 'That must be jolly rotten for her. *Ow, ow.*'

'But it *wasn't* my fault!' My three friends shake their heads, agreeing with me luckily. I show them my picture of Mercy.

'This was what she looked like,' I say, smoothing the paper out on the floor.

'She's sad,' says Sarah and we agree she looks sad.

All of a sudden, I remember how I could see right through Mercy's dress, which was peculiar. I could see Mummy sitting on her hand even though Mercy was in the way. I tell them that.

'I think I know what you saw,' Sarah says. 'My mum knows about this sort of thing. Remember she has crystals.'

We all know this. We stare at Sarah, waiting for the answer. She looks down again at my picture and then at me.

'You saw a ghost, Melia. Mercy is a ghost.'

'Crikey,' Melanie-Anne says. 'Does that mean Mercy is dead?'

Sarah says she must be, if she's a ghost.

'But her ghost is alive.'

Annabel's eyes are like two giant saucers. Sarah is pale and Melanie-Anne finishes her milk.

I have read about ghosts in books but I have never seen one, well not until Saturday at least. I now wonder if Finn's *Thing* is a ghost. We talk about the *Thing,* what it could be and why only Finn sees it.

I spot Miss Wiggins by the door. She'll be wondering what we're doing, sitting on the floor. I grab the picture, fold it up and suggest we run about a bit.

While we play hopscotch without any chalk or squares, we agree that all four of us will try and find out what we can about ghosts. How lucky I am that my friends are properly interested, but it might be too much for Finn.

On the way home with Nanny Jan I remember how I heard the words *please help me* when I saw Mercy. Why would Mercy be saying that? *Please help me* with what?

When we arrive home Finn is standing on the doorstep, holding a dustpan and brush. He's done lots of sweeping up. Nanny Jan says it's my favourite for pudding, banana fritters. I beam at Finn as I hang my satchel up.

'You're a good boy, Finn,' I say, opening the door to the nursery which is warm and filled with light.

After lunch I will ask Nanny Jan very carefully if she knows anything about ghosts. After all she knows where witches keep their keys.

NANNY JAN

Camellia asked me a funny question after lunch today. She asked me what I thought a ghost was, and whether the 'woman' she saw when Mrs Devon fell off was a ghost.

I hardly knew how to answer her, but I had to give her some explanation because, once Camellia gets a bee in her bonnet, she won't let go. It's a balance really of giving enough information to satisfy her curiosity, but not adding fuel to the fire. I really don't want the children getting themselves terrified of ghosts and ghouls, finding them round every corner. I'd only just about got Finn settled after his so-called *Thing* on the terrace.

She asked me quietly while Finn was pushing his tractor over the rug, doing his 'I'm a farmer boy' song.

I told her I didn't know much about ghosts but I'm afraid that was a lie. My mother saw a ghost once at our old home. She said it was a man who sat clear as day in the front parlour. She observed him for a good two minutes, and then he melted away in front of her eyes. She said she wasn't exactly frightened, more curious, but she did wonder what he was doing there. We never saw him again but that didn't make him any less real.

Of course, I didn't tell Camellia any of this. Instead I told her that some people believed in ghosts and some people didn't, and she looked thoughtful at that.

'But Nanny Jan, do *you* believe in ghosts? Do you have to believe in them to see them?' Her voice was loud enough for Finn to hear. He looked up from his tractor, peering at us with his good eye.

'What's a ghost?' Now we were going to have some fun. Camellia looked at me and then Finn.

'Mercy might be a ghost,' she said. 'But that's quite interesting actually and nothing to be worried about.'

'Is Mercy a Holy Ghost?'

Finn's question was quite a sensible one because the vicar talks about the Holy Ghost in church. I couldn't help smiling.

'What about Mr Magpie? Was he a ghost?'

I shook my head and assured him that Mr Magpie was *not* a ghost. He was a just a bird that got into the nursery and gave poor Nanny Jan a fright, that was all.

Finn then stood up and looked out of the window.

'Am I a ghost?'

Camellia took charge then, telling Finn that he most certainly was *not* a ghost because ghosts don't eat banana fritters. I reminded Finn he ate two for lunch.

That was the end of the conversation fortunately. However, just as we were putting on our coats and boots for the afternoon walk and Camellia was deciding which doll should go in her pram, she tackled me again.

'Do you think you have to *believe* in ghosts to see one?' I busied myself with doing up Finn's duffle coat, making an '*I'm not sure*' face. It was when we were standing in front of the house, watching the dogs run about in excitement, that she turned to me.

'Well I believe in ghosts, Nanny Jan, because I want to see Mercy again. I think she's sad and needs help.'

Then we set off for our walk.

CAMELLIA

I love being useful and I love helping people, so I've decided I shall do all I can to help poor Mercy. I feel very sorry for her, wandering about the fields in just her dress and necklace, getting cold. And I did hear her say *please help me*. I'm not sure ghosts can feel the cold and fog as we do, but it's awful to think of her all by herself, feeling sad and lonely.

I definitely believe in her because I saw her, and it doesn't really matter what Nanny Jan says. I know she wasn't being straight with me before the walk. She did what grown-ups do when they don't want to give you a proper answer. They just say something completely useless or they talk about something different. As if I don't notice when they're doing that!

I know my friends will come up with bright ideas, because they are brave, like me. We've agreed that on the last day of term, which is tomorrow, we will have a big *pow-wow* about what to do. One of my questions will be how to make Mercy appear again in a safe way. We don't want any more people falling off their horses!

I'm alone in the nursery, busy changing my dolls into their prettiest dresses for Nearly Christmas Time. Luckily, I have lots of beautiful clothes for my dolls to wear, and I sit surrounded with dresses, cardigans, coats and hats.

It's nearly teatime and getting dark outside. Finn is upstairs with Nanny Jan looking out some smart winter trousers. But I've had enough of dolls' clothes for the moment, so I get up to stretch my legs. I go over to the window.

Mr Magpie is in the tree, and beyond him standing on the lawn is what looks like a thin white statue. I rub the window pane with my sleeve to see better. The white statue is spinning, but how can this be? Do statues spin? I know if I call for Nanny Jan it will probably disappear, so I stand and stare, watching it spin faster and faster. I'm only a *bit* frightened because of course I'm safe in the nursery. Out of the corner of my eye I see a flash of black and white. Mr Magpie has flown away, and now the spinning statue has disappeared as well.

I draw the curtains and go back to my dolls. I decide not to tell Nanny Jan about what I saw out there, but I will definitely tell my friends.

CAMELLIA

We are all here for the last day of term! Miss Wiggins is wearing a red dress with a grey shaw, the same colour as her hair. She's in a kind mood today and I notice her cane isn't on the shelf.

There's so much excitement in the air that some of us are actually bouncing in our seats. We aren't having proper lessons today. Instead we are allowed to draw pictures of anything we like, so long as it's something to do with Christmas. Then we have an extra-long break-time to talk and play. Miss Wiggins says she's brought some mince pies to school, baked by her sister. I absolutely love mince pies and hope there might be one left over for Finn.

We are busy with our Christmas pictures and I'm having lots of fun drawing a reindeer. Miss Wiggins looks over my shoulder and says how drawing a reindeer is very advanced. I smile up at her but again wish she would say something about Sarah's picture. Sarah has drawn and coloured in an enormous present with a red and green bow. I glance over at Melanie-Anne who holds up her picture. She's made a good effort at drawing her pony, standing by his stable with a Christmas star in the background. Miss Wiggins gets round to Annabel and asks her why she's only drawn two blue eyes.

'It is a picture of my cat Snowy in the snow,' says Annabel.

Miss Wiggins raises her eyebrows, but she can't help smiling.

Soon it's time for break and mince pies. Because it is nearly Christmas everyone is allowed orange juice and coloured straws, and the hall has been decorated with a few bits of tinsel here and there. I know I'm a lucky girl to have such a nicely decorated nursery at home.

I gather my girls around me.

'*So*!!' I say. 'I have more news!'

When I tell them about the spinning statue, Melanie-Anne gives a great big shiver.

'Weren't you scared?'

It's a good question. I stop and think about it, trying to remember how I felt. I always tell the truth to my friends.

'Yes, I was a bit.'

'So, what was it, do you think?' Annabel asks. 'Another ghost?'

We turn to Sarah. Her mum might have come across spinning statues before.

'Only you saw it?'

'Does that make a difference?' asks Melanie-Anne.

'Well it makes it more difficult, if you want grown-ups to believe you. And we know what they can be like.' Sarah rolls her eyes. 'Although my mum's pretty good.'

'You're lucky,' says Melanie-Anne.

'So, what do you think it was, Sarah,' I ask. We wait for the answer. While we're waiting, Annabel says she loved that mince pie. She could do with another one.

'Could it be a mirage?' This is an interesting idea from Melanie-Anne, but none of us know what a mirage is, and Melanie-Anne isn't sure she does either. She says she heard her brother talking about one the other day, something to do with the desert.

'Not very likely,' Sarah says but in a lovely, kind voice. 'But actually, I *have* got an idea. I think you might have seen a portal.'

For the rest of us, the word portal is no better than mirage. But Sarah tells us it's like a magical, spinning doorway. Her mum's got a book on fairy portals. Perhaps something is coming through? Not just fairies though.

I don't like the sound of this. Annabel asks if my father has a dictionary at home, then maybe I could look up *mirage* and *portal*. I will have to get into Daddy's study and I'm sure I can do that.

Miss Wiggins is staring at us from across the hall. We know it's time to stop the meeting. As we climb to our feet, Sarah asks if I'm sure the magpie flew off when the statue disappeared. I tell her I'm pretty sure that's what happened.

'Then the magpie could have flown *into* the portal,' she says. I stare at her and she frowns.

'If the magpie flew *into* the portal, then it can fly *out* again. Whenever it likes.'

On the way home from school with Nanny Jan, I have a think. The nursery magpie might have flown out of a portal and, if a magpie can fly in and out, so might other things. Finn's *Thing* might have come through a portal. There might be one in the nursery and one on the lawn. And maybe we can't always see them? Did Mercy appear out of a portal, a hunting portal? That would explain how she disappeared so quickly. I have a horrible thought ... *I* might disappear into a portal. And what about Mummy and Daddy and Nanny Jan and Finn?

This is a nightmare! But I don't tell Nanny Jan.

Finn's mince pie, wrapped in greaseproof paper, balances on my knee. There *was* one left over and Miss Wiggins said of course I could take it home for Finn.

It's sleeting once we are home, and Nanny Jan says it might be too cold for our walk. We don't want to catch a cold for Christmas, do we? As I get out of the car, she tells me the Christmas tree is arriving tomorrow. That's good news, but I wish I didn't feel so worried.

Could a whole Christmas tree disappear into a portal? And what if Mummy's new tinsel and plastic tree disappeared too? She would be terribly upset. If we don't have to go for a walk, I will get into Daddy's study and look up *portal* and *mirage*.

In the meantime, I show my reindeer picture to Finn and give him his mince pie. 'It's really Christmas time now, Finn.'

'No more school, Melia?'

'No more school for now, no.'

I glance around the room. Is there a portal here now, right here in the nursery? How would I know? Then I have a brainwave.

Mr Magpie is the clue.

NANNY JAN

Camellia was very quiet in the car coming back from school. Usually she's full of it on the last day of term. She held up her little package which she said was a mince pie for her brother. She's such a kind girl sometimes.

After lunch she wanted to go through to Mr Devon's study to search for a dictionary. I asked her what she wanted it for, and she gave me such a look as if to say never you mind, Nanny Jan!

Mr and Mrs Devon were at the races today, so I gave her permission to slip through the big oak door to the other side. I noticed she took an exercise book with her and a pencil. Finn wanted to follow her through, but I managed to distract him with the promise of the Woodentops on television.

When she came back she was rather troubled. I offered to have a chat about whatever it was that was bothering her, but she said she was fine, just a bit tired. I suggested a little rest on the sofa with some of her favourite books. Then perhaps we could find the Christmas tree decorations, ready for tomorrow.

Camellia tucked herself up and very soon I noticed her eyelids drooping. It was most unusual for her to fall asleep like that, and I hoped she wasn't coming down with something. I got a jigsaw puzzle for Finn and me to put together, and that gave Camellia some peace. And so we had a very quiet afternoon.

When Camellia went up for her bath, she left her exercise book behind and I confess I did have a look in it. She had written in her best handwriting:

PORTAL: *grand doorway, gateway, around the church or castle doorway, entrance to bridge or tunnel.*

MIRAGE: optical illusion, apparition, trick, unrealistic hope.

Goodness, we had some words there! I wondered what she was up to? But if I knew Camellia, this wouldn't be the end of it.

Once the children were settled in bed and I had read them a story, I thought again about Camellia's words, but couldn't make much sense of them. After supper I watched Dr Kildare on television. I must say that Richard Chamberlain is ever so handsome.

The children were peaceful when I looked in on them before bed. I've never liked bolting Finn into his room. It doesn't seem right somehow.

CAMELLIA

Why was I so very tired yesterday? Once I'd looked the words up in Daddy's heavy dictionary, the only thing I wanted to do was sleep. I tried to look up other words like *illusion* and *apparition* but I could hardly keep my eyes open, and then Nanny Jan was very kind to me, tucking me up under a rug on the sofa.

This morning I feel different and I'm not sure how exactly. It's as if I'm more awake and my eyes can see everything, even *invisible* things.

The Christmas tree comes today and surely that will make the nursery happy. I just hope our tree doesn't vanish but, if we decorate it really well, then perhaps it will be safe.

I hear Mummy running into the airing cupboard! It's what she does in the morning when it's very cold weather. Our airing cupboard is big and warm, so it's a good place for getting dressed.

'Brrrrrrrr!' I hear Mummy shouting from behind the door. This means she's in a good mood. Perhaps Mummy's horse won at the races.

She comes out, dressed in her vest and pants and gives me a great big smile. She's happy.

'Mummy!' I cry.

'It's Christmas tree day, Camellia,' she says with her hands on her hips. 'And we know how to decorate trees, don't we?'

'We jolly well do!'

In that moment I forget all about portals. Mummy is happy and that's what matters.

CAMELLIA

Mummy says she has lots of things to do before lunch, but she promises we shall decorate both trees this afternoon. I'm allowed to help her put the beautiful fairies on her new tree in the drawing room, before we set about the nursery tree.

I can't *wait* for the afternoon to arrive! It's now eleven o'clock and we are having our elevenses. As a treat I'm having some milky coffee. It's delicious but I have to drink it as quickly as I can without burning my tongue. If I leave it for more than a minute, it forms a disgusting skin on the top. Nanny Jan says this is the trouble with hot milk and the secret is to keep stirring. Finn's having cold milk with a straw, and he's busy blowing bubbles through it.

We have found our Christmas tree decorations, and Nanny Jan checks the precious coloured lights. They can be the very devil she says because if one fairy light doesn't work, then the whole lot go on strike. Our lights are working, thank goodness.

We set up our little white church on the big chest. It has a nightlight inside it as well as a key to wind. Then it plays 'Silent Night', one of my favourite carols. Nanny Jan says 'Silent Night' is a German tune. It's much more beautiful than 'While Shepherds Watched Their Flocks by Night'. The only word for that one is boring.

Mr Gibbs, the gardener, staggers in with our Christmas tree, already planted in a big bucket of earth. He says it's very heavy and sets it down with a big sigh of relief. We give him a big smile and say thank you. Our tree is here! Nanny Jan puts some old wrapping-up paper around the bucket and I breathe in the smell of Christmas.

'Oh, Nanny Jan! Isn't that smell just like a Christmas tree forest?'

Nanny Jan smiles and Finn admires his paper-chain which hangs down over the pile of books.

'I did that,' he reminds us.

'And *so* you did,' Nanny Jan says. 'And this afternoon you will help decorate our tree.'

'You can do the lower branches, Finn,' I tell him. 'And you can choose your decorations from the box.' Finn is happy with that.

Nanny Jan says we are going on a morning walk. We can look for some holly and ivy to add to our decorations.

It's sunny and bright with frost on the grass and I'm wearing my pretty woollen gloves. I carry a baby trug over my arm, feeling just like Mummy. Finn is pulling his little cart. We begin by walking down the lawn towards the lost pond, and Finn runs ahead of me, making little footsteps in the frost. I hear Mr Magpie chattering in the tree above, very noisy. Is there a portal nearby? Finn carries on, pulling his cart into the sun. When I look back at the tree, Mr Magpie has gone but I can still hear chattering.

A voice in my head says '*I am kind, I am kind,*' and then Finn stops, pointing into the sunlight. I catch up with him.

'What is it, Finn?' I know what he is going to say.

'*THING,*' says Finn. He turns around. 'I want to go the other way.' He tugs at his cart crossly. There's something in it already. It's a small fir cone.

Nanny Jan joins us, wondering what's the matter. Finn tells her. She says she's sorry Finn saw his *Thing*, but, if we go to the west side of the garden, we'll be completely safe because his *Thing* doesn't live there. I check her face when she says this and am amazed that it looks the same as usual. Grown-ups are very good at telling fibs! It fools Finn in any case and we set off the other way.

It's much easier to spot the holly and ivy with the sun behind us. I find some holly with a few berries left, and Nanny Jan snips off a sprig for my trug. She gives another bit of holly to Finn who throws it into his cart. He has collected quite a few fir cones and I tell him how we could easily paint them for the nursery table.

Finn's cheeks are pink with cold and my feet have gone numb. I march to warm them up and Finn copies me. I know he has gone sad. Nanny Jan knows this too because she starts talking about lunch and having a game with him this afternoon.

As we cross the lawn by the rose beds, I spot three magpies having a meeting. They are chattering to one another. Chatter, chatter, chatter! If *only* I knew what they were saying.

They finish their meeting and take off towards the lost pond.

CAMELLIA

Mummy and I are off to the cellar to fetch her tree. She switches on the light for us to see down the stairs. We pass the boiler room and I remind myself that we must *never* touch the boiler. If we do touch the boiler it will blow up! It's a new one which is even more dangerous apparently, or so we're told.

We hurry past and Mummy finds her Christmas tree box. I help her carry it back upstairs and we laugh because it's a bit awkward. Her finger is mending nicely but she has to be careful. I feel very grown-up helping Mummy, and I thank Nanny Jan as she holds the big oak door open. Now we're into the hall and then the drawing room.

The drawing room is *beautiful* with the softest, pale carpet and heavy green brocade curtains. Mummy has already lit the fire and Banger lies asleep in front of it, her favourite place. Bramble is out with Daddy, shooting probably.

Mummy sets the tree up on a little low table, bending the branches out, and asks what I think of it.

'It's like a Christmas tree covered with snow!'

We agree that's exactly what it's like and Mummy says it was well worth £18. She warns me not to tell Daddy how much it cost.

Mummy winds the white lights round first and then we begin hanging the floating angels on to the tinsel branches. This is something we're both good at, and I feel a surge of happiness. I catch Mummy's eye and she smiles.

'Very good, Camellia.' She switches on the white lights and I hold my breath.

'It's brilliant isn't it Mummy?' I clap my hands for joy.

Mummy suggests we draw the curtains and turn off all the other lights. Then we stand back and admire the tree. It's perfect. This moment is just perfect. There never was a more beautiful tree.

Mummy asks if I would like Nanny Jan and Finn to see the tree, and her telephone rings as I run out of the room.

NANNY JAN

Oh, I did feel sorry for Camellia this afternoon. She had set her heart on Mrs Devon's helping us decorate the nursery tree, and she was ever so disappointed when her mother said she had to go out to deal with something (we never discovered what).

Mrs Devon was on the telephone when Finn and I went through to admire the new tree and very pretty it looked too. Camellia's face was a picture.

Eventually Mrs Devon put the receiver down with a frown, saying she had to go out in the car immediately. Camellia said: 'But what about our tree, Mummy?' and was told that her mother was very sorry, but something had come up. We three could have lots of fun decorating the nursery tree.

Camellia said quite rightly 'It's not the *same*' and 'It's not *fair*.' Then her shoulders drooped but she didn't plead with her mother any more.

Back in the nursery Finn handed her one of his favourite decorations. She could put it up on one of her high branches. Camellia brushed away a tear at that point and said she needed to go upstairs to fetch Dorothy Baby.

When she came back downstairs again, she didn't have her doll with her, but her eyes were red. I switched my wireless on and luckily it was playing Christmas carols.

So, the three of us set about decorating the tree. Camellia's heart wasn't in it to begin with but then Finn made us laugh, trying to balance his fir cones on the lower branches. He would say 'Oh blast it' every time a fir cone fell off and Camellia got the giggles.

'It's really very difficult,' Finn said. 'They won't stick!'

'I hope the Christmas fairy won't fall off,' I said, offering to pop her on. We wished the fairy luck. She said she had good balance.

Once the Christmas fairy was in place, I switched on the lights and the tree was done. Camellia wound up the little church and we listened to one verse of 'Silent Night'.

Banger was scratching at the door, so I let her out. However, she was back in almost immediately with her tail down. Perhaps she didn't like the sound of chattering in the dark. I heard it too. Do magpies chatter in the dark?

At the time I thought it odd, but by then it was time for tea.

CAMELLIA

Mummy came in to see me last night. I was tucked up in bed with my books, Dorothy Baby asleep in her cot beside me. She said she was very sorry she couldn't help with the nursery tree, so I suppose that was something. She looked very pretty as usual but quite tired.

I decided to show her my picture of Mercy. What would Mummy think of it?

'She can't have been a foot-follower, not wearing that?' Mummy said, crossing her legs. 'Quite some necklace!' Already I knew Mummy wasn't concentrating. This often happens with grown-ups.

'I *saw* her, and she surprised Robin,' I said, smoothing my eiderdown down. 'Robin saw her!' I could tell Mummy wanted to go, but I pressed on.

'Who does that big window in church belong to? The one near the pulpit.' I could tell Mummy was surprised at my question.

'It's for one of Daddy's relations. Her husband made sure she was never forgotten by having a stained-glass window dedicated to her.' Mummy was looking at her watch, saying something about needing to talk to Cook about the party tomorrow night.

'You and Finn are going to stay with Gran and Grandpop, remember. Nanny Jan will come with you. It will be fun to stay there.' Now I knew Mummy was saying things to make her feel better, and that made me annoyed. I thought it was selfish of her actually.

I had one more question for Mummy. She'd already kissed me goodnight and was moving towards the door.

'Why are you so scared of magpies, Mummy?'

I was feeling hurt and I meant to hurt her. Afterwards I felt sorry about that but right then I saw her back go stiff.

'One for sorrow, Camellia. One for sorrow.'

She left to say goodnight to Finn. There was no more for me.

That was yesterday, and now I am sitting with Finn in Gran's smoky sitting room. It's not a drawing room because it's too small. Gran's fire has 'a tendency to smoke' which means there's quite a lot of fog hanging in the room. Gran doesn't seem to notice though. I don't know where Grandpop is.

We had to have our tea at the dining room table, because Gran doesn't have a nursery. Finn sat on a cushion to reach his tea. He had milk in his own mug, but Gran gave me her special China tea, pouring it into one of her beautiful green and white china cups. She says her tea is called Lapsang Suchong and I love it, even if it does taste like a bonfire. I also love Gran's gingerbread cake which has real bits of ginger in it.

Nanny Jan is in Horsham, doing a last bit of Christmas shopping but she'll be with us for bath time. I hate the spare bathroom here. It has a horrible feeling, not friendly at all. I certainly don't want to be left alone in it, so I'll ask Nanny Jan if Finn and I can have our bath together.

I can tell Gran doesn't really know what to talk about because she's not used to little children. So, I suggest that maybe we could play a game of Ludo or something. Gran goes to her big chest of drawers, brings out several games and we let Finn choose.

While Finn is choosing, I wander over to Gran's desk to have a look at her photographs. There, in a small silver frame, is a picture of Mercy! It has to be her! She's wearing the very same dress and necklace, and I could hardly forget those big staring eyes. I hold out the picture.

'Who's this, Gran?' My heart is beating fast.

Gran takes the silver frame from me, puts on her glasses, looks at the photograph and hands it back to me. Her face is stern.

'That's a picture of my mother.'

'I saw her out hunting when Mummy broke her finger.' I just come out with it.

Gran's back goes stiff and she says that's not possible because her mother is dead. She says she died when Gran was a baby.

'Well I saw her ghost then. She surprised Robin and then Mummy fell off and broke her finger.'

Gran's face goes very white. The fire puffs out some more smoke and I hear the ticking of the mantlepiece clock. Finn has stopped his sorting and is staring at us. I smile, hoping Gran will smile back, but she's not smiling, not one bit.

'That's impossible, Camellia.' Gran's voice sounds like Miss Wiggins when she's telling someone off.

'But I saw her. I think she was a ghost. It was her!' Now Gran's face has shut down, her eyes scrunched up and small.

'The Church forbids us to talk of ghosts, Camellia. It's wicked to believe in such things.' It as if she wants to say something more, but instead she turns her back on me, asking Finn if he has found a game to play.

Finn looks at me and then Gran. He holds out the Ludo box and Gran sets the game up, red for Finn and blue for her and she doesn't include me. Ludo's no fun with just two people. I would have been yellow. I put the photograph back on the desk. What do I do now? What can I do? I have made Gran angry.

She doesn't take any notice when I walk past. I run upstairs to my room. I should *never* have asked about Mercy, but I don't understand why she's so cross. I can't help it if Mercy is Gran's

Mummy. It isn't my fault she died. But I'm in trouble, that I do know.

I wish I was at home and not in this beastly room. There's a *horrible* picture on the wall. It's of a miser counting his money, at least that's what Nanny Jan says. Why would Gran want a picture of a miser in her spare room?

I'm not welcome downstairs because I've done something wrong, very wrong. I am worn out and fed up, so I climb up on my bed, pressing my face into the satin eiderdown. I'm crying again, but I can't help it. I *hate* being told off. I want Nanny Jan to come back.

Then I remember I have my picture of Mercy with me, so I unfold it to study her face and dress. It's definitely the same person as Gran's photo. Anyone can see that.

I lie there, patiently waiting for my tears to dry up. Then, for something to do, I sit in front of my dressing-table mirror and start to brush my hair. I have to blink a few times because my face in the mirror is hazy for some reason, but it doesn't seem to make any difference. I stare down at my hairbrush and see it perfectly well, so there's nothing wrong with my eyes. Then I hear a funny ticking sound, and I dare myself to look back into the mirror. I wish I hadn't because a face suddenly appears behind me, hovering in mid-air. I blink hard only to see its yawning grey mouth and half-closed eyes flickering like a ciné film. I quickly look down. Why would I want to see such a horrible face? It's worse than the miser's. Go *away*. *Please* go away. And why has my back turned to ice? Go *away*! I don't want you here.

It works. When I turn around, it's gone and the ticking has stopped. But what if it comes back? I take a deep breath and stand up, my hands in fists.

I ask a question out loud.

Who are you?

But you know who I am, don't you?

How do I know?

You've always known.

Am I going mad? Who does this voice belong to? I must get out of this awful room! But then I know. How could I not know? The air warms up around me, like a soft breeze in summer.

Of course it's Mercy. Poor Mercy, and she needs my help. But goodness I will need a lot of courage. She didn't look very nice in the mirror with her face all grey and yawning, not as pretty as out hunting, but that's probably because she's so unhappy. I tuck the picture down my vest, and it makes me feel braver. I don't dare look in the mirror again.

I run downstairs to find Gran and Finn. They have finished their game of Ludo and now they're playing snap. I say I'm sorry to Gran. She smiles a tight smile.

'No more talk like that, Camellia.'

She makes me feel as if I'm about three years old. Why doesn't Gran have a Christmas tree? But I don't dare ask her that!

I want Nanny Jan to come back.

NANNY JAN

I feel for those children, I really do. When I got back yesterday afternoon, having done a bit of shopping for myself, I found Finn wearing his patch (I had expressly said he could take it off after tea) and Camellia in one of her sulks.

I know Old Mrs Devon tries her best with the children, and I've no doubt she's very fond of them, even if they are not of her blood, but she's so very Victorian! I wish she could show a bit of *humour* sometimes. She comes across as ever so strict. I wouldn't dream of telling her how to be with the children because she wouldn't like it, and anyway it isn't my place. That's just the way she is. But goodness it makes more work for me!

The children stuck to me like glue once I was back, almost shrinking away from their grandmother. I know that hurts her, but what those two children need are laughs and cuddles, and a listening ear. I'm not sure how much Finn takes in to be honest, but Camellia can become very despondent if she isn't listened to or encouraged.

So, I had a pair of very subdued children to bath. Camellia

insisted she wanted to share her bath with Finn, and I must say they did have fun, being as I let them have some of my Radox bubble bath. Camellia claimed it was going to soak her aches and pains away, that she thought her Gran could do with some as well. It might cheer her up, she said.

Once in bed, Camellia owned up to being told off by her grandmother, and I wasn't sure what to say. I suggested that perhaps the reason her Gran was strict was because she was upset about her own poor mother, especially at Christmas time. I thought we were going to have more tears then, but instead Camellia said she'd had enough of crying. She was all cried out.

She asked me whether I could find out any more information about Old Mrs Devon's poor dead mother. She said if she knew more, then she could better help her ghost. I promised her I would.

It was only when I was tucking her bedclothes in tight that she told me about the mirror. I didn't like the sound of it, but I made sure I didn't tell her that.

Tomorrow I will ask Mrs Betts if she knows any family history. That's if poor Mrs Betts has a moment to spare with all the clearing up. I might get a moment during morning coffee.

CAMELLIA

I'm awake and in the dark. I look for my china mouse night-light, but it isn't there. I remember I'm in Gran and Grandpop's house, worst luck. I hear a knocking sound over by the door. Perhaps someone wants to come in?

There's a sudden loud BANG and my heart starts to thump. It's going to jump right out of my chest at this rate! I know Mummy says radiators can make funny noises in the night, especially new ones like ours, but could a radiator make a bang as loud as that? I wonder Nanny Jan didn't hear it. She and Finn are next door. I listen, hearing taps and knocks.

I know I'm not brave enough to investigate, so I stay under the covers, and now all I can hear is the wind blowing outside.

Perhaps that's the reason. My window is rattling a fair bit.

It's no good! I turn on my bedside light to look at my watch. It's five minutes past three in the morning! I'm never awake at this time, not unless I have a temperature, and I know I'm not ill. I would hate to be ill in this awful bedroom.

Dorothy Baby is asleep, her eyes tightly closed. I know she prefers to be in her pretty cot, but Nanny Jan said it wasn't worth bringing it here for one night. It's a great comfort to have her tucked in beside me.

The knocks have stopped now, thank goodness. Instead I hear someone crying from far, far away. Maybe it's Finn and of course his crying would sound quiet from next door. There are big walls between us. Nanny Jan is there for him though, so I mustn't worry. I strain my ears to listen more, but now the only thing I can hear is my window rattling in the wind.

I don't know why I want to sing 'Rock-a-Bye Baby'. I don't sing the last bit because it's rather horrible. There's no more crying or knocking, and everything is quiet. I switch off my light and settle down.

'*Rock a bye baby on the tree top. When the wind blows, the cradle will rock.*'

CAMELLIA

I have loads more information now! I know who Mercy is and I know her real name, although I prefer to call her Mercy. I can't wait to tell my friends, but I won't see any of them until after Christmas, when Melanie-Anne has her Christmas Party. I will make a list of everything I know and take it to the party on 29th December, but that's *ages* away!

Nanny Jan was kind and understanding when I told her about Gran. I saved it up until after bath time because, if you share something with Finn, he can repeat it at just the wrong moment. I wouldn't want to upset Gran any more, and I would hate to be told off again. But I want to find out more.

It was while we were having our elevenses with Mrs Betts that Nanny Jan asked the question. We were sitting at the kitchen table for a change because the nursery was being put back to normal after the party. Mrs Betts had the answer immediately, fixing me with a knowing look.

'Your great-grandmother, dear, that is Old Mrs Devon's mother, died on Christmas Eve in 1896. Ever so sad it must have been to leave your little baby like that, but I suppose if you're dying, you're dying, and you can't help it. Colonel Devon was that sad he had to have a big window made in church, the one you see today.'

I stirred my milky coffee.

'Do you think that's why Gran doesn't have a Christmas tree? She's just too sad?'

Mrs Betts said she thought as much. It must be a very sorrowful time for Old Mrs Devon. I was about to ask Mrs Betts if she believed in ghosts when I caught Nanny Jan's eye and she shook her head. Not in front of Finn.

So, we went back to talking about how many glasses there were to wash up and the funny places some of them were left. Mrs Betts said she found one in the yellow bathroom!

'What a lark!' she said. 'Now where did I put that duster?'

Then she asked me a question.

'Do you reckon it looks like snow, Camellia? What if we had snow for Christmas?'

'What a lark!' said Finn, and we all laughed.

CAMELLIA

It's Christmas Eve morning. After breakfast Nanny Jan is going to take us for a walk up to the stables, so we can give Henry his present, and also for Finn to have a practice sit on Robin. Finn doesn't really want to do this, but I tell him it's good for him and it might make his legs grow.

We're having porridge as usual and I watch my brown sugar melt into treacly circles. It's just the sort of weather for porridge because it's foggy yet again. I tell Finn we can be dragons on our walk and ask him what colour dragon he wants to be.

'Tangerine,' he says. It's often tangerine with Finn, and I tell him tangerine dragons are the best.

We take the dogs with us. Finn's wearing his jodhpurs and they're far too big for him. He says he can't walk properly. I huff and I puff, showing him how to make dragon smoke in the freezing air and that gets his legs going. There's lots of chattering up ahead. Magpies again, five of them in the apple tree. They're very smart. Finn hasn't noticed them because he's concentrating on being a dragon.

Henry greets us and thanks Nanny Jan for the present. He's dressed in his camel-coloured overall with his hair sticking up. He says he's been working very hard this morning but there's always time for us. He tacks up Robin and brings him out.

Finn sits on Robin with his feet in the leathers, not the stirrups, and Henry asks how that feels. I know that Finn is never going to be a jockey, but I don't say so. His hat is so big it slips down over his eyes, and Nanny Jan has to push it back up. Then she takes Finn's patch off because she wants to take a photo. I hold the patch while Henry leads Robin to a spot in front of the gate.

Nanny Jan takes two or three photos, telling Finn he's sitting very nicely, but suddenly the dogs bark, making Robin jump. He pitches forward and Finn slides sideways, lucky that Henry catches him. Once safe in Henry's arms, Finn's face crumples. He's thinking about wailing I know.

The magpies chatter away in the apple tree and all at once I know something. Mr Magpie is a useful messenger! He's able to warn us when something is about to happen. Finn doesn't want to sit on Robin any more and Nanny Jan says she understands.

'Poor old Finn,' she says. 'What a shock!'

'Didn't like that,' Finn says as we walk back home.

'Robin is *not* reliable,' I say to Nanny Jan as well as Finn.

'But *you* are,' Nanny Jan says, taking the patch back. 'Now let's think about wrapping up presents.'

I help Finn hunt for fir cones on the way.

CAMELLIA

It's been decided that I am to go to church this afternoon for a special Christmas Eve service, starting at 5 o'clock. Mummy came in before lunch and said that Gran would take me in her car.

I'm a bit nervous about Gran because she might tell me off again. Nanny Jan says during lunch that Gran might be sorry she was sharp with me and this might be her way of making up.

'I will just ask her nice questions,' I say. 'Like what is her favourite carol, that sort of thing.'

Nanny Jan says that would be good, and I could also show her how well I know my carols by singing like a nightingale. I have never heard a nightingale sing but Nanny Jan has. She says nightingales sing like angels, mostly at night which is when angels sing. This is news to me.

Finn will stay behind as he's still a bit young for church in the evening, and it would take an awful lot of sweets to keep him quiet. I'm too grown up for sweets, but Nanny Jan pops a couple of toffees into my coat pocket while Gran is waiting in her car. I thank her and hear Finn asking for a toffee as the back door closes.

'Well, here we are together, Camellia,' says Gran, steering the car out of the driveway. 'Off to church!'

It's as if we're off to the pantomime! I know she's trying her best, so I tell her how much I like going out in the dark. It's foggy still and Gran has to drive very slowly. Luckily, she knows the road to church very well and it's only about a mile.

I'm warm enough in my navy-blue coat and Gran is top to toe in fur. As usual people stare at us coming into church. Already the pews are full up, and from the back I hear a baby crying. We can see the huge crib on the side with the figures of Mary and Joseph, but there's no Baby Jesus yet. He arrives in the manger tomorrow. Then it will be Christmas.

Gran sinks to her knees and I feel a bit embarrassed. She does some praying with her eyes closed but her lips are moving. I shut my eyes and stay sitting. Then I look up the carols in my hymn book, remembering to ask Gran which is her favourite.

'It's always been "O Little Town of Bethlehem",' she says with a smile.

'That's a lovely one,' I say, and I mean it.

'Which is your favourite?' she asks.

I tell her it's 'Silent Night' and Gran's purses her lips. Perhaps 'Silent Night' is *not* a favourite of hers, but I don't dare ask why not. When I look across at Mercy's window, it's dark. I wonder what time she died? Was it about now?

'Isn't the Christmas tree pretty, Gran?' I point out the church tree with its fairy lights. If I'm honest, it's not nearly as cheerful as ours.

Gran then does something strange. She reaches out for my hand, holding it fast. I stare up into her face and it's as white as chalk. Her eyes seem very blue because they are watery. I smile and she smiles back.

The organ starts up and Gran lets go of my hand. We sing 'Once in Royal David's City' and our happy singing fills the church. Gran's voice is weak, so I sing for both of us. I know this carol backwards! The service is for children, so it isn't boring. No sermon thank goodness! Instead the vicar tells us he's already hung up his stocking! But is he too old for presents?

I don't know if Gran has noticed but there's a magpie on one of the organ pipes. I know he's real because a boy on the other side of the church is pointing. The magpie watches us, still as a statue. Does this mean there's a portal in church? Surely not in such a Holy Place?

He's still there when we start 'O Little Town of Bethlehem'. I lean in towards Gran, her fur coat feeling soft against my face. She sings this one in a much stronger voice, and she smiles down at me halfway through the second verse.

We sit down and the baby starts crying again. I look up to check on the magpie and it has vanished. Suddenly I feel a bit funny, wondering why there's a great red whooshing in my ears as if a hundred wings are beating. What's the matter with me? I put my head down low and take some deep breaths, telling myself not to panic. Everyone is praying now so I don't think Gran has noticed. I clench and unclench my fists and stare at my shoes. I mustn't make a fuss in church.

Perhaps the church portal is trying to take me?! Perhaps I'm wrong and I *can* disappear into one. My heart thuds and I try my very best to listen to the prayers. When that doesn't work, I think about Finn and Nanny Jan and my stocking and everything at home. I have to concentrate very hard.

But now I'm feeling better. I take another deep breath and wonder whether it's time for a toffee. I chew as quietly as possible and hear that same voice again whispering: '*I am Gone, I am Gone.*' I look at Gran but it's obvious she didn't hear it. She's finding her place in the hymn book, ready for the last carol.

What a day! I shall add what happened in church to my list. That was very scary, but at least I wasn't swallowed up by the portal. As we leave our pew, Gran looks up quickly towards Mercy's window but then she starts talking to someone from the village. They smile kindly at me, saying how much I've grown. I don't know who they are, but I smile back politely.

'Well, wasn't that a lovely service?' Gran says happily as soon as we're in the car. The usual after church conversation! The fog has lifted slightly but, if anything, it's even colder. My watch says six o'clock. Only six hours till Christmas Day!

Gran delivers me to the back door. I kiss her goodnight and remember my second toffee. I ask for her hand, telling her to close her eyes. Then I place the toffee in her palm, wrapping her fingers around it. Now she's allowed to open them.

'That's for you, Gran. Thank you for taking me to church.' Gran is lost for a second, but then she recovers.

'Thank you, darling Camellia. Happy Christmas.' She shuts the door behind her, off into the dark again.

I dance into the nursery to find Nanny Jan and Finn, sitting on the sofa with the Christmas tree twinkling. Our stockings are laid out flat on the little table, ready to be taken upstairs. There's a Christmas Eve mince pie for me and a cup of tea. I breathe in the scent of the tree and take off my coat.

Gran called me darling!

CAMELLIA
Christmas Eve

I wake to a funny, scrabbling noise. Goodness, is it Father Christmas? I must pretend to be asleep otherwise he won't leave me any presents.

There's more scrabbling, so I push my feet down the bed to test if my stocking is heavy or not. I can't feel anything which means Father Christmas can't have been yet, but now I'm worried because I'm awake and I might see him. Ever since ever I've been worried about seeing him.

The scrabbling stops. I lie on my back like a church statue, wondering if I imagined it. What's the time? I open my eyes just a tiny bit, and there is the comforting pink glow of my china mouse nightlight. I tell myself I must go back to sleep and then Father Christmas will come, and then it will be Christmas Day.

More scrabbling and this time it's louder. It seems to be coming from my dressing table, as far as I can tell. I dare to open my eyes properly, reaching for the little torch on my bedside table. When I check my watch, it says a quarter past eleven, so that's very late indeed!

The scrabbling has stopped, so I shine my torch towards my dressing table. The drawer is open! This is odd because I know I didn't leave it like that. I keep my hairbrush in there, along with some beads and other precious things. My picture of Mercy's in there too. Why is the drawer open now?

I keep the torch beam on the drawer, and it's then that I see a most horrible thing. In front of my eyes, the drawer slides shut all by itself. It's as if it's alive! Everything in me knows this isn't possible. A drawer does *not* shut itself, not unless someone pushes it. I don't know what to do!

If I switch on my light, Father Christmas will know I'm awake. I had better sit in the dark, watching the drawer with my torch, but if it opens again, I will scream. I won't be able to help it. My room is freezing cold, and I'm shivering. I must lie down again to get warm.

I seem to have a drawer that can move all by itself as well as making horrible scrabbling noises. It's half past eleven, and I've been awake for a quarter of an hour. I will *have* to go to sleep soon otherwise Father Christmas will not come.

I shine my torch around the room to make sure a magpie isn't perched on the curtain rail, hiding in the shadows. Perhaps it was Mercy searching for her picture? I switch off the torch and go right down under the bedclothes, pulling them over my head. This way I can't see or hear anything. It's quite hard to breathe but it's definitely safer like this. I pray that Finn is fast asleep next door.

I try to think of happy things like our Christmas tree and Mummy's tinsel tree, as well Mrs Betts's kindness and the Clitheroe Kid. Of course, all I can think about is Mercy.

Mercy, Mercy, Mercy.

What does she want? I must sleep.

CAMELLIA
Christmas morning
I'm awake and it's Christmas morning! It's still dark but it must be past seven o'clock surely? I stretch out my foot and feel for my stocking. Yes, there it is, as heavy as an elephant! So, Father Christmas did come after all.

The drawer! Was it a dream? Well, more of a nightmare really. But I'm not going to think about that now, not on Christmas morning! I switch on my light and see my great big stocking. There are all sorts of funny shaped things inside and at the top is what looks like a book. I reach in and draw out my first present. It is indeed a book and, even better, a diary. Just what I need!

Next are some pencils and a beautiful wooden pencil case. Now a woolly hat with a robin on the front. That will be useful! Reaching even further into the stocking, I pull out a rolled-up colouring book. It's of Snow White and the Seven Dwarfs. Next there's a big tube of Fruit Pastilles which are my favourite, then a pair of red socks and right at the end a tangerine.

What presents! Father Christmas has done very well indeed. I put on my hat and eat the tangerine. Then I draw the curtains. There's only the faintest pink and grey Christmas light coming up in the east, but soon it will be daytime.

I wonder if Finn's awake. I open my door slowly and peer through Finn's chicken wire. I can't actually see him from here, just his chest of drawers and window.

I whisper loudly 'Finn, are you awake?' I hear him get down from his bed and pad towards me. His hair is sticking up on one side and his pyjama bottoms are too long. They were mine.

'Yes. I'm awake,' he says. 'And my stocking's full.'

I suggest he puts his dressing gown on and comes into my room. I unbolt his wire door and he comes through, staggering under the weight of his stocking. He climbs into my bed and sits there, like a little owl. His eye is mending nicely and it looks straight at me.

'Come on then, Finn,' I say. 'Let's see what Father Christmas has brought you!' Finn makes a start pulling everything out. He finds his hat which has a Christmas pudding on the front. He puts it on. Now we are both in our hats, and we laugh, pointing at each other.

And that's how Nanny Jan finds us, dressed in her quilted dressing gown of the prettiest sky blue. She kisses us both, wishing us Happy Christmas. Finn holds up his tube of Fruit Pastilles for her to take one. He can't speak as his mouth is full. We show Nanny Jan our wonderful presents and she says we're very lucky children, but we know that already.

It's a bit early to go in to see Mummy and Daddy, so Nanny Jan says we can creep downstairs in our dressing gowns, have a hot drink in the nursery and look at the Christmas tree. Nanny Jan goes to find her slippers, followed by Finn, and I search for mine. It's only then I notice Dorothy Baby is missing. She's not in her cot. Perhaps she fell out? But that doesn't seem very likely. I don't understand it. Where could she have gone? I check my other dolls on the shelf, and they are all there.

'Come on Melia,' calls Finn. 'Hurry up!'

I must think! I remember again what happened in the night and go over to my dressing table. I carefully open the drawer. My picture of Mercy has gone! I search under all the beads and my hairbrush, but the picture is nowhere to be seen.

I'm in the middle of my room, my hands on my head. That helps me think. All the presents on my bed cannot make up for no Dorothy Baby. Mercy must have taken her, along with her picture, but *WHY*? I drop my hands after a bit. I know what's happened. And it's not fair.

Dorothy Baby and my picture have gone into the portal.

ANGELA

Well I think I can safely say I am utterly, utterly exhausted. That party! Why Gerald thinks it's a good idea to have a party right before Christmas I have no idea. But I always have to go along with it.

Of course, it was a success because we know our parties are the best. But it does take one hell of a lot of organising and then clearing up afterwards. It just adds to all the things I have to sort out every single day. If it isn't one thing after another! What I would really like to do is sit quietly in the drawing room in front of the fire doing absolutely nothing! Fat chance.

I feel permanently harassed because Gerald spends most of his time telling me to hurry up. Hurry up, Angela, for God's sake hurry up. I can hear his voice now.

I did very well filling the children's Christmas stockings after the midnight service, remembering which hat to put in which stocking. I cannot expect Nanny Jan to do this although she does pretty much everything else. The children are very attached to her and I know it's a good thing, but it doesn't leave much room for me.

The fact that I couldn't help Camellia with the nursery tree didn't improve things. Mind you, we did have fun with my new tree, and it was good to see Camellia's funny side there. She's mostly so serious. Then she went into the most dreadful sulk because I had to go out. I simply couldn't put that off and we all know why. Well, I do.

So, then I felt most frightfully guilty and I hate that. Finn doesn't mind because he's too young, but the one thing I hate is being judged by Camellia.

Something obviously happened when the children went to Constance. I haven't discovered what but often it's easier not to ask. All I know is that Camellia was even more hunched up and scowling. And it isn't as if my father hasn't told her a hundred times to put her shoulders back.

We have everyone coming to lunch today, and I must check that Cook knows what she's doing with the turkey. I told her it needed to go in at 8.30am.

And now on Christmas Day of all days we have Camellia in high dudgeon because her best doll has gone missing. As if I hadn't got enough to worry about! Gerald didn't help the situation by reminding Camellia she had plenty of other dolls. Even I know she loves that one the best. What she doesn't know is that I am giving her a very expensive NEW doll. I bought her in Harrods only last week.

The children looked adorable in their hats, especially Finn. Luckily, I remembered to remove the labels, because Camellia doesn't miss a trick. At least she seemed pleased with her red diary. I don't know where I would be without my diary! It's absolutely essential with all the hundred and one things I have to do.

I do wish my hair wasn't such a trial. It looked quite nice for the midnight, but jamming it under that hat hasn't done it any favours. I will have to do some backcombing which always takes time, and this little finger of mine makes it even more difficult. As if I hadn't got enough to do!

The drawing room fire needs to be lit as soon as we get back from church. I will let the children off coming as I'm not sure I can face Camellia's scowls. I had better do my backcombing when I come back. No point before because I have got to wear another bloody hat.

I must get on. There's so much to do. Church, presents, Christmas lunch and then dinner with Jack and Constance. I shall be on my knees!

CAMELLIA

I've spent all morning searching for Dorothy Baby, and it's ruined my Christmas Day so far. I can't *bear* to think she's disappeared into the portal, and I'm still searching. Nanny Jan has been helping and even Finn's been doing his best. He must have looked under that nursery cushion a hundred times!

Mummy and Daddy do *not* understand. When we went in to see them and I told them about poor Dorothy Baby, Daddy said that I had plenty of other dolls. How could he?! I was furious and gave him my worst stare. Mummy was kinder and said she was very sorry but perhaps I'd left Dorothy Baby somewhere and forgotten where I'd put her. Mummy said she did that all the time with her glasses. I could have screamed! Glasses are not the same as dolls, and Mummy knows that *perfectly* well.

We have searched all the cupboards, under the sofas and chairs, under the spare room beds, in the bathroom cupboards, the kitchen cupboards (Cook was not very pleased), in the airing cupboard (that took quite a long time) but Dorothy Baby is nowhere to be seen.

I go back to my bedroom *again* to see if by some miracle she has appeared in her little cot. She has not. I open my drawer and my picture is not there.

Nanny Jan calls up the stairs, time for elevenses. I bring my red diary down, along with the pencil case and pencils. I know I must write about poor Dorothy Baby, but my diary doesn't start until 1st January 1963. I stare at the page, hearing the word *sorrow* in my head. I close my eyes, hoping the *sorrow* will disappear.

'Magpie, Melia,' says Finn.

I am praying the magpie isn't actually in the nursery. Finn

points at the terrace. There's a magpie staring in at us. He is quite still. I walk over to the door and bang on the window.

'Where have you taken Dorothy Baby?' The magpie puts his head on one side, opens his beak and chatters one word. It sounds like *home*. His eye is very bright.

Finn comes over to the window, patch in place and says to the magpie.

'Where's Melia's doll?

'The magpie says Dorothy Baby has gone *home*.'

Finn bites on his iced biscuit and gives a big sigh.

'Poor Melia,' he says, patting my back.

The magpie turns and takes off. He has delivered his Christmas message.

NANNY JAN

I did feel for the poor child this morning. We have searched high and low for Dorothy Baby and Camellia is quite devastated. She knows she put her to bed in her cot last night and I do believe her. Camellia's mothering skills are second to none, and it seems inconceivable that Camellia could have mislaid her.

Our Christmas breakfast was spoiled as there was *nothing* I could say to cheer her up. Finn trailed after his sister doing his best, and it was such a shame because the children should have been having fun, enjoying their stocking presents.

For the life of me I can't think where that doll has gone. Mr and Mrs Devon went off to church and I thought it sensible that the children were excused. As it turned out we used all that time to search.

I got the children changed after elevenses, posting them through to the drawing room so they could open their presents. There were quite a few from godparents and the like. I retired back to the nursery for a bit of tidying up.

I saw that blessed magpie on the terrace again. I don't like him! Magpies always mean trouble in my book. I banged the window and shooed him away.

We are all in the dining room for Christmas lunch, so I hope the children are on best behaviour. Once lunch is finished, we can settle down in the nursery and watch some television. They will be over the top by then and need calming down.

Where *can* that doll have got to?

CAMELLIA

We are in the drawing room with Mummy and Daddy. The fire is crackling with both dogs lying in front of it. I pat Banger's rough white coat and she stretches out her little legs. Her tummy's getting hot.

Mummy and Daddy are smiling at us. Mummy's hair looks a bit odd, sort of flat on top and bushy at the back. I know she finds it difficult with her broken finger to get her hair just right. You can tell she's been wearing a hat.

I ask Mummy if the Baby Jesus has arrived in the manger. Mummy looks puzzled for a moment as if that's a very difficult question.

'You *know*, Mummy! The Baby Jesus in the crib, with Mary and Joseph and the shepherds. He wasn't in the manger when I was there with Gran. He's never there on Christmas Eve. He arrives on Christmas Day. He's meant to be there today. So, *was* he?' Mummy's annoyed because I'm getting worked up, I know it.

'Baby Jesus was there, Camellia, just as he should be. You needn't worry.'

But I *am* worried about Baby Jesus! What if he disappeared into the portal like Dorothy Baby? There was a magpie in church after all. Mummy doesn't really understand. She never really understands.

Mummy points at her Christmas present for me.

'There, Camellia, open that one first.' I kneel to tear off the Christmas paper. There in a cardboard box is the most beautiful doll. She has golden hair down to her shoulders and bright blue eyes which fly open when I tip her upright. Her dress is pale green and white with a bow at the front. Her shoes are rose pink. She's heavenly!

'Oh, thank you, Mummy!' I go over to give her a kiss.

Daddy's about to say something, but Mummy stops him. She's watching Finn scrabble with his paper, trying to get into his present. It's quite a big box and Mummy has to help him. Soon she lifts out a little wooden wheelbarrow. It's just the right size for Finn and I can tell he is delighted.

'You can collect lots of fir cones in that,' I tell him. He beams and pushes his new wheelbarrow around the drawing room. He offers to give my new doll a ride, but I think of Dorothy Baby. It wouldn't be right. I shake my head.

Mummy hands me another present. She says this is a special one from Mrs Martinswood. I'm a bit surprised because Mrs Martinswood has never *ever* given me a present. Mummy tells me it's because I was such a brave girl that day out hunting.

I pull the paper off and my face falls. It's a glove-puppet like Sooty but this one is a fox glove-puppet with a face that makes me want to look away. He's not pretty, like my dolls! His nose is thin and his glass eyes are yellow. His coat is made of old red velvet which I suppose means he's smartly dressed. I put my hand inside and wave him about.

'Well, he's a very fine fellow!' laughs Daddy. 'You'll have lots of fun with him.'

'I think he looks mean,' Finn says and Mummy agrees, but she says all the same I must remember to write and thank Mrs Martinswood.

I fold up my wrapping-up paper, weary of having to pretend. I have a beautiful new doll and a mean fox glove-puppet, but I do *not* have Dorothy Baby. At least Finn's happy with his wheel-barrow, piling his presents into it.

The fire is warm and I pat Banger's back. Soon everyone will be arriving for lunch. We will be on show.

CAMELLIA

Everyone is arriving! Mummy and Daddy go to the front door to welcome our Christmas guests. Finn and I stand to attention in front of Mummy's new tree, feeling the cold Christmas air rushing in around our feet. Finn has been let off wearing his patch because it's Christmas Day and he is smart in his green tartan trousers and white shirt. His new wheelbarrow is beside him.

In they all come, so many old relations. There are Mummy's parents, Granny and Grandad, Cousins Eva and Edith in their hats, Cousin John who stays with Cousins Eva and Edith, Old Nanny (she was Mummy's nanny) and last of all Gran and Grandpop.

Everyone takes off their coats and hats (not Cousins Eva and Edith of course) and Mummy rushes about. Daddy offers them drinks and nearly all of them have sherry. My neck is tired from staring up while they ask the usual questions, mainly about how much I've grown. As if I don't know! They don't say that to Finn, mind you.

Gran stands back in the hallway, a bundle in her arms. She beckons me over and tells me to close my eyes with my arms stretched out. She passes me the bundle and I don't wait for permission to open my eyes. It's Dorothy Baby! Fast asleep in a beautiful pale pink shawl.

'I think you left her behind, Camellia,' says Gran. 'I found her this morning.' I hug Dorothy Baby tightly to my chest. I'll never let her go.

'WHERE WAS SHE?!' I cry. Gran frowns, smiling at the same time.

'Why, in the room where you slept of course. She was on the bed.'

'Thank you, Gran. Thank you! I've been looking for her *everywhere.*'

'The shawl is for you, Camellia. It was mine once. I think it suits her very well.'

Relief makes me dizzy. I must have been holding my breath. I rush over to Finn and show him Dorothy Baby. He laughs out loud and says Dorothy Baby must try out his new wheelbarrow. He looks disappointed when I say no, but I can't let her go.

I run through to find Nanny Jan. As soon as she sees my face, she knows I'm happy again. I will work out how this could have happened later. Dorothy Baby will sit beside me for Christmas lunch because I can't bear to let her out of my sight. I skip back through to the drawing room and Old Nanny beckons me over. She wants to see my baby.

Old Nanny is about the oldest person I know, even older than Miss Wiggins. She looked after me when I was a tiny baby. I think she's about seventy-eight. She has white hair and small, kind eyes and she knows *everything* about babies. She's sitting on the sofa because her legs are old and tired, dressed in a pretty blue and grey skirt, with a pale lilac cardigan. I tuck myself in beside her and tell her how Dorothy Baby went missing.

'I was worried sick,' I tell her.

'Of course you were, pet,' Old Nanny says. 'That's because you have a good, kind heart. But she's come back to you now, hasn't she? Babies always come back.' When she says that, I let out a big sigh of relief.

Old Nanny pats my hand and says: 'There now.'

NANNY JAN

Oh, it was such good news that Camellia was reunited with her doll. When she came running through to me her face was radiant, and I was so very pleased for her. Goodness only knows how Dorothy Baby came to be back with Old Mrs Devon, especially after Camellia swears she tucked her doll into her crib last night. We have a mystery there to be sure.

However, all's well that ends well. We had a lovely Christmas lunch and the children did very well coping with the grown-up conversation. We sat Finn on two big cushions and he ate a good lunch, apart from the Brussels sprouts and I wasn't going to tick him off about that. He loved the crackers, putting his little toy and hat in the new wheelbarrow. I noticed Camellia cradled Dorothy Baby as soon as she'd finished eating, and her face was a picture.

I was ever so happy to see Old Nanny. She's coming to look

after the children when I have a week off in January, and of course they will love that. Camellia will be able to share her worries with her I'm sure. Old Nanny never judges and that's remarkable in someone so old. I suppose she's seen it all. I know I can share my feelings about the children with her, knowing she will keep my secrets.

After lunch we watched the Queen and then, when the grown-ups went back through to the drawing room for coffee, the children stayed in the nursery with me, watching Billy Smart's Circus. They were both tired, but they had done very well indeed. Finn's eyes were closing at the start of the pantomime, which was *Puss in Boots*, so we let him sleep.

While Camellia was getting ready for bed she opened and shut her dressing-table drawer, studying it very closely. I think she thought her Mercy picture might have reappeared, but it had not. She said she might draw another one with her new Derwent coloured pencils. She didn't tuck Dorothy Baby into her crib, but took the doll into bed with her, still wrapped in the beautiful shawl.

Her bedroom was icy cold, so I offered to make her a hot-water bottle. Her face lit up at that. She knows she has to be careful in case it burns her legs, but she said she'd wrap it up in an old jersey. I left her writing in her diary. Luckily there were a few blank pages before 1st January 1963.

'Thank you for helping me look for Dorothy Baby today, Nanny Jan,' she said when I gave her the hot-water bottle. 'I know you understand.'

'Let's hope nothing peculiar happens tomorrow,' I replied. 'And we can have a getting back to normal sort of day.'

'And thank-you letters!' She rolled her eyes. 'Of course, we'll have to help Finn with his.'

It was bitterly cold when I let the dogs out last thing, a steely sort of cold with the usual fog. Mr and Mrs Devon were having Christmas supper with Colonel and Old Mrs Devon. I didn't envy them. I'm sure I couldn't have eaten another thing! I suppose it's their tradition, but to have to get into evening clothes and start all over again would make me very weary. I was more than grateful to have my bath, *Woman's Own* and my bed!

Another Christmas Day done. Until next year.

CAMELLIA

Christmas Day evening

I've got so many things to think about but at least I have my new red diary. It will be useful for writing things down as they happen. And so much has happened! I hardly know where to start and there isn't much room at the beginning of the diary. I will have to make my writing very small.

I'm keeping Dorothy Baby in with me tonight. I don't trust her cot in case it's a portal, but I wonder if my new doll might fancy it. Mind you, she's a grown-up doll and perhaps a cot is too babyish for her. For the moment she sits on my chair, looking as if she doesn't understand where she is. I feel a bit mean leaving her there, but Dorothy Baby needs me more.

No, it won't do. The new doll is miserable, so I climb out of bed to wrap a little blanket around her shoulders. What shall I call her? She looks like a Heidi to me with all that yellow hair. Heidi it is. Now I'm out of bed I take a look at the drawer again. It might be safer if I took it out completely, so I pull and pull and out the drawer comes. I place it carefully on the carpet underneath. I say goodnight to the china mice and get back into bed.

It really is most dreadfully cold. Surely, it's cold enough for snow? I wonder what time Mummy and Daddy will get back from their supper with Gran and Grandpop? Mummy looked perfectly lovely in her long black dress and pearls when she looked in on me, and this time I could smell a different scent. She said it was *Madame Rochas*. Daddy put his head round the door to say goodnight too. That was nice I thought, because normally I just hear him go down the stairs. I heard Finn shout 'Goodnight, Daddy' from next door. He has his wheelbarrow in with him and Nanny Jan had to carry it up the stairs. He will have to wear his patch tomorrow and write thank-you letters, and that's hard for him, even without the patch. His letters are usually very short.

Where is Mercy now? What do ghosts do in the portal? And however many magpies are in there now? At least Gran and I understand each other a bit more, and it was kind of her to give me her very own shawl. I know she thought I had left Dorothy Baby in the miser's room, but I did *not*. Luckily Nanny Jan knows that too.

I shall think about it more tomorrow. For now I must go to sleep. My hot-water bottle means I'm cosy and warm. Father Christmas doesn't come again tonight which is a relief, and my drawer is on the floor so no one can push it shut.

I'm very sleepy. I let go.

CAMELLIA

I wake and I'm freezing, even in bed! It must be morning because there's white light under my curtains. I feel for Dorothy Baby and she's not there. Immediately my head starts rushing and my heart thumping and I jump out of bed, pulling my bedclothes back. *Not there!* Oh please, please not again. I'm not sure I can bear it. I shouldn't have let go.

But what am I doing? I need to draw the curtains properly. I snatch them back to find an iron grey day, the tree branches hanging like skeleton bones, as if they are stiff and old.

I throw my pillow off the bed and it's then that I see Dorothy Baby. She's in her cot, tucked in tight. How can this be? Who tucked her in? Gran's shawl is the top covering, folded neatly. Even more strange, her eyes are wide open, and they are *never* like that when she lies down. If she lies down, she should be asleep! I touch her blue eyes to shut them and they will not close.

I spin round to check my other dolls, and they are all watching me. Heidi sits by herself with the blanket around her shoulders. Then I notice my drawer is back in the dressing table. But I know I left it on the floor! I don't like the thought of someone pushing it back while I was asleep. That's horrible! I tug on the drawer carefully and it catches a bit. Now it's open I find something that wasn't in there before.

It's my red diary. I pull the diary from the drawer and open it. Mercy's picture falls out.

NANNY JAN

I found Camellia already dressed when I went in to her this morning. She had two jumpers on, wondering if I thought two pairs of socks a good idea. I said she might have trouble getting her shoes on over them. I must say her room was really icy. I checked the radiator to see if it was on and it was hot, so nothing wrong there. It was then that she showed me Dorothy Baby in her cot. Poor Camellia was really fussed about her, and then it all came out about the drawer and finding the picture in her new diary.

'What's going on, Nanny Jan?' Her voice was a whisper. 'Why are Dorothy Baby's eyes open like that, even when she's asleep?' I couldn't answer that one and suggested we brought her doll downstairs for breakfast. She kindly offered to help get Finn dressed, and we laughed when she tried to push his arms into his second jumper. It was difficult because Finn didn't want to wear it.

'I'd rather wear my hat,' he complained, waving his stiff arms around. 'And this is Melia's jumper!' I told him it would keep him warm.

'My bedroom's gone very strange,' I heard Camellia tell Finn as they went downstairs. She was carrying both Dorothy Baby and the new doll because she said she didn't want her new doll to feel left out. Her name is Heidi apparently.

I made a start on breakfast. We decided it was another porridge sort of day, being as it was so cold. Mrs Betts came in while I was stirring the pan, declaring that this time it really *was* cold enough for snow.

'That sky's got snow written all over it,' she said. I told the children and Camellia laughed, saying did the sky really have the words *snow, snow, snow* written on it? She said she hadn't noticed. I said I thought it probably did, but of course the words might be invisible.

I brought an extra little convector heater into the nursery to warm us up. Finn put his hat on after breakfast and marched about like a soldier. It was all I could do to get him to settle down to write a couple of thank-you letters. Mrs Devon insists they are done on Boxing Day, but she doesn't have to oversee it. Camellia encouraged Finn to write *Thank you* and then draw a little picture with *Finn* underneath and some kisses and hugs.

I never need to oversee Camellia because she knows exactly what she's doing. I did catch her staring out the window several times, her eyes weary. I really can't make head nor tail of what happened in her room.

I'm not sure how much I should share with Mrs Devon. If things get worse, then I will have to put her in the picture. I'm not sure either if I should talk to Mrs Betts because she's dreadfully superstitious. She was worse than me over the magpie! Old Nanny is the person I think; Old Nanny to Young Nanny.

But I hate to see Camellia troubled like this. She is not her usual self. She seems flat somehow. We'll have a little walk later, as long as it's not too bitter. A bit of fresh air always does us good.

CAMELLIA

I've written down as best as I can all the strange things that have happened, starting from when Mercy first appeared and Mummy broke her finger.

I think I may have to make separate columns rather like we do when we're adding up our sums. I will need a column for Mercy, a column for magpies, a column for the *Thing*, a column for Dorothy Baby and a column for the drawer. But that might get even more complicated. I also need a column for the portal. They are all linked up of course. But how? Oh, and a column for the words I hear in my head.

Perhaps it would be easier to make picture columns. Then I

can draw magpies and spinning statues and portals. I have done all my thank-you letters, including one to Mrs Martinswood, but I didn't really know what to say to her. I ended up writing: 'Thank you very much for the fox glove-puppet. Daddy says we will have lots of fun with it.' That's about as truthful as I can be. The fox is sitting upside down in Finn's wheelbarrow. That means we can't see his mean face and eyes. I wonder where on earth Mrs Martinswood found him? Nanny Jan said she thought he might be one of Mrs Martinswood's old toys, one she didn't want any more.

Dorothy Baby's eyes have gone back to normal. They wouldn't shut during breakfast, but now they're working fine. Heidi prefers to have her eyes open. They only shut sometimes but that's probably because she isn't a baby doll.

Mummy and Daddy have gone off shooting. I think Mummy will need three jumpers and a big coat to keep warm in this weather. Luckily Nanny Jan says we only need do a short walk today. It's that cold.

Mummy and Daddy are out and Nanny Jan is busy, so I wander through to the drawing room to say hello to Mummy's tree. It looks rather plain and tired in the flat light of Boxing Day. Mrs Betts comes in with her Ewbank floor sweeper, which is what she uses when she doesn't want to get the big hoover out.

I offer to dust the little tables and empty the ash trays and Mrs Betts says she's glad of the help. I help plump up the cushions, feeling brave enough to tell her what happened over Christmas.

Mrs Betts says she doesn't like the sound of any of it. She says things are being stirred up, probably because the old house was pulled down to make way for the new house. That can stir things up and no mistake. I look up at her, willing her to tell me more.

'A house doesn't like to be pulled down, Camellia, especially one so fine as the old one, even if it did have over twenty chimneys. Your Daddy said he didn't want to live in the old

house as it was too old fashioned or something, and that's why
it was pulled down for the new house to be built over it.' Mrs
Betts pauses to catch her breath.

'What gets stirred up?' I ask her.

'All sorts of things. And it can take a while for them to settle
down again.' She pauses again. 'I saw it at the other grand house
and, if I am honest, the mistress was never the same again.'

I'm dying for Mrs Betts to tell me more about how the
mistress was never the same again, but Finn comes in, pushing
his wheelbarrow, asking us if we need any help. Mrs Betts tells
him that we're just about done but gives him an empty packet
of cigarettes. Finn is delighted, placing the box carefully into
his wheelbarrow. I notice the fox is no longer on board.

I will question Mrs Betts another day. I think she could
tell me lots of useful things. I go back to the nursery and add
another column for Mrs Betts, writing her name in green.

CAMELLIA
The snow

We're having our tea in the nursery. Nanny Jan gives us some
Christmas cake and I carefully cut away the marzipan with my
knife. Finn makes such a face when he eats some by mistake
that Nanny Jan takes his whole plate away. He says it makes
him feel sick.

Mummy and Daddy aren't back yet. I'm sure they must get
tired of rushing about so much. We had our walk round the
garden, but the air was so cold it hurt my face. Finn tried to
push his wheelbarrow, but he got fed up very quickly, so we left
it by the sundial. The sky was full of brown and grey clouds and
I couldn't hear a single bird singing, not even a robin. It was
as if the sky was closing in. Nanny Jan went back to fetch the
wheelbarrow and we called for the dogs to come back in. We
didn't see any magpies.

But now we're back inside with the curtains left open.
Outside the light is going and I'm half worried I might see the
spinning statue again. I don't want any more surprises. I want

everything to go back to normal. Do I dare look out of the window? Just once?

I *do* dare and something magical is happening.

Nanny Jan and Finn are busy at the table. They don't know yet what I can see. I cannot believe my eyes! Hundreds and thousands of snowflakes are floating down, and the sky is a swirling mass.

'Finn!' I shout, banging the window with both hands.

'Magpie?' because this is what Finn expects now.

'*SNOW*! Finn, it's *snowing*!' Finn jumps down from the table, running to the French windows. He looks up into the sky.

'*Snow*!' He laughs and laughs, pushing off his patch to see better. Nanny Jan stands with us while we watch the snow falling and falling. The flakes are huge!

'Well, Mrs Betts was right,' she says. 'What a wonderful sight!'

'*Please* can we go out, Nanny Jan?' I'm already unlocking the door, and Finn is dancing up and down. Before Nanny Jan can answer, I'm out on the terrace with my head tipped back. I want to feel the snowflakes on my face. Now I am twirling around with my arms out wide.

'Finn! Look this is fun!' Finn copies me, sticking his tongue out to taste the snowflakes.

I'm perfectly and utterly happy in this moment, spinning round with the snow falling. I don't feel the cold at all! It should be dark by four o'clock, but right now it seems the world is becoming brighter. The snow is lying, turning the lawns white, like the icing on the Christmas cake.

Finn brings his wheelbarrow out and runs around making tracks which are covered up as soon as he makes them. The dogs have joined us and scamper about. I can barely feel the snow, only little touches of cold and there another, and another. I've never felt so alive!

After a while Nanny Jan says we ought to come in. My shoes are soaked through and my jersey has a thick covering of snow. Finn looks like a little snowman and his teeth are chattering.

Nanny Jan shakes the snow off his wheelbarrow, and it drips on the mat.

My cheeks are glowing but my hands feel numb. Nanny Jan brings a warm towel to rub us dry, while the dogs shake snow out over the carpet. I'm in love with the falling snow so I stay by the window, staring out. I hope Mummy and Daddy get back all right.

The snow is still falling when we go up for our bath and *still* falling when we go to bed. I jam Heidi into the cot, telling her she will get a good night's sleep in there. I put my red diary under my pillow and then I fill my drawer with socks because I can't believe anyone would want to look through those.

I take one last look out of my window and can't believe how fast the snow is coming down, as much as ever. It's been snowing for over three hours now. Nanny Jan brings in my hot-water bottle and tells me that Mummy and Daddy have just arrived back safe. I wonder if Mummy will look in on me.

I try very hard to stay awake, but I have to let go.

ANGELA

Well, it was a blessed relief Constance found that doll. Camellia must have left it behind, even though she absolutely insists she did not. I *think* she was quite pleased with her Harrods doll. You never know with Camellia. Finn absolutely loved his wheelbarrow as I knew he would. What a little darling he was, pushing it around.

Lunch went well I thought, at least nobody went to sleep! I noticed Constance taking her Bisodol before the Christmas pudding. Honestly! Surely lunch doesn't sit *that* heavy on the stomach. But the turkey was a triumph and I do so love my chestnuts.

It was wonderful having Old Nanny there. I caught her looking at me quite a few times, but always in a loving way. She fills me with confidence every time I see her.

I rather envied the children and Nanny Jan after lunch. To be able to just flop and watch the Circus would be heaven. I had to keep things going in the drawing room, making sure everyone had their coffee.

I find going out for supper on Christmas night quite a trial. I'm not quite sure why we do it? Constance gives us cold turkey and salad, followed by cold mince pies which is most uncheerful. That fire of theirs smokes like the Battersea Power Station. It can't be good for us, but for some reason Constance never seems to notice.

Then of course we had to go shooting today. I could have done without *that*! But shooting is better than hunting. Let's face it *anything* is better than hunting, and at least I'm not expected to do anything clever. I got terribly cold and thought my feet would never unfreeze. My Badedas bath was never so welcome as this evening!

I knew it wasn't a good idea to go for drinks with David and Tessa. The snow was coming down fast, but Gerald insisted we would get through. As it was, the drive home was difficult, the snow making it almost impossible to see the road. We only *just* got up our hill. At one point I thought I was going to have to get out and push, and that would have been the giddy limit. I would have refused anyway as my finger is still mending.

I looked in on the children before my bath, but they were asleep. I was pleased to see Camellia had tucked her new doll into the cot beside her.

It was still snowing when Gerald put the dogs out at half past ten. We can have some fun with the sledges tomorrow. The children will love that. And the snow means we can't hunt!

CAMELLIA
December 27ᵗʰ

All is white! I stare out at the day, hardly able to believe my eyes. The snow is dazzling in the sun. I can't see where the driveway begins or ends because the walls are covered and smothered. It's as if a gigantic snow blanket has been laid all over our world. The branches of the trees are covered in white, and overhead the sky is the palest blue. No footsteps in the snow, *yet*.

I open my window just a little, leaning out to breathe in the winter air. It smells of snow, sharp and bitter at the same time. There isn't a *single* sound. All is silent. No birds, nothing but snow.

I shut my window and check to see if Heidi is in her cot. She has one eye open and one eye closed, but I think that's the way Heidi is. My drawer is in place, full of socks. Dorothy Baby is wrapped in her shawl in my bed. My red diary is under my pillow.

All is well. I run back to the window. It's a sparkling, magical day.

CAMELLIA
Walking in the snow

We have finished our breakfast and Finn and I are dancing up and down, wanting to play outside. The snow is banked up against the French windows. Will we manage to open the door? Outside the sun is shining and the snow is sparkling. It's waiting for us!

Nanny Jan says that it really does look like a Winter Wonderland, and who would have thought we would have so much snow. She's never seen anything like it, certainly not in Sussex.

Mummy came in to see us at breakfast and promised that we would go sledging. She said our sledges are somewhere in the garage. Daddy might come with us as well.

'Nanny Jan,' I cry, 'We absolutely *have* to go out now!'

Finn is searching for his hat and now he's found it. He puts it on.

'I'm ready,' he says, standing in the middle of the nursery. But he's not. He needs his duffle coat, his gloves, his boots and his patch.

'Nearly ready, Finn,' says Nanny Jan kindly. 'But let's make sure you're really warm this time.' She brings in all Finn's stuff.

Now we are ready. We stand by the door, waiting for Nanny Jan to push it open which she manages to do with a great shove.

Finn reaches out a mittened hand to pat the snow. It's about a foot deep. I know that because it's about the same as my ruler.

'Gosh,' Finn says. 'Almost as tall as me.'

I step out into snow which feels like icing sugar. It's so soft! I kick some into the air and the sunlight catches it, shining like tiny snowy stars. I bring my hands together and throw more up into the air. Finn brings his wheelbarrow out and puts snow in it, but he's finding it very hard to push. Banger rushes out past me and disappears. It's as if the snow has eaten her up. Bramble is next and all we can see is a black tail wagging. It's very funny!

I don't know where the steps are, but I walk towards them, suddenly finding I'm up to my waist in snow. I feel forwards with my boots, turning around to warn Finn to be careful. I tell him if he follows in my footsteps, he should be all right.

Of course, Finn doesn't follow in my footsteps. He goes down the steps a different way, so all I see of him is a red hat with a Christmas pudding on it. Then the hat disappears because Finn has sat down. The snow is that deep! I wade back to Finn and help him to his feet. He's covered in snow and he laughs and laughs.

'Oopsadaisy!' he says, brushing himself down. Nanny Jan calls from the nursery window, wanting to know what's happening. I shout back to tell her the snow's too deep. We need someone with taller legs to show us the way. The dogs find us, taking great leaps as if they're cantering. Their eyes are shining, their noses white with snow.

Mummy appears at the door and waves.

'What fun!' she cries. We wave back.

'Come on, Mummy!' I shout, but Mummy hasn't heard. She carries on waving at Finn because he looks so funny. He looks like a snowball with a hat on, a snowball wearing a patch.

Mummy tells us the snow is too deep for sledging. We would have trouble reaching the big hill, but she says Daddy's going to organise for a tractor to clear the drives. She says *tomorrow* will be the sledging day. She will ring up our cousins, the

Cordleys, and invite them to come over tomorrow afternoon. Then we will have a high old time she says.

'Oh but...' Finn says. I know how he feels.

'Why not build a snowman?' Mummy suggests. She's holding her breakfast coffee cup. Nanny Jan appears behind her in a blue anorak with a furry hood. Mummy steps aside to let her through. Nanny Jan holds out her arms.

'Snowman time, children!' she cries. 'This is *just* the right sort of snow. Now where shall we build him?' Finn claps his mittens together, showing her the way down the steps.

Nanny Jan helps us to build a really fine snowman. He's about the same height as me, and we build him in a place where we can see him from the nursery. Nanny Jan gets us started with his body and we go through two pairs of gloves, adding to it and making it bigger. I gather most of the snow and Finn does lots of patting it into place. The dogs run around us, barking for joy. I wish Mummy could help us, but I suppose she's busy on her telephone.

Then we make our snowman a head, and Nanny Jan balances it on his shoulders. I pat in more snow to make sure it doesn't fall off. Then it's time for a break.

We are inside now, thawing out. I'm drinking my milky coffee and Finn's watching his snowball melt in the wheelbarrow. He wonders if he could drink the snow-water? Nanny Jan says she wouldn't advise it.

We find some coal for his eyes and a carrot for his nose, as well as some extra bits of coal for buttons down his front. I catch Daddy passing through the kitchen, and ask him for an old hat and scarf. Daddy does very well actually, finding us an old trilby hat, as well as a violet and blue school scarf. All we need now is a curved stick for our snowman's mouth.

I offer to search for this when we go out again. I tramp out towards what I think is the flowerbed and have a feel around for branches. I find just the one and manage to break it off. It has an evergreen leaf stuck on the end, and Nanny Jan says it adds character. I can tell that Finn's a bit tired because he's not really helping. He's mainly sitting down in the snow and watching.

We put the eyes, nose and mouth in, and Nanny Jan encourages Finn to put in the coal buttons for his coat. Later Mummy and Daddy come into the nursery to admire our work, and I feel very proud when Daddy says the snowman is a splendid fellow, especially in his hat and scarf. Finn shows Mummy his snow-water.

After lunch Mummy takes us to see the sledges in the garage, as well as the huge Canadian toboggans hanging on the wall.

'We're all set for tomorrow afternoon,' she says.

I wonder how Henry is getting on with the horses. They won't be able to go out into the snow-fields, and Robin will have to be given extra pony nuts. The snow's far too deep for us to walk up to the stables, but Daddy says the snow-plough tractor will be very good at clearing the roads. We will be able to get about tomorrow.

We tidy up the nursery before bath time and I can't find the fox puppet anywhere. I wouldn't mind if *he* disappeared into the portal.

NANNY JAN
I know I shouldn't judge but I thought it was a *real* shame Mrs Devon didn't help the children build their snowman. Anyone could see they were clamouring for their mother to join in, and honestly she could have done. All that telephoning doesn't take an entire morning. I think she uses the telephone as an excuse not to get involved. Of course, I could never say that to anybody, not even Old Nanny.

She misses so much though. She doesn't get to see how funny the children can be, forever rushing off to organise the next thing. It breaks my heart sometimes, witnessing their dismay, especially Camellia's. Finn goes his own sweet way mind you, and he always has Camellia to follow.

In the end we built a wonderful snowman and were quite exhausted by the time we finished. I think Finn found the brightness of the snow a bit much for his eye, so tomorrow I will find his seaside sunglasses. Who would have thought there would be so much snow? It's the same all over the country according to the news, with people struggling to get about. Now there's even talk of coal strikes! What a time to strike, I'm sure.

Mrs Betts couldn't get through today but Mr Devon has organised for the roads to be cleared. At least Mr and Mrs Devon have promised to come sledging tomorrow. That will mean the world to the children.

I'm glad to report that all was normal with Camellia's dolls today. Perhaps we are over all that now. We did wonder about the whereabouts of that fox glove-puppet. He has completely disappeared. I can't say I am sorry.

CAMELLIA

My room is like an icebox this morning! It must have frozen very hard again last night. I put my hand out to check that Dorothy Baby's still in bed with me and she is. Next I run to the window to see whether it has snowed any more. Everything is just the same, all except for the big snow-plough tracks in the driveway. That means we'll be able to go sledging!

I don't know whether it's my imagination or not, but a strange, dark shape spreads and glides over the snow, from under the house towards the end of the garden. I blink and it's gone. Could that have been Finn's *Thing*? I rub my eyes and stare some more. Whatever it was, I won't tell him.

I check my dressing table and the drawer's still there but for some reason Heidi is upside down under my chair. I *know* I put her to bed in the cot last night, so what's happened this time? I walk round to the other side of my bed and there I see the most dreadful sight.

The fox puppet is tucked up in the cot, under the little sheets and blankets. His head is sticking out and he stares up at me with his mean yellow eyes. Mean, mean! I don't want him in there! How dare he sleep in the cot! I must get him *OUT* but I need to find Nanny Jan. She must help me. I know I can't bear to touch him.

I have a sudden thought. I couldn't have done that, could I? We know he disappeared last night so where did he go? Where was he hiding, before waiting to climb into the cot? I *can't* think about that! I run to Nanny Jan's room and she's still in bed.

'Nanny Jan!' It doesn't sound like my voice at all, and it's too loud. I should be keeping quiet because Mummy and Daddy might be asleep. 'Come quickly please! It's the fox puppet!' Nanny Jan understands immediately because she's out of bed in a flash, following me back to my room. Finn stands behind his chicken wire, half-asleep.

I show her the cot, and she puts her hand to her chest in shock. I look away. He's horrible and mean, and he shouldn't be there. How did he get there? How?

'I *hate* him!' I cry. 'Look at the way he stares at you, with his head tipped to one side!' Nanny Jan looks, but I don't. I hear Finn's voice calling 'Melia' from next door. He wants to be let out. Nanny Jan bends down to pull the fox puppet out of the cot, saying that's quite enough for now. She promises she will lock him in a cupboard.

CAMELLIA

I'm all shaky and confused because I *cannot* understand how the fox puppet could have climbed into the cot by himself. I will have to be extra careful about protecting my room from whoever's doing this. I wonder what I could use to keep me and my dolls safe, and of course there's Finn too.

The idea of him creeping round my bed, his eyes mean and yellow with his body all flattened and empty. It is too horrible! I wish I had a stick to hit him with. Perhaps I could borrow one of Daddy's umbrellas? He has so many in the hall that I don't think he would miss one, if I borrowed it. That makes me feel a bit braver, imagining myself whacking Mr Fox with an umbrella.

Nanny Jan says she's going to lock him in a cupboard, but what if he jumps into the portal from the cupboard and then out again into my room? He might easily do that.

I shall have to make another column for the fox puppet, but I don't really want to draw him. I wish Mrs Martinswood had *never* given him to me! Perhaps she gave him to me because she couldn't bear him any more.

It's not safe to have the cot in my room. It needs to go somewhere else. Then, even if Mr Fox manages to get into my room through the portal, he won't be able to go to bed. I have a look in my drawer and it's full of socks, so that's a relief.

I pick up the cot to carry it downstairs to the nursery, but really and truly it needs to go all the way into the cellar. I shall ask Mummy to take it down for me. Then I have a brainwave. The little white church would be good protection for my room, and comforting to hear 'Silent Night'.

I ask Nanny Jan during breakfast if that would be possible, and she says she doesn't see why not. I will have a church instead of a cot. It might do the trick, but I would like more.

I go in search of Mrs Betts and this time she's busy hoovering the spare rooms. Her duster lies across her shoulder and she's wearing a flowery pinafore. She never *ever* minds if I interrupt her, not like Mummy or Daddy. Mrs Betts says wasn't she right about the snow and aren't we lucky to have a tractor to clear the roads. Others are not so lucky. She says the tractor man gave her a lift this morning and it was such a lark.

'Mrs Betts,' I begin, standing on one leg.

'What is it, my duck?'

'What would be good to protect my room. Make it safe?'

I tell her about the fox puppet, the cot and now the little church. She bends down to unplug the hoover and pushes it along to the next room. I follow her.

'Does your room feel creepy?' she asks. I nod. 'I read somewhere that mistletoe is very good for that sort of thing.'

What a bright idea from Mrs Betts! I ask if she could reach up to the hall mistletoe, and cut a little sprig off for me. At the same time, I will borrow an umbrella from the stand.

'You mustn't eat the berries, mind,' she warns. 'They're poisonous.' I promise her I won't, and nor will Finn.

Mrs Betts says of course she will do that just as soon as she's finished these rooms, and perhaps I could give her a hand. She says she often feels a bit funny right here at the top of the front staircase.

At last I have the mistletoe in my hand, and I carefully lay it beside the little white church. The umbrella leans behind the door, ready for action. The dolls watch and I tell them it's for their own good. I wonder if I should put some mistletoe in Finn's room.

Whatever it is doesn't seem to have spread to his room. *Yet.*

NANNY JAN

I've hidden the fox puppet right at the back of the sweets cupboard which I always keep locked. It's not as if Camellia or Finn would ever steal sweets, but Mrs Devon says you never know with other children.

Camellia came rushing into my room this morning in a dreadful state. I think I was hoping for too much yesterday. Things have *not* settled down. In fact I would say whatever it is has escalated. There was a peculiar atmosphere in Camellia's bedroom this morning, a creeping sort of menace and, when the poor child showed me the fox in the cot, I was shocked. His expression was horrible, a sort of half-sideways stare which didn't half unnerve me.

Naturally I didn't tell her any of this. I merely removed the fox, taking it back to my room. Then I let Finn out and he went through to Camellia while I got dressed.

When I came back Finn was sitting on the floor chatting to Heidi, while Camellia sat motionless on the bed, her face as white as a ghost. Already she was worried the fox might escape from his prison.

She said she *never* wanted to see him again, and I assured her she didn't have to. Finn got wind of the general situation and all through breakfast he kept saying 'What a bad fox.' I had to tell him to be quiet in the end.

After breakfast I took the little church up to Camellia's room. She wound it up there and then, sitting quietly while it played 'Silent Night'. She said she knew it would keep her safe and I was happy she believed that. I kept on catching her looking around, checking that everything was in its place.

After lunch I went back up to her room with some ironed clothes and noticed that she had placed a sprig of mistletoe beside the church.

Somehow that made me feel very sad.

CAMELLIA
Sledging

The fog comes down after lunch but luckily our sledging party is still going ahead. Daddy says he'll get the tractor to pull the Cordleys' car up the drive because otherwise they might have trouble. That tractor driver must be very busy. He had to take Mrs Betts home at lunchtime.

Everyone has arrived and we set off walking to Robin's hill which is the best for sledging. This is because it's very steep. We all look as if we are going skiing with big coats and hats and gloves. My gloves are a bit damp so already my hands are cold.

Mummy is as pretty as ever in her black ski jacket and white bobble hat, and she's the first to set off, pulling one of the toboggans behind her. They are easy to pull as they skim along the flat snow. Daddy pulls the other toboggan and Nanny Jan has the little upright sledge. We children march along behind and it's quite hard to stay standing up. The road is white with flattened snow and it's really icy and slippery. We have to walk with short steps.

Nanny Jan notices Finn is already getting left behind so she offers him a lift on her sledge. Lucky Finn! He's delighted and waves at the rest of us.

Lorna, my cousin, who's two years older than me, is annoyed

that she can't get a lift on one of the sledges. Her mother, Aunt Daphne, pulls a very old battered sledge and tells Lorna off when she sits on it. Lorna is always being told off, but then Lorna is *always* getting herself into trouble. She stamps along beside me and I tell her about our snowman. Lorna says she and Julia, her younger sister, made a snowman too but that its head fell off.

'No, it did not!' It's Julia behind me. Julia's only five and a half and is walking along well. She has lots of curly brown hair under her green hat, and dark eyes that sparkle. We both know Lorna's making things up again. We let her run ahead to Daddy to see if she can get a lift there. I bet she doesn't.

The fog is so thick that I can hardly see Nanny Jan and Finn up ahead. The dogs run backwards and forwards between us. They are lucky to have four legs to run on the road. We don't dare run. We would fall straight over! I find it helps my balance if I stick my arms out either side. Julia does the same. We are like acrobats in the circus!

'Come on everyone!' I hear Daddy's voice at the front. I certainly can't see him through the fog.

'What did you get for Christmas?' Julia asks but, before I can answer, there's a chattering in the oak tree above us. I stop to look up. A magpie is peering down.

'Hello,' I say. Julia's face is a picture, as if to say I'm mad talking to a magpie.

'They're unlucky,' she says.

'Who says?'

'Mummy says so.'

'They're only *messengers*, Julia. Very useful actually.' She doesn't look that convinced. As if by magic the magpie flies down to stand in front of her. He puts his head on one side and opens his beak, chattering *I'm not unlucky, I love being a magpie.* Julia steps back, afraid of what she thinks he is. I thank him politely and he flies off behind us. Now Julia is frozen to the road. Honestly, another one frightened of a magpie.

'Come *on* you two,' says Aunt Daphne. 'You're getting left

behind.' She's right, we are getting left behind. But we're not the last.

I've seen a figure behind us, wearing a dress and necklace.

ANGELA

Heavens that was fun! We were quite the party to go sledging and the fog didn't spoil things at all. Those Canadian toboggans go like the very wind. I don't think I've ever laughed so much as when Daphne came off on our second run. I managed to persuade her to come on my toboggan with Lorna, Camellia, and she very gingerly sat at the back. How she thought she would go anywhere on that ancient thing she brought was beyond me.

As it was, we flew down the hill and she came off at the first bump. Unfortunately, Lorna turned round just as her mother fell off. That upset our balance and my steering, and we only missed the oak tree at the bottom by a whisker. Camellia absolutely loved it, clamouring to go again. Lorna berated her mother for falling off and for being so utterly useless. But goodness we did laugh.

Nanny Jan was very good with Finn, taking him for short runs on the little sledge. She sensibly stuck to the lower slopes and they just had to dodge fast if they saw us heading in their direction. Finn found this frightfully funny.

We had a race with Gerald, Lorna and Julia on one toboggan and me, Camellia and Daphne on the other. Daphne's weight definitely contributed to our winning, and the fact that she didn't fall off this time certainly helped.

We were a very happy party walking back for tea. Camellia really enjoyed herself, laughing her head off and completely trusting me to steer the toboggan. Much more fun than riding a horse quite frankly.

Gerald let Lorna ride on his toboggan going home, and Julia hopped on mine. I was impressed that Camellia walked the whole way herself, and all was well until she went to check on her snowman.

I knew my job was to make sure tea was ready.

CAMELLIA

I saw Mercy again while we were walking back. I wish she had a coat on in this freezing weather, and I know that's silly because of course she's a ghost. I must be the only person who sees her because Julia looked back with me and saw nothing. It's strange to see her moving, rather than just standing and staring. Her long dress covers her feet, and she glides over the ice. She must be dreadfully lonely, all by herself. I can feel her sorrow.

Once we are back, I run as fast as I can round the house to check on our snowman. I find a most peculiar thing has happened. His coal buttons are facing the nursery like before, but his face is turned around towards the Downs. Even his carrot nose has moved. Who did this? Who would *want* to play this sort of trick? And for what? I follow my tracks to the back door where everyone is taking off their boots and coats.

'Come in for tea!' Mummy is saying. 'We've got crumpets and plenty of Christmas cake.'

'The snowman's *face* is the wrong way round!' I shout and everyone stares at me.

'Let's sort it out in the morning,' Mummy says firmly. 'Not now after we've all had such fun.'

Mummy makes me feel stupid for making a fuss and Nanny Jan winks at me, as if to say not now. I take my coat off, throwing it down amongst the piles of coats, hats and boots in the hallway. Everywhere there are puddles of snow-water. I try to forget about the snowman while we have tea. Mummy reminds Daddy how her toboggan went faster than his. She knows she can steer a toboggan better than a horse and bumps are safer than jumps. She catches my eye and smiles.

I go out again with a torch after everyone has gone home. What is *happening* with my snowman? Will his face have changed again? No, it's still the same but now his scarf is missing! I come flying back up the steps to tell Nanny Jan.

'What next?' she says. 'Will his hat still be there in the morning?'

'Or his *head*?' I cry. He's not about to fly off into the portal, is he? Bit by bit?

I sit in the bath, my toes tingling. I hope I don't get chilblains! There is a long night ahead of me, but I have the church and mistletoe. I can't be sure they will work, but I must have faith.

Heidi sits on the chair while Dorothy Baby is safely tucked up beside me. The cot is in the cellar and the fox puppet is locked up in Nanny Jan's prison. I'm too tired to write in my red diary.

I'm almost asleep when Mummy comes in to say goodnight. She says Aunt Daphne rang to say that, when she got home, she found Daddy's violet and blue scarf underneath Lorna's coat. Why does Lorna have to be so naughty? Mummy says she's in big trouble and won't be allowed to come sledging again. Not for at least a week.

'We had fun, didn't we Mummy?'

I hope it's safe to say that. Mummy kisses me and says didn't we just. I ask her to wind up the little church. She's a bit surprised it's there, so I say it's because I love it so. When she spots the mistletoe, I tell her it's for luck. Mummy quietly shuts my door and I listen to 'Silent Night'.

I'm on my own.

CAMELLIA

The little church and mistletoe worked! I slept really well and feel quite different this morning. Heidi stayed on her chair all night and Dorothy Baby's eyes are working properly. Finn is singing 'Little Donkey' next door. He doesn't realise you don't need to sing carols after Christmas.

When I go to see him, I find he's unbolted his gate himself. There's a big pile of books inside the doorway and he tells me that, if he stands on them, he can reach the bolt. I mustn't tell anybody though. He brought the books up one by one from the nursery while Nanny Jan was ironing. I am impressed.

'Well done Finn. That's such a good idea but you need to put them away for now otherwise the grown-ups will guess.' Finn picks up the first big book and hides it under his bed.

'And you must promise *not* to come into my room too early and wake me up. That's why Mummy had the gate made, remember.' Finn makes a face. I laugh and pat him on the head.

I'm first into the nursery and I run over to the window to see what the snowman is up to. He's looking at us again!

'Nanny Jan! Finn! The snowman!' Nanny Jan and Finn hurry to the window. They see what I see. I wonder if I imagined it last night, that he was facing the wrong way? Am I going mad?

'Where are my boots?' I shout, running to the hall. 'I must go and check him up close!' Nanny Jan gives Finn his boots as well, even though we haven't had breakfast, and warns him to be careful on the icy steps.

We study the snowman carefully. Finn says he's pleased his pieces of coal stayed stuck in. But I'm already round the back, finding the holes made by his coal eyes and carrot nose. There's even a trace of coal in one of the eye holes. That's proof he turned his head. He looks a bit bare without his scarf. I know I couldn't have done this because I was sledging. It's another mystery.

We come back in for breakfast. When Nanny Jan hears our news, she says what we have here is a two-faced snowman, adding she knows a few people like that. She tells us that Aunt Daphne is going to bring the scarf to Melanie-Anne's party this afternoon, but that Lorna isn't allowed to go.

Lorna must have done something else naughty. Mummy said last night that her punishment was *no sledging*. She didn't say anything about parties.

I can't wait to be with my friends again, although Melanie-Anne will probably be very busy as it's her party. I'm worried the fog might come down again like yesterday. Nanny Jan says this fog is something else, and what we need is a nice strong wind to blow it away.

CAMELLIA

I have decided to wear my dark green party dress with pink and white smocking, and I can just about squeeze into my bridesmaid ballet shoes. I will wear my furry boots in the car and change once I'm there.

Mummy is taking me and she's driving very carefully down our drive, out on to the road to Cowfold. The main road seems very black against the piled-up snow on the side. They must have used a huge snow-plough for clearing the big roads. What a lot of work! I wanted Mummy to set off a bit earlier, but she said she had a hundred and one things to do this afternoon and now we are late.

When I go through the front door it's obvious the games have already started. Mummy hands me my pink ballet shoes and says she'll be back at six for pick-up. It will be very dark by then, but Mummy says we'll be able to get up the hill because Daddy has organised for the tractor to wait for us.

I quickly change into my ballet shoes, then put my head round the corner of the dining room. Melanie-Anne's mother spots me immediately and brings me into the game. It's musical bumps and already there are children on the side who are out. They're trying to pretend they're still enjoying the game which I know they're not. Melanie-Anne waves at me from the kitchen doorway. I join in with the eight children left, Sarah being one of them. She's wearing a beautiful pink dress with a blue sash and her hair is fairer than ever.

I'm very good at musical bumps. I can drop like a stone when the music stops, and I have learned that, if you watch the person lifting the arm of the record player, you can always tell when the music's going to stop. They always give it away.

Now it's just three of us left, Sarah, a girl with bunches and me. The girl with bunches trips over her feet, so she's out. Sarah is laughing and getting quite puffed but she's as good as I am. The other children watch closely now, wanting to know which one of us is going to win the bag of jelly babies, held up by Melanie-Anne's mother.

After three more rounds, when we both sit down at exactly the same time, Melanie-Anne's mother declares it a dead heat. We need to get on with the next game after all. We can share the jelly babies.

I don't get a chance to talk to any of my friends properly until after tea, and even then we're being hurried through to the drawing room for a puppet show. I dread this and Sarah says she understands. I've already told her about the horrible fox puppet and how he's locked up in Nanny Jan's cupboard. Annabel's more interested in the snowman's face, wondering if Mercy could have moved the eyes and nose round.

'I suppose she could have done,' I say. 'She was around yesterday when we were sledging.'

'Can ghosts move things?' Annabel asks, settling herself down beside me and crossing her legs.

'I will have to ask my Mum,' says Sarah.

Annabel has got me thinking though. It *could* be Mercy but surely she wouldn't be so mean? I remember the black shape, gliding away from the house and ask for ideas.

'My Mum says that sort of thing is dark energy,' Sarah says. 'Not very nice.' We exchange glances. *Not very nice.*

I explain about my little church and mistletoe, and Sarah asks if I've ever thought about rowan? Sarah says it's a very powerful tree.

Melanie-Anne is stuck on the other side of the room. She keeps looking towards us, wanting to be part of our conversation, but she has to be polite to her other guests. Her mother would be cross if she wasn't. I know the feeling. Her cheeks are quite pink with the effort.

Annabel says I must come over for tea soon. She has a feeling that Mercy might well be musical, and she has a piano in her dining room. She says a tractor had to bring it all the way across the fields. I think this is wonderful! I wonder if I might have a piano one day. Do I dare ask Mummy?

The lights go off and we sit quietly while the puppet show starts. What's the story this time? It's about a witch who lives in the woods, and what she likes to do most is capture children and throw them in her cupboard. The witch has bright orange hair and emerald green eyes, and her pet is a stupid black cat called Horace. I don't think it's a very good story at all. Not nearly as good as Hansel and Gretel!

The witch is cackling in her kitchen, plotting her next trick and stirring her cauldron. Her bed is set up in the kitchen, very high with about eight mattresses, and a ladder. We watch as Horace climbs the ladder, sits on the mattresses and goes off to sleep. In the corner of her kitchen the witch has a little crib which reminds me of my cot in the cellar.

All the children are laughing at Horace who's snoring loudly, but I want to look back at that crib, and it's then that I see Mr Fox, peeping over the top. *Where has he come from?* His head knocks on the crib, once, twice, three times, his yellow eyes gleaming. Surely other people can see and hear this? I look at Annabel who's watching the witch. I turn to Sarah whose eyes are open wide.

'Can you see him, Sarah?' I whisper.

'I see him,' she says. Why can't anyone else? He's hiding behind the bed now. We can just make out the tip of his ear. It's black.

'Keep watching,' I warn Sarah. 'See where he goes.'

But now the witch is dancing about, trying to wake Horace up. She knows there are children approaching her cottage and she must put her cauldron soup into bowls.

'Yuk!' says Sarah.

Where is he now? How can he just disappear like that? *Where has he gone?* My heart is hammering because Mr Fox has managed to escape from prison. He has followed me here! There must be a portal in Melanie-Anne's house. That means there are portals everywhere, and *that* means nowhere is safe! I don't enjoy the rest of the puppet show, because I don't dare watch any more. Mr Fox could appear at *any* time! I keep my eyes on my ballet shoes, wishing I had brought some mistletoe with me. I need to find some rowan as quickly as possible.

The show finishes and everyone claps. The witch got squashed under all the mattresses, thank goodness. I ask Annabel whether she saw the fox and she shakes her head. Melanie-Anne didn't see the fox either.

I turn to Sarah and take both her hands in mine. Her black velvet hairband has slipped a bit and her hair looks like a halo.

'You saw him, didn't you, Sarah?'

'I saw him,' Sarah replies. 'He was *there*.'

ANGELA

Collecting in the car

It didn't take me long to realise it wasn't a good idea to drive into Horsham this afternoon. Although the roads were clear, they were still pretty icy and I had to crawl along in some places. All the time the temperature was plummeting, and it was freezing in the car. However, I had success in Wakefields, finding a smart top to go with my black velvet trousers. I want to look my best for Monday night after all.

I met poor Daphne in the driveway. She'd been waiting for me to arrive and of course we were late. She handed over Gerald's scarf, saying she was terribly sorry. Lorna has received a sharp ticking off and is not allowed to come sledging for at least a week. I feel a bit sorry for Lorna actually, being punished so often. Nanny says I was very naughty as a child, but I don't remember getting into that much trouble. Nanny could forgive me anything!

I gathered it was a very good party. Camellia told me that she had won the musical bumps with Sarah, but she hadn't enjoyed the puppet show at all. I do wonder sometimes about the suitability of these entertainers. What exactly is the point of terrifying children? Camellia said there was a little boy crying at the front who had to be taken out.

She spotted the scarf in the back seat and also the Wakefields bag. Her eyes lit up, so I said I would show it to her once we were home. Perhaps I should take Camellia shopping more often?

The tractor was waiting for us. We slithered down past the pond and stopped at the entrance to the farm. Kind Bert fixed a rope to our bumper, just as it began to snow again.

'More snow, Mummy,' Camellia said. 'My snowman will need his scarf tonight.'

'But he's made of snow surely? Does a snowman feel the cold?'

'He will *need* his scarf,' Camellia repeated firmly, sounding cross.

We were off. I must say I rather enjoyed being pulled uphill. All I had to remember was to keep the car in second gear and press very gently on the accelerator. The snow was swirling down by the time we reached the house. Before I could stop her, Camellia had taken the torch from the glove compartment, disappearing round the house with the scarf flying behind her. I was glad she was in her furry boots at least.

I was in the kitchen talking to Cook when she crashed through the door. She stood there, covered in snow, about to lose control.

'His face has changed *again*! Now he looks *sad*!' It was if she wanted me to fix it, there and then, and in the dark. It was all too much at the end of a long day.

'It's probably changed because of the snow,' I ventured. But at this she actually stamped her foot, shouting 'NO!' This was most unlike her, but I knew I had to be firm.

'Camellia! I will *not* be spoken to like that!' She glared at me, and there were tears in her eyes. Now she was angry.

'You *never* listen properly, Mummy.' After that remark, I had to put my foot down. Do as you mean to go on. All this in front of Cook too. I would never live it down.

'Now listen here, young lady. You were a very lucky girl to go to such a lovely party. And I came and picked you up in the dark. I think it's about time you went upstairs to bed.'

'What about your top, Mummy?' I couldn't cave in at this point.

'Tomorrow,' I said firmly, leaving the kitchen. I heard her

calling after me, something about a rowan tree, but I'd had enough by then. What I really needed was a drink. That was one hell of a drive. And now we've got more snow. Gerald wants me to organise a skating party here on Sunday. As if I hadn't got enough to do.

Nanny Jan can cope with her. That's what we pay her for.

NANNY JAN

I had expected Camellia to be in a good mood after her party, but she wasn't. She came thundering up the stairs, still in her snowy boots, and found us in the bathroom, Finn happy in his Radox bubbles.

'How was the party, Melia?' he asked.

'The snowman's gone sad,' she announced. 'His mouth has gone upside down. And it's snowing again. I put his scarf back though. He might be cold otherwise.' She took a deep breath.

'Mummy's *mean!*' she cried, much to our surprise and then she ran to her bedroom, slamming the door. Finn and I stared at one another. What on earth had happened? While I was towelling Finn dry, I could hear the poor child crying, huge great sobs. I wanted to go to her there and then, but first I needed to sort Finn out.

Of course, he wanted to go to his sister to find out what was wrong, but I thought it best not at this stage. Once into his pyjamas, he spent a lot of time looking under his bed for some reason. I read him Andy Pandy and told him that Andy Pandy and Teddy were going to sleep and so should he.

I couldn't hear any more crying when I knocked on Camellia's door. There was no answer, so I gently pushed the door open. Camellia was lying face down on her bed, Dorothy Baby underneath, her snowy boots making marks on the eiderdown.

'What is it, my love?' I put out a hand to stroke her back. She half sat up then and, all of a sudden, she was clinging to me. She made a strange sound, almost as if she were going to be sick, then more sobbing. All I could do was hold her and let her cry it out. This wasn't like Camellia at all. We very rarely see her cry.

Once she'd calmed down, she asked me to wind up her church, and we sat quietly listening to 'Silent Night'. Then she told me about the party, the fox puppet, the snowman but worst of all her mother's sharp words. It all came out in a rush and, at the end, when she asked if I knew why her Mummy never listened properly, I didn't know what to say. I actually think Mrs Devon has completely forgotten what it's like to be a child, always wrapped up in her social whirl.

I suggested her mother was probably worried about the icy drive and that she was tired, just like we all get sometimes. I knew Camellia didn't believe me, but she accepted it. I asked if, as a treat, she would like me to bring her a big glass of Ribena to drink in her bath, and perhaps she would like a tangerine as well.

Camellia's eyes shone at that, not just with tears. There was real gratitude there and, as I ran the bath for her with some of my Radox, I thought to myself: *That is why I'm a nanny to these children.*

FINN

I don't like it when Melia is upset. I heard her crying. Nanny Jan thought I couldn't. But I could.

I've hidden my big books under my bed. It's my secret.

I know how to escape.

Poor Melia.

My room is cold.

CAMELLIA

I wake to the sound of dreadful screaming, and I can't tell where it is coming from. Perhaps it's Finn! Something's wrong with Finn! I switch on my light and fly out of bed, pulling my door open. Finn's on the other side of the chicken wire, his hair standing up on end, struggling to put one of his big books in place.

'Finn!' I cry. 'Was that you screaming?'

'No,' he says. 'But it woke me up. I need two more books to get out.'

'Who could it have been?'

I unbolt his door and my teeth are chattering.

'It was an *awful* sound.' Could we have had the same night-mare? I bring Finn into my room and wind up the little church. We listen to 'Silent Night'. Then I go and fetch his dressing gown and help him into it. I put mine on too and we look at each other, not knowing what to do next. Finn rubs his eyes.

'I didn't like it,' he says.

'Nor did I,' I agree. 'Do you think it was a woman screaming?'

Finn says he thinks it was. It sounded more like a woman.

'Why was she screaming?'

Finn thinks about it for a moment.

'Perhaps she saw a mouse. Or a rat. Mummy might have seen Samuel Whiskers.'

'But Mummy's still asleep,' I tell him. 'It was someone else.' Finn pats his dressing-gown cord and says something very interesting.

'Do you think it was Mercy?'

'Yes, Finn. I do!' I *know* it was Mercy. She was screaming about something and we both heard her. There's not a single sound coming from Daddy and Mummy's room and Nanny Jan hasn't come along the corridor, so they must have slept through it.

My watch says it's nearly three o'clock. I peer out into the darkness to see if it is snowing, but I can't see anything.

'I don't want to go back to my room, Melia,' says Finn.

'You don't have to,' I tell him. 'You climb into my bed. There'll just about be room for both of us. Move Dorothy Baby over a bit.'

'My book!' Finn looks worried.

'I'll put it back under your bed and I'll say I unbolted your door.'

I go into his room to replace the big book. I find there's *quite* a lot of other stuff under his bed. That done, I put the sprig of mistletoe on my bedside table beside my watch. Tomorrow I will ask Nanny Jan about the rowan tree.

Finn is already under the bedclothes. He says he promises not to kick. We wedge Dorothy Baby between us, and I switch off the light.

'We need to go to sleep for four hours, Finn. Then it will be morning time. If we hear Mercy screaming again, we can always put our fingers in our ears.'

'Do you think Mercy was screaming because she saw a rat?'

'I suppose she might have done.'

'Your feet are cold, Melia.'

'So are yours, Finn. But they will warm up when we are asleep.'

'Night night,' says Finn, and I tell him to sleep tight. I listen to his breathing and know exactly when he falls asleep. All this has made me forget about Mummy. I blink my eyes in the dark. They still feel funny after the crying, stiff and sore.

I'm so weary. What on earth is going to happen next? The room feels like winter, and from far away I hear the sound of chattering. *Chatter, chatter, chatter.*

No more screaming or chattering thank you. I want to go to sleep.

Finn snores beside me.

NANNY JAN

When I came along to the children this morning, I was alarmed to see Finn's gate wide open and then, even more so, to find him not in bed.

I opened Camellia's door to discover the children tucked up together like the Babes in the Wood. They were fast asleep, and Finn was in his dressing gown with his arm stretched out. What could have happened? Why hadn't I heard anything?

I drew the curtains back and Camellia stirred. She blinked up at me and said good morning. Then she carefully climbed out of bed, retrieving Dorothy Baby from halfway down, and whispered that she had rescued Finn from the screaming. She said she thought it was probably Mercy doing the screaming, and something about seeing a rat. I put my hand on my heart when she said that. I cannot abide rats. Nor can Mrs Devon and nor can Mrs Betts. Camellia shook her head at this and laughed.

'No, Nanny Jan. I think it was probably a ghost rat.' She pick ed her mistletoe up and put it beside the little church. 'But...' she paused. 'I think she was screaming about something else. By the way, Nanny Jan, what do you know about the rowan tree?'

I was pleased to see her mood had improved after last night's tears, but I wondered how she was being so calm. I followed her into the bathroom while she brushed her teeth.

'It didn't last very long, Nanny Jan,' she assured me. 'It just gave us a bit of a shock, that's all.' We knew Finn was awake then because he shouted from Camellia's bedroom.

'Camellia needs a rowan tree.' There was a pause. 'And so do I.'

'And I need to check on the snowman,' Camellia said. 'What will happen to him today, I wonder?'

I couldn't quite pinpoint it, but something had shifted within Camellia. She seemed to be more at ease and confident. Either that or she was putting on a very good act. I helped Finn dress and followed Camellia down to the nursery.

There was even more snow. Camellia pointed towards the snowman's face.

'See, Nanny Jan! His face has gone all sad!' Even with the extra snow I could see that the upward curve of the snowman's smiley mouth had been turned the other way.

He didn't look sad to me. He looked angry.

CAMELLIA

Mummy comes into the nursery after breakfast with her Wakefields bag. I don't feel like saying sorry, so I don't. But I do say her top is pretty, which it is. I tell her she looks nice in pale green, which she does. She says she's going to wear it with her black velvet trousers to the New Year's Eve Party tomorrow night. I know she's trying to make up, but I feel a bit closed and so I'm more polite than friendly.

'Now, where's that snowman of yours?' she says gaily. 'Ah, I see him! Yes, he does look a bit down in the mouth.' And that's it. We are treading carefully around each other.

Finn is wearing his Christmas hat indoors. He says it's his protection hat. Mummy looks confused and, even more so when Finn says he wants a rowan tree.

'I need a protection hat and a protection tree,' he says, offering Mummy a tangerine from the fruit bowl.

'What's all this about?' Mummy asks, putting the tangerine back. 'Why do you need protection, Finn?' Here we go.

But Finn's on a roll. He lists all the people who need protection: Camellia, Finn (he points to his chest), Nanny Jan, Mummy, Daddy, Mrs Betts, Banger, Bramble, Robin, Henry and his wheelbarrow.

'You forgot the snowman, Finn,' I say.

'What from,' Mummy asks innocently.

'The Screaming, Mercy, the *Thing*, the bad fox puppet.' He takes a deep breath. 'And the RAT!' Mummy screams and Finn gives me a knowing look.

'Ha ha ha!' he says. 'Got you Mummy!' Mummy leans back in relief and does her laugh that isn't real.

'We forgot the *magpie*, Finn,' I say. Mummy takes a sharp breath.

'What side is the magpie on, Melia? I forgot.' Finn taps his head. Mummy, Nanny Jan and Finn are all staring at me. I give them the answer.

'Both,' I say, and then very quietly '*Always*.'

When I say the word '*always*', Mummy gets up off her chair and says she would like to have a word with Nanny Jan outside, if she would be so kind.

I know it's not very nice of me, but I enjoy the feeling of scaring Mummy. It serves her right. I go over to find my drawing pad and colours. It's time to add to my columns. I shall draw Mercy screaming in her column.

Poor Mercy. Poor Mummy.

NANNY JAN

I've been told in no uncertain terms that I have to put a stop to all this nonsense. I felt ticked off good and proper when Mrs Devon took me through to the drawing room.

I don't see how I can stop peculiar things happening. If the children say they heard screaming in the night, then they did. I remember as a child what it was like not to be believed. I have locked that fox up in the sweets cupboard, so at least he's out of sight, out of mind. If Camellia wants to worry about her snowman, I can't exactly stop her.

It would be unkind to take away her pictures because it helps her make sense of everything. I didn't much like her drawing of Mercy screaming, mind you, but she obviously needs to do it. And if Finn wants to wear his red hat indoors for protection, where's the harm?

I think Mrs Devon is still upset over what happened between her and Camellia yesterday. This is the sort of thing I would like to discuss with Old Nanny. I must say I was surprised at Camellia when she brought the magpie up. There was a funny, hard look in her eye as if she wanted to hurt her mother. I haven't seen it before. Dear oh dear.

I promised I would keep a close eye on the children and do my best to divert them if and when they talked about 'strange things'. Perhaps everything will calm down in the New Year. Mind you, Camellia has set her heart on a rowan tree (even putting it on her birthday list), and I think she's going to ask her grandmother whether there is one in the wild garden. Once Camellia has set her mind on something, there's no stopping her.

Mrs Devon told me later that she has organised for Camellia to go to Annabel's for tea on New Year's Day. Apparently the roads are still passable after last night's snow. I noticed the snow didn't stop Mr and Mrs Devon going out to lunch with some friends.

We had a funny sort of day, neither one thing nor the other. We went out for a little walk, but it never really got light.

Camellia found the snowman another branch for his mouth. Now he looks fed up! I didn't have the heart to stop the children collecting various toys from the nursery cupboards and taking them upstairs. How can I say no to a blue tractor that's going to keep Finn safe or a wooden castle with a flag on top? Camellia wanted more mistletoe, but I managed to dissuade her from that. We found a china angel ornament to put beside her little church. Let them feel safe. I remember what it was like to feel afraid.

Bath and bedtime came and went without incident. I do wish their bedrooms weren't quite so cold. I suppose it's because they face north.

CAMELLIA

Nanny Jan has said we can go sledging in Gran and Grandpop's garden. Their garden has just the right sort of steep hill for sledging.

We set off after lunch with the dogs. I pull one sledge and Nanny Jan pulls the other. Finn has to walk this time, but we have given him a little stick for keeping his balance. It's all right if we trudge slowly along the edge of the drive. The weather is grey and foggy again, the air like frozen iron.

While we walk along Finn sings 'Silent Night'. He says it protects him outside. He never gets the words quite right and always makes a muddle of the last two lines where the tune goes very high. This makes him laugh, and then he starts again.

I'm pleased Nanny Jan said yes to sledging. She's been a bit funny peculiar since Mummy 'had a word' with her. I know what 'having a word' means. It means a telling off. Nowadays Nanny Jan changes the subject if we talk about Mercy or magpies or even the fox puppet, although I don't want to talk about him much.

As well as sledging, Nanny Jan doesn't yet know I'm going to look for a rowan tree. I looked it up in Daddy's book of trees when they were out to lunch. I copied it in my drawing pad, and I know it has leaves like the ash tree and bright red berries, although the birds eat them. There might not be any left! There certainly won't be any leaves.

If we see Gran, and I will make *sure* I do, I will ask if she has a rowan tree. I'm hoping Mummy hasn't talked to Gran about how we're in trouble, so I should get away with it.

'Magpie Melia,' says Finn pointing upwards. I look up and there he is, watching. I like to think that the magpie is telling me I'm on the right track, so I ask him to show me which way to go. He flies off to the right, way down the garden. I walk in his direction, pulling my sledge.

'Wait!' shouts Nanny Jan. 'We should be going down the middle of the garden.' I trudge back. The snow is very deep here, going right over my boots. Finn sits down and says his legs are tired. I line my sledge up at the top and push off. I cruise down as slow as a snail. It's because the snow is too thick.

'These sledges aren't nearly as good as the toboggans!' I shout back up the hill. Nanny Jan lifts Finn onto the sledge with her and I stand out of the way while they go past. Nanny Jan tries to speed up using her legs.

'Hopeless,' says Finn as they come to a halt.

'Not much speed,' Nanny Jan says but then adds 'Probably safer for you and me.'

I've had enough of sledging already, so I tell Nanny Jan that I want to say hello to Gran. She warns me to be careful going down the rockery steps. Because the steps are steep, I go the long way round under the big cedar tree, but already I'm out of my depth. My boots are completely stuck and the old grey branches overhead block out the sky. They are heavy and weighed down by all that snow. How do I get out of here? My legs have frozen. It would be easier to just lie down.

A magpie chatters behind me as if saying '*This way, this way*'. But I know that way is scary. Someone or something is waiting patiently up there. I take a deep breath, forcing my boots through the snow. Come on Camellia, come on! But the snow is hard, like scrunchy sugar and I can't get through. I want to rage against the beastly stuff. Why did I come this way?

But then, to my relief, my legs get their strength back and I push on slowly but surely, at last reaching the house with the frozen pond in front. There is the familiar stone heron, only now he doesn't see goldfish. He just peers into the ice. Whatever was behind me has gone. I am out of breath!

I peer through the window and see Gran in the little sitting room, doing her tapestry under a spotlight. I bang on the French doors and she looks up with a worried face, but then smiles when she sees it's me. She opens the door.

'Goodness,' she says. 'What a little snowman!' I tell her we're sledging, and Nanny Jan and Finn are busy halfway up the hill. I get straight to the point because I don't like wasting time.

'Gran, I was wondering, is there a rowan tree in your garden?' She is surprised at my question, but I quickly tell her I know what a rowan looks like because we're learning about trees at school. This is a bit of a fib, but it works. Gran puts her tapestry wool back in a bag.

'We do indeed have a rowan tree,' she says, 'And, if I look in my little gardening diary, I can tell you when we planted it.' I wait politely while she goes to her desk. Gran holds her diary up and finds the page.

'Sorbus aucuparia,' she says. 'That is Latin for rowan tree, planted June 1956.'

'My birthday's in June 1956!' I cry, but I think she already knows. 'So, your rowan tree is exactly the same age as me!'

Gran smiles and says she supposes it is. I want to know more of course.

'Where's the tree, Gran?'

Gran says she knows exactly where it is, and it's doing very well indeed. She points towards the cedar tree and says the rowan is up beyond that. It's on the east side of the garden because it doesn't mind the winter sun in the morning. She says the camellias don't like the morning sun if it's frosty. It burns their flowers.

'I'm a Camellia,' I say. 'I don't mind the morning sun!' Gran says she's glad to hear it. She wonders if I would like some tea, but I tell her I'd better get back to Nanny Jan and Finn. I tell her Dorothy Baby is very well indeed, that she loves her shawl.

Gran does a real smile when I say this, looking almost pretty. I wave goodbye and follow my tracks across the white lawn. It's not easy to find a rowan tree in the snow, but I march with strong legs towards the east side of the garden and I find it.

My birthday tree stands in a clearing all by itself and it's a very fine, young tree. There are no leaves or berries left because of hungry birds, but I know it's my tree. I reach up to a lower branch and break off a twig.

'Thank you, rowan tree.'

I put the twig in my pocket and answer Nanny Jan's calls. She wants to know where I have got to.

'I'm here, Nanny Jan!' I shout and appear, as if by magic, on the middle track. I collect my sledge from under the bushes. 'Gran was very well.'

Nanny Jan says she's pleased to hear it.

Finn says that there's no way he's walking back up the hill again, so Nanny Jan hauls him up on the sledge. She says she must be losing weight with all this winter exercise. I walk beside her, my legs tired now. I don't tell her about the rowan twig in my pocket.

It's my secret.

NANNY JAN

I got the fright of my life last night while I was watching television in the nursery. The children went to bed at seven o'clock as usual, and Mr and Mrs Devon were out at their New Year's Eve party. I had the dogs in with me and everything was quiet. I rather foolishly decided to watch the play after the news. It was called *On the Night of the Murder*, but it was only an hour long and I thought let's just see what it's like.

It was during the second half that I knew something wasn't right. The dogs raised their heads at something, ears pricked. I turned round and much to my astonishment I saw the nursery door handle turning very slowly, all by itself. There was nothing

I could do but keep my eyes on the door, fearful of who or what was on the other side. I was afraid, but the dogs weren't. They knew who was coming.

Our New Year's Eve ghost walked into the room as quiet as a mouse, a little figure in pink and green pyjamas. Camellia's eyes were open, but I knew she was asleep. She walked over to the sweets cupboard and bent down. Then she pulled at the door knob and of course it wouldn't open because it was locked. I found this very unsettling because all sorts of thoughts began to chase through my mind. Was Camellia responsible for moving the fox puppet? Did she knowingly play the trick herself, or was she doing it all in her sleep?

I called her name softly. She heard me and stood up, staring, her eyes half-open. Her head turned slightly, as if puzzled, her arms hanging down by her sides. Her face had no expression. I can't say I wasn't afraid.

I've always been told that you should never wake a sleep-walking child, so I put my arm around her and gently suggested we needed to get her back to bed. I wondered if I would have to carry her. Banger was up and wagging her tail as if to encourage us.

I managed to walk her back up the stairs and into her bedroom. She didn't say a single word. As I drew back the bedclothes, I noticed a small twig halfway down. I removed it, replacing it on her bedside table and Camellia stared at me then, as if she was looking right through me.

'Come on, you,' I said quietly. 'Back to sleep and sweet dreams.' After I tucked her in, I wondered about winding up the little church but decided against it. She found Dorothy Baby in her sleep, hugging her tight.

I looked in on Finn, carefully stepping over the blue tractor and castle in the doorway. He was fast asleep, wearing his red hat. By the time I returned to the nursery, the play was just finishing. I thought I had better check the sweets cupboard, so I found the key and unlocked the door. The sweets tin was there as usual, but just to make absolutely sure, I stretched my hand out towards the back.

The fox puppet had gone.

I heard faint crying as I went up the back stairs, having put the dogs out. How I shivered on the back step! I wasn't keen on looking out into the darkness, but the dogs came back quickly. I checked both children again, and they were asleep. I didn't expect Mr and Mrs Devon to be back for over an hour yet, and fortunately I wasn't expected to wait up for them.

I was that glad of my hot-water bottle. This house may be brand new but it's freezing cold at night. I've decided I won't mention the sleep-walking to Camellia because she has enough to worry about. I *am* concerned about the fox puppet though. He must have gone somewhere. Fox puppets do not just vanish into thin air.

I will worry about whether I mention any of this to Mrs Devon in the morning. I don't want to get the children or me into any more trouble. They will probably be very tired after their party.

Why can I still hear crying? So far away…

PART II

CAMELLIA
1ˢᵗ January 1963

It's a brand new year! At last I can write properly in my 1963 diary. It's morning and I've drawn my curtains. As usual our world is white and frozen, and already it's hard to remember how it was before the snow came. I feel sorry for the poor birds and I'm going to ask Nanny Jan if we can clear a place on the terrace and put out some food for them. I can't bear to think of them starving.

I know I tucked my rowan twig in with Dorothy Baby and me last night, but this morning it's on my bedside table. Did I do that? I had a horrible dream in the night. The fox puppet was sitting on top of my curtain rail. One minute he was peering down at me with his mean yellow eyes and the next minute he was gone. But then he would appear over and over again. I shouted *go away*, but it didn't make any difference.

I check Heidi who's quite happy sitting on my chair, wrapped up in her blanket. Nanny Jan reckons she looks a bit drunk with one eye open and one eye shut. You have to shake her to make both eyes open, but I don't like to do this.

Today I'm going to have tea with Annabel, and I'm hoping Nanny Jan takes me because Mummy will probably be tired and cross after her party. She usually is.

While we're having breakfast, I tell Nanny Jan about my fox puppet dream, and she looks at me in an odd way. It makes me nervous, as if she knows something I don't.

'Bad fox puppet,' says Finn, spooning in porridge. Nanny Jan agrees and goes out of the room to fetch some toast.

'I hope he's still in prison,' I say. 'Do you think we ought to ask Nanny Jan to make sure he's there?'

'He needs to be in prison,' says Finn, smiling. 'Because he's *bad*!'

When Nanny Jan returns with the toast, I ask her if she wouldn't mind checking to see if the fox puppet is still safely locked up. She spins round with her mouth open. It's as if she is guilty of something!

'Be a saint!' says Finn and I laugh because that's what Mummy says.

'Do you really want me to?' Nanny Jan's hand is shaking. She can hardly hold her cup of tea! We both nod at the same time. We need to know, and I need to make sure he's not still hiding at the top of my curtain rail. Nanny Jan finds the key and bends down to open the cupboard. She reaches in and I know she has found something because her face changes.

She pulls her hand out, empty.

'He's there.'

'Phew,' says Finn. 'That's a mercy.'

Nanny Jan locks the cupboard up and puts away the key. She sits down at the table, shivering. She butters her toast and puts strawberry jam on it, but she doesn't eat it.

Something has frightened Nanny Jan. I know what I must do! I run upstairs to fetch my rowan twig. After I place it next to her plate, I tell her it's magical and it will make everything all right again. Finn wants to know all about the twig, so I tell him. I'm not sure Nanny Jan is listening but, when I glance sideways, I'm sure I can see tears in her eyes. I ask to get down and Finn and I go over to the window.

Our snowman's eyes have gone.

NANNY JAN

How on earth is this possible? How did he get back in? I know full well he wasn't there last night when I checked. Camellia *can't* have done this? Then I have an awful thought. I hope it isn't me? Have I started to sleep-walk too? Oh, but she was kind to run upstairs, fetching her rowan twig for me. I struggled not to cry. They are such dear children.

And then after breakfast they shouted that the snowman's eyes had gone. Well, we know that can't have been Camellia. There's absolutely no way she could have gone out in the middle of the night in her pyjamas. I suggested we find two more bits of coal. At least his hat and scarf were still there.

Camellia wanted to put some food out for the birds, and I said I thought that a very good idea. We asked Cook for some scraps of bread and raisins and maybe some old cheese, if she could spare it. Camellia said she wanted to save the birds from starving. At least this hadn't got anything to do with ghosts or fox puppets or missing eyes.

I am in a quandary now because I don't know whether to tell Mrs Devon or not. Do I let her know Camellia has been sleep-walking? Do I miss out the bit about the cupboard?

There's something most peculiar happening in this house. I wonder if Mrs Betts can tell me any more about its history, when the old house was built and if anyone died in the house. Her family have lived round here for years.

I go upstairs to make the children's beds. Camellia's busy drawing birds in the nursery, and Finn is looking out the window for magpies.

On the subject of magpies, we never did work out how that magpie got in.

CAMELLIA

I'm getting quite used to all the strange goings-on. I was scared the first time our snowman's face turned around, but just now when we saw his eyes were missing, it seemed almost normal.

After breakfast Finn and I go out with two new bits of coal. Soon our snowman will be able to see again. But what we find is odd. His old eyes haven't disappeared. They're in the snow in front of him.

'Which ones shall we put in?' Finn asks. We decide on the new bits.

Now our snowman can see, we set about clearing a space on the terrace for feeding the birds. Nanny Jan has given us our seaside metal spades and they're quite good. Finn has a bucket as well and he tries his best to make a snow-castle, but the snow gets stuck.

'Blast,' he says. I give his bucket a whack. We tip it over together and the snow falls out.

'Sand is better,' I tell him. We clear a good space and Nanny Jan brings out food for the birds. She gives us some grated cheese as well as bits of suet. There's even a slice of stale Christmas cake which we crumble up. Already a robin is sitting on the wall. He's hungry!

We go inside to watch the birds. Blue tits swoop in and then a blackbird. They are gobbling up the food! I worry about where they go to sleep at night. Nanny Jan says she's afraid some of them won't survive the winter, and she heard on the wireless that gales are forecast for tomorrow.

We must do *all* we can to feed the birds. I go to the cupboard to fetch my pad and colours. I sigh because Finn says he wants to do some drawing too.

Why does Nanny Jan keep looking at the sweets cupboard?

CAMELLIA

It's decided that Mummy will take me to Annabel's house. Mummy seemed in a good mood when she came into the nursery before lunch. She said that it had been a terrific New Year's Eve party and everyone had danced like mad, especially at midnight. I'm longing to be old enough to dance at midnight! But I want my dress to stay beautiful and not turn to rags like Cinderella's.

I'm busy packing my pad with my different columns into my satchel. I need to show Annabel what I've sorted out. Mummy comes in at exactly this moment and asks to see what I have drawn. I'm not sure I want to show her, but perhaps she will like the way I've coloured things in.

I hand them over to her and I can't tell what she thinks of them. She's certainly not smiling. She goes through them again. I shouldn't have shown them! Now I know I'm in trouble because she's frowning. She pushes them back towards me.

'What do you think, Mummy?' I ask bravely.

'They're not exactly jolly, are they?'

She hates them! I follow her out to the car telling myself that Annabel will be interested, even if Mummy isn't. I also know that no matter what I do, Mummy always thinks Finn's drawings are more *amusing*. My columns are definitely not amusing. They are scary perhaps, but true. I wish Mummy could understand.

She doesn't say a word on the way to Annabel's, so I stay quiet. I'm often in the wrong with Mummy. Annabel's mother is never cross and sure enough, she's at the front door with Annabel, saying 'Come in, darling. Come and get warm. You two girls are going to have *lots* of fun.'

Why can't Mummy be more like this? She says she will pick me up at six. I don't feel like waving her goodbye, but I do all the same.

Even though it isn't teatime, we are given a little cup of tea each and a Penguin biscuit. Annabel's mum says that will help us with our games. I love being at Annabel's house and I tell her so. For one thing it's warm and cosy in the dining room but also there's Annabel's fine piano! We drink our tea and eat our Penguins. I show Annabel my columns.

'Wow, Camellia,' she says. 'These are great! It's as if you are telling the story with pictures.'

'That's exactly what I am doing.' I scrunch up my silver Penguin paper with a sigh. 'Mummy doesn't understand though. She's not like your mum at all.'

Annabel understands. She's lucky because she has a grown-up brother and sister and her mum treats Annabel like them. I know she's allowed to go to bed much later than Finn and me.

'So how can we help your ghost, Camellia?' Annabel goes over to the piano, sits on the stool and starts playing a tune.

'What's that?' I am entranced.

'Bit of Beethoven,' Annabel says. 'I haven't got it *exactly*, but my sister taught it to me. It's got something to do with

Moonlight.' I watch her fingers on the keys and ask if I can learn it. Annabel budges up on the piano stool and we begin. It's only a few notes and I have it pretty quickly. Now we are playing it together. I am on the high notes and Annabel is on the low.

'*Wow!*' we say at the same time.

I ask Annabel if she knows how to play 'Silent Night'. She says we could try and work it out. She can play by ear.

'Do you like "Silent Night" then?'

'It's my Being Safe tune,' I tell her.

This is why I love seeing Annabel. She's the one friend I can do music with. Now we're free to work out as many tunes as we like.

'You have a go by yourself,' says Annabel.

Because I have the tune in my head, I'm able to find the notes on the piano keys. This is like drawing but with music! Annabel joins in.

Soon we can play 'Silent Night' together. Annabel's mum comes in to say she has never heard anything so lovely, in fact she thinks our playing is *absolutely fab*, and would we like our tea now? She has baked a cake specially.

During tea Annabel's mum tells us how she once saw a ghost or rather she saw where the ghost walked, because it opened one door and then the other, while her dog watched it cross the room. She says she wasn't frightened at all. Annabel's mum says all this as if she is making the most ordinary conversation. If only Mummy could be like that!

After tea there's still time for the piano. Annabel says perhaps we can work out a tune specially for Mercy. This is such a lovely idea that I have to give her a hug. We will make it the most beautiful tune in the world. Even more beautiful than Beethoven's Moonlight!

I am in a bubble of happiness when Mummy collects me. I tell her what we have been doing, and then I bravely ask her if we could ever have a piano at home. I can't believe it when she says yes.

'Really Mummy? You *really* mean it?' She turns the car into the drive, and we see the tractor waiting for us.

'I really mean it,' she says.

Mummy and I are friends again!

ANGELA

As if I haven't got enough to worry about, I'm now *worried sick* about Camellia. Those drawings! Where on earth do those ideas come from? It's as if I don't know her at all, which of course I don't.

I find her so difficult to understand. Of course, she's very unlike me, but then again what am I like? I do whatever Gerald tells me to do and usually that works out for the best, all except the hunting of course because that terrifies me. What would it be like to actually say no? I think Camellia's entirely capable of saying no, and she's made that perfectly clear over the last few days.

She's actually far braver than me, and I admire her for that. But then it shows up how weak I am, and who likes feeling weak? I hate it. I know I was a bit hard on her over the snowman business, but it had been a very long day. I think she got the message. Gerald's always saying you have to be as you mean to go on. God knows I try.

It would help if I knew who I was meant to be and where I was meant to be going. I feel I'm forever flying about, organising things that I don't necessarily want to organise. And now we've got the skating party on Sunday. So that will be drinks and sausage rolls and perhaps we might try to make glühwein. Gerald loves that. And then some tin trays or something for the children to sledge down the banks. I will have to look out my skates and heaven knows where they are.

I think Nanny Jan took in what I said to her over the children. We need to forget about all this nonsense as soon as possible otherwise heaven knows where it will lead.

Well I think we know exactly where it's led. It's led to Camellia drawing those frightful pictures. I wonder if I ought to ring Dr Byng and ask for his advice? Perhaps Camellia is disturbed? What an awful thought! I'm sure he wouldn't mind coming over to have a quiet word with her. We could make it very casual, over a cup of tea in the nursery. If that doesn't do the trick, and he doesn't know what's wrong, then Gerald has suggested the vicar.

I know the vicar's a bit too young and progressive for Gerald's liking, but we could give him a try. He's very approachable and I think I might ring him tomorrow and ask him to pop over as well. Anything to get this household back on an even keel.

Heavens, I've got a lot of telephone calls to make! I must also ring Sheelagh to ask her if she knows where we can get hold of a piano for Camellia. The piano is a very good idea. I don't think Camellia could believe it when I said yes. Gerald doesn't have a musical bone in his body, but I like the odd bit of classical musical and I *love* the ballet, not that we ever get a chance to go. Camellia is obviously musical, and I think we should encourage her. And if she's playing the piano, she's not drawing frightful pictures.

But first Dr Byng. He can look at my little finger while he's here. I think it's mending quite well.

NANNY JAN

I found Mrs Betts in her upstairs hoover cupboard and asked her if I could talk to her about the history of the old house. She raised her eyebrows, saying she would certainly try to find a moment. Perhaps directly after coffee? I said that was a good idea and I would set the children up with something in the nursery. Mrs Devon was at her desk as usual and Mr Devon was out and about, so we thought we would be able to talk in private. She said she would have a think while she was doing upstairs.

In the end Mrs Devon was through in the kitchen talking to Cook, and the children were weaving in and out of everything, eager to get out and feed the birds again. I helped Mrs Betts wash up the coffee cups and announced that I was going to take some clothes through to the wash room, and did Mrs Betts want to help sort the loads out?

Mrs Betts took my cue, carrying armfuls of washing. Once through and into the safety of the wash room, I firmly shut the door. Mrs Betts told me what she knew, while I sorted the laundry.

'The old house was built in the 1880s, that I do know. No expense was spared in making it as modern as possible. And warm, come to that, hence all those chimneys. The old Colonel built it and took a long time getting married, but eventually he married a very nice young lady, well not so young actually, she was thirty-two I believe. They lived happily at the old house, or new house as it was then. The Colonel was very big in the Hunt, and I believe Mrs Goodridge also hunted a bit.'

'How do you know all this, Mrs Betts?'

Mrs Betts said her mother kept a diary of all the comings and goings of the village. Mrs Betts loved to read about the old days, always interested to know what the ladies and gentlemen were getting up to. More to the point her mother had a friend who worked as a maid at the old house.

'Then Mrs Goodridge was expecting so she stopped hunting. She gave birth to a baby daughter, that's Old Mrs Devon, in the August and it was said that she never really recovered after that.'

'Do you think she gave birth in the old house?'

'Sure to. People didn't go into hospitals in those days. Not even high-born ladies like Mrs Goodridge. Then she got ill in the December of that year and died on Christmas Eve.' Mrs Betts paused for breath. 'Ever so sad it was.'

'So, she probably died in the old house as well?'

'Most probably. Her room was most likely very close to where the front stairs meet the top landing. That's where I often get the shivers.' Mrs Betts paused for breath.

'Then of course young Mr Devon goes and pulls the old house down because he wants to build his fine new house. I always thought that a bit of a shame, even though I wouldn't fancy cleaning all those rooms with fireplaces. Can you imagine the soot?!' I agreed it would make for an awful lot of work.

'But what I say is that if you build a fine new house on top of an old one, as it were, using the same stone mind, don't go thinking you can wipe out what's happened. Things get stirred up. Story went that poor Mrs Goodridge wasn't allowed to see her baby in her final few weeks because the doctors were afraid the baby would catch the disease. I believe it was the influenza that did for her in the end, but she was already weak.'

Mrs Betts helped me load the washing machine at this point. We had been rather a long time talking, but I thanked her very much for her history lesson and she smiled and said any time.

I went through to the nursery and the children held up their food for the birds.

'Where were you, Nanny Jan?' Finn asked.

'Sorting out the washing, Finn.'

'Why did you take so long?'

I gave him my answer.

'*Because.*'

CAMELLIA

Snow magpies

I thought we were going sledging this afternoon. Mummy promised she would come with us, that we could take the big toboggan out, but now she says the doctor is coming over to look at her little finger. She says we can always go tomorrow. This is what grown-ups say when they break a promise. I'm very annoyed and so is Finn because Mummy said he could have his first go on the toboggan.

Mummy says she's not quite sure what time Dr Byng will come because he's a very busy man. She also says he would like a little word with me. That makes me feel sick. Why does the doctor want a *little word* with me? I suppose it isn't as bad as a *word* because that would mean I was in *big* trouble. But why does he want to have any sort of word with me?

So now we can't go out for a proper walk because Dr Byng

could arrive at any time. Nanny Jan says why don't we go and play in the snow under the terrace, and she can always call us in when the doctor arrives.

Finn is very grumpy and, once we are outside, he sits down in his wheelbarrow. He doesn't have to wear his patch this afternoon. Instead he's wearing his seaside sunglasses. First, I check the snowman's face is in exactly the right place. It is! He hasn't melted one tiny bit. In fact, I think he's grown!

'Let's go and look for magpies, Finn.'

Finn thinks this a good idea and follows me to the lower steps. On the far lawn I spot our magpie. He's having a bath in the snow. One minute his head is diving in, then he's sitting and then he's flapping his wings, so they shine in the sun. The snow is flying up in the air like a fountain.

'Look Finn!' I shout, pointing at the magpie. Finn laughs and says he wants to have a snow bath too. We search around to find just the right snow and then we roll around, waving our arms and kicking our legs. I laugh so much I'm nearly sick and Finn holds onto his snowy tummy with his mittens. He thinks he might be sick too.

That's how Mummy and Dr Byng find us. We are covered in snow, even our faces, and Finn's sunglasses have been thrown into a bush. We stand there like magpies who have had a snow bath.

As we trudge up the steps, Finn tells Mummy we were just copying the magpie, that was all and I can tell she's annoyed. She takes Finn by the hand, through the nursery into the kitchen, leaving me to stand and stare at Dr Byng. I take off my coat and boots, dropping them on the mat. I leave the door open, for the bright winter air to support me, and we sit down opposite each other on the sofa. *Far apart.*

I will have to be very clever. I find it always helps to smile.

NANNY JAN

I was told firmly by Mrs Devon to stay put in the little room off the kitchen, where I could get on with my ironing. She said this to me when the doctor arrived, insisting that Camellia and Dr Byng needed to have a private talk. I couldn't argue. It wasn't my place. But I did feel as if poor Camellia had been ambushed. She's understandably wary of any doctor, getting herself in a fair old state if ever we have to go down to the surgery.

Mrs Devon marched Finn through to the drawing room to help take her Christmas tree down. I knew Finn wanted to stay in the nursery with his sister, but Mrs Devon firmly took his hand, saying 'Come ON.'

Oh, to be a fly on the nursery wall! I wondered what Camellia would say to the doctor. I had little doubt he would repeat the conversation back to Mrs Devon, probably word for word, but at least I knew I would hear Camellia's side later.

I suppose our Christmas tree has to come down too.

CAMELLIA

Dr Byng has a funny little moustache and I keep my eyes on that, rather than his beady eyes which remind me of Samuel Whiskers. His horrible black bag is beside him. Holding his hands between his knees, he opens his mouth to speak but I beat him to it.

'How's Mummy's little finger?' This takes him by surprise and in that moment I know he hasn't even checked Mummy's finger. I am the one he's come to see.

'It's doing very well and almost completely healed after about three weeks of mending.' Dr Byng is making a big mistake. He's talking down to me. I smile, wondering what I can do to annoy him.

'It was the ghost, you know.'

He raises his eyebrows.

'The ghost of my grandmother's mother appeared, just like that, in front of my pony Robin. Robin didn't like it, and he went backwards. Then Mummy fell off and broke her little finger.

'And', I continue, leaning forward, 'She wouldn't have broken her finger if she'd been holding the leading rein properly. You must never *ever* wrap it around your hand. It's a cardinal sin, you know.'

The doctor looks surprised. He admits he didn't know that. I'm getting a surge of confidence, filling me up. It's as if the words are coming out of my mouth, just like that.

'What have you come to see me about?' Dr Byng gapes at me. He's not very sure.

'How can I help you?' I ask. Another smile. I sit there and wait, my back as straight as a soldier.

'Well...' he starts. 'Your mother was wondering if you were upset about anything. She says you have been doing some funny drawings...'

'I love drawing,' I tell him. 'Perhaps you are not aware, Dr Byng, that I'm adopted and drawing is what I do. It's not what Mummy and Daddy do but it's what I do. Actually, Finn's also quite good at art. All I have done is draw what has been happening to me and this house. What I'm doing in effect is trying to make sense of it. Mummy doesn't want to believe, but Nanny Jan does and so does Finn.'

Dr Byng asks what sort of things have been happening, and I tell him truthfully. He looks through some of my drawings while I carry on telling him.

'Poor Nanny Jan was dreadfully frightened yesterday over the fox puppet, and Finn and I had to comfort her. Also, our poor snowman can never be sure which way he's facing, towards the house or the Downs.' Another smile. I make sure he sees it.

'As I said before, Mummy doesn't want to believe in any of this, and I think it's probably making the situation worse.' I'm surprised I say the last bit as I haven't thought of it before. I carry on.

'Mrs Betts, our daily help, also thinks there's something funny going on in this house. I suggest you try standing at the top of the front stairs when it's getting dark. Finn and I have heard screaming and Nanny Jan has heard crying.'

Dr Byng looks a bit confused. I can tell he doesn't really know what to say. I offer to show him the rest of my drawings, but he says no, he really must be getting on with his rounds. He gets to his feet.

'I can play the piano by ear, Dr Byng.' He moves towards the door with his bag.

'Mummy can't.' One last smile. 'Happy New Year, Dr Byng.'

The doctor opens the door and hurries out. I take a deep breath and lean back against the sofa. I am *so* pleased with myself! That taught him a lesson!

At the same time, I wonder where all those grown-up words came from? I run through the kitchen and find Nanny Jan who is ironing.

ANGELA

Well that was a fat lot of good! Dr Byng can't have been with Camellia for more than ten minutes. Finn and I had hardly got started on the tree, and there was Dr Byng at the door with his hair standing on end. He was carrying his bag and I specifically told him *not* to take his bag into the nursery as it upsets the children. So, he'd got that wrong to start with.

I managed to bundle Finn out, shouting for Nanny Jan as I did so. I could hear Finn from the other side of the door shouting 'Not fair, Mummy. Not fair!' What's got into these children? I'm only trying to do my best to get things sorted out. I shut the door firmly.

'Well?', I said to Dr Byng inviting him to sit down. I positioned myself in front of the fire and gave him one of my inquiring looks.

'Your daughter is remarkable,' Dr Byng said, folding his arms. 'She's highly intelligent and her language is very mature. She quite put me in my place.'

This didn't help at all. I needed advice as to how to put a stop to all the supernatural nonsense. I needed Camellia to understand none of it was real. I said as much to Dr Byng. He uncrossed his arms and put his hands in the air. I suppose his arms were saying he had no idea. I asked him about the drawings, and he said he thought they were very good.

'But what about the content, Dr Byng? Why is she drawing these things? Some of the pictures are plain frightful.' I was beginning to sound shrill. I took a deep breath and carried on. 'As you know, Camellia is adopted. Could it be that something is coming out, something that we don't know about … something in her background?'

Dr Byng then asked an uncomfortable question.

'Is this more about you, Mrs Devon? Camellia tells me you are very frightened of magpies. Could it be you who are over-superstitious?'

This really was the end. How dare Camellia tell Dr Byng about me and magpies. I could tell I wasn't getting anywhere so I asked him plainly whether he could do anything at all to help.

Dr Byng said no. Camellia was a perfectly fit and intelligent young lady, and it wasn't often that he was outsmarted by someone so young. He added that he felt she was a very truthful child. So that was that. No helpful advice from the medical quarter. Dr Byng was giving me a look as if he felt sorry for me.

'How is your finger, Mrs Devon?'

'Still bloody sore, if you must know.' Dr Byng was surprised at my sharp remark, and I felt ashamed for saying what I said.

'No, it's getting there, thank you. Your splint was very helpful.' Dr Byng said he was glad and now he had to be getting on. He did say something useful as I was seeing him out the front door.

'You might try our vicar if you're still worried. He might put Camellia's mind at rest, if she really is being haunted.'

I didn't like the sound of Camellia's *being haunted* one bit. In that case I would ring the vicar first thing. Gerald was right about bringing him in.

I'll tell Nanny Jan to take the nursery tree down tomorrow. It's not quite Twelfth Night but really, once we are through New Year, the Christmas decorations look very dreary. I had better finish this tree myself. Finn was a bit rough with the angels. I must say, they do seem reluctant to come off the tinsel.

With a bit of luck, the vicar might be able to visit tomorrow? I'll tell him it's very urgent.

NANNY JAN

We had quite a to-do with our nursery tree this evening. Mrs Devon had been in to tell us that it should come down tomorrow, and so after tea I switched the lights on while Camellia sang 'Silent Night'. We were saying goodbye to our tree. It was its last night with us. Finn asked why it couldn't stay until his birthday which is in July.

'It would just be twigs, Finn,' Camellia said. 'Look it's going bald already.' She tapped a branch to show him.

'They don't grow back?' Finn asked.

'They do not,' Camellia told him. 'It turns into one big twig.' At that moment the fairy lights went off.

'Oh NO!' shouted Camellia.

I'd only got halfway across the nursery when the lights came on again. About five minutes later they went off and two minutes later they came on. This happened several times. Camellia began to time it on her watch.

'One minute that time, Nanny Jan!'

'What a lark,' said Finn.

Camellia said she wanted to show her mother and I didn't see the harm, so she ran off through to the drawing room. Mrs Devon had just got off the telephone so the timing was good.

As they came into the nursery, the lights went off again.

'See!' said Finn, waving at the tree.

'See what?' Mrs Devon looked puzzled. She didn't understand. Almost immediately the lights came on again and promptly went off.

We watched for about ten minutes and at one point they were actually flashing. Camellia danced around, saying she thought the tree was talking to us, saying *goodbye* she said, but in a lovely way.

Mrs Devon had to admit she'd never seen anything like it and wondered if it was something to do with the fuse?

'It's *magic*, Mummy!' Camellia cried. 'Look they've gone again!'

'Magic, Mummy,' repeated Finn.

I did sense that Mrs Devon was caught up in the excitement, even if just a little. Whatever was happening, it made the children happy and I was more than pleased their mother could share it for once.

Camellia didn't tell me much about the doctor. She said she had forgotten most of it. I'm assuming all went well because Mrs Devon didn't mention it again.

The children went to bed quite happily. The tree had returned to normal by the time I came back downstairs. I double-checked the sweets cupboard and the fox puppet was still in his prison.

If only it wasn't so cold.

CAMELLIA

What a good sleep! I wake up feeling full of beans. When I draw the curtains back, our world looks a bit different. The branches of the trees are waving about madly, pitching this way and that. The sky is a dark grey and, even though it's gone eight o'clock, it hardly feels like morning at all. The gloomy skies don't bother me though. I feel sunny.

Heidi is well, Dorothy Baby is asleep in bed, and my dolls are sitting happily on their shelf. Perhaps it's time to change their dresses again? It's no longer Christmas after all and today our tree has to come down.

It was magical last night with the lights going on and off. Mummy can say it's the fuse as much as she likes, but I know it was magic. Finn and I laughed and laughed, mainly because Mummy looked so surprised.

I don't want to say goodbye to my little church, but I know Mummy will say it has to go back to the cellar. My mistletoe is old and tired, the milky berries shrivelled up. I still have my rowan twig though and it must be extra magical because nothing bad has happened since I picked it. I don't count the tree lights as bad. They were wonderful!

I write in my diary as much as I can remember about my talk with Dr Byng. It's odd that I can only remember the beginning and the end. Mummy didn't say any more about it, so I don't think I will have to see the doctor again.

Goodness, it's windy! Above the trees there are rooks or crows wheeling about in the stormy sky. It's as if they are dancing in the wind. Yesterday Mrs Betts warned of more snow on the way. How can there be any *more* snow? We have so much already. Nanny Jan says they have even more in the North.

It's porridge *again* for breakfast because Nanny Jan says it's that sort of day.

'This is a gale, Camellia. Not just a wind.' Finn and I eat our breakfast and think about gales.

'Thank goodness there's no hunting in the snow,' I say.

'That's a mercy,' says Finn.

'If you get snow *and* a gale,' explains Nanny Jan, 'Then you get drifting, and huge, big drifts of snow build up and that can cause chaos.' Finn wants to know what sort of chaos, and Nanny Jan says that you can get fifteen-foot drifts, blocking roads and railway lines.

'Then people really get stuck?' I ask.

'They really do,' says Nanny Jan.

Mummy comes in and says: 'Isn't it windy?' I see her hair is looking a bit flat, so she'll be wanting to go to the hairdresser pretty soon.

'Now Camellia,' she says. 'I've had such a nice chat with Mr Impey.' I look blank.

'Who's Mr Impey?'

'He's our vicar, Camellia. He's coming over here after lunch because he wants to see if he can help with all the funny goings-on.'

I smell a Samuel Whiskers sort of rat. Mummy wants me to talk to the vicar now. But he might be more help than the doctor because he's quite young.

'I'll give him a lovely cup of coffee in the drawing room and then bring him through,' Mummy says. I spread strawberry jam on my toast. Finn drinks his milk. It's all arranged then.

'Do you think the vicar would like to see my wheelbarrow?' asks Finn.

'Almost certainly,' Mummy says, moving towards the door. 'But only after he's had a nice chat with Camellia.'

'Good,' says Finn. 'But we won't show him the bad fox puppet.' Mummy has left before Finn says this. Nanny Jan and I stare at him.

'No,' I say. 'But we may have to.'

I don't feel sunny any more.

NANNY JAN

We took the Christmas tree down this morning.

All the time it was getting windier and windier. Mrs Betts arrived, saying her hair had been blown into a right old bird's nest, in spite of her scarf. She said it was bitter again and the wind wasn't helping. It was getting into her bones.

Once Camellia had brought down her little church, even though she wanted to keep it, we decided to make our expedition down to the cellar.

I *never* like going down to the cellar. It gives me the creeps, and what makes me feel even more claustrophobic is the idea of the weight of the building sitting on top. This cellar is huge, running below the length and breadth of the house, with that many rooms off the main passage. It always smells of chalk and old water.

Camellia led the way and I followed, all the while keeping an eye on Finn who was carrying his paper-chain in a special bag.

'This way,' said Camellia. 'Finn, don't touch the boiler!' Finn stopped dead in his tracks. 'This is where Mummy puts the decorations. Look, there's her tinsel tree box.' She paused and glanced around. 'I wonder where Mummy has put Dorothy Baby's cot?'

'If I was a ghost, I would live down here,' Finn said, wandering into one of the rooms. 'Then I would jump out on people.'

Camellia was searching for the cot. She wanted to bring it

back up because Dorothy Baby was getting squashed in bed with her.

We spent a good ten minutes searching with Finn jumping out behind us. He hid behind suitcases and tables and chairs for the summer, old cots and armchairs and boxes and more boxes. There is nothing like laughing in the face of fear. Mind you I don't find that fox puppet very funny, and I still haven't told Mrs Devon about the sleep-walking.

Camellia was searching in the very last room when she cried out. We found her in Mr Devon's wine cellar, staring at something behind the door. It was Dorothy Baby's cot, smashed into pieces. I knew it was her cot because of the little bird transfer on the side.

'Oh Camellia,' I cried. 'I *am* sorry!' Camellia blinked hard, bending down to touch the pieces of splintered wood.

'How could this have happened?' She held up a sharp piece. Finn appeared in the doorway behind us, surveying the scene.

'We will need a policeman,' he said. Camellia turned on him then.

'Oh Finn, of course you don't need a policeman for a broken cot.'

I helped her pick up some of the pieces. The cot was beyond repair sadly. Finn offered to fetch his paper-chain bag to carry the broken pieces upstairs, and we were a sorry party, walking back up into the daylight. Who on earth would do such a thing? Camellia was given that cot for her second birthday.

'Well that's that, Nanny Jan,' she said. 'I wonder what will happen next?' and then quietly 'I loved that cot.'

I filled the kettle up for elevenses, surveying the weather outside. The wind was buffeting against the house and the sky had turned pewter.

We were in for a storm.

ANGELA
Mr Impey arrives
The Reverend Francis Impey was very punctual. He arrived,

distinctly windswept, because he had to walk up the drive. He said he didn't think his little car would be able to get up the hill, and he was probably right. It's now dreadfully icy. He wore a pair of stout walking boots with studs (he showed me), and he even carried a pair of ski sticks which he propped up outside the front door. His cassock was flapping like a sail in the wind, and his coat and hat looked good enough for Russia.

The children were peering round the nursery door when I took him through to the drawing room, carrying his cup of coffee. I needed to make my position clear, and I made sure Gerald was busy because I didn't want him sticking his oar in.

I took up my customary position in front of the fire, and Mr Impey sat on the sofa. It struck me in that moment how very handsome he was. His eyes were astonishingly blue and he had very good teeth, not to mention a charming smile.

'Now Mr Impey, we really need your help to settle Camellia down. Dr Byng suggested that you might be able to shed some light on the situation.' I didn't mention Gerald.

'We've had some funny comings and goings recently,' I continued, getting into my stride. 'Camellia says she saw a ghost out hunting. I broke my finger as a result.' I held it out to show him. 'And then we've had disappearing dolls and flashing Christmas lights, not to mention the snowman.'

Mr Impey listened politely without commenting.

'But most worrying of all are Camellia's drawings. I don't think she should be drawing that sort of thing.' Outside the wind was picking up even more, as if it was hurling itself against the house. Mr Impey spotted me tut-tutting. He gave a big smile. Goodness, he was good looking.

'It's a bit like the Wizard of Oz, isn't it?' he said. 'Where will we be blown to, I wonder?' He finished his coffee and put down his cup.

'I think the best thing would be for me to talk to Camellia and then we can see where we are.' Another charming smile. Was he flirting by any chance?

I didn't want this ending up like Dr Byng, so I told Mr Impey firmly that I wanted all talk of ghosts and strange goings-on to be discounted. What we needed was to get everything back on an even keel. I didn't want people to think my child was disturbed. I didn't actually tell him that, but I thought he got the gist.

Nanny Jan and Finn can come in here and do a puzzle or something while Mr Impey is talking to Camellia.

That *infernal* wind!

CAMELLIA

Mr Impey and I sit alone in the rather bare nursery. I am perched on the sofa and surprisingly Mr Impey sits cross-legged on the floor, so I'm higher than him. He's dressed in black, his long coat spread about him. His white collar is very smart indeed. The remains of my poor cot sit in Finn's bag and I show them first, tipping out the splintered pieces. On the little table are my pictures, spread out.

'Oh, what a *shame*!' he cries and in that moment I know I have a friend. 'Whose cot was it? Which one of your dolls?' It's as if he knows!

'It was Dorothy Baby's cot,' I tell him. 'We had to put the cot downstairs after the bad fox puppet got into it. That really scared me.' I glance towards the sweets cupboard and Mr Impey notices.

'What's in there?' he asks.

'The fox! He has to be kept in prison because he's so *bad*.' Mr Impey thinks about this, putting his head on one side. Then he says something funny.

'I could *murder* a jelly baby!' I cannot believe a grown-up has said this. I ask him what he means exactly, and he tells me he needs to eat a jelly baby *right* now. It would make our talk go even better. I tell him that the sweets cupboard is always locked. I will need Nanny Jan to open it with the key.

'Where's Nanny Jan then?' Mr Impey says, his blue eyes dancing. '*Where's* that key?'

I run through to the drawing room to find Nanny Jan. Finn's

busy with his easy puzzle and Mummy's on the telephone as usual. Nanny Jan gets up, following me out of the room. I hear Finn say he would like a jelly baby too.

Mr Impey studies my drawings while Nanny Jan unlocks the cupboard. He has set them out around him on the carpet, and he picks them up one by one. Nanny Jan offers him the little bag of jelly babies and he gives her a wink.

'A black one, my favourite. Thank you. And one for Camellia too.' He smiles at me. This is *fun*! 'And perhaps leave the cupboard open in case we need any more.'

Nanny Jan doesn't know what to make of this and shuts the nursery door behind her. I'm worried Mr Fox might escape now the cupboard is open, and I tell Mr Impey this. I eat my jelly baby slowly.

'We will talk to Mr Fox later,' he says. 'But first tell me about your drawings. I'm not as clever as you and I need you to explain everything.'

There's something about Mr Impey that makes me feel safe. I know I can tell him all my worries, and never feel stupid for having them. He's not like other grown-ups at all. Every two minutes or so he says he needs another jelly baby, and soon they're all finished. He says we might need to move on to the Smarties next.

He listens to *everything*. I've told him all I can remember, even the bit about feeling strange in church on Christmas Eve, as well as the beautiful window and the portals. He's most interested in the rowan tree.

Not once does he tell me I'm silly. Now we are talking about Mercy and Mr Impey tells me he's seen several ghosts.

'But my Gran says we're not allowed to believe in ghosts, except the Holy Ghost of course.' Mr Impey smiles at this.

'There are all sorts of ghosts,' he says. 'Including Holy ones. The great thing is to keep an open mind. Most of the time the ghosts, or spirits as they are sometimes called, are confused. Either they don't know they are dead, or they're trapped here because they haven't gone to the Light.'

'So, Mercy is stuck?'

'Most probably,' Mr Impey says.

'What can we do to help her?'

Mr Impey stretches out his legs across the nursery floor and takes a deep breath.

'Send love,' he says. 'Even ghosts need love.' This is a surprise. I tell him I didn't know that.

'Even Mr Fox needs love,' Mr Impey says, glancing towards the open cupboard. 'In fact, Mr Fox *especially* needs love. Now I dare you to put your hand in that cupboard and bring him out. I'd like to meet your Mr Fox.'

My heart speeds up. He's not *my* Mr Fox!

'But before you do that,' Mr Impey says, noticing my hesitation, 'I want you to fill your heart with as much love as you possibly can.' I tell him I'm not sure how.

'Think of *all* the people you love,' Mr Impey says. 'Your dolls, your most favourite things, your dogs, the seaside, your best flowers, the sunshine, your favourite song...'

I nod slowly and close my eyes. I concentrate on all the people I love, as well as Banger and the seaside and then I try my best to fill my heart with love. After a bit I think I'm ready. It's time to bring out Mr Fox. Mr Impey watches me, holding out his hands, ready to receive.

I put my hands in the cupboard, feeling about. Where is he? Behind the big tin of sweets? No. I feel about some more. The cupboard's dark, but he's here somewhere, and I pray I don't get bitten. I stretch my hands further in and touch his red velvet coat. I've got him! I take a deep breath, pull him out and give him to Mr Impey. It worked! Mr Fox doesn't look nearly so scary now my heart is full of love.

Mr Impey turns the fox puppet over in his hands.

'Well, he's obviously very old. His velvet coat's a bit mangy.'

'I think his yellow eyes look rather mean,' I say. 'Even when my heart is full of love.'

'Well,' says Mr Impey. 'He can't help that his eyes are yellow and rather close together.' He puts his hand inside Mr Fox, drawing the puppet's paws together as if in prayer.

'Hello Mr Fox,' Mr Impey says kindly. Then he brings Mr Fox's nose up to his ear, as if listening to whatever he's saying.

'I think Mr Fox needs a blessing. He has probably never been blessed in his long life.'

'What shall we bless him with?' I look around the nursery for something. Outside it's snowing again. Blown by the gale, the flakes are whirling around, rising and falling. Mr Impey knows what I'm thinking.

'We shall bless him with snowflakes,' he says. 'Can you catch some for me, Camellia?'

It isn't easy to open the door against the wind, but I manage it somehow and now the snowflakes are pouring into the nursery. I reach out and catch some in my hand, and they are melted by the time I tip them on to Mr Fox's head, the snow-water flowing over his face and eyes. Mr Impey says a blessing. It's not very long.

'He's crying!' I say.

'He is blessed,' says Mr Impey. I have to say Mr Fox looks less bad.

'Everyone deserves to be loved,' he says, giving a big sigh. Then he sits Mr Fox on the sofa, his back against a cushion, and I shut the door. Snow melts on the carpet. Winter has come into the nursery. But not for Mr Fox! Snowflakes have cured him.

'Now Camellia, I will keep an eye out for your Mercy in church. I can always come back again next week, if you like. It might be a good idea to give the house a blessing as well.'

'Do you think my Gran could ever believe in ghosts?' I ask.

'Only when she's ready. You will know when she's ready,' he adds mysteriously. I say I'm not sure I will. Mr Fox sits on the sofa with tears in his eyes. I think he enjoyed his blessing.

'Thank you, Mr Impey.'

'Thank *you*, Camellia,' he says. 'When are you getting your piano, by the way?' Has Mummy told him this? I don't think so.

'You play by ear, don't you? So do I! Not everyone can play by ear or see ghosts like us.'

He sets off to walk through to the drawing room but then he stops and turns.

'By the way, ghosts love music.' My heart leaps.

I love Mr Impey!

Mummy helps him into his big coat and gives him his hat. Mr Impey and I are all smiles, so she thinks it has gone well. Of course, she's right but not in the way she would have liked.

Mummy invites Mr Impey to the skating party on Sunday, and he says he will come along if he can. It just depends on what happens after church. We stand on the front doorstep, waving him goodbye as he walks off into the snow and wind, digging his ski sticks in with every step. The snow swirls and dances and soon he has disappeared into the white.

When Mummy asks me how it went, I tell her truthfully that Mr Impey made me feel calm and collected. I don't tell her he believes in ghosts.

Finn peers at Mr Fox on the sofa and then into the sweets cupboard. I tell him how Mr Impey blessed Mr Fox with snow-flakes, and how Mr Fox isn't bad any more because he's loved. Finn looks inside the cupboard again.

'Yes, but where have all the jelly babies gone?'

I don't tell him.

CAMELLIA

I'm in pitch darkness! My eyes are open, but I can't see my nightlight. Have I gone blind? Am I in the portal? I can't see anything! I listen for the wind and hear nothing. Have I gone deaf as well?

I stretch out my hand, feeling for my bedside light. I switch it on and see nothing! I've definitely gone blind! Why now? My eyes were all right yesterday! I must THINK! I'm nearly seven after all. What I *can* do is test if I've gone blind by using my torch. It isn't on my bedside table so it must have fallen off. I lean over, scrabbling on the carpet, and I find it. Now what if I can't see the torchlight? Then I'll *know* I've gone blind.

I press the switch and see a beam of yellow light. Relief makes my teeth chatter, as I swing the beam around the room. Perhaps the wind made the electricity go off? It happened when we had thunderstorm last summer. Yes, I'm sure that's what has happened. My watch says it's quarter past three, and my throat feels dry.

I must be thirsty, so I pad over the corridor to the bathroom to fill up my tooth mug. Bathroom water never tastes very nice, but it will have to do. I balance my torch on the basin shelf and turn on the cold tap. While the water runs, I look in the mirror because for a moment I think I'm brushing my teeth.

There is nobody there. *I'm not in the mirror.* I am not in the bathroom. I turn around, expecting to see myself behind me, but there is no one. I turn off the tap and drink the water, but the only thing I see in the mirror is the empty bathroom. How can this be? I have an awful thought. I'm in the portal! But am I really in the portal? I feel as if I'm still here in the bathroom. Perhaps I'm dreaming?

I run back to my room to fetch Dorothy Baby. Will I be able to see her in the mirror? I shine my torch up on to the ceiling to spread the light, and Dorothy Baby has a reflection, hanging in the air as I hold her up. But *I am not there.* I wave the torch around a bit, wondering if that will bring me back.

And then I know I'm not alone. Mercy stands in the doorway. I know it's her because I can see her reflection. Her face is twisted up as if she's crying. I watch as she puts her hands up to her mouth, and I don't dare turn around. All I can do is stand and watch her misery, and not a single sound. I hold Dorothy Baby as tight as I can. Mercy must be standing very close, because I can feel her, and now my back is turning to ice. I am turning to ice. Please don't let her touch me. Please NOT.

But then I remember Mr Impey's advice. I must send her love! That's what she needs. I close my eyes and think about Finn and Banger and 'Silent Night', filling my heart with love. I say bless you, bless you, bless you, hoping Mercy can hear. I imagine the softest snowflakes landing gently on her face, whispering bless you, bless you, bless you over and over again.

Dorothy Baby falls out of my arms! I scramble to pick her up and when I look into the mirror again, I'm back. I can see myself, but I'm so pale and peaky that now I look like a ghost! I turn around and Mercy is gone. That was close!

Mr Impey will be very proud of me! I can't wait for him to know how clever and brave I've been. He *must* come to the skating party! I hug Dorothy Baby tight, telling myself how well I've done. It's amazing what you can do when you fill your heart up with love!

I wish I had a hot-water bottle, at least a hot hot-water bottle. Mine is freezing so I throw it out of bed. I put on some socks and then I notice Mr Fox is not where I left him on the shelf. He has moved two dolls to the right. I blow him a kiss and bless him for luck. Then I put a cardigan on over my pyjamas and climb back into bed.

I curl up into a ball, wrapping myself around Dorothy Baby. Perhaps I really did fall into the bathroom portal? But I am back now. What a relief! I leave my torch on because I don't want to be in the pitch dark again, and I'll ask Nanny Jan for a new battery tomorrow. My feet are freezing, even in socks.

Someone is crying right outside my door, and I know it isn't Finn. I'm too tired, Mercy. I'm too tired to bless you again.

NANNY JAN

When I went into the children's rooms this morning they were absolutely freezing. The radiators hadn't come on for some reason and I hoped we didn't have a broken boiler. Finn swore he didn't touch it when we were in the cellar.

We soon discovered what had happened. There had been a power cut in the night, altering all the timings for the heating. Fortunately, it didn't take long for Mr Devon to get the boiler going again. Camellia said during breakfast that she knew there had been a power cut and wondered if she could have a new battery for her torch.

Our snowman was still standing after all the wind, although

his hat had blown off. There was a bank of snow on his eastern side and the landscape of the garden was changed in that there were now drifts of snow wherever the wind had come up against walls, trees or shrubs.

I was very much looking forward to my week off. I hadn't spent Christmas with my parents after all, and I knew how much they were looking forward to seeing me. Old Nanny was due to arrive before lunch and the children were very excited. Camellia drew her a picture of two snowmen and a magpie, with the sun and a fir tree in the background. I was just grateful it wasn't a picture of a ghost.

Camellia seemed very chirpy after her talk with Mr Impey. She was amused he ate so many jelly babies. I don't think Finn was! And who would have thought that Mr Fox could be so redeemed? Camellia maintained he was no longer bad, just misunderstood. He was allowed to come upstairs with her at bedtime, and she promptly set him up on the shelf between two dolls. She said they would look after him.

The skating party will go ahead, in spite of the snowdrifts. Mrs Devon said the guests are going to do their best to get here on Sunday. Sadly, I shall miss it. I would have enjoyed seeing Mr Impey skating.

I know I will benefit from a few days off. The house isn't friendly any more. Whether it's my imagination or not, I daren't look to the left when I come out of my room at night. It's as if someone or something is watching me at the top of the main staircase. I hear crying too. I tell myself it's not Finn or Camellia because it's not. Last night I convinced myself it was the wind, even though it had died down.

Mrs Betts arrived after breakfast. She's a marvel and I told her so, getting through whatever the weather. Camellia asked if she could help get Old Nanny's room ready, and Mrs Betts said she couldn't do without her. Camellia so loves to feel useful. Finn helped me with my packing. He told me very seriously that I would need fourteen pairs of socks due to the *shocking cold*. We ran out of socks at ten, so he went to his room and fetched four pairs of his own. As we went back downstairs, he put his hand out for me to hold.

'Will you send me a postcard?'

I was only staying in the next-door village, but I promised I would. I also told him I would have my photographs developed, and then we would see Finn as a fine horseman.

'Hmmmm,' said Finn.

ANGELA

I set off to collect Nanny just after ten. I had quite expected to see the whole world turned upside down after that bloody wind, with twenty-foot snowdrifts everywhere. As it was, we were lucky. I think it's far worse in the west. I'm sick to the back teeth of this snow, if truth be told. It was pretty in the beginning but now I want to get on.

Fortunately, there's absolutely no chance of going hunting in this weather, so Camellia and I are spared. Even if we didn't have the snow, I'd tell Gerald my little finger was much, much too sore to hold the reins.

Thank heavens my finger doesn't stop me driving. That would have been the limit. Pulling up in my parents' drive, I congratulated myself that I had dealt with the Camellia business pretty well. It hadn't gone quite as I hoped with Dr Byng, but dear Mr Impey has worked wonders with Camellia. She seemed very bright this morning and showed me her picture for Nanny. I'm putting Nanny in the pink room as it has a nicer view than Nanny Jan's room. I'm sure the children will be all right. I will tell them they can come to our room in the night, if there is a crisis.

Of course, Nanny was ready for me. If there's one person in the world I can rely on, it's Nanny.

'Well Angela,' she said. 'Here I am.' I supported her arm, walking across the ice to the car and, once in the front seat, I gave her a rug to put over her knees. I didn't talk too much about what had been going on with the children. I just gave Nanny a brief outline and told her how nice Mr Impey had been. She reassured me by saying what she always says.

'It always turns out for the best in the end.' I sincerely hoped
so.

Nanny has magical powers with children. I don't remember
her ever getting cross with me as a child, and I always wanted
to do my best for her. I could not say the same for my mother.
She was never there.

The children were framed charmingly in the back door as
we pulled up. Finn was wearing his red hat and Camellia had
a little posy of holly. I let Nanny greet them in her own way,
breathing a huge sigh of relief.

What would I do without Nanny?

CAMELLIA

It's very different having Old Nanny here. I have to remind her
when we have our elevenses and what Finn and I have to drink.
She doesn't know about feeding the birds (she does now), and
she didn't even know what time we have lunch.

Nanny Jan is often busy doing stuff like washing, ironing,
and making our beds although I do my best to help with mine.
Because Old Nanny is old, she doesn't do much of that. This
means she's with us more.

She sits in the nursery and watches and listens. She also does
a lot of knitting. She never says anything horrid about anybody.
If I ever say I'm cross with someone because they haven't been
very nice, Old Nanny says you never know what's been going
on for that person. I learn a lot from Old Nanny.

Finn's being a bit naughty because he tells Old Nanny we're
allowed two lots of sweets a day because it's January and there's
snow. Nanny shakes her head at this and smiles. Finn tries
again.

'We give sweets to the birds sometimes.' This is a *huge* fib
from Finn, and I give him a look. I'm busy changing my dolls'
dresses.

'All in good time,' Old Nanny says vaguely.

Mummy joins us for lunch today which is a great treat.

Daddy has gone to a meeting. Mummy tells us the skating party plans are coming along, and Finn and I bounce on our chairs. Mr Gibbs is going to brush all the snow off the pond this afternoon, and Mummy says Henry will probably help too as it's quite a big job.

'When can I have skates?' I ask Mummy.

'Soon,' Mummy says, and I know what that means. 'Now this afternoon you can help me look for things like tin trays, old plates and mugs and little glasses. I need someone who can count well. Then we need old chairs for people to push on the ice. And I need to look for the big metal dustbin for our fire, and a grate, so we can roast the sausages on the top. I've already got the bridge rolls for the sausages.'

Finn bounces on his chair some more. This is so exciting! Mummy is different with Old Nanny around. I think she's more herself.

It's too icy for Old Nanny to come for a walk, so we leave her in the nursery and follow Mummy to the pond to see how Mr Gibbs and Henry are getting on. They have swept the snow off the pond with great big brooms and we admire their hard work. We can't stop the dogs running down the bank and we laugh as they skid across the ice. Now it's our turn, and we practise sliding down the bank on tin trays.

We are in heaven. We find we can slide down the bank and get halfway across. It's difficult to walk on the ice without falling over so we use the trays to push ourselves on our tummies. It's like we're swimming on ice!

Mummy laughs and says: 'Isn't this fun?' It's always fun if Mummy's in a good mood. But now it's getting dark and we have our last slide across the pond.

We walk back either side of Mummy, back to the lights and warm and tea and toast, leaving the dark behind us.

CAMELLIA
The skating party
Finn and I wake bright and early because today's the day of the

skating party. Everything is as it should be. Mr Fox is tucked up between the same two dolls. He didn't move. Heidi sits on her chair and I feel a bit sorry for her. I'm not sure I pay her enough attention and perhaps that's why she looks drunk. I really don't like to shake her. She can't help it if her eyes don't work properly.

'FOGGY!' I hear Finn shout from next door. Not too foggy, I hope! I look out the window and it's really, really foggy, about as foggy as the day when I first saw Mercy. I go to see Finn and he's sitting on his windowsill, wearing his hat.

Old Nanny didn't bolt him in because she said she'd never heard such a thing in her life. I'm not sure Mummy liked hearing that because she smiled a tight smile. When Old Nanny tucked Finn in after his bath, she told him he was ever such a grown-up boy of four and a half, and she knew he would stay in his room and not disturb Camellia. He didn't need a gate, did he? I know she said this because she shared it with me when it was my turn to be tucked in tight.

I told her that we'd been having some scary things going on and Old Nanny said that we could talk about all that tomorrow.

'Now's the time for getting sleepy, my pet,' she said. 'Nanny's here and she makes everything safe. You tell me everything tomorrow. Doesn't your Dorothy Baby look pretty in that shawl? She's lucky to have you as a mummy.'

I looked into Old Nanny's small blue eyes and I saw love, the sort of love that keeps going whatever. I liked that very much.

But that was yesterday and today is today! Finn and I promised Mummy we'd do lots of fetching and carrying. Mrs Betts is also coming in to help, even though it's a Sunday. Mrs Betts loves a party.

Mummy goes running into the airing cupboard. She shouts 'Brrrrr!' and laughs. That means it's going to be a good day! I help Finn get dressed although he's pretty good at it now. He struggles with his jumper, saying his head's too big. I wear my navy polo neck with my fair isle jersey on top. I wish all this wool didn't itch so much, but better itchy than cold.

I wonder if Nanny likes porridge? I go through to the kitchen and ask Cook if I can make it. She laughs, saying she will do it for me, and she'll make enough for Old Nanny too. Mummy comes flying through the kitchen, telling us she's got a hundred and one things to do. I can tell she is happy though.

Old Nanny comes down. She says Finn has been showing her his sock collection. I have laid the breakfast table and done a very good job. I notice our snowman has lost an eye. I will replace it when I feed the birds. I'm dancing with impatience. I can't *wait* for the skating party to begin. Finn's telling Old Nanny that he's faster than me on the tin tray and I don't argue. I'm too excited.

Mummy has lots of her own friends coming to the party. From my list I know Sarah and Melanie-Anne said yes. Annabel can't come because she's going to a musical party with her big sister. The Cordleys are definitely coming, bringing their new Nanny Mae. I hope there will be enough sausages! Mummy says that Daddy has tons of them.

We finish our breakfast and Old Nanny can't get over how we can bounce on our chairs, eating porridge at the same time. She says it would give her indigestion.

I'm very useful in the morning, running errands for Mummy and Daddy. Daddy's in a good mood, getting in Cook's way in the kitchen. He has found a huge saucepan for the hot wine, so now he's even happier. Mrs Betts is dressed in trousers today, not a skirt. Safer, she says.

We make sure Old Nanny has plenty of warm clothes for sitting and watching. Daddy is going to drive her up towards the stables, and then walk her carefully along the flat. Then she will sit in a chair and watch everyone skating.

We are ready! It's midday and people are starting to arrive. They emerge from the fog walking towards us, most of them carrying their skates round their necks. They head up towards the pond where Daddy has set up 'putting on skates chairs' as well as the huge dustbin with smoke billowing up. The hot wine saucepan is bubbling, and Daddy beckons the grown-ups towards him to try his Swiss glühwein. He's laughing out loud because he loves to entertain his friends. Mummy has set up a table on the ice for the plates and mugs and glasses. This is where the children get their drinks, and we hope the orange squash doesn't freeze! Mummy hasn't put her skates on yet, but she tells people she will once she's had a drink.

The six old kitchen chairs in the middle of the pond are for nervous skaters. Soon they're all being used with people pushing round the pond in a circle. I can't help laughing at grown-ups being scared of the ice.

I am waiting patiently for Melanie-Anne and Sarah. Aunt Daphne arrives, carrying her black skates. She says she wishes they were white but there you are, you can't have everything. Lorna and Julia are trying to climb the bank and pushing them up is their new nanny. She has a kind, rosy face and is young! And she can't be strict because she is laughing.

Finn hands out the tin trays, pointing any children towards the far side of the pond. He understands that we have to keep to our nursery end. Mummy has put her skates on now and she doesn't need a chair because she skates beautifully. One day I will skate as well as Mummy.

Melanie-Anne and Sarah are here! They were dropped off together and they can stay until three. Melanie-Anne is wearing an enormous blue woolly hat which comes down over her eyes, and she has to keep pushing it back. She says it belongs to her brother. Sarah wears a beautiful green anorak with a furry hood.

'Our trays,' I say, giving them one each. Sarah's eyes sparkle. We walk along to the nursery end.

Soon we are sliding down across the ice. We find it helps if you give a great shout of 'mind out' as this at least makes the skaters change course. There is much shouting and laughing. Some of the skaters are even more wobbly, probably because of Daddy's gluühwein.

The sausages are cooking on the fire in the dustbin and I feel my tummy rumbling. It's already half past one. When will Mr

Impey arrive? Will he have time? I do so want him to meet Sarah and Melanie-Anne.

As if by magic and at that very moment Mr Impey comes marching up the drive. My heart lifts. He's wearing his huge coat and hat and he walks using his ski sticks. I wave at him and he comes over.

'Hello, hello, hello,' he says to all three of us. He has a pair of brown skates around his neck.

'Can you actually skate, Mr Impey?' I ask.

'What do you *think*?' he says. 'What do you think these are for?' He points. 'I'm sorry they're brown! Frightfully slack!' Melanie-Anne's eyes widen.

'I can skate,' he says, laughing and then, 'I can *even* skate backwards!' That actually makes me laugh out loud. Mr Impey is so *funny*. He is here and I love him, and I can tell my friends love him too.

I walk him over to the grown-up end. I have a sudden worry. Will the ice be strong enough for all these people? Mr Impey isn't worried one bit. He raises his glass to me and I smile back, wondering how soon I can tell him about blessing Mercy in the bathroom.

He puts on his brown skates and sets off without a chair. He does one circle round the pond and then, with the three of us watching, he turns to skate a circle backwards. We cheer out loud. Mummy has spotted him and beckons him over. We have lost him for now, but he will come back, I'm sure.

We eat our sausages wrapped in bridge rolls, and I feel a bubble of pure joy brimming up. I think this is the happiest I have *ever* been. Finn says he's on to his third sausage and might easily have five or six. I take Melanie-Anne and Sarah away from the others to tell them about Mercy in the mirror.

'I would have been petrified,' Melanie-Anne says. 'What does it mean when you can't see yourself in the mirror?'

'I'll ask mum,' says Sarah.

'I thought I had fallen into the portal. It wasn't fun.'

Gran is walking up the north drive. She looks a bit lonely, so

I wave and she gives a sad wave back. She joins us, but it's not as easy introducing my friends to Gran as it is to Mr Impey. It feels a bit stiff but Gran gives them a friendly smile, asking if they're having fun.

Melanie-Anne and Sarah nod politely. This is the grandmother I've been talking about after all. Finn comes over to ask Gran if she would like a sausage roll. He says there are some left. Melanie-Anne fancies another one and she joins Finn to walk back over to the food.

Gran, Sarah and I stand quietly together. A magpie chatters behind us, and I can't help turning round. There is Mercy standing beneath a tall ash tree. I know it's an ash because of the keys. I touch Sarah's arm for her to turn, and her eyes widen. Then Mr Impey is walking towards us with his skates back round his neck and he gives us a merry smile. I don't say a word, but I do point at Mercy. Gran wonders what I am pointing at. She looks puzzled.

Now is a good time to test if Gran can see her, with Sarah and Mr Impey here.

'I can't remember what that tree is called, Gran.' She follows the direction of my finger, and Mercy stares. I can feel her eyes from here.

'What's it called, that tree with the keys?' Mercy stands there waiting but Gran doesn't see her.

'Why, that's an ash tree, Camellia,' Gran says. 'Such a useful tree because you can burn the wood, even when it's green.' I nod politely.

When I look back, Mercy has gone. Finn is coming along with two sausage rolls, and how they're still on the plate I have no idea. Gran thanks him very much and takes a bite. Then she walks away towards Daddy and the other grown-ups.

Sarah nods her head. She knows what she saw. Mr Impey says he really must go because he has old people to visit, but he's had the greatest fun.

'And I saw your ghost, Camellia,' he says, his blue eyes serious. 'I saw Mercy.'

'I think she wanted to join in the skating party. She's always on her own.'

'A lonely ghost, your Mercy,' says Mr Impey, gathering his ski sticks.

'We shall see what we can do for her,' he calls over his shoulder as he walks down the bank. 'I'll be back in a week.'

I smile at Sarah.

'I told you he was lovely.'

I'm not going mad! What a relief! I can't be mad if both Sarah and Mr Impey can see Mercy. What a pity Melanie-Anne wasn't with us. We go in search of her and already the party is breaking up. People are saying goodbye, returning to their cars or walking down the drive.

Gran is already making her way home. One day she'll be able to see Mercy, I know it. She disappears into the fog. I didn't get to say goodbye, and I didn't get to tell Mr Impey about blessing Mercy. We were too busy. I tell myself he knows it already.

We carry things back to the house. Mummy says we can leave the table, chairs and dustbin until tomorrow. She asks me what I thought about the day.

'Really lovely Mummy. That was a marvellous party.' I don't tell her about Mercy, because I want to keep her happy.

We are back in the house and I will ask Old Nanny if she would like to watch a bit of television. I help Finn take off his coat and boots. He's almost asleep already.

Our nursery is light and warm. Old Nanny smiles at us from the sofa and for now we are safe.

CAMELLIA

Old Nanny and I have a quiet moment together. This afternoon Mummy has taken Finn off to the eye doctor to check his left eye. The doctor needs to see how well it's mended after the squint operation. Finn might be able to throw his patch away completely.

Nanny and I are in the nursery as usual, and she's knitting a cover for my hot-water bottle. I was allowed to choose a colour from Nanny's big patchwork bag. I chose the lightest, palest lilac-blue and Nanny said I'd chosen well, she just hoped it wouldn't show the dirt too much. I promised I wouldn't go rolling around the mud wearing my nightie. She laughed at that.

While Nanny knits, I tell her about seeing Mercy out hunting, how Mummy doesn't really understand me, how Gran doesn't believe in ghosts and how Mercy is her Mummy who died on Christmas Eve and that is the window in the church. It's rather a lot for Nanny to take in. She nods and knits as I tell her my worries. I'm pretty sure she guesses what's coming next.

'What happened to my Mummy, Old Nanny, before I was adopted?' I take a deep breath and I think Nanny does too.

'I believe your Mummy died, Camellia,' Old Nanny says gently.

'Poor her,' I say. 'It must be awful to die when you've got a little baby.' I have a sudden thought! 'So, my Mummy was like Mercy!'

'I'm not sure what happened, pet,' says Old Nanny, unravelling more blue wool, 'But you came to Mummy and Daddy when you were about six weeks old. I was with you, and you were the dearest little baby. You hardly cried at all and took your bottle beautifully. I knew you were very special even then.'

'And Finn?' I have to ask.

Old Nanny says he was very small when he was born because his mummy wasn't very well. I say I remember helping bath him in the first few days.

'Did his Mummy die?' So many Mummies *dying*! Old Nanny said she thought she did.

'Your Mummy and Daddy were so happy when you two children came along. They couldn't have babies you see.' I think about this and it makes me sad.

'That means Finn and I are here to cheer Mummy and Daddy up?' Old Nanny laughs at this.

'I think you do a bit more than that, dear. They love you very much indeed.' Now I have another question!

'Do you think my Mummy who died is a ghost as well?' I'm not sure if I can bear that idea. Mercy is enough to be worrying about. Old Nanny changes the subject by holding up the new hot-water bottle cover. She has finished it.

'What do you think? Why not run and fetch your hot-water bottle and then we can see how it fits.'

I run upstairs and Mr Fox smiles down at me from his shelf. He loves sitting between the dolls because they are kind dolls after all. I pick up the hot-water bottle as well as Heidi. She can come downstairs for a bit. I feel sad for our mummies, but I don't think I will dare ask how they died. That would upset Mummy.

The cover fits perfectly, and Old Nanny goes to the kitchen to boil the kettle. Then she fills the hot-water bottle, screws it up tight and hands it to me.

'There's nothing like a hot-water bottle,' she says.

ANGELA

As if I hadn't got enough to worry about! Nanny told me this evening that Camellia asked about her other mother. Straightaway, I went into full-blown panic. Nanny was soothing as ever, saying Camellia had accepted the fact that her mother had died, as had Finn's.

Of course, we know this isn't true. However, that was what the Agency advised us to say, and I'm grateful to Nanny for remembering. After all she was with us when we collected Camellia from the Knightsbridge Agency. And thank God she was, because I had absolutely no idea what to do with a six-week-old baby. Nanny held her all the way back in the car. We knew Camellia and Finn were handed over for adoption at the request of their respective mothers, and I appreciate we were lucky being able to match Gerald and me with background, colouring and height. I think Finn has turned out small because he was so premature.

I don't want to think about any of this! It was pretty awful having to accept I couldn't have a baby of my own. How I cried about that! But now I'm making a pretty useless job as an adoptive mother. I know I am! Let's face it, I don't really know *how* to be a mother. Where was my own mother when I was growing up? Busy being a doctor that's where. Nanny was my mother. She was a mother to Peter and me. But of course, she wasn't our real mother. How I longed for *her* attention. Perhaps that's why I was so naughty.

Mr Dyle was very pleased with Finn's eye. He can throw his patch away, but Nanny Jan was quite right about Finn needing to wear sunglasses on sunny days, especially with the snow. Finn does look priceless in them plus the red hat. I took him out for tea after the appointment and he ate three teacakes.

The skating party was a great success, although I thought Constance looked a bit tucked up. I was surprised she didn't bring her skates. She used to be a great skater after all. The children absolutely loved the trays. I know Lorna got in everyone's way, and Daphne was hard on her again, but she's very funny and reminds me of myself. Gerald's glühwein was wonderful, if a bit strong, but that added to the fun. I know I skate better once I've had a drink, just as I ski better after lunch.

I've found a second-hand piano for Camellia and we shall get it delivered just as soon as the snow has gone.

The atmosphere at home is kinder and calmer with Nanny here. She brings out the best in me and the children. Gerald respects her hugely. She read the children a bedtime story this evening. That took me right back to Norfolk.

I do hope Camellia doesn't ask me any more questions. I couldn't bear it.

CAMELLIA

We have settled into a different routine with Old Nanny, in that Mummy always joins us for breakfast when we talk plans for the day. We're actually having rather a quiet time, before school next week. There's far too much snow and ice for Old Nanny to walk outside, so instead Finn and I tramp about the garden with the dogs. Finn didn't want to walk all the way down to Gran's garden today, so I went by myself. I wanted to talk to the rowan tree again, and I found lots of twigs, scattered on the ground. They must have been blown off in the gale. I carefully put some of them into my pocket, storing them up for when I need protection.

Mercy is peaceful for the time being. I think my blessing must have helped her, making me as proud as proud can be! My room doesn't feel as cold, even though Daddy says we are having the most dreadful frosts at night. I make sure I feed the birds every day.

The time I like best is when Old Nanny reads us a bedtime story. After our bath, we come downstairs in our dressing gowns. Then we climb under Old Nanny's rug on the sofa, often with Mummy listening as well.

Finn's gate is never bolted these days and doesn't need to be. He's been such a good boy, not once waking me up. Nothing peculiar has happened since Old Nanny has been here, and I hope it stays like that for Nanny Jan.

She's back tomorrow so this is our last bedtime story. Old Nanny says she will come back in April.

'Just like the swallow,' she says. 'But fortunately, I only have to come from Norfolk, not all the way from Africa.'

NANNY JAN

When I arrived back this morning, the children gave me such a lovely welcome. The first thing Camellia said was that Mr Fox had behaved himself since the blessing. She said he'd been as good as gold, sitting on the shelf with her dolls.

I must say the house felt happier and I just hoped it would last. Old Nanny said how much she had enjoyed her stay and hoped I'd benefited from a break. Once back at home, I understood how much I needed the rest. I slept like a top and woke feeling refreshed, quite a contrast to the exhaustion over Christmas and New Year.

I mentioned the sleep-walking to Old Nanny and she put my mind at rest by saying that most children do that, even if only now and then. If Camellia were sleep-walking every night, then that would be different. She said the children were well, that they'd looked after her wonderfully. Finn no longer needed his gate and they had loved their bedtime story. The skating party had been a huge success and the children had been very helpful.

Whilst being pleased that everything had gone so well in my absence, there was a part of me worrying I was doing something wrong. Should I be ignoring all supernatural conversation from the children? I talked to my mother about it. 'Always listen to the child,' she said. 'Really listen for what they're *not* saying.' I shall bear this in mind if things start up again.

Finn helped me unpack while Camellia fed her birds. He brought me a tiny piece of wood which he said was a bit of rowan. He assured me it would keep me safe.

'Thank you, Finn. We'll go for a lovely walk today because the sun is shining.'

'Not too far!' Finn made a face. Then he beamed. 'I've thrown my patch away! In the waste paper basket!' I congratulated him. Then I remembered my photographs.

'We can look through my photos later. They came out very well.'

I shivered once Finn had gone downstairs. In spite of the house feeling happier, my bedroom is colder than ever.

CAMELLIA

We're looking at Nanny Jan's photographs, especially the ones of Finn on Robin. Nanny Jan says her camera is a Kodak 127 Brownie. I must say it takes very good pictures. I spread out the three Finn photos on the nursery table.

'Which one do you think is best, Finn?' Finn peers at them very closely. He says he thinks they're all the same. They *all* make his legs look short. I have a closer look at the third one. Little teeth are shining out from a shadow underneath Robin. There are no teeth in the other two.

'What's this, Nanny Jan?' I say. 'Under Robin's tummy. Is it a creature with teeth? And are those eyes?' Nanny Jan comes over.

'I think that's probably Bramble,' she says. I glance at Finn who's got his tractor out, busy attaching its trailer.

'You don't think it's Finn's *Thing*?' I whisper. Nanny Jan takes the photo over to the window. She frowns.

'Remember how the dogs barked and Finn nearly fell off.' She says she does, and Finn looks up.

'What are you whispering about?'

'Nothing,' I say. Finn is up from the floor.

'Why are you whispering about nothing?' Nanny Jan puts the photo back on the table and checks the other two for any sign of Bramble. Bramble is not there.

'I think it's just a trick of the light,' she says. Finn is now studying the photos.

'What's so funny about the pictures?' He wants an answer. I have to think of something.

'We're playing that game where you have to spot the difference.'

Finn rubs his ear. He knows something's up. Nanny Jan switches her wireless on and luckily it's *Two-Way Family Favourites*. We hope it will stop Finn asking questions.

The song is 'Walking Back to Happiness' which has a good beat. I start to dance and Finn can't resist. He loves dancing around the nursery. Nanny Jan puts the photos away, but I will ask to see them later. Something made Robin jump, not just a trick of the light.

We go out for our walk with Finn wearing his seaside sun-glasses, and Nanny Jan says he looks like a film star. He doesn't really need to wear them because the sky has become dark and dull.

'Brown sky in the afternoon,' I say. 'Big trouble.'

Nanny Jan laughs. She's not familiar with that saying. She agrees the sky looks full of snow. *Again.*

We trudge up to the stables to say hello to Henry. He says he's going mad with the snow because he can't get the horses out, and there's a lot of mucking out to be done. He says he has to walk the horses round and round the yard which luckily he has cleared, using some special red salt which melts the ice on the cobbles. He doesn't know what he'd do without it.

I go into Robin's box and he gives me the eye.

'Are you getting fat, Robin?' I say, patting his woolly neck. He tries to reach into my coat pocket in case there's a carrot there. I feel around and all I've got is a bit of rowan twig. I find a couple of pony nuts on the floor and hold them out for him. Robin eats them but I know he finds pony nuts boring. He wants carrots or, even better, grass. Suddenly I know I'm not alone. I turn around and freeze.

Mercy is looking over the stable door.

CAMELLIA

Mercy and I stare at one other. Her face is calm with a pretty smile. We are very close and I'm able to see that her necklace is made up of green stones. She beckons me with her hand, turning her back as if to walk away. Does she want me to follow her? Robin munches his hay at the back of his box, not bothered by Mercy this time.

I take a step closer to the stable door and she beckons again. What does she want? I *must* be brave. She might have something to show me. I pull back the bolt and follow her across the salty yard, aware of a blurry shape scampering around her feet. It's a little dog and, as far as I can tell, a terrier, the colour of Henry's red salt. So, Mercy isn't alone any more. She has a little ghost dog.

She glides towards the mounting block. On her shoulder she has a magpie, balancing like an acrobat. His beak is pressed close to her ear and his tail reaches long down her back. He's not a real magpie because his wings are dull. He must be a ghost magpie.

To my surprise Mercy drops down to lie on the icy ground. She curls up, tucking her knees into her chest while her little dog puts his head on her neck, as if in sorrow. All the time the magpie watches me. I hear a whisper in my head, but I can't understand the words. They are too quiet.

My legs have turned to jelly, and I try hard not to fall over. Mercy is pulling at me to lie down, but I don't want to lie down on the ice! She's trying to tell me something, but I don't understand. I don't know how long I can keep my balance. It's as if something is moving underneath me, sliding away. Is this the portal? I don't know where I am any more.

But I *do* know what to do! I must fill my heart with love. While my world is spinning and the ice moving, I try and fill my heart with love for Finn. I love Finn, I love Finn. Please let this stop. I can't hold on any more. I'm going to fall.

But now Mercy is fading, disappearing into the ice, with the ghost magpie the last to go, his grey wings flapping in the icy air. When I look down, all I see is the frozen road. I shake my head to clear it, stamping my feet to warm them up. Mercy is gone and her little dog too.

I call out for Nanny Jan and Finn and find them in Henry's little kitchen. Henry is giving them tea and wonders if I would like a cup. I keep quiet about Mercy because I don't want to scare Finn. I'll save it for school on Monday. Henry notices I'm not myself and asks me if a ginger nut would help.

As I bite into the biscuit, I know what the whisper in my head was saying.

'*I am dying.*'

NANNY JAN

We've spent the last couple of days sorting things out for Camellia's return to school. Mrs Devon and I took the children to Horsham to buy some new shoes for Camellia because her toes have reached the end of her sandals.

The country seems to be getting about pretty well in spite of the weather. We haven't had any more snow, but there are great blocks of it piled up along the roads. They will take an age to melt! I don't think the daytime temperature has risen above freezing since Boxing Day. They're saying this winter is as cold as 1947.

The house remains quiet, if chilly. For some reason my room is particularly cold, and Mrs Devon has kindly suggested I can move into the double south-facing room in February, that's if we're still in the depths of winter. I must say I would appreciate that. It's only a few more steps from the children, and all the time they're growing up after all.

Camellia writes in her diary every day. She never shows it to me and I respect her privacy. She says she's looking forward to seeing her friends at school and I'm not surprised. This has been a funny old holidays. She wishes Mr Impey would call again. I said that I thought he was probably very busy with his parishioners, and that he would call just as soon as he could.

She did tell me that Mr Impey and her friend Sarah saw the ghost at the skating party. Having told me out of Finn's earshot, she confessed she was worried I wouldn't believe her. Camellia has always been a very truthful child, so I saw no reason not to, but I did feel for her. She's very passionate about her ghost, wanting to do all she can do to help. She owned up to finding Mercy scary, wondering whether she's responsible for moving stuff around her bedroom. Will I ever be able to see her? I must say I rather dread it. Camellia seems to have accepted the situation now, and Mr Fox's transformation from bad Fox into kind Mr Fox has helped hugely. We have to thank Mr Impey for that!

I have told her to always come to me if she's worried. We had another look at the photo and Camellia thought it might be Mercy's little ghost dog. I let that one go. We can't really be sure what Finn saw on the other occasions, and it will be interesting to find out if not wearing his patch makes a difference. He hasn't mentioned his *Thing* since Christmas.

Tomorrow school starts so I will have to think of some activities for Finn. He does miss his sister when she's at school. One more term to go and then he starts. I shall have the mornings to myself!

Mrs Devon came in after tea to say that Miss Wiggins had telephoned to say that two children wouldn't be coming back to school due to chickenpox. If there's ever a good time to have chickenpox, then I suppose winter is the best. They say the itching is much less severe in cold weather, and this is surely cold enough. I must remember to stock up on calamine lotion.

'What's chickenpox?' asked Finn.

'Spots,' Camellia told him.

'No chickens?'

'No chickens, Finn.'

Poor children. They are bound to catch it.

CAMELLIA
Back at school

I've packed my red diary in my satchel. I need to remember *everything* when I see my friends. It's such a relief not to hold anything back. At home I have to be careful of not upsetting Mummy, scaring Finn or worrying Nanny Jan. Mr Impey is more like one of the girls except he's a grown-up man of about thirty. I wish he would visit again.

Finn can't hide his tears waving me off to school. He's worried I will catch the spots. I say I will try *not* to. It's a freezing morning as usual, and Mrs Betts scoops Finn up, just as Nanny Jan and I are leaving.

'*Bone* cold!' she calls out. Then she tells Finn how much she needs him and his wheelbarrow to help clear up the hall. There's that much dog hair and bits to pick up after the weekend.

It's good to know Mrs Betts will take care of Finn until Nanny Jan gets back. It's a Monday morning so Mummy will be in the drawing room on the telephone. I will never have a telephone when I'm a mummy because it really spoils things.

Nanny Jan says goodbye at the door. While we're hanging our hats and coats up, Melanie-Anne rushes over. She says she had a very boring weekend, sitting in the stable for hours. Something to do with watching her mother's mare. She says she had to eat some pony nuts and even tried a mouthful of bran mash.

'I'm pleased to be back at school actually.' I tell her I'm not surprised.

Children are pouring in through the door and everyone is happy to see their friends again. We run into the classroom and quickly find our desks. Sarah's here but there is no Annabel.

Miss Wiggins quietens us all down. She's wearing an olive-green dress with a cream Arran cardigan which looks like it was made about fifty years ago, as does her dress. It's *that* old fashioned. I notice her cane is back on the shelf. So is the Radio Malt. I hope she doesn't give it to us this morning because it's disgusting.

'Now children,' she says. 'We are missing two for the start of this term. Annabel has chickenpox and so does Fiona.' I remember Fiona was at Melanie-Anne's party. Poor Annabel! Miss Wiggins continues:

'Now it's more than likely some of you will get chickenpox. I have telephoned your parents and informed them as to the incubation period. I can see from your faces that you don't know what that means. It means how long the chickenpox sits inside you before the spots appear.' She pauses.

'If YOU, Camellia,' she says, making me jump, 'were to mix with another child with chickenpox or, more to the point, who was just *about* to get chickenpox, then it would take between ten and twenty-one days for you to come down with it. That period of time is called the incubation period.'

I'm in trouble! I saw Annabel for tea which means I will catch chickenpox. I bet Annabel's mum is making a lovely fuss of her, baking special cakes. And if I catch it, then Finn is bound to catch it too.

Miss Wiggins now tells us what we will be learning this term. We are different age groups, and this is for the older children which includes me.

'I'm going to teach you some Latin. We do French already of course, but Latin is so very useful. Many doctors use Latin, as do lawyers. Several of our English words derive from Latin and I've found you big children some excellent Latin primers. I think you are going to find it very interesting indeed.'

I look at Sarah and Melanie-Anne. We're not so sure! Melanie-Anne has enough trouble with French and long divisional sums of money. I pat my beautiful wooden pencil case, then slide the top back, admiring my new pencils. I suppose one day I'll be allowed to use a fountain pen like Mummy.

Miss Wiggins teaches us Latin for about an hour. We learn about *amo* and *mensa*. I'm quite lucky because I pick up new subjects quickly. I write in my new Latin exercise book and my handwriting is nice and neat. Sarah's nose is about two inches from her exercise book, and she keeps looking back at the primer. Melanie-Anne stares up at the ceiling.

But now it's the time we've all been waiting for! At last we are freed from our Latin primers and, collecting our milk (orange for Sarah) and biscuit, we hurry along to the hall. I have the red diary tucked under my arm. We sit on the stage and I tell them everything, checking in my diary to make sure I don't miss anything out.

'Wow!' says Melanie-Anne. 'So spooky.' Sarah has something to say about *Ghosts in the mirror* and *Not seeing your own reflection*. I listen with my pencil poised.

'My mum says two things about *Not seeing your own reflection*. It means either you are a vampire,' Melanie-Anne looks horrified. 'Or,' Sarah carries on, 'Part of your soul is missing.'

'But both of those are horrible!' I say.

'They are pretty serious,' Sarah agrees.

'I *can't* be a vampire,' I cry. 'I haven't got funny teeth and I eat crumpets, and porridge and roast chicken. Do vampires eat those things? I thought they only drank blood?' I hear Mummy's voice in my head. As if I haven't got enough to worry about! Melanie-Anne chews on her biscuit. She's managing to make it last a long time.

'A bit of your soul could have fallen into the portal,' she says. 'Maybe that's why you couldn't see yourself.' I quickly change the subject. I don't want to think of myself as a vampire, or with a bit of soul missing.

'What about ghosts moving things, Sarah?' Sarah re-crosses her legs and shakes her hair. Then she pushes her hairband back.

'Now they *can* do that my mum says. It's hard for them because they don't belong in our world, but they definitely *can* move things.' Julia comes over and asks to join in. I feel mean when I say we're having a private grown-up conversation. It's only because I don't want to frighten her.

'I hate doing that,' I say.

'She's too young to hear this stuff,' says Sarah. Melanie-Anne asks why Robin wasn't scared of Mercy when she looked over the stable door.

'Perhaps he's used to her now,' I reply. 'He was busy munching his hay as well.

'Now I think it would be good to find out what Mercy is trying to say to me.' I don't need to talk any more about Robin. 'So, any ideas from Sarah's mum on that? How do you talk to a ghost who doesn't talk?' We sit and think for a bit.

'When do you think we'll get chickenpox?' Melanie-Anne asks the question and none of us know.

'I might be first,' I say, shutting my diary. 'I saw Annabel for tea. I bet I'm first.' Sarah says she's heard the spots can be terribly itchy and you mustn't scratch them, otherwise you get scars.

Miss Wiggins has spotted us. What are we up to, sitting on the stage? On the way back to the classroom I find Julia and explain that we were talking about scary things. She mustn't think we were being mean.

On the way home I tell Nanny Jan how we've started learning Latin. Nanny Jan reckons that's ever so grown up. She says I'll be going to Oxford next! I tell her I'm going to teach Finn some Latin.

I *really* hope I'm not a vampire. Nanny Jan says it's shepherd's pie for lunch. Surely vampires don't eat that?

CAMELLIA

While we're eating our shepherd's pie, I tell Finn about the Latin lesson. I know he's a bit young, so I teach him one word only and that's *Amo*. He likes it and uses it immediately.

'*Amo* my wheelbarrow.'

'Very good Finn.'

I ask Nanny Jan for a second helping of shepherd's pie. I want to make quite sure I'm not a vampire. I'm also extremely hungry.

'I don't *amo* long walks,' says Finn. Nanny Jan says that as long as the snow stays around, we can't go on long walks. It will give Finn a bit of time for his legs to grow.

'*Amo* snow.' Nanny Jan thinks there might be a lot more snow coming. Mrs Betts said she could feel it in her bones. I change the subject by asking Nanny Jan if she knows what chickenpox spots look like.

'They look like little blisters, Camellia, as if you've got yourself a tiny little burn. That's how they start. Then they scab over and get itchy. After that the scabs fall off and you're through the chickenpox.'

So, I will be on the look-out for tiny little blisters. I wonder whether vampires get chickenpox?

Mummy comes in after lunch and I tell her about Annabel. I say I might draw a card to cheer her up and then Mummy might post it? She says that's a very good idea and of course she will do that for me.

I think about what Annabel would like on her card. A picture of her cat Snowy would be perfect! I don't need to put Snowy in the snow because I'm rather good at drawing cats. So, I draw her in a beautiful garden with spring flowers and green grass. I add some trees and then the sun.

Why do I suddenly want to put Mercy in the picture? The only way I can stop myself is by actually dropping the pencil.

I wait for the moment to pass. Instead I draw a tiny magpie in the tree. It means there's a part of Mercy in the card and that makes me feel easier. Inside I write:

'Dear Annabel, I hope you haven't got too many spots and they aren't really itchy. We miss you at school. Have you been able to play your Moonlight? Get better soon. Love Camellia xox.'

I take it through to Mummy, who's writing a letter. Luckily the magpie is so small she can't really see it, and she finds me an envelope and stamp. She says Nanny Jan will pop it in the letter box on the way to school tomorrow. I scowl at her, but she doesn't notice. She's busy at her desk again. She *promised* she would post it today. Such a little thing as well. Why doesn't Mummy do anything for me? I march out with the card.

Now I'm in bed, my diary written up. I've brushed my teeth and made sure my reflection is there. I'm forever worried I might not be there, especially at night-time. But perhaps it will never happen again.

I unfold my picture of Mercy. How can I help her? I hope Sarah asks her mum what she thinks is the best way to speak to Mercy or how she can speak to us. It's hard for me to know.

I open my new book, *Five on a Treasure Island*. It's very exciting and I bet the Famous Five would know how to talk to ghosts. I say goodnight to Mr Fox. He looks happy, leaning up against one of the dolls. Heidi has both eyes shut, even though she's sitting up. I suppose she's asleep.

I feel along my teeth with my finger. Are they getting longer? My front teeth are in, but those aren't the ones I'm worried about. It's the ones on the sides. My rowan twigs sit on my bedside table as usual and Dorothy Baby is fast asleep next to me.

I can't think of anything more and I turn off my light, remembering to bless myself and everything in my room. I'm falling asleep with a tune playing in my head. It has only one word and the word is *amo*.

I love. I let go.

NANNY JAN

Finn's got *amo* on the brain. He's just like a parrot at the moment and we had a lot of what he did *amo* and what he did not *amo* all through breakfast. I really hope Camellia comes back with another word at lunchtime.

Dancing class starts today. Finn's too young to start dancing unfortunately, but I know he's longing to. He asked to sit and watch Camellia today and I thought why not? Our walks in the snow are a bit limited, so it will be a good alternative.

The house is calm, but my room is *still* an icebox. We had a nice man come round to look at the radiator this morning, and he said there was nothing wrong with it. It's just not powerful enough. I'm having to take two hot-water bottles to bed. I'll need to sleep in a hat next, just like Finn!

There are power cuts going on in London with theatres and cinemas coming to a stop mid-performance. Can you imagine? Heaven knows what's happening with the hospitals. It would seem there are problems moving coal down from the north. There's no sign of an end to the arctic weather, and there's even talk of the sea freezing over.

Well, there's absolutely nothing I can do about the sea freezing over. My job is to look after the children, and I need to build up my strength for the inevitable chickenpox. It's bound to be circulating at dancing class. Camellia keeps checking her tummy for spots, as does Finn, as well as feeling along her canine teeth. She won't tell me why she keeps doing this.

Mr and Mrs Devon are going away for a few days, so I am to call on Old Mrs Devon if I need support. Thank heavens for Mrs Betts! She always sees the funny side of life, knowing the house like the back of her hand. If something goes wrong, she will know who to contact. Finn is singing in the nursery. He has made up an entire song about himself with two words. The tune changes with each rendition but the words don't.

'*Amo* FINN. FINN *amo*.'

CAMELLIA
Dancing class

I can't help smiling as I change into my ballet shoes for dancing class. I hang my coat up on exactly the same peg as school, because of course we're in the very same building. Miss Grant runs her dancing class in our break-time hall.

Miss Grant's friend plays the piano up on the stage and she has to play *very* loudly. Miss Grant is quite old but not as old as Miss Wiggins. This afternoon she's dressed in a thick mauve dress with a big brooch.

Today is special because Nanny Jan and Finn are going to watch. Finn is excited and waves at me, bouncing on his chair. Nanny Jan has told him he has to sit still and be a good boy.

I run into the middle in my beautiful red ballet shoes and practise some curtseying. Sarah comes flying up to me and makes a face as if to say she has some interesting Mercy news. Melanie-Anne is next through the door, pulling at one of her shoes. She doesn't enjoy dancing class nearly as much as Sarah and me, because she doesn't know her left from her right.

The others arrive and run into the middle. Sarah and I get the giggles curtseying to each other. There's only one boy in our class and his name is Ian. He comes over to us and gives a nice bow. Sarah smiles her lovely smile and Ian blushes. I think he loves Sarah!

Miss Grant gathers us all together and says, in order to warm up, we can run on our very tippy toes right around the hall. She gives her friend a nod to get started on the piano. We can wave our arms nicely as we run but we must remember to look as graceful as possible.

Each time I run past Finn I give him a big smile. He likes to know he isn't forgotten. Now we're all holding hands in a circle and Miss Grant tells us to go one way and then the other. She says *now left* and *now right* and poor Melanie-Anne is rolling her eyes.

We spend most of the lesson learning how to dance the waltz which is actually quite complicated. It's in three time and we listen as Miss Grant's friend plays her version of 'The Skaters' Waltz'. It's such a pretty tune it makes me feel quite dreamy. We practise our steps, and for now all of us waltz as ladies, even Ian. Miss Grant says, as the term goes on, we will learn how to dance as gentlemen. Sarah winks at me, putting her hands on her hips.

Miss Grant's friend is playing her last round of 'The Skaters' Waltz' when Sarah digs me in the ribs.

'Look, Melia,' she says, pointing. Miss Grant warns Sarah we are not using hands yet. But I *do* look and there is Mercy dancing in her beautiful dress. She's dancing the waltz as a lady and she's very good at it. She's at the furthest end of the hall and Sarah and I watch her while we dance our own steps.

Mercy must be musical! She wouldn't be dancing otherwise. Can Nanny Jan and Finn see her? No, they are watching the others. As the music comes to an end, Mercy fades and disappears. At least she's not lying on that icy road any more.

Miss Grant finishes the lesson with some curtsey practice. She tells us we must remember to hold our skirts out in a ladylike way. Ian isn't expected to curtsey, so he does some bowing. While we are putting on our coats, Sarah tells me what her mum said at lunchtime.

'Ghosts can use the wireless or the television to send a message.' She buttons up her coat. 'What happens is the television can go all fuzzy and then you hear the ghost. Same with the wireless. Perhaps you can borrow your Nanny's wireless?' I button up my coat.

'So that's how she can talk to me. Maybe?' Sarah nods.

'I'll ask her.'

Nanny Jan and Finn are coming up the passage.

'Did you enjoy that, Finn?' I ask. He actually laughs out loud because he absolutely *loved* it. As soon as we're home, Finn starts practising his curtsey. I tell him he's a boy. He should bow like Ian, but he waves me away.

'*Amo* curtsey,' he says, and does another one.

CAMELLIA
Chickenpox

I wake up feeling rather hot and bothered. It's a Saturday morning and I force myself out of bed to look at the day. Everything is covered in a peculiar thick frost. The morning is dull, grey and freezing. In that case why do I feel so hot?

I run to the bathroom to check my teeth and, while I brush them, my skin feels as if it is hurting all over. Although I've slept for about eleven hours I feel as tired as tired can be. I check my tummy for tiny blisters but there are none. I go back to bed and hug Dorothy Baby and my cold hot-water bottle. I'm not sure now if I'm hot or cold. I feel horrible.

I hear Finn calling me, but it sounds so far away. What's happening to me and why do I feel like this? It can't be chickenpox because I haven't got any blisters. Finn comes running into my room.

'Will you read me an early morning story, Melia?' He has the book. I open my eyes and squint at him. I'm feeling shivery now.

'I'm too tired, sorry,' I tell him. My head feels funny and my back hurts. I turn over and face the window, away from Finn.

'I'll go and find Nanny Jan and tell her you're tired.' I hear his footsteps running away down the passage. When Nanny Jan comes in and puts her hand on my forehead, I feel tears coming and blink them back. It's hard.

'Your forehead *is* rather hot, Camellia,' she says. 'I'll fetch the thermometer.'

Finn feels my forehead and says he hopes it's not the spots. I'm too tired to reply. Nanny Jan comes back and puts the thermometer under my tongue, telling me to keep my mouth firmly closed. We shall wait for two minutes. Finn sits on the chair, watching me with Heidi on his knee. Nanny Jan reads the thermometer.

'You're over a hundred, Camellia. I reckon you're coming down with something.' She asks if I feel like any breakfast. I don't. Instead, I ask for my hot-water bottle to be filled because my feet are like blocks of ice.

I'm in bed all morning and I do my best to read my Famous Five book, but my eyes sting and my back aches. Nanny Jan brings me two hot-water bottles, promising to look in on me every half hour. I couldn't really face breakfast, so Finn brought me an orange. He tells me he's fed the birds. I find talking to him tiring so Nanny Jan takes him back down to the nursery.

Mummy and Daddy are away this weekend, so it's just Nanny Jan, Finn and me. Nanny Jan takes my temperature at lunchtime and says it's gone up again. She gives me some Ribena as a treat. She says I must drink and drink with a temperature. After lunch, which is two digestive biscuits, I fall asleep.

When I wake it's nearly dark. My head aches dreadfully and my teeth are chattering. I feel awful and I know someone else is in the room. Mercy's here and I'm too tired, too tired to do anything.

I hear my dressing-table drawer being opened. Not *again*. Because I feel so ill, I hardly care what I see. Moving very slowly because everything hurts, I push my eiderdown back to peer over my bedclothes.

The drawer is opening and shutting by itself. I begin to count and I'm up to twelve when I see Mercy standing by my cupboard, her eyes fixed on the drawer. She's doing this I'm sure. I'm too tired to be scared.

Then I see my dolls fall off the shelf, one by one. She's pushing them off with her mind. Is this really happening? I pull the eiderdown up around my neck and straightaway I feel unbearably hot. Now she leans over me, stretching out her hands. She wants Dorothy Baby.

I shout 'NO!' and 'Please Go Away!' and rock from side to side. *Please* Mercy, leave me in peace. To my relief the landing light comes on and I hear footsteps coming up the stairs. It's Nanny Jan and she switches on my bedside light. She notices the dolls on the floor.

'What's been going on here, then?' she asks, bending down.

'All of them on the floor, except Mr Fox. He's still on the shelf.'

'It wasn't me,' I whisper. 'I think I'm really ill.'

Nanny Jan comforts me by saying it will soon pass and I'm being ever such a brave girl. She says she'll give me a junior aspirin to bring my temperature down. Finn's missing me dreadfully and wishes he could be with me upstairs.

She takes my temperature again and it's over 101. Then she asks if she can check my tummy and back for spots. There are none there and it's only when she's straightening my pyjama top that she notices something on the front of my neck. It's a tiny blister.

'That's why you are feeling so rotten, Camellia. It's the chickenpox. It's always uncomfortable at the start, so don't you worry.' She gives me a junior aspirin with another drink. Then she asks me if I need anything else. In spite of feeling so ill I remember what Sarah said at dancing class.

'Could I listen to your wireless?' Nanny Jan says of course I can, and she'll bring it straight up. The wireless is just the thing when you are feeling rotten with chickenpox. I hope Mercy will play with the wireless and leave my drawer alone.

I lie very still, waiting for the aspirin to work.

NANNY JAN

So now we know Camellia has chickenpox. She was that miserable and I did feel for the poor child. Her temperature is rather high and I'm hoping the junior aspirin will make her feel more comfortable.

I really missed her today, both in the nursery and on our very short walk. We went round the house and garden, mostly to give the dogs a run. It was an extraordinary day in that I have never seen such a thick white frost. I believe it's called a *rime* frost. The fog never lifted, leaving us in a silent world, not even a robin singing. As far as birds are concerned, it's a question of survival and I'm sure there will be casualties this winter. We do our best, putting food on the terrace, and Finn has taken on this duty because he knows how much Camellia loves her birds.

Mr and Mrs Devon are not due back until tomorrow evening, and I'm sure I can hold the fort until then. Finn asks me every five minutes how I think Camellia is getting on because he wants to be with her. He's very interested in the number of spots. Mind you, Finn can only count up to twenty and I fear Camellia will have many more than that.

She asked for my wireless and I tuned it to the *Light Programme*. She had it on very quietly, providing some comforting background noise. I know how one can feel lonely, stuck in bed feeling miserable, so I was more than pleased to lend it to her. I can always borrow Mr Devon's wireless.

Camellia didn't want a bath this evening because she felt too shivery. After bathing Finn, I let him go in and say goodnight. He offered to tell her a bedtime story which I thought very sweet of him. Camellia shook her head, saying she felt too tired.

'Poor Melia,' he said as I tucked him in. 'I don't like it when she's ill.'

I told him I was sure she would get better very soon and what she really needed to do was sleep.

'Sleep is the best medicine,' I said, giving him a goodnight kiss.

'What colour medicine is it?' He stretched out his arm. 'Need my hat.' I helped him put it on.

'Sleep coloured. Night night, Finn.'

I looked in on the children before bed. Camellia murmured a bit in her sleep when I felt her forehead, wrapping herself around her doll. I switched the wireless off because there are no programmes through the night. If I wake later, I'll come and check on her again. She had plenty of water in her glass. I left it sitting amongst her rowan twigs on her bedside table.

There'll be more spots in the morning, I'll be bound.

CAMELLIA
The nightmare
I'm awake and I feel *really* awful. I can just about make out my nightlight, but it seems miles away. My throat is sore and dry,

so I reach out for my water glass but, when I see it, I snatch my hand back.

It's *alive*. There are creatures swimming in my water glass. They are blue and brown and silver, and they swim round and round the glass, watching me. I know they're bad and mean, and they want to break free of the glass and bite me.

I look down at my hand and it's huge. I switch on my bedside light, hoping that will help, but NO it's worse. The creatures in my glass swim about, faster and faster, growing and growing. My glass is alive and it's enormous. But my hands are as tiny as mouse's paws. I'm going mad.

Somehow I crawl over my bed to my dressing table which has shrunk. I want to find out if I've changed in the mirror but, before I dare do this, I want to see my dolls on the shelves. They have grown huge and Mr Fox has become small, so small I can hardly see him.

I shake my head which feels as if it could fall off any minute. I am tipping over and have to grab the edge of the stool, keeping my eyes fixed on my knees. Why are my knees normal when my hands are paws?

I lift my head to see what's in the mirror. Thank goodness I have a reflection, but it takes a few moments for me to realise it isn't actually me. It's another child. Her dress is pale and her face solemn. I raise my arm and she raises her arm. I turn my head and she does too. I wave my tiny paw at her and she waves her hand. She isn't me. She's someone else.

When I say 'Who are you?' her mouth replies 'Who are you?' Who are we? Are we the same? And now the mirror is growing ever bigger and the mirror-child becomes a giant. I can't bear to look at her any more and I throw myself back onto the bed. I am *lost*! I am frozen and I don't know where anything is any more.

My world is sliding sideways, and I know I'm falling. I shout out 'FINN' and then again even louder 'FINN!'

I scream when Finn appears in the doorway. He's the size of a mouse.

NANNY JAN

Finn came tearing into my bedroom last night, shouting that Camellia had gone mad. I followed him down the corridor to find Camellia rocking backwards and forwards on her bed, her hands over her eyes. My immediate thought was that the poor child was having a night terror. I gently placed my hand on her back and spoke her name quietly, so as not to frighten her.

She moaned then and rocked some more. 'No, no, no,' and 'Just go away.'

'She's gone mad,' said Finn behind me. I turned to tell him his sister had most certainly *not* gone mad. Unfortunately, Camellia heard me and I could have kicked myself when she whispered '*I know I've gone mad.*' I asked if she could take her hands away from her eyes and try and open them, but she threw herself backwards.

'Everything's the wrong size!' she shouted.

'What's the matter with her, Nanny Jan?' Finn's voice was low.

'We're soon going to find out, Finn.'

I found Camellia's dressing gown and put it around her shoulders. The poor child's teeth were chattering. Finn fetched Heidi from the chair and sat the doll beside his sister. All the time I kept talking to Camellia in a soothing voice, assuring her that she was safe, that we were there with her and that it was going to be all right. Her fingers remained pressed to her eyes.

'I just want everything to go back to normal!' she cried. 'Finn was the same size as a mouse and my hands were horrible little paws.' She began to rock again.

'I'm bigger than a mouse, Melia,' Finn said. 'I'm bigger than a rat actually. Of course, I am!' Any mention of a rat gives me the shivers, so I told Finn to be quiet. However, within seconds Camellia's shoulders relaxed and she gave a big sigh. Finn had broken the spell.

When she looked around the room she began to cry. She said she was crying because everything was the right size again.

She hadn't gone mad. I told her that her temperature probably caused it and offered to boil the kettle for another hot-water bottle. I felt her forehead and it was cooler.

I wondered if either of them would fancy a warm milky drink. Then we could have a midnight feast together. I said I could make them some hot chocolate. Of course, Finn wanted a biscuit as well.

Camellia said she might manage a sip of hot chocolate and I took this to be a good sign. While I was downstairs boiling the kettle and waiting for the milk to warm, I remembered something my mother had said about when children see things all topsy-turvy. I think she called it Alice in Wonderland Syndrome. Of course, Lewis Carroll might have had similar episodes himself, inspiring him to write. I'm not fond of the books myself. I find them rather cruel.

I brought three little mugs of hot chocolate up on a tray, the hot-water bottle tucked under my arm. By this time Finn was sitting on Camellia's bed in his dressing gown and red hat. Camellia was very pale but calm and she took the mug from me quite readily.

'Did you bring a spoon, Nanny Jan?' I said I had, it was here in my pocket, along with Finn's biscuit. I gave Finn a straw for his, telling him to drink it carefully.

'Now Camellia,' I said, settling myself down at the end of the bed. 'I think you had a go of the Alice in Wonderland Syndrome.'

'What's that?' Finn asked. 'What's a syndrome? Is it an aeroplane?'

I explained what it was and how my mother had told me about it. Camellia leaned back on her pillow once I confirmed it was quite common. I knew she was relieved. I also knew it was better to talk about Alice in Wonderland Syndrome than hallucinations.

'But I don't want it to happen again, Nanny Jan,' she said. 'I really don't. It was horrible.'

How could I promise her it wouldn't happen again? I said

I thought it was very unlikely. We finished our drinks and then I told the two of them to go and brush their teeth. Finn said he thought it was very funny to be brushing his teeth in the middle of the night. When I tucked him in, he thanked me for looking after his sister so well. I thought that was really nice.

Camellia said she didn't want to be left alone, so I read a chapter of her Famous Five book until she was sleepy. I must say Enid Blyton knows how to tell an exciting story.

It was 4.30am when I climbed into bed again. Not only had I borrowed Mr Devon's wireless from his dressing room but his early morning kettle too. It was very useful for refilling my hot-water bottle in the middle of the night.

I fear there will be more spots in the morning.

CAMELLIA

Light is pouring into my room. My watch says it's nine o'clock, and I'm on my second day of chickenpox.

I think about what happened in the night. Was it a nightmare? Perhaps it was. But my mug of hot chocolate is sitting on the chest of drawers. It *was* real. I lift up my pyjama top and count five new blisters on my tummy. Who knows what's on my back?

I can't hear Finn next door, so perhaps he's already having breakfast with Nanny Jan. I walk around the room, testing my legs which are luckily working quite well. I don't feel as awful as yesterday.

I put on my dressing gown and go downstairs. All is very quiet. I push the nursery door open to find Finn sitting at the table, eating a boiled egg with soldiers. Banger is under his feet, waiting for crumbs. When she sees me, she walks forwards wagging her tail.

'Hello Banger,' I say. 'Hello Finn. Where's Nanny Jan?'

'She's talking to someone on the telephone,' Finn says. 'How's your Alice Syndrome? Did it come back?' I tell him that it didn't and once was bad enough.

'It looked very bad,' Finn says.

'I'm sorry, Finn. I couldn't help it.' I pat Banger's head and don't feel as well as I thought. Nanny Jan comes in and asks what on earth do I think I am doing? I shouldn't be out of bed! She says Gran rang to ask how we were getting on.

'I told her about your chickenpox. She's going to church, but she'll call in here afterwards. She wants to see you.'

'I wonder if she will tell Mr Impey?' Nanny Jan says she thinks she might. She pulls out a chair for me.

When I sit down I feel a bit teary. Nanny Jan asks if I want to have a bit of breakfast with Finn or go back upstairs. I say I would rather be here with Finn. The nursery is sunny and warm.

Nanny Jan says that's just fine. Do I think I could manage a bit of porridge? I shake my head. Just a piece of toast and marmite then. Nanny Jan says tea is just the thing for a temperature and offers to make me a special pot. My tears are trying to come, so I blink like mad. Nanny Jan says she'll go upstairs and make my bedroom fresh and tidy, just as soon as she's made my breakfast.

'Nanny Jan is kind,' Finn says with strawberry jam on his chin. I nod. I'm not used to being looked after like this.

'Soon be better, Melia.' He reaches out for a banana. 'How many spots have you got this morning?'

'Six in all,' I tell him. 'That was when I last looked. But probably more now.' Finn eats his banana slowly. Then Nanny Jan comes in with my tea and toast.

My legs feel like lead climbing back up the stairs. Nanny Jan suggests a morning bath and while I'm in it she counts my spots.

I am up to 28 now.

NANNY JAN

Old Mrs Devon arrived after church, dressed in her furs as usual. I offered her a cup of coffee and a quick chat, before going up to see Camellia. I didn't say anything about the Alice in Wonderland episode because I didn't want to worry her any more than I had to. Of course, Finn might mention it. I have to be prepared for that.

Looking out over the driveway while I prepared lunch, I wondered when we would ever see any green. The snowy landscape was such a familiar one now. Would it last right the way into February? It seemed very likely.

Finn called out from the nursery. He wanted help with his Lego. Camellia would have sorted that out for him in no time, but now he needed me.

There was a pair of magpies hopping about on the terrace, pecking at the snow. Who knows what they find to eat in this weather? It's the same for all the birds, poor things. I stood watching them for a bit and found I was admiring their appearance, truly as smart as paint. Two months ago, you would never have caught me being nice about magpies. That's Camellia for you!

I looked up at the kitchen clock. Old Mrs Devon had been with Camellia for quite a while now.

CAMELLIA

I'm listening to Nanny Jan's wireless and it's quite boring actually. This is because it's a Sunday when there are a lot of hymns. I try to get on with my book but it's a big effort. I wish someone could read to me. I hug my hot-water bottle which is luckily quite warm. Nanny Jan took my temperature at 11 o'clock and said I'd gone down to 99.

There are footsteps on the stairs and Gran is calling *coo-ee*. She does this in the garden when she wants to find us, but why does she call *coo-ee* when she knows exactly where I am, stuck in my bedroom with chickenpox.

She stands in the doorway, still wearing her fur hat. She must have left her coat downstairs. Her cardigan is a pretty green, a bit like the sea on a winter's day.

'Poor Camellia,' she says. 'I understand you've got the pox.'

'Chickenpox.' I put her right.

'It's a rite of passage. Of childhood that is,' Gran says, and I have no idea what she's talking about.

'I've got twenty-eight spots,' I tell her. 'At least it was twenty-eight when we last checked. It's probably more now. None on my face yet.'

Gran wonders if she can sit on my bed? Then she asks me how I am feeling. Her face is kind.

'Pretty rubbish actually, Gran. But at least I have Nanny Jan's wireless to listen to and look, here's Dorothy Baby. Your beautiful shawl is folded up on the shelf because she gets a bit hot.' Gran notices my red diary on my bedside table. She says nothing about the rowan twigs.

'Do you write in your diary every day, Camellia?'

'I do,' I tell her. 'How about you?'

'I used to, when I was a girl, but then I stopped. Life became too busy.'

'Mummy has a diary,' I say. 'But her diary says things like *Ring Old Nanny* and *Go to the hairdresser* and *Go hunting*. Things like that. She doesn't write her thoughts down about what happened.'

'That's what makes a diary interesting,' says Gran. 'Your perspective on life.' She explains how perspective means view. 'Samuel Pepys wrote a very interesting diary in the 1600s.'

I listen as Gran talks about why it's so interesting. I actually think it sounds boring because Samuel Pepys was an old man. I don't tell Gran this of course.

'Do you know anyone else who wrote a diary?' As soon as I ask the question, Mercy appears in the corner of the room. She stares at Gran, and the wireless stops. Now there's just a hiss. I watch Mercy's mouth move as a voice speaks from the wireless. Three words.

'*Find my diary.*' I look from Mercy to the wireless, and then to Gran. Did she hear the words? I don't think she did. All she's doing is twisting her wedding ring round and round her finger. She can't have heard them, so I say them again, quite loudly.

'*FIND MY DIARY.*'

Gran frowns, her face stern. I'm in trouble! *Again*. She asks what I mean by saying such a thing. I know I have to be brave and ask the question I've been wanting to ask.

'Did your Mummy have a diary?' After I say this, Mercy steps forward to listen, leaning in for the reply.

'I really have no idea,' says Gran. Immediately a doll comes flying off the shelf. It lands on the carpet behind Gran, and she turns in surprise to pick it up. I watch as Mercy steps back into her corner.

'However did that happen?' Gran is puzzled. I turn my palms upwards and shrug. Gran peers at me now as if she doesn't understand. Of course, she doesn't understand. I do though.

'Do you think you might be able to find your Mummy's diary?' I can't believe I'm saying this. Gran's face has gone from stern to shocked.

'I wouldn't know where to find it,' she replies. Another doll crashes to the floor. Mercy must be more careful! There'll be broken arms and legs next. Mr Fox views us from above as if to say *I'm safe because I am blessed.*

The wireless comes back on and Mercy disappears.

'I wonder how long you will have to be off school, Camellia,' Gran says, as if nothing has happened. 'It's such a bore, isn't it, missing out on school because then you can get left behind.' She straightens one of the doll's arms. The other one is still on the floor.

'I never get left behind,' I tell Gran. 'By the way, do you think your Mummy liked to dance?'

If I wanted to, I could tell her right now how much Mercy enjoyed waltzing at dancing class, but I think it would be too much for her. Gran looks pale and shocked enough as it is, and I feel a bit sorry for her. I decide to change the subject. I am used to dolls flying about, but Gran is not. She keeps looking over her shoulder.

'How was Mr Impey?' Gran is relieved to answer such a normal question. She says he preached a very nice sermon.

'Did you tell him I had chickenpox?' I really hope she did.

'Yes, I did, and he said he was sorry to hear it. He says there were quite a few children missing from Sunday School.'

'Mr Impey was very good at skating,' I say. I don't say that Mr Impey saw her mother standing under an ash tree. Gran smiles and says she used to skate quite a bit until she broke her ankle. That put an end to skating. And now she says that she must be getting back home to see what her cook has prepared for lunch. Grandpop didn't come to church because he has a cough.

As Gran is hovering in the doorway about to leave, she says something lovely.

'The rowan tree has beautiful white flowers in early summer, Camellia. You will love them.' I thank her for coming to see me, and it's what she says next that makes my heart sing.

'I will have a think about my mother's diary and where she might have kept it. Perhaps it's hidden away in a box somewhere. Get well soon, darling.'

And she is gone.

ANGELA

That was rather a frightful weekend. They did manage to shoot but only three drives and how sorry I felt for the beaters having to wade through all that snow and ice. It was bad enough for the guns. It doesn't seem sporting to shoot pheasants in this weather. They are trying hard to keep alive as it is, and then we go and bloody well shoot them. The bag was thirty-two, plus the woodcock. All I know is that my feet froze solid, standing around, and it was rather a miserable affair.

At least dinner was delicious, in spite of the company. I knew Shirley didn't want to give me that recipe for pudding, but I managed to get it out of her. She dropped her guard at breakfast! I managed to write it down too, although whether Cook will be able to decipher my scrawl is another matter entirely.

The journey home was slow. Hampshire is under more snow than Sussex so we must thank our lucky stars. We made it home before dark but only just. The kitchen lights were on, as was the light in Camellia's bedroom. I wondered why.

I soon found out. Nanny Jan told me Camellia had gone down with chickenpox. Finn came rushing into my arms in the kitchen, something about Camellia having 'Alice Syndrome'.

'I thought she had chickenpox?' Nanny Jan was quick to explain.

'Camellia had a bit of a fright in the night. It was just her high temperature. We had a midnight feast, didn't we Finn?' Why did I think Nanny Jan was hiding something?

Finn said he had a biscuit too. He wanted to take me up to see Camellia, there and then. He actually pulled me by the hand. Gerald had already gone through to his study with a cup of tea, and I hoped he would light the fire on the way. Finn told me to *come on* all the way up the back stairs. We reached the top and he pushed open Camellia's door.

'Here she is,' announced Finn. 'Poor Melia.'

She did indeed look very sorry for herself, sitting in bed with her favourite doll. Her eyes filled with tears when she saw me, and I worried we were going to have a scene. I'd only just got back!

'Poor old Camellia,' I said and then I felt awful because I didn't know what else to say. She gave me one of her frowns, a single tear running down her cheek. Finn noticed this as well and rushed round to bring a handkerchief from the dressing table. He gave it to *me* to give to Camellia. That made me feel even more dreadful. I was being shown up by my four-year-old son. The handkerchief was one Nanny had given Camellia for Christmas.

'I'm all right,' Camellia said, reaching out, then snatching her hand away. 'I've got Nanny Jan's wireless and it's *Pick of the Pops* in a minute.'

'That's nice,' I said feebly. 'Now is there anything I can bring you?' Camellia shrugged. Finn patted her book on the side.

'She's nearly finished this one, Mummy.' I was so grateful for Finn's observation because it gave me an idea.

'Would you like me to go to Horsham tomorrow and buy you the next Famous Five book?' At least I could do this for her.

Camellia's face lit up immediately and, opening her *Five on a Treasure Island*, she checked the front pages. She told me the next one was called *Five Go Adventuring Again*. I said I'd write that down in my diary and see what I could do.

I will need to talk to Nanny Jan about whether Dr Byng should visit, and it would be useful to know more about the itching. How soon does that start? I was thinking this through while Camellia was reeling off other Famous Five books. She gave me a glare then, as if she knew I wasn't really listening. To be honest I wasn't.

I said I really needed to get unpacked and sorted and Finn asked if he could help. He said he loved that sort of thing and would give me a hand. Once we were in my bedroom, Finn sat himself down on my button-backed chair. He wanted to say something important.

'I know how to look after Melia,' he said.

He does, but I don't. What's the matter with me?

FINN

Mummy must love Melia more.

I love Melia very much.

Even when she's bossy.

Melia is kind.

I'm going to help look after Melia.

But Mummy must love Melia *more*.

CAMELLIA

I really don't like being ill. Usually I'm happy on my own, but not when I'm ill. My thoughts are all jumbled. I'm not scared *all* the time, of course. It sort of comes and goes. I'm actually bored of feeling ill and, all the time I'm stuck here in bed, the rest of the house gets on with the day. Nanny Jan says my temperature is sitting at about 99 and that means I'm fighting the chickenpox very well.

I don't know what I would do without the wireless. It's my friend but sadly not through the night. That's when all the programmes stop, and of course it wouldn't matter if I were asleep. What happens is that I wake up feeling uncomfortable or thirsty, and then I worry that *any* minute the Alice in Wonderland Syndrome will start. I absolutely dread it. It hasn't happened yet, but it *might*.

After Mummy came to see me, promising she would try to buy me a new Famous Five book, Daddy appeared in the doorway. He said he was very sorry to hear I'd got the '*pox*.' Why do he and Gran have to call it *pox*. It's as if he's making fun of me. When I told him it was called chickenpox, he just laughed. Why are grown-ups so annoying? I glared at him for being so stupid and he said, if I wasn't going to laugh, then he was going downstairs.

How can I laugh at that sort of joke? It's not even funny. He'd interrupted *Pick of the Pops* in any case, so I was better off without him.

We've lost count of the number of spots now, there are that many. Nanny Jan says I'll feel much better once they've all come out. I've found three new ones on my face. Soon my temperature should come down, but then the itching will start.

I think it's already started. I concentrate hard on the wireless. 'Bobby's Girl' has fallen down to Number 19.

CAMELLIA

I've had the chickenpox for five whole days and today I feel much stronger, although the spots are so very ticklish I can hardly stand it. Nanny Jan has forbidden me from scratching, but it's very hard not to!

The spots on my face make me look an absolute fright. When Mummy came in with the new Famous Five book, she peered at my spotty face, warning me that any scratching could leave scars. What if I scratch them in my sleep?

Mummy said she didn't think Dr Byng needed to visit because he had quite enough to do. She asked the surgery for advice and they suggested bicarb baths as well as pink calamine lotion. So now I have two bicarb baths a day which makes the itching go away, if only for a little while.

Mrs Betts always looks in for a chat when she's doing upstairs.

She said she remembered her children having chickenpox and it nearly drove her round the bend. I asked her if she wrote a diary every day, and she said chance would be a fine thing.

Finn visits me often. Nanny Jan bans him from my room from two o'clock to half past three when she says I need an afternoon rest. As if I'm not getting enough rest stuck in bed!

Now it's Thursday morning and Finn rushes in, waving a letter. He says it's for me. He's brought me another orange too. I tear open the envelope. It's from Annabel.

'*Dear Camellia, Thank you for your card. It looked just like Snowy. It cheered me up. So sorry you've got chickenpox. Mine is finished. I went back to school yesterday. Sarah and Melanie-Anne are ill now. Come back soon. Have you seen Mercy? Love Annabel. PS. Yes, I've been playing the piano. xoxox.*'

Finn wants me to read him the letter, so I do.

'I love Annabel,' says Finn.

Poor Sarah and poor Melanie-Anne! So many missing in Miss Wiggins's classroom. She'll have to put her Latin lessons off for a while. Mummy comes in with some good news. She says Mr Impey has asked if he can call this afternoon.

'Yes please!' I cry. Finn says he'd better tell Nanny Jan to hide the jelly babies and runs off downstairs.

'I thought you'd be pleased, Camellia. He says he can be here for an early cup of tea. Then he has to go to choir practice.'

'Thank you, Mummy!' I say.

Mummy gives me one of her true smiles. She likes Mr Impey too!

My heart feels like it's singing. It's the best news! I have so much to share with Mr Impey that I hardly know where to start. I shall make a list in my diary.

I hope Mr Impey has had chickenpox already?

CAMELLIA
Mr Impey calls

When I hear Mr Impey's car, I run to the window. He's wearing his Russian hat again, and Mummy greets him at the front door.

I wonder how long she will keep him. Not too long, surely!

Finn comes running in and says he can't be long because he's busy guarding the sweets cupboard. I laugh and promise him the sweets will be safe today. He says he has a message from Nanny Jan. Would I like a cup of tea and some biscuits when Mr Impey comes to see me?

'Yes please, Finn,' I say, 'You're such a useful messenger!'

Finn says he already knows. He can deliver messages *all around* the house *fast*. No one is faster than Finn.

Mummy brings Mr Impey up, followed by Nanny Jan with a tray of tea and Jaffa cakes. When Mr Impey catches sight of me, he claps his hands to the sides of his face.

'LAWKS!' he cries. Mummy and I stare. Mummy asks him what he means exactly.

'Just felt like saying it,' says Mr Impey. 'It's what you say when you see a Camellia with chickenpox.' He looks around for a chair and asks Heidi if she would mind if he sat on her. Mummy looks confused but I feel laughter bubbling up inside.

'Do move her, Mr Impey,' I say. 'Her name is Heidi. She won't mind at all.' Mr Impey picks Heidi up and peers at her face.

'Is she all there?'

'It's her eyes,' I tell him. 'They're all over the place.'

'She's from Harrods,' Mummy says.

If Mummy doesn't go now, I will explode, and I can tell Mr Impey's trying hard not to laugh as well. Mummy says perhaps Mr Impey could be very kind and pour out the tea, then she will be able to get on with her telephone calls downstairs.

'I can only stay for fifteen minutes,' Mr Impey says. 'But that will be enough time for tea and Jaffa cakes.'

I can't believe Mr Impey is really sitting in my bedroom, drinking tea and eating his Jaffa cake in a funny way. He says he likes to chew off all the chocolate first.

'So, what's new?' he asks. 'Have you seen your ghost again?' I nod with a mouthful of Jaffa cake. He narrows his eyes. 'I haven't seen her in church by the way.'

'I think she prefers to be near me,' I tell him. 'She was a bit

naughty with Gran. She threw two of my dolls off that shelf.'
Mr Impey looks up at the shelf and spots Mr Fox. He takes
him down.

'Hello, old friend. Have you been behaving?'

I tell Mr Impey that Mr Fox has been as good as gold since
his blessing. He hasn't put a foot wrong.

We talk about what it's like to have chickenpox and Mr Impey
says he remembers it well. He reckons he had over a hundred
spots, but you wouldn't know it now. I tell him about the Alice
in Wonderland Syndrome and he practically falls off the chair.

'The Big Smalls?' he cries. 'Goodness me, I've had them!'
He makes two circles with his finger and thumb. 'As if you are
looking through binoculars the wrong way?'

'Exactly!' I say. 'And my hands were tiny! Finn was no bigger
than a mouse!'

'Do you know the book *The Borrowers*?' Mr Impey says,
offering me the last Jaffa cake. I shake my head. 'Well, whoever
wrote that must have experienced the Big Smalls as well. It's a
most peculiar book.'

I show him my Famous Five books. He says they look much
more interesting. He likes a good adventure story. Then I give
him the rest of the news, checking my notes in the red diary.
I don't want to miss anything out. Mr Impey says he's proud
of me for blessing Mercy in the bathroom, and he's particularly interested in Mercy's voice coming through the wireless,
saying he's heard of that sort of thing before.

'Do you think I'm a vampire, Mr Impey?'

I have to ask him. He laughs heartily at that, and I laugh
nervously. But soon he makes me feel better. He says that
vampires can't give blessings. It's one of their failings, that and
sharp teeth.

Then he looks at his watch and says sadly it's nearly time to
go, but before he does, he's going to bless my bedroom. While
I'm recovering from chickenpox, I don't need dolls flying about.

'And I shall include *not* having the Big Smalls again in my
blessing, both for you *and* me.' Mr Impey thinks of everything!

He closes his eyes while he sits on the chair, his hands together in his lap. I do the same. When I open them again, he gives me the merriest smile.

'All done! Now I must away to choir practice, and I fear my choir is still a work in progress. Some of them can't even sing in tune. It's very vexing!'

I give him a rowan twig as a thank you, and Mr Impey says he has always loved the rowan tree. Then he asks if he could borrow my *Five on a Treasure Island*? I give it to him gladly, and he says he'll take good care of it. He won't read it in the bath.

'I can feel your ghost here, Camellia,' he says. 'She will be quiet while you're recovering. Once you're completely well, we can think about how best to help her.'

He stands in the doorway, the Famous Five under his arm and the rowan twig safe in his pocket. He says '*Adio*' which is Greek for goodbye apparently. He will see me again very soon.

'When's that piano of yours arriving?' he shouts from the stairs.

'Soon!' I shout back.

'Good!'

And he is gone.

CAMELLIA

I'm on day twelve of chickenpox and feeling *much* better. The itching isn't nearly as bad now, and I haven't scratched any of the spots on my face, so Mummy is very pleased with me.

I'm well enough to be up and dressed in the nursery but I'm not going back to school until next Monday. I haven't been outside, apart from putting food out for the birds and that doesn't really count. There has been *even* more snow and our snowman isn't a snowman any more, more a standing block. We are letting him return to nature, as Nanny Jan calls it.

Every day we check Finn for spots. I'm to blame if he gets ill, because I'm the one who brought it home, but it's not as if I did it on purpose. Today he's being a bit of a crosspatch, so I reckon we're not far off. He fell asleep while we were watching the Woodentops, and I covered him up with a rug.

I'm eating like a horse, well certainly like Robin. I'm very pleased I'm not a vampire and of course I've been blessed for the Big Smalls. I haven't seen Mercy since Mr Impey called but I wonder, now I'm very nearly recovered, how soon she will return. I've finished my second Famous Five book and suppose I'll have to wait until Easter for the next one.

I don't think Gran has spoken to Mummy about what happened in my room. At least Mummy hasn't said anything about it. I hope Gran remembers to search for Mercy's diary. It must have been in the old house when Mercy died, but it could have been packed up when Gran moved to her house at the bottom of the garden.

I keep myself busy writing in my diary and drawing lots of pictures, mostly of birds. Daddy has lent me his big bird book and I copy a few of them as carefully as I can. Of course, I've drawn a magpie!

We're having tea and Finn doesn't want to finish his crumpet. I've already eaten two and I tell Nanny Jan that, if Finn doesn't want his, I'll have it.

'I feel funny,' says Finn, shaking his head. His eyes are over-bright and his cheeks are pink. I look at Nanny Jan who raises her eyebrows.

'Let's feel your forehead, Finn,' she says, but before Nanny Jan has a chance to reach Finn, I jump down off my chair and kiss his forehead.

'Hot!' I say. Nanny Jan asks why I did that.

'Old Nanny taught me. She said it's the quickest way to tell if someone has a temperature. Of course, it only works if you haven't got a temperature yourself.' Nanny Jan bends down to kiss Finn's forehead and then she kisses mine.

'You're right,' she says. 'Finn's much hotter than you.'

'I feel very, very bad,' Finn says, rolling his eyes.

'Tummy,' I say to Finn. 'Let's check your tummy for spots.' I'm quite the expert now. I pull up Finn's jersey and vest. There are three tiny blisters.

'Three,' I say. 'You've got three on your tummy, Finn.'

His eyes fill with tears.

'I want Mummy to see them,' he says quietly.

I know Mummy is in the drawing room, so I ask Nanny Jan if I can run through with the news. She says of course. I knock on the drawing room door quite loudly. Mummy always says we have to knock in case she's having a very important conversation with someone.

When I shout 'Finn's got chickenpox!' Mummy opens the door immediately! We hurry back to find Finn, tucked up on the sofa with a thermometer in his mouth. As soon as he sees Mummy, he bursts into tears. Nanny Jan asks him to be a good boy, to try and keep his mouth closed, but it's hopeless. She says he's up to 100, even after a minute.

Mummy draws Finn on to her lap and gives him a hug. I'm pleased she's comforting him, but I wonder why I didn't get a hug when Mummy got back from her weekend.

'Poor darling,' Mummy says, stroking Finn's hair. When Mummy says this, I can't help putting my hands on my hips. It's not quite fair.

Very soon we have Finn safely in bed. He's been given a junior aspirin to see him through the night. Nanny Jan checked him for spots when she put him into his pyjamas, and she counted twelve.

Now poor Finn's teeth are chattering just like mine at the start of chickenpox, and I promise him they will soon stop. He insists on wearing his hat, even with a temperature. I offer to read him a bedtime story as a special treat.

Halfway through the story he interrupts me.

'Melia, I don't want to get Alice Syndrome!' He's about to cry again, and this time I know exactly what to do, thanks to Mr Impey.

'I shall bless you for *not* getting Alice Syndrome,' I say. 'Just lie there quietly while I do the blessing.' I shut my eyes and tell him to do the same. He closes his eyes, wishing his teeth would stop chattering. I say I will add his teeth to the blessing.

I bless Finn and know he will be safe.

'All done, Finn,' I say. 'You can open your eyes now.' He blinks, looking around the room. He says his teeth are better already.

I finish the story and Mummy comes in to say goodnight. She thanks me for being so helpful. I go back into my room and wait for Nanny Jan to bring me my hot-water bottle.

I must be better because Mercy is back. She's standing in her corner, watching me.

NANNY JAN
We couldn't leave Finn upstairs all by himself, so Mrs Devon arranged for a day-bed to be set up in the nursery. It means he can come down at breakfast time and climb into his nursery bed. When he gets tired, he drops off to sleep, all the time knowing that people are around. He goes to bed upstairs at night as usual.

We are up to day three with Finn's chickenpox and I'm happy to say he's doing much better than Camellia. She had many more spots by this stage, and she's convinced Finn's getting off lightly because of her blessing.

She's been a great help. Never can it be said that Camellia is not a helpful child. She sees what needs to be done, even before I've thought of it. She gives Finn his lunch while we sit at the table, and he eats as much as he can. She reads to him until his eyes close. Then she gets on with her bird drawings which I must say are remarkable for someone her age. She goes back to school tomorrow. She might get rather tired for the first couple of days, but I know she's eager to see her friends.

Once Finn is recovered, I can move into the south-facing bedroom. As far as the weather forecasters are concerned, there's no end in sight for the Big Freeze. They're now saying it's the coldest winter this century. There was talk of someone driving a car across the Thames at Oxford, although why anyone would want to do that is beyond me. February is proving to be as cold, if not colder, than January. Here's hoping for a thaw in March!

The house has been quiet for the last two weeks, ever since Old Mrs Devon called to visit Camellia, and Mr Impey cheered Camellia up no end of course. I think we could do with Mr Impey on the National Health Service!

Finn will miss Camellia when she goes back to school but at least he isn't stuck upstairs. He does look a little poppet in his pyjamas and red hat.

Mrs Devon is being pretty good with calling into the nursery, asking if she can do anything. The trouble is I never know what to suggest. If she were actually *with* the children more, it would be easier. They need more day-to-day contact with their mother, doing ordinary things like overseeing bath time or laughing with Finn when he brushes his teeth.

A nanny cannot tell an employer how to be more of a mother. She must concentrate on being the best nanny she can be. Even so, I wish Mrs Devon would join in more. The children do love her so.

CAMELLIA

It's odd being at school with so many people missing. Sarah and Melanie-Anne aren't here, and neither is little Julia. At least I have Annabel with me, and we can talk about music. She says she's *befogged* by Latin. I like that word very much and Annabel says she made it up.

I tell her about the Big Smalls. Luckily, she didn't get them. She says the chickenpox made her feel quite tired, and we wonder why people have to get chickenpox at all.

I ask Miss Wiggins if she writes a diary and she says she does, even if it's a few lines, every day. She says it's a good discipline. I'm trying to work out how old Miss Wiggins is and when she was born. Mummy guesses she's about seventy-five, so I do a sum: 1963 minus 75. I make that 1888 (lots of eights!). If Mercy died in 1896, I need to do another sum to work out how old

Miss Wiggins was then. She was eight years old, another eight!

Miss Wiggins catches me doing sums she hasn't set. I tell her I'm mad about drawing the figure eight, and luckily she believes me. If Miss Wiggins was living in the village when Mercy died, she might remember something about it. I decide to be brave and ask at break-time.

I stand in front of her with my milk.

'Miss Wiggins, did you know that my great-grandmother died on Christmas Eve in 1896.'

Miss Wiggins shifts in her chair, giving me her full attention. I'm not used to this because Mummy hardly ever gives me her full attention. It makes me nervous. I take a sip of milk and continue.

'She has a beautiful window in the church. I've seen it and it was made specially for her.' I pause. 'Were you there then?'

Miss Wiggins nods, saying she grew up in the village. She doesn't say how old she was, but she was old enough to remember the window being built. Her father took her into church to see the new stained glass being fitted. She remembered how beautiful it was with the sun shining through.

'So, you were probably just a bit older than me?' I ask.

'Just a little,' she says. 'I remember my father said he thought it was a shame they had to smash out the old window.'

I hadn't thought of that. I wondered what was there before.

'Everything is about change, Camellia,' she says. 'And because your great-grandfather had money, he was allowed to alter the fabric of the church.'

Am I being told off? I'm not sure. It wasn't Mercy's fault the old window was smashed out. She was dead, poor thing! I say it was very sad anyway. I don't know what else to add. Miss Wiggins agrees with me.

'Very sad indeed,' she says, and that's the end of our talk. I find Annabel and tell her about Miss Wiggins's father.

'I shouldn't worry, Camellia. It was probably a ghastly old window and needed smashing.'

I wish I could think that.

ANGELA

Thank heavens we're nearly at the end of the chickenpox. Nanny Jan has done a sterling job coping with it all. Finn was much luckier than Camellia, far fewer spots, and how he loved being looked after in the nursery. He isn't that good at amusing himself, unlike Camellia.

What a relief to be getting back to normal. It's been quite a winter what with one thing and another. Thank God Gerald and I didn't plan a ski trip this year because I'm sick of snow. Talking of Gerald, he's champing at the bit because of no hunting and not that much to do on the farm. Shooting finished at the end of January so now the pheasants are safe.

I've found a piano for Camellia and we've put a provisional date for delivery in the third week of March. Surely the snow will have gone by then? I'm hoping this will give her something to get her teeth into. She says she's longing to work out tunes. I suppose I will have to think about piano lessons. I might ask Miss Wiggins about that.

Nanny Jan is due to move rooms next week. It must be dark and miserable in that north-facing room. It never gets any light. She'll enjoy the sun in her new room.

I've been very efficient and bought Camellia's new Famous Five book for Easter, hoping it's the right one. I don't think she likes Harrods Heidi much.

I'm pretty sure the strange goings-on are behind us. Camellia has been drawing beautiful bird pictures instead of ghosts. She has settled back at school and fingers crossed we're on an even keel.

Camellia and I walked the dogs round the garden this afternoon because Nanny Jan had the afternoon off. We were trying to see if we could find any snowdrop leaves, and Camellia discovered some under the Scots pine. We are more than halfway through February now, so they're very late. However, bearing in mind the freezing temperatures, it is a miracle they've managed to come up at all. We still have about six inches of lying snow.

Oh, for a thaw! Surely spring is around the corner.

CAMELLIA
Finding Bo's grave

Mummy says she's found me a piano! She tells me while we're searching for snowdrops. She says it's an upright piano made of light brown wood, and we must think about where it will go in the nursery. I give Mummy my best smile and thank her.

'Was it very expensive?' I brush the snow from the snowdrop leaves to give them a bit more light.

'Yes, it was. But only quite expensive for a piano. It's not as if we are buying a grand piano. That would take up the entire nursery!'

From the corner of my eye I see Mercy has joined us. I don't tell Mummy of course because it's safer to talk about the new piano. Mercy is with me a lot these days, but she isn't any trouble.

Now the snowdrop leaves are free, I wander off down the lawn, my footsteps crunching in the icy snow. The sun is bright and the air is sparkling with frost. A magpie sits in the oak tree above me, and I stop to say hello. Mummy is by the ha-ha now. She wants to know where I'm going.

'I'm going down to the end of the garden.' Mercy is already ahead, gliding over the snow and shadows.

'I need to stay close to the house because of Finn,' Mummy calls across the snow.

I follow Mercy down the lawn with Banger trotting behind me. She's used to Mercy now and doesn't bother to bark. We come round the corner to find Mercy in front of the yew trees, pointing at the ground. I try to understand what she wants me to do, but Banger already knows.

Mercy moves back for Banger to dig in the snow. She makes quite a good job of it and I help her by brushing the snow away. Soon she uncovers flattened winter grass, more like frozen hay. What's so important about *this* piece of grass? Banger keeps on digging madly and I praise her when we discover a flat round stone. She stops, panting after all her hard work.

The stone has some writing on it, so I push away the last pieces of frozen mud with my gloves. It's a gravestone and it says: *Bo 1896*. Who is Bo? 1896 is Mercy's year. How does Bo fit in? I look around for Mercy. Where is she now?

She is standing *right* over me, so close that the air crackles with cold. Banger starts whining and in that moment I know that Bo is Mercy's little red dog. There's not much of December left after Christmas Eve, so Bo must have died soon after Mercy. I feel the ice creeping down my back, the same as in the bathroom.

I wish I could tell Mr Impey *right now.* Oh, if only he were here! There might be other dog graves around this place? Perhaps Daddy would know. This is where he grew up after all, and he doesn't mind talking about dogs or horses.

When I stand up, I'm shivering. It's probably because I've been in the shade all this time. I walk round the yew trees, back on to the main lawn, following my own footprints. Mercy has gone.

It is only when I'm at the back door that I notice Banger hasn't followed me. Mummy says not to worry, she's probably gone after a rabbit and will be back soon for her dinner.

I'm not so sure.

CAMELLIA

After tea we search and search for Banger but she's nowhere to be seen. It's dark and Mummy and I are out with our torches, calling her name over and over again. My tummy lurches and churns. Where can she have gone? I tell Mummy I last saw her down by the lost pond, that Banger dug up a gravestone with the name Bo 1896 on it. I don't tell her about Mercy.

It's very, very cold. The air feels like iron. I crunch over the snow, searching the east side of the garden while Mummy calls for Banger round by the garage. Could she have gone down to Gran's garden?

Daddy arrives back and joins in our hunt. He rings Gran,

asking her to search as well. Daddy brings Bramble out, hoping she can help. I am to blame and *wish* I hadn't taken Banger with me. She must be very hungry now because she hasn't had her dinner. She never wears a collar.

Nanny Jan comes back from her day off and calls me in. It's bath time and she says I mustn't catch my death of cold, especially after chickenpox. Mummy and Daddy are still searching.

I'm in my pyjamas, ready for bed, but how can I sleep when I know Banger's out there somewhere? Finn tries to cheer me up by saying her white coat is very thick, but it's no good. I'm miserable. Banger isn't a polar bear after all. She loves lying by the fire.

Mummy comes in to see me. There's still no sign. Gran has called and called but Banger isn't there. We just have to hope she hasn't gone down a rabbit hole and got stuck. Then she'll freeze to death. She's been out for over four hours now.

I turn off my light, trying my hardest not to cry as I hear Mummy and Nanny Jan go out again to call *'Banger, Banger'*. I feel as if we have been calling her name for ever.

There's no sign of Mercy. She's not in her corner.

Later I wake to the sound of whining, right outside my window. Is it Banger? Could she have come home? My watch tells me it's nearly midnight, so everyone must be asleep. I will be brave and deal with this on my own. I put on my dressing gown and run downstairs as fast as I can. Who knows if I will be able to manage the key in the back door, but I use all my strength and turn it. Then I heave the door open.

I can hardly believe my eyes.

'Banger!' I cry. 'Where have you been?'

Her tail is wagging. She's happy to be back, but she is not alone.

Mercy is behind her, standing in the shadows.

NANNY JAN

Camellia woke me up with the news that Banger had come back. She said she was downstairs, wrapped in a tea towel.

While I put my dressing gown on, Camellia danced about around me.

'Isn't it just wonderful, Nanny Jan?'

'It certainly is, Camellia,' I said, following her downstairs.

There was Banger, wrapped up like a mummy, sitting in her basket. I quickly checked her over. Her eyes were bright, her nose cold.

'I've checked her nose already, Nanny Jan,' Camellia said, laughing. 'Although I think her nose would be cold enough after being outside all that time. Where do you think she went?'

I said I couldn't imagine and suggested Camellia give Banger a good rub down. I wanted to check on the back door for myself, wondering what else might be out there. I pulled it open and the cold air rushed in. The night seemed more frozen than ever. For a moment, only a moment mind, I fancied I saw a figure, sliding into the shadows. Of course, I could have been mistaken. Camellia joined me then.

'I must let your mother know,' I said, closing the door and locking it. 'You stay here with Banger. What a bit of luck you heard her crying!'

I never like disturbing Mr and Mrs Devon while they are asleep, but this was different. Soon we were all in the kitchen, even Finn, who had woken when he heard our voices. It was a very happy scene with Camellia in the middle of it, holding her little dog. Mr Devon was giving Banger a pretend telling off for getting lost, and Camellia told him to do no such thing.

Who would have thought it? To be out in the cold for so long and she didn't seem to be any worse for wear. Mr Devon gave her some food and she wolfed it down. I made us some hot chocolate and Finn asked for a biscuit. Because we were all so happy, I gave him two.

CAMELLIA

It's the beginning of March and every bit of snow has melted! It doesn't feel like spring though. The world was bright and snowy before and now it's plain dull. The grass isn't even a proper green. It's a muddy brown and the trees need time to recover from the cold as well. No sign of any proper buds yet.

Finn's much better now, spending most of his time marching about and singing Latin songs. I know it drives Nanny Jan mad. On the other hand, it means he's well.

Nanny Jan has moved into the big spare room, with its beautiful view of the Downs. We helped her move her stuff in. What we like is that there's plenty of room in her double bed for Finn and me!

Sarah and Melanie-Anne are back at school. Melanie-Anne said she had the most dreadful time with over three hundred spots, but Sarah got off lightly. Not a single spot on her face.

Miss Wiggins has started our Latin classes again, and we try to learn the words for farmer and war, as well as left and right, but it's hard work. This is because there are seven different ways you can say each word.

Sarah's mum is busy thinking about how ghosts can spirit away live dogs. We can't be absolutely sure it was Mercy who took Banger away for nearly ten hours, but I'm pretty certain it wasn't anyone else.

She didn't appear for a few days after that. If only Banger could talk! I went down to Bo's grave yesterday, keeping Banger on the lead. The little gravestone was bare and lonely, so I ran back up to pick some nearly-out snowdrops. I laid them on the grave, all three of them and then Banger and I stood quietly for a moment. I heard a magpie chatter but I didn't see Mercy.

She could be anywhere.

CAMELLIA

I decide to ask Daddy if there are any more animals buried at the end of the garden. It's a Saturday and Daddy is in his study. We've been for our short afternoon walk in our dull brown world and there's still half an hour until tea, so now is perfect.

I knock on Daddy's study door, and he says come in. He's sitting at his desk, tying a fly. He likes to make his own flies for catching fish and he's working on a very pretty one in yellow and blue. I don't like the hook though because it's very sharp. I wouldn't like to be a fish with that in my mouth! I don't say this of course. Banger is with me. I tell her to sit, and Daddy smiles.

'Very good, Camellia.' I decide to get straight to the point.

'Are there dogs buried at the end of the garden, Daddy?' Daddy puts down his magnifying glass and leans back in his chair.

'There are indeed many dogs buried down there. My mother's three terriers, my father's four Labradors, my sister's Norwich and the list goes on.'

'Who's Bo?' I'm not interested in the other dogs, but I don't tell him that. Daddy shakes his head. He's not sure he's ever heard of Bo. I tell him there's a grave down there for Bo.

'What sort of terrier is red-coloured?' I ask. I'm not going to tell him about Mercy's ghost dog, and luckily Daddy doesn't think it's a funny question.

'Norwich, Norfolk, Welsh, Irish, Patterdale.' Goodness Daddy knows about red terriers. 'Airedale,' he adds. 'That one is huge.'

'A small one,' I say.

'Then that would be a Norwich. They're often a sort of reddish brown and pretty small. They bark like mad!'

'Ah,' I say. 'Do we have a dog book, Daddy?'

Daddy searches the top two shelves and brings down an old book called *Working Terriers*. He tells me to look in the index under N for Norwich. I know how to do that, but I don't tell him. I find the Norwich terrier on page fifty-four and there's quite a good photo. It's Mercy's little ghost dog. It is Bo.

Daddy says I can borrow the book to practise my dog drawing. Then he stands up, pressing his hands down on his desk. His knuckles are white.

'My grandfather buried his favourite hunter down there. Just beyond the ha-ha. Said it took the devil of a lot of work digging a hole big enough.'

I know a hunter means a horse. I'm not sure how much I like the idea of a great big horse being buried there. What with the favourite hunter and all the terriers and Labradors, no wonder it feels strange.

Now I understand why it's one of Mercy's favourite places. She likes being close to the dead, especially her Bo. If I'm not careful Daddy is going to start talking about hunting, so I tell him I promised to play a board game with Finn. I thank him very much, and Banger and I go back to our side of the house.

I need to find just the right red-brown colour for Bo.

PART III

ANGELA

Gerald has announced we're hunting on Saturday. The hounds are itching to get out according to the kennels, and I fear Camellia and I are expected to go out with the rest of the Field. I have given Camellia the news, and she's as gloomy as me. She asked about my finger, and I made a face, holding it up, as if to say *what do you think?* That excuse won't do.

Of course, Gerald is as pleased as punch. He says the foxes need stirring up. Why are men like this? Actually, when I say men, there are some pretty awful women who hunt, shouting at you as if they own the place and demanding you keep off their verges.

Gerald has said Camellia can be off the leading rein and, while I'm relieved about my finger, I worry for Camellia on that pony. It has a mind of its own and hasn't had any exercise since Christmas. I'll make damn sure my cigarette case is full.

The weather is dreary. I feel dreary. Oh, for some sun! Nanny Jan said she saw an early primrose while out walking with the children. What heaven, a little primrose sun.

I'll have to find my hunting jacket. Did I take it to the dry cleaners after that fall? I must have done, surely? I'll ask Gibbs to polish my hunting boots. Gerald has no bloody idea how much I loathe hunting. One of these days I shall probably fall and break my neck and that will serve him right.

I'm dreading Saturday. Once more into the breach I suppose.

CAMELLIA
Hunting – 8th March 1963
It's simply dreadful. Mummy and I are having to hunt, and we thought we'd got away with it for this season. Mummy tried to

tell Daddy that her finger was sore, but Daddy said 'stuff and nonsense', that it would do her good to have her liver shaken up a bit. He also said I didn't need to be on the leading rein, seeing as I was nearly seven years old. I'm a bit nervous about this but on the other hand I can't pull Mummy off.

It's a cloudy day, not that cold but it's drizzling which is dreary. Dreary days are good for scent apparently, and today the hounds are going mad, sniffing around everywhere. I look at my watch and it says half past eleven. We have to get through three hours of this.

I know Mummy is terrified. She's always terrified. Her face is pale and she keeps biting her lip. She's probably even more nervous having fallen off last time. I kick Robin on to keep up with her. He blows a bit because he hasn't had any exercise.

There are lots of people out because this is the last day of the season but, when I look around, I can't see any other children on ponies. Just my luck to have to go out. The ground is soft and muddy and we slide around quite a bit. Robin is already covered in mud. The trees are bare and spikey.

Mummy and I are keeping up quite well. At least we're not too cold and I have five sweets to keep me going. I keep looking around for magpies, knowing they'll warn me if Mercy's near.

For two long hours we go charging over fields and through the woods, forever following the sound of the horn. Mummy and I are exhausted, while others say they could keep going forever. Mrs Martinswood is out today and I tell her truthfully that her fox puppet is happy at home. She says she's so pleased.

At *last* we're on the final run of the day. The hounds are gathered at the bottom of the field, making a great noise and milling about. We all trot down the hill and suddenly I hear the most terrible cry, something I've never heard before and never want to hear again. It's the fox! It's being killed. It can't be anything else. I try to cover my ears but it's hopeless. I can still hear. I tug on Robin's reins, trying to pull him up, letting the other riders go past, Mummy too. I'm the only one left behind, but luckily nobody has noticed. Of course, Robin wants to walk on, so we have to go forward. I keep the reins short. Slowly, Robin, slowly.

The hounds are in a group now, snapping and grabbing at something and eventually the huntsman calls them off. Through a gap I see a mangled mess of red fur, stretched out. The fox *must* be dead. Please let him be dead and no longer suffering. I close my eyes, swaying in the saddle and Robin puts his head down to eat grass. There's a great cheer from the Field. *How can they cheer?* Where is Mummy? She's looking down, her face grim. She hates this too.

The huntsman is bending down and now he stands, holding something up in his hand. It's the fox's tail. I wonder if I'm going to be sick. I hear Daddy's voice calling my name 'Camellia!' It sounds as if he's got a treat for me, something special. But it is not.

Daddy jumps down off his horse and walks up to me, his blue eyes sparkling, a smile on his face. He's almost laughing! He takes hold of Robin's reins, pulling his head up. No more grass for Robin. I turn away and it's then that I see the huntsman. He's getting nearer and nearer and in his hand is the fox's bloody tail.

'First fox you've seen killed, Camellia,' Daddy says. 'That means you're a lucky girl and can be blooded.'

I freeze. I cannot move a muscle. I stay like this while the huntsman dips his hand in the blood from the stump of the tail. Then he wipes the blood across my cheeks. He even puts some on my nose.

'Well done, Camellia,' says the huntsman, giving a broad smile. Daddy says it's a great honour, but all I can smell is the fox's blood, and it's revolting. Any minute I could faint. Either that or be sick. I shut my eyes yet again.

'Well, what do you say, Camellia?' Daddy asks. He turns back towards the Field. 'I bet she won't wash her face for a week!'

He laughs and, to my horror, I hear other people laughing. How *dare* they? I'm trapped because he's still holding onto the reins. I force myself to open my eyes. Perhaps if I glare at the huntsman he might go away. But no, he's still there, holding the bloody tail. There's a big streak of blood on his jodhpurs. I wish he would stop smiling.

'Does she want to keep the brush, Gerald?' the huntsman asks, holding it up. Daddy waits for my reply.

I have *nothing* to say. But Mercy does. She has suddenly appeared in front of the huntsman and she's shouting and screaming, leaning in, her shoulders hunched. Her mouth is stretched wide and she shakes her fists at him. She makes no sound. We are both silently screaming. When Robin flattens his ears and throws up his head, Daddy has to pull him back. His face is all astonishment. He can't understand why I'm not happy about the blooding.

I have *never* seen Mercy angry before. Not like this, in any case. She's just like the bad fairy-godmother in *Sleeping Beauty*! But it seems I'm the only person who can see her. I watch her curse the huntsman. She's doing *exactly* what I want to do. I hear a chatter in my ear and a touch on my shoulder. It's a magpie, if only for a moment. I saw the black and white, I know I did.

Daddy has given up waiting for an answer. He has stopped smiling, and people are staring at us. He lets go of Robin's reins, thanks the huntsman and gets back on his horse. Mercy has disappeared.

Now the huntsman sounds his horn, calling in the hounds. They gather round him, some of them with blood on their faces. I see he has somehow hooked the fox's tail to the saddle and it dangles there. The rest of the fox is left by the hedge I suppose. A magpie is perched in the hazel, and I see two riders salute. The smell of the fox blood is sour, and all I want to do is get home and wash it off.

The huntsman blows and blows on his horn, unaware of Mercy who has appeared again in her pretty dress. She hasn't finished with him. Now she stands before his horse and pulls at the reins. No one can understand why the huntsman's horse rears up suddenly, but I do. He goes tumbling to the ground and at last his horn is silent.

All is commotion! A rider goes to his rescue, helping him to his feet. The huntsman is holding his right arm as if in great pain. I see Daddy get off his horse to talk to him. Mummy is near enough to hear. She nods and walks Amber back up to me.

'He thinks he has broken his arm, so it's all over for today.'

The blood is already drying on my face, feeling tight across my cheeks. I'm glad the huntsman has broken his arm. It serves him right.

'That was dreadful,' I say to Mummy. 'I hated it.'

'I'm sorry, Camellia,' Mummy says. 'But at least you only get blooded once.' I know I *never* want to go hunting again.

'How could they be so horrible, Mummy? How *could* Daddy think I wanted to be blooded?' I'm so shocked I can't even cry. If I cried it might wash the blood off.

We walk back home through the gloomy afternoon, and soon we're on the last stretch. I see some early primroses in the ditch, but I don't bother to point them out. I've had enough. Primroses are gentle and hunting is mean.

'That was the worst thing that's ever happened to me,' I tell Mummy. 'Even worse than having my tonsils out!' I'm not sure she is listening properly. We both know we won't tell Daddy how we feel. It's easier to say nothing.

I don't want anyone to see the fox blood on my face, so I run home from the stables, not waiting for Mummy. I *must* get to the bathroom. I slam the door and look at my reflection. For once I wish it wasn't there because my face looks terrible, as if I've been in a fight. I tear off my hat and start filling the basin. My heart hurts and my face crumples. That *poor* fox. The tears come now, more and more and I let them fall. At least I'm on my own. I scrub my face with my flannel until it hurts. I will *never* forgive Daddy for letting that happen and even worse, for thinking I would enjoy it.

I go to my room and get changed. My face is stinging! I clench my fists and pace about, before something makes me look at Mr Fox on the shelf. He has water around his eyes, but there are no snowflakes in my room!

I carry him to the window, put my hand inside his red coat and draw his paws together. I make sure I say *bless you*, and then I bring his head round to me.

Mr Fox is crying.

CAMELLIA

I haven't spoken to Daddy since the dreadful blooding. Mummy is being kind enough though, and this afternoon she came in with charts of colours for painting the nursery.

'I think we need cheering up,' she says. The charts are mainly different shades of yellow. Mummy obviously thinks we need to paint the nursery yellow! I agree with her. Finn comes over for a look.

'Pah!' he says to Mummy. He seizes the one green chart and points to the bottom one. 'What about this one?'

'*Peapod Green*, Finn?' I'm not so sure.

'It's better than yellow,' he says firmly.

'I like *Pale Primrose*, Mummy,' I say, pointing at a little yellow rectangle. It reminds me of the primroses in the ditch. Mummy thinks it's a very nice colour, and it will brighten up the nursery no end.

Finn is cross, I can tell. Nanny Jan comes in and says she also likes *Pale Primrose*. She notices Finn's expression and, when he shows her the *Peapod Green*, she says why don't we have a section of *Peapod Green* under the radiator by the French windows.

'Right,' says Mummy, 'I will order *Pale Primrose* for the walls and a small pot of *Peapod Green* for Finn.' She gets up from the sofa. Finn looks unsure. He can't tell if he's won or not.

'And then the new piano arrives tomorrow!' she says, smiling. I beam at her.

I bounce on my chair. A piano for me! And surely it will help me forget about the dreadful hunting day. Mr Fox now sleeps on my bed because I felt very sorry for him crying like that.

He's quite happy there, even if he sometimes falls off in the night.

Mercy is with me most evenings. She stands watch while I go to sleep, and sometimes I worry about how tired she must be, standing for so long. I have forgiven her for taking Banger off like that. Well, I have blessed her which is about the same as forgiving.

I can't forgive Daddy. I just can't.

CAMELLIA
The new piano

I'm back from school and Mummy greets me, holding the back door open. She says the piano has arrived.

I walk into the sunny nursery and there it is. My new piano! It's the very same colour as Bo and the keys shine white and black. I run over to sit on the stool, immediately feeling at home. I play a bit of Annabel's Moonlight and it sounds wonderful.

Finn has a big smile on his face.

'I've played it already,' he says. 'I didn't play that though. I did more stuff at the low end.'

Mummy asks me what I think. Nanny Jan comes in from the kitchen and even Daddy's here. They all want to know. I play 'Silent Night', having practised that one with Annabel. Finn claps his hands together and says we don't need the little church any more.

Mummy looks at me and says 'Well…?'

I feel a surge of pure white happiness welling up and I'm not sure I can speak. It's too much! In this moment I love everyone, even Daddy. I turn and face my audience.

'It's quite, quite perfect. Thank you! Thank you!'

I know I'm about to cry, so I invite Finn to join me on the piano stool. He hops up and we perform our first duet of 'Silent Night' with Finn adding his stuff at the low end.

Daddy laughs out loud at our performance and says 'Bravo!' Nanny Jan says it'll be the Albert Hall next.

'Well that's a hit,' says Mummy.

CAMELLIA

Nanny Jan, Finn and I are in the woods searching for primroses for Mothering Sunday. Mercy follows us as usual, gliding along the path, with the dogs running behind.

It's a sunny afternoon and the breeze feels warm and spring-like. There are fat buds on the trees now, and Nanny Jan points out a flowering blackthorn bush. She tells us that March is sometimes known as a blackthorn-winter, due to cold east winds and sleet. We walk past celandines which are shiny and as yellow as Mrs Betts's duster, but leave them alone because we are after primroses.

'Mind you,' Nanny Jan adds, 'After the winter we've had, I think we deserve a blackthorn-spring.' All around us the black-birds are singing their hearts out, and over in the ditch we spot the pale lilac of the cuckoo pint flower.

Finn complains that this is quite a long primrose walk. He's carrying a little wicker basket as if he's Dick Whittington, swinging it around on a stick.

'That won't be much good once you've got primroses in it, Finn,' I say.

'I'm not going to pick very many,' he says, making a face.

I *know* I'm the best primrose-picker. Nanny Jan says I'm clever to make sure I pick them *right* at the bottom of the stem. Finn tends to snatch them up, so his primroses are all different lengths, mostly quite short. His bunches look best in egg cups.

We arrive at our special primrose place and for a moment we stop and stare. There are are literally hundreds and thousands of little pale-yellow faces, even more than last year, and in amongst them masses of violets. A song thrush welcomes us, high in a nearby oak.

'Just look at all the violets!' I cry.

Nanny Jan agrees they are very pretty but difficult to pick. Finn has already begun his snatching, tossing primroses into his basket. I wish Mummy would come primrosing with us, but she's always busy.

Before I start picking, I look around for Mercy. To my surprise she has a companion, a young girl about the same height as me, dressed in palest blue. They are picking primroses together, or at least they seem to be. The girl has light brown hair with a plait down her back. I can't really see her face.

'Come on slow coach!' Nanny Jan says. She can't see the figures of course.

'Magpie, Melia,' says Finn, pointing at the tall ash tree. Two magpies, smart as paint, are chattering away.

I settle into picking the primroses, every now and then glancing towards Mercy and her friend. They are there still, shimmering in the dappled light, every now and then bending down. The violets are asking me to pick them but I leave them be, remembering Nanny Jan's advice.

The sun warms my back and we work quietly for a while. Soon Finn comes over to say he's had enough. I keep on going. I could spend ages picking primroses, especially when all around is birdsong and spring. The green world has come back.

'That will do,' says Nanny Jan, with a sigh. 'My poor back's aching anyway.' I show her my basket proudly, and she admires my neat bunches. Then she peers into Finn's basket and says he's done pretty well.

'Now we must get back home to put them in water, ready for taking to church tomorrow.'

Mercy and the girl are no longer with us. Nanny Jan carries Finn's basket for him, while I'm quite happy carrying my own. Every now and then I lift the basket to my nose and breathe in the precious primrose scent.

Mummy welcomes us back, giving us the news that Gran will join us for the Mothering Sunday service tomorrow. It's at three o'clock and afterwards we're invited back for tea. Has Gran started searching for Mercy's diary? She did promise, but you never know with grown-ups.

I tip my primroses out on to the nursery table, ready to bunch them up, and find a surprise underneath. Violets! I *know* I didn't pick them. I call Nanny Jan over and she asks if I'm certain. Of course I'm certain! I gently float the tiny violets in a white saucer, and they swim around happily. Then I put the saucer on top of my piano.

Thank you, Mercy and the girl.

CAMELLIA
Mothering Sunday
The morning sun lights up my curtains. Spring is coming! I can feel it. I fling open my window and listen to the birdsong. Any bird strong and brave enough to survive that winter has a lot to sing about. A thrush and a blackbird sing a spring duet, just like Finn and me on the piano.

For some reason Mercy is waiting outside the big front door. Does she want to come in that way? In slow motion she turns her head towards me, Bo in her arms. Her mouth moves as if she's trying to say something. I wave from my window and she smiles.

I brush my teeth and, when I come back, Mercy is standing in her corner. She isn't holding Bo any more because he's curled up on my bed. When I stretch out my hand, it goes right through him, and all I feel is eiderdown. Both Bo and Mercy slowly fade away, and I study at the spot where Bo was lying. There is a dip in the eiderdown! I lean forward and catch the faintest smell of roses, as well as something rotting, like compost.

The window slams with a bang, making my heart jump. There's no wind outside so how could this happen? I fasten the window and then my bedroom door opens by itself. Mercy's playing games, but I'm getting used to it. Mr Fox is close to the edge of his shelf, peering down. Heidi stares at me, one eye shut and one eye open and then she throws herself off the chair.

Mercy reappears in her corner. Her eyes are dancing. She wants to be noticed. She's going to play more games, all the time growing stronger.

'I'll ask Gran about the diary again today,' I tell her. 'I promise.' She stares some more.

'Cross my heart and hope to die.'

And she is gone.

CAMELLIA

Mothering Sunday service

Mummy is driving us to church, and it seems odd to be going to church in the afternoon, when we would normally be having our walk. Nanny Jan is in the front, with Finn and me in the back.

My two bunches of primroses are on my lap, their stems wrapped in silver foil. Nanny Jan carries the other two, because Finn's hands are too hot for primroses.

We walk along the path through dappled sunlight. There are magpies hopping around the gravestones, and I count seven but there could be more, hiding. Finn waves his basket at them and keeps marching.

'Don't worry about the magpies, Mummy,' he says. 'These are friendly ones.' Mummy isn't so sure and I catch her doing a little salute. Today she wears a pretty pink coat, but no hat, because it's only a children's afternoon service. I'm in my light green dress with navy-blue smocking and long white socks. I'm actually quite pleased with my outfit, apart from my dreadful sandals.

Bo is sitting among the magpies, so Mercy must be close. Perhaps she's already in church. It *is* Mothering Sunday after all. Mr Impey is at the door to greet us. He says good afternoon to Mummy and Nanny Jan, and then he bends down to me.

'Your Mercy's already here. I'm afraid she has thrown some prayer books around.' Finn is listening, his eyes big and round, his ears almost flapping. Luckily Mummy and Nanny Jan have gone ahead to find our pew.

'Gosh,' I say. 'I'm so sorry! I think she wants more people to take notice of her.' Mr Impey gives his merry smile.

'Don't you worry. I've blessed her and now she's sitting quietly at the back.'

'Where is she? Where's Mercy?' I do my best to point her out, but of course she's invisible to Finn.

Finn is still saying 'Where is she?' when I shove him into our pew. I tell him to be quiet. There are not that many people here for the special service. I should think most other children are having their afternoon walk.

When Gran arrives, dressed in her blue spring coat, she takes her usual pew in front of us. I'm sure she must be lonely all by herself so I ask Mummy if I can join her. Mummy says of course and I think Gran must be happy with me because she gives a lovely smile. Once I'm beside her, she asks if I'm looking forward to extra sticky ginger cake for tea. You bet I say.

Mr Impey comes to the front to welcome us all. He's dressed in purple because we're in the middle of Lent. While he says the opening prayer, he closes his eyes, so I do the same. But when I open them again Mr Impey is staring at me and the space to my right, moving his head from side to side.

Mercy has come forward to sit beside me, so close I could reach out and touch her. I stare across at her window and then her, wondering if Gran has *any* idea. Perhaps if I moved up a bit, she could sit next to Gran. But then I would have to move *through* her. I don't really want to do that.

Mr Impey clears his throat.

'Now is the time for you children to give your spring flowers to your mothers or grandmothers or sisters or aunts!' I have my two bunches so I give one to Gran and the other to Mercy. Of course, her primroses fall straight through her on to the pew. Finn makes a lot of noise giving his bunches to Mummy and Nanny Jan.

We sing a hymn and, while we are singing, my prayer book goes sailing into the pew in front. Luckily there's no one sitting there. It's usually empty, only now it isn't. Surely Gran can feel this? Mercy stands right in front of her staring, and all Gran is doing is singing with her eyes down! Mercy leans in towards Gran, but she doesn't look up once. I hear Finn doing his la-la-las behind me and now he's asking Mummy for a sweet. She tells him to hush.

The hymn finishes and we all sit down. Mercy has disappeared, and I turn to see if she's at the back of the church. She's not, but I bet she's up to something. We don't have to wait long to find out.

As if out of nowhere there is a huge commotion with magpies flying up and down the aisle, over people's heads and up towards the altar. Mummy and Nanny Jan actually scream! Finn shouts 'Magpies, Melia!' so these are real magpies.

There are flashes of black and white all around us and the sound of feathers whirring. This is big magic from Mercy, I just know it. Gran has to duck as one dives down right over her head. There's the loudest chattering from the noisy magpies and the children are laughing and shouting, pointing up at them as they fly this way and that. There must be over twenty of them, swooping around the church. I am actually rather thrilled.

Mr Impey stares at them in wonder. They are a wonderful sight! All the same, some of his congregation are getting themselves into a state, so he walks quickly to the big church door, pushing it open.

The magpies escape immediately, all except one who perches on the pulpit, his wings shining violet and green as he turns in a circle. I don't dare turn round to see how Mummy's getting on. She might have fainted! But she must be all right because I hear Finn tell Mummy and Nanny Jan that magpies are kind. You have to laugh at Finn!

Mr Impey walks back to the pulpit and commands the magpie to leave. I understand what happens next and I'm guessing Mr Impey does too, but I should think the children and their parents will talk about this for months. And I know Gran sees it too.

The magpie disappears into thin air, right in front of our eyes.

Oh dear! I know Mummy won't like this, and she will probably say it's my fault. Somehow Mr Impey continues with the service and, when we are leaving church, I shake his hand.

'Gosh,' I say. What else is there to say?

'That was quite some show,' Mr Impey says, and that's the end of our conversation sadly because the people behind are pushing us along. *Why would magpies do that* they are saying.

Mercy is waiting for us by the churchyard gate. She's very pleased with herself I can tell because she's smiling, almost laughing. Gran doesn't say a word about the magpies, but we *may* talk about them at tea. The disappearing magpie is perched on Mercy's shoulder, as if whispering in her ear. They both vanish as we walk through.

I must ask Gran about the diary. Surely, I will get a chance.

ANGELA

How I didn't pass out with all those bloody magpies flying about I have *no* idea. Nanny Jan was having a dreadful time too, crouching down into our pew, hanging on for dear life. I felt ashamed of myself for screaming!

Poor Constance had to duck down when a bird came flying right over her head. I have to confess there was a part of me wishing Gerald was there with his gun so he could shoot the damn things. However, I'm pretty sure you're not allowed to shoot birds in church and certainly not in Lent. More's the pity quite frankly.

Why on earth would magpies fly round a church like that, and again how the hell did they get through a closed church door? We're all in for the most terrible bad luck, I just know it. There must have been over twenty of them! Twenty-times bad luck.

And then, as for that one on the pulpit, disappearing in front of our eyes, like some sort of conjuring trick! Surely Mr Impey couldn't have staged it, could he?

Camellia didn't say a word about any of it on the way back. I noticed she acknowledged someone at the churchyard gate, but there was no one there.

I didn't bring the subject up in the car because I wanted to avoid Camellia working herself up into one of her passions. If she does, and I don't agree, then she sulks, saying nobody ever understands her. Finn did say 'naughty magpies', but we left it at that. I think Nanny Jan was still in shock!

I think it would best if we forgot all about it. Much safer.

CAMELLIA

Absolutely typical! Nobody talked about the magpies on the way home. Now I know how Mercy feels. What do you need to do to get noticed? Finn said 'naughty magpies' to me in the back, and I gave him a big grin. But Mummy and Nanny Jan didn't say anything to that.

We arrive at Gran's house and she says why don't Finn and I have a little play in the garden while she gets tea ready. It's sunny and warm and we run about on the lawn. Finn starts to flap his arms like a magpie, and I can't resist doing the same.

'Chatter, chatter, chatter!' shouts Finn and I follow him, wheeling my arms in the air. At least Finn's on my side! Mummy and Nanny Jan are having a talk on the terrace, probably about us but I don't care. I need to run this off. I'm fed up with being a good girl all the time, and now we've got all this space for flying and chattering.

Grandpop joins us for tea and says he's very thirsty after spending all afternoon working in the garden. He's been pulling up brambles around the cedar tree. You would have thought Gran might tell Grandpop about the magpies in church, but she does not. I decide to go about it in a roundabout way.

'Grandpop,' I say. He looks up from putting jam on his bread. 'What family of birds do magpies belong to?' Mummy tenses up but I press on. 'We're doing bird families at school.' This is a fib of course, but Grandpop won't know.

'The Corvus family,' he says. 'That includes crows, rooks, jackdaws, magpies, jays and even the ravens at the Tower!'

'Do you remember Gerald had a pet jackdaw?' Gran says. 'When he was about twelve. He taught it to say a few words.' Grandpop says he does. Then he tells us that any bird from the Corvus family is a clever one, including Daddy's pet jackdaw. If he's not mistaken, the cage is in the garage.

'Please could you show it to us after tea?' I check Mummy's face before I ask this. If anything, she looks bored. Grandpop says he doesn't see why not. Then I ask Gran for another cup of Lapsang and tell her the ginger cake is wonderful, which it is. I

wonder when I'll have a chance to ask her about Mercy's diary.
I certainly can't bring it up round the tea table.

After tea Grandpop takes Finn and me to the garage. He goes
all the way to the back, returning with a huge wooden cage.

'It's made of bamboo as well as wood, so not too heavy.' He
brings it out into the driveway and Mummy and Nanny Jan
come to have a look. I ask who made it? Grandpop says he
doesn't know but, when Gran joins us, she says she remembers
it when she was a child growing up at the Old House.

'Do you think we could borrow it, Grandpop?' I ask. I
don't know how I know, but this cage is important for Mercy.
Grandpop says it'll need a bit of washing down because it's
very dusty, and I tell him that Finn and I would be good at that.

Mummy says she could just about fit the cage in the boot of
the car, with the back seats down, but then there would be no
room for us. Nanny Jan says she would love to walk us back
home, but she has got lots to do, ironing etc. Finn says he's
got lots to do as well and can he sit on her lap in the front? Of
course, Nanny Jan agrees.

I'm very pleased with this plan. It means I can ask Gran to
walk me up the garden.

CAMELLIA

At last Gran and I have a chance to talk. The others have gone
home in the car with the bird cage. We walk slowly up the hill
because it's very steep! All around us the birds are singing and
singing. They just can't help it! The bluebell leaves are pushing
through the grass, and Gran points out the lily of the valley,
peeping out beneath the rhododendrons.

'I know my mother was fond of lily of the valley,' she says. I'm
pleased Gran has started the conversation like this!

'My father told me,' she adds sadly.

'What do the flowers look like?'

Gran tells me they are like little white bells and the scent is
heavenly. She will pick some for me when they come out in
May.

I can't wait any longer. I'm nervous to ask about the diary, but I take a deep breath and come out with it.

'Have you been looking for your Mummy's diary?' My heart is thudding. Gran stops and sighs. She says searching for the diary makes her feel a bit funny, but she promises me she has started.

'I'm taking each and every book down from the library. It will take me some time, but then I will know.' I reach out to squeeze her hand.

'Thank you, Gran.' We walk on and come to another stop by the rowan tree. Its buds are pink and copper, and Gran says give it a couple of weeks and the pretty leaves will be breaking.

I feel even braver now, so I ask Gran what did she think of all the magpies? She thought it was extraordinary, especially the one which disappeared. We reach the top of the hill where Gran's garden turns into ours. I thank her again for the delicious tea and then I say something I hadn't planned.

'I was very close to you in church.' Gran looks at me in surprise, and I say the words again, 'I was very close to you in church.'

Gran whispers 'I know.' Her face is sad and drawn, not stern at all. I'm afraid she's going to burst into tears! We wait for the moment to pass.

We kiss each other goodbye and I run back over the drive into our garden. I slow up beside the big pine trees to catch my breath. I'm sorry I upset Gran but now I know she has to cry and cry *properly*. Then she will be able to see Mercy.

Finn's waiting for me on the terrace. He says the bird cage has been put into the garage for now. We can ask Daddy about his jackdaw later. He runs about flapping his arms again. When I ask him what sort of Corvus bird he is, he tells me with a grin.

'I am the Holy Magpie.'

I laugh. You have to laugh at Finn.

CAMELLIA

The nursery is being painted today and the weather is sunny

and warm. This means Finn and I can play outside while Mr Pym, the painter, does his work. He has a little wireless covered in paint, playing all sorts of tunes which he whistles along to. He slaps the *Pale Primrose* paint on happily, using a great big brush and he's told Finn when it comes to the *Peapod Green*, he'll let him help.

Meanwhile Finn and I are busy cleaning the jackdaw cage. We have two buckets of soapy water and sponges, and Finn tries to whistle like Mr Pym but soon gives up. He says you need bigger teeth to whistle properly.

'More clean water, Melia.' He drops his sponge into the bucket. 'Why do you think Daddy called his jackdaw Jack?'

I sigh. I must say I was a bit disappointed with the name.

'Because he couldn't think of anything else? That's why.' Daddy told us Jack was with him for about a year and that he only went into his cage at night. For the rest of the time he was allowed to fly around. Daddy said Jack really enjoyed fruit cake.

I go inside to ask Mrs Betts if she would fill our buckets again. Nothing's ever too much trouble for Mrs Betts, and she helps us carry them back to the terrace. She admires our cleaning.

'You're doing a super job,' she says. 'It's coming up a treat.' I have a thought. The jackdaw cage would make a useful outdoor room for my dolls. They would enjoy that.

Finn's getting tired of cleaning, so I finish the last bit. Now it needs to dry out, and we drag it to the sunniest spot. It needs the wind to blow through.

Mercy appears. She watches us as we stand back and admire our hard work.

'Mercy's here,' I tell Finn.

'Where?'

I point at her. He waves at Mercy even though he can't see her. She waves back!

'Why can't I see her?' He makes a face. 'It's not fair.'

'Shall I ask her to come closer?' Now poor Finn is worried.

'I want to go and talk to Mr Pym,' he says. 'It might be time for *green*.' I watch him running into the nursery. He's so little.

I turn back to Mercy and she's gone. The wind rustles the branches of the copper beech overhead and in between the sky is very blue. I hear a chattering from the cage.

There's a magpie watching me from within. I want Finn to see and call his name, but he won't hear over Mr Pym's wireless. The cage might be a portal and sure enough, when I blink, the magpie is gone.

I *know* a magpie once lived in this cage. Did the magpie belong to Mercy? If only Gran could find her diary! I hope she's looking right now.

It will soon be time for lunch. Mr Pym is whistling *We're all going on a summer holiday* and Finn sings along. I'm drawn back into their world, away from Mercy and her magpies.

But she's waiting for me. Just round the corner...

CAMELLIA

Our primrose nursery is so bright and fresh! We've been in it for two days now, but the smell of paint is still pretty strong. Nanny Jan opens the windows at breakfast, and they stay open all day. Bumblebees keep buzzing in and I have to stop whatever I am busy with to shoo them out.

Sarah's coming over to play today and we're going to see what we can do to help Mercy. The plan is for us to go down to the end of the garden, and I'm going to ask Nanny Jan if she would help us with the bird cage.

It's sunny again with a little breeze. I step out on to the terrace and for a moment remember what it was like covered in snow, and how our snowman stood over there, with his face turning round. He took a long time to melt into the lawn.

I hope Mercy will come and play today. Then Sarah and I will be able to help her. Somehow we need to keep Finn happy, and I will ask Nanny Jan to keep him up here. I'm sure she won't mind. It is no good asking Mummy to help with Finn. She's either too busy or Finn gets bored when she's on the telephone. Then he comes to find me.

Sarah arrives just before lunch and I welcome her in. Her

mum is with her, dressed in beautiful colours, turquoise and pink with lots and lots of beads. Her hair is fair, like Sarah's and she wears it in a ponytail.

'Have fun, you two,' she says in a soft, kind voice. 'Be careful though.' It's as if she knows what we are going to play.

'Remember to protect yourself.'

'Of course, Mum,' Sarah says. We say goodbye and run into the nursery. We know how to protect ourselves. We're nearly seven after all.

NANNY JAN

Camellia was that pleased to have her friend Sarah over for the day. Sarah's a dear, sweet girl and very kind too.

As soon as she was through the door with Camellia, Finn took her over to his *Peapod Green* wall. He wanted to know what she thought.

'I did it nearly all by myself,' he announced proudly.

'It's a brilliant green,' Sarah said.

I must say the smell of paint is quite overpowering, even after two days of having the windows open. The nursery looks bright and clean though, and I do *not* want any magpies getting in here, making a mess, and as for that lot in the church! Camellia didn't seem that bothered and neither did Finn. I do worry about Camellia. Sometimes it's as though she's very far away.

She told me her grandmother was going to look for the ghost's diary. I only hope it doesn't stir things up even more. I hear crying most nights and I could swear it's coming from inside my new room. I haven't told Camellia because I don't see what good that would do.

The piano has helped hugely to encourage her creativity. She has spent ages trying to play *We're all going on a summer holiday*, forever correcting her wrong notes, and never giving up. And we are getting quite used to hearing 'Silent Night' in April.

While we were having lunch, Camellia asked if I would help her carry the jackdaw cage down to the bottom of the garden. She said she was going to see how her dolls liked sitting in it. I said I would take Finn for a walk up to the stables to see Henry, and that would give the girls a bit of peace.

'I love apple crumble,' Sarah said to persuade Finn to finish his plate. 'Yum yum!'

'Maybe Henry will give you a cup of tea and a biscuit?' Camellia said, giving Finn her brightest of smiles. Finn didn't look convinced. He said he didn't really like ginger nuts.

CAMELLIA

We are settled at the end of the garden. The yew trees loom over us, blocking out the sun, so we sit in their shade with our cardigans on.

Nanny Jan brought the jackdaw cage down for us, balancing it in the big wheelbarrow. Sarah and I walked either side in case it fell out. We let Finn carry two of my dolls in his wheelbarrow but they kept falling out. I felt sorry for him, trailing after us. He knew he wasn't included in our game.

Now we're sitting cross-legged on our tartan rug with the dolls arranged around us. As well as the jackdaw cage, I've brought my little pram with Dorothy Baby on board. I have to keep checking to make sure she stays in there! The yew trees give off a strange, dusty smell and I have a funny feeling crawling down my back. I wish it would go away.

I show Sarah Bo's grave which is fast disappearing under grass and daisies. So far no sign of Mercy, nor any magpies.

'We need our protection,' Sarah says, buttoning up her cardigan. I ask how her mum does that. I already know how to fill my heart with love. That works on most things.

'We imagine wrapping ourselves up in a beautiful cloak of protection,' Sarah tells me. 'Whatever colour you like.'

We sit for a minute while Sarah puts on her golden cloak and I choose a lilac one. We keep our eyes closed.

'All safe now,' she says. I sigh, feeling rather tired in my lilac cloak.

'I wonder where Mercy's got to.'

Sarah says she knows exactly where Mercy's got to.

'She's right behind you, Melia.'

Of course she is. It feels as if Mercy has poured a whole load of snow down my back, but I suppose she can't help it. I try to shake it off. Mercy stands straight and tall with the magpie on her shoulder, then he flies down to hop into the jackdaw cage.

Sarah and I stay very still and, because we're watching the magpie, we don't notice what else is happening. I hear a funny squeak and, to my horror, I see my little pram rolling away. She's not going to take Dorothy Baby again! Not if I can help it. I scramble up, ready to run but Mercy's already there. We watch as she pushes the pram back. Was that a mean trick, or not? I'm not sure. In any case Bo has appeared, trotting in front of her.

'Wow,' says Sarah. 'What a dear little dog.' She stretches her hand out, but he sits down on his grave and begins to whine. It's a sorrowful sound.

'Oh Sarah, I'm so glad you can see what I see!' My heart is full and I can feel tears coming. Sarah says she understands.

'Why's Bo crying?' she asks. 'What's he crying about?'

I don't reply because I'm staring into the ha-ha where the earth is heaving, just like an earthquake, the mud of the field splitting into pieces. All of a sudden, and with a dreadful sound, a horse's hoof breaks out of the grass. It's horrible!

I want to scream, but I can't.

Sarah jumps up. She wants to see what's happening. There's half a leg now, kicking as it tries to break free. Mercy stands with us, silently watching this sickening sight. I find my voice.

'NO!' I shout. 'Stop it, Mercy. Stop it!' Bo's whining grows louder, and Sarah falls to her knees, putting her hands over her ears. Mercy knows how to stop this because she's making it happen. It's too much for us! We back away.

Suddenly it stops. I peer back over the edge and all I see is grass and a few nettles. No horse's leg. It's all over.

'Are you all right, Sarah?' I whisper. She nods, her eyes tightly closed.

'You can open your eyes now.'

But what's happened makes me feel rather sick. The jackdaw cage is on its side, the pram has tipped over and the dolls are scattered higgledy-piggledy. I pick up Dorothy Baby, safe and sound. Mercy has gone, taking Bo and her magpie with her.

'That was *awful*!' Sarah says. 'Why was a horse's leg trying to get out of the ground?' I know why.

'That was a hunter-horse. He was buried there. He's big.'

'I'm glad I had my golden cloak on,' Sarah says. 'Why do you think the hunter-horse wants to come out now?'

I tap my head, trying to clear it. Why did that happen? *Why*?

'I think Mercy wants more help. Maybe she loved that horse?'

We gather up the dolls, putting as many into the pram as we can. The bottom of the garden doesn't feel safe any more, and I'm scared the ground might heave up again. We leave the jackdaw cage behind.

'Why do you think Mercy did that?' Sarah asks as we carry our stuff back up to the house. I know exactly why Mercy did that.

'It's because she's angry.' Heidi falls out of the pram again. She's too big.

'Angry Mercy,' Sarah says, picking up Heidi.

'And she's running out of patience.'

CAMELLIA

I'm worried about what Mercy might do next, especially now she's angry. The anger's making her more powerful, meaning she can make *real* magpies fly around the church, make a magpie disappear, make my little pram go down the path and then wake up the dead hunter-horse in the ha-ha.

All this in the last few days! I can't tell Finn about the hunter-horse because he would be too scared and that's not fair on him. Nanny Jan wouldn't like it either. She was a bit surprised to find Sarah and me playing in the nursery, saying she was sure we'd be down the garden for much longer.

Sarah and I have made a promise that we won't tell anyone about the hunter-horse. We wouldn't be believed anyway. Then we agree that we *can* tell Sarah's mum and Mr Impey. After all we need to share this with trusted grown-ups. Mercy is too strong for me now, and I'm running out of things to keep her happy. I can't do it all by myself.

It's a lot to worry about. Sarah has promised to talk to her mum, and she'll give me more news at Lorna's ninth birthday party. Mummy says it's to be a paper-chase, with children running through our primrose woods. I only hope Mercy doesn't take one of the children. I have no idea how to stop her doing that.

I don't want to go down to the bottom of the garden again. The jackdaw cage is there still, but it should be safe.

I sit at my piano and play three verses of 'Silent Night'. I know Mercy likes that.

CAMELLIA
April 6th
I'm in the nursery with Annabel and we're sitting at my new piano. The French windows are open, and Banger sits in the sun on the terrace. Finn is busy outside putting things in his wheelbarrow and the longer he does that the better, because it's not easy when Finn wants to learn the piano too. He can't play by ear.

Annabel plays her Moonlight and says she thinks my piano has very good tone. I tell Annabel I've been trying to work out a few tunes.

'Bobby's Girl's quite difficult, and Locomotion's just impossible!'

'Do you know those tunes off by heart?' Annabel asks. I shake my head. 'Because,' she explains, 'If you don't, then it's impossible to get them right.' We sit quietly, wondering which tunes we know by heart.

'Away in a Manger'? 'Silent Night' obviously, but those are carols. We're nearly at Easter! Annabel agrees. Her grandmother's coming for Easter.

'Nanny Jan likes Elvis as well as Cliff Richard. She says he's got some very good songs. 'It's now or never' is one of her favourites.'

Finn appears in the doorway and says he's nearly had enough of outside. I ask him to find me a magpie feather and this works. He sets off and I see him on the lower lawn peering into bushes. We have some more time.

'We said we would compose a beautiful tune for Mercy,' Annabel says. She has said exactly what I wanted to hear. But how are we going to do that?

The door opens behind us and a familiar voice says:

'I see two musicians hard at work!'

It's Mr Impey! He says he was just passing and thought he would call in. He says his old parishioners are tiring him out, and he needs to talk to people nearer his age.

'We're trying to compose a beautiful tune for Mercy,' I explain. 'And you said ghosts are musical.'

'Some ghosts. Not all.'

Finn's back in the nursery. He hasn't found a magpie feather yet and says he looked jolly hard. He tells Mr Impey there are *no* jelly babies in the sweets cupboard. Mr Impey says he's sorry to hear that, and sits down on the floor as usual. He says he has an important question for each one of us.

'What's your favourite fairy story?' he asks. 'I know what mine is.'

'*Snow White*,' I say.

'*The Little Mermaid*,' says Annabel.

It's Finn's turn now. He scratches his head.

'*Hansel and Gretel* but I'm not sure why. I hate that witch!'

'Well,' Mr Impey says, 'I think I have found Mercy a beautiful tune. Hansel and Gretel was turned into an opera nearly a hundred years ago.' Finn says he doesn't know what an opera is. Annabel does of course.

'It's like a play with a lot of loud singing.' Mr Impey smiles at this.

'It is indeed. Some are better than others of course, but *Hansel and Gretel is* a very special opera.' Finn rubs his ear. Has

Mr Impey seen it.

'Not only have I seen it, but I have a record of the opera!'

Annabel and I sit up at this news. Mr Impey says he could bring it over and then we could all listen to the 'Evening Prayer'. He says Hansel and Gretel sing it when they're lost in the wood, and they call on fourteen angels to keep them safe. I tell Mr Impey our record player is hopeless, and he says we can borrow his.

Then he jumps up and asks if I would allow him to play the piano. Annabel and I move out of the way. He runs his fingers over the keys and says the piano has a lovely tone. Annabel and I smile. We can't help it.

'This is the "Evening Prayer",' he says. 'I don't need piano music because I play by ear. Also, I know this tune by heart.'

Mr Impey plays, and I don't think I have ever heard such a beautiful tune. It's both sad and happy at the same time, and I feel tears prickling my eyes. He plays it through twice and then turns around.

'Well?'

'It's heavenly,' I tell him. He says having teary eyes is a sign of being *very* musical. This shall be Mercy's tune. Finn asks if the witch has a tune and Mr Impey tells him that indeed she does, but not very beautiful. Finn can listen to it and see what he thinks.

'I don't think Mercy wants to hear the witch's tune,' I tell Finn. 'Not unless she's in a bad mood.' I want to talk to Mr Impey about the hunter-horse, but I can't in front of Nanny Jan and Finn.

Mummy will be sorry to miss Mr Impey! He says he'll arrange for a good time to come back with his record player. He might even lend it to us for a few days. I'll have to wait until then to tell him about the hunter-horse. I only hope Mercy behaves in the meantime.

We wave him off in his little car. Annabel says she's never met a musical vicar before, but then she hasn't met many vicars.

I *think* I can just about remember the 'Evening Prayer'. It's as if it's ringing in my soul. We're back in the nursery and I feel like dancing. I spread my arms out wide like a bird.

'Annabel', Finn says. 'Will you help me find a magpie feather?' He tells her he knows just where to find one and I follow them out onto the terrace and down into the garden.

The sun is warm and the air feels soft. The grass is the shiniest green and there's birdsong in every tree. I spin round and round in the April morning. I've found Mercy's song.

CAMELLIA
Lorna's Party – 9th April

Nanny Jan is driving me to Lorna's party. Finn's in the back of the car too, annoyed he isn't invited.

'Even I will be quite young for this party, Finn,' I tell him. 'Lorna's nine today and I am not seven yet, and it's a paper-chase, remember. Lots of running through the primrose woods chasing bits of paper and looking for clues.' I admire my new gym shoes, ready for running. Finn goes quiet.

Mummy's going to join the party later, and she will bring me home. Mummy loves a party after all.

It's another bright sunny day, little clouds sailing in the sky. The breeze dances in the trees while we gather to start the race. I'm wearing shorts and a tee shirt and feel a bit nervous amongst the older children. Sarah and I decide to run together, and on the way round she can tell me what her mum said about the hunter-horse.

I count twenty children altogether and we hop about, eager to get started. Aunt Daphne reads us a few rules and says it should take us about three quarters of an hour. Sarah rolls her eyes. That's quite a lot of running! There will be seven clues for us to collect along the way, and we can put them in our pockets. If we miss anything out, we won't win.

Lorna has a big grin on her face. I get the feeling she already knows the clues. It's her party after all. Nanny Mae is standing to the side with Julia who's too young to race. She has a list of the children running and she calls our names out, like the register at school. This is so we'll know if anybody goes missing in the woods.

Aunt Daphne fires the starting pistol and we're off! The older children charge off into the distance, leaving Sarah and me to run happily at the back.

'I've had nightmares about that horse,' Sarah says as we run along. I tell her I haven't been down to the bottom of the garden since. I'm too scared. A boy in white shorts and tee shirt comes running up behind and overtakes us. He has dark hair and is already miles ahead.

'I thought we were at the back?' I say. 'Where did he come from?'

'Hope he's not a ghost!' Sarah laughs. 'How long do you think we've been running?' I look at my watch which isn't easy.

'About five minutes I should think.' I've already got a stitch. Sarah tells me to run with my arm in the air because she's heard that helps. I try this but it feels silly and makes me laugh. Now my stitch is even *worse*!

All around us the woods are shimmering with pale green leaves and dappled light. Sarah and I are out of breath, so we walk for a bit. The bits of paper on the ground are not that easy to follow because they've been trampled into the path by the runners ahead. Some of them have even flown into the bushes on the side.

'So, my mum says Mercy could be using our energy. She can do more things if there are lots of people around.'

'All the people in church, you mean? And you and me for the hunter-horse? And she likes our energy?'

We stop at the first clue which asks us to find an acorn. We look around and luckily there's an oak tree right in front of us. We set off again.

'So, you're saying Mercy gets her power from the people around her?'

'Yes,' Sarah says. 'Something like that and she likes your energy best.' As soon as Sarah says this, Mercy appears, gliding through the trees to our left. She has her child with her. Sarah hasn't seen the child before.

'Bless you, Mercy. Bless you!' I pant, running along. 'No hunter-horses please. Bring me some violets.' Sarah doesn't know about the violets, so I explain.

'I feel I have to keep her happy all the time,' I tell her. 'It's exhausting.'

Mercy is gliding fast. She overtakes us and disappears. We stop at the second clue. Sarah takes off her gym shoe and shakes a twig out of it. She asks what we need to find this time.

'A feather.'

As if on cue, we hear a most beautiful sound. It's like tinkling water, but it's definitely birdsong. I've never heard a song like it, yet my heart is bursting. But I *do* know this, just like I know the 'Evening Prayer'. The song flows on and on, sometimes bubbling, sometimes soaring and every now and then it goes *pi, pi, pi.*

'What bird is that?' Sarah asks. We can't tell where it's coming from.

'Not a blackbird,' I say. 'Not a thrush, not a wren. I know those well.' Sarah searches on the ground for her feather and says she'll find one for me too. I stand and listen, enchanted. Of course I have *always* known which bird sings this song.

'It's the nightingale, Sarah. It's the *nightingale!*'

We run on and finish the race. I think we missed out two clues, but it doesn't really matter. We heard the nightingale! We clock in with Nanny Mae, who ticks our names off. She asks us whether we saw Ian or Fiona, as they haven't returned yet. We didn't see them and it's a bit strange because we thought we were at the back. Nanny Mae says not to worry, go in and have some tea. Ian and Fiona are bound to turn up soon.

CAMELLIA

We're having tea round the long dining room table, and we certainly won't go hungry! We have orange and lemon squash to drink, as well as plates of sandwiches, little fairy cakes, sausages and bowls of twiglets, crisps and chocolate biscuits.

I pile up my plate. I'm hungry after all that running. I wrap a sausage in a piece of buttered bread and take a bite. It's heaven! I look around the table and see lots of pink faces from all that running, some of them as red as tomatoes. I'm glad my face never goes that red.

Nanny Mae brings the cake in and we sing Happy Birthday to Lorna. It's a chocolate cake decorated with primroses and nine purple candles.

I see Nanny Mae whisper something to Aunt Daphne. I know exactly what they're whispering about. Ian and Fiona are still missing. Sure enough, Aunt Daphne says she must tell us something, if we could just be quiet for a minute. She takes a deep breath.

'Ian and Fiona haven't come home yet, and it's getting quite late now. Did any of you see them on the run?' Some of the children put up their hands. Ian and Fiona *were* seen on the run but not at the end. Sarah gives me a nudge. She can't seriously expect me to say that Mercy has taken them. I put my hand up to speak. Aunt Daphne is waiting.

'Perhaps a grown-up should go and search for them,' I say bravely. At that very moment Mummy appears in the doorway, dressed in a dark green trouser suit.

'Yes, a grown-up!' shouts Lorna. 'We're all too tired!' She throws herself off her chair to make her point. Aunt Daphne is all of a dither. She says she doesn't know what to do. She can hardly give the prizes out while two children are missing in the woods.

Mummy offers to go and search. I'm proud of Mummy, knowing how she gets herself lost in the woods, but maybe that's just when we're hunting. Aunt Daphne agrees and says she'd better get a move on as parents are due to pick up in half an hour.

I know I must be the one to help Mummy, even though my legs are tired. I feel a bit sick from the chocolate cake, not sure if I'll be able to run. Sarah says she'll come with me, and I feel guilty for not telling the grown-ups about Mercy.

Mummy strides out along the path and Sarah and I follow her, trying to keep up. We both have stitches after tea, so we trot with our arms up.

'Ian!' Mummy shouts. 'Fiona!' We walk and call for about fifteen minutes and there's nothing. I look out for Mercy but she's nowhere to be seen. Now I feel afraid for Ian and Fiona. They might have to sing the 'Evening Prayer' like Hansel and Gretel!

Suddenly Mummy stops.

'Listen!' she says. We listen as hard as we can.

'Over here!' comes a voice. We round the bend and there's Ian standing beside Fiona on the edge of the path. She's crying and, when Mummy asks her what's wrong, she says her ankle hurts.

'I can't walk on it!'

'I saw her fall,' Ian says, puffing out his chest when he sees Sarah. 'And so I stayed with her until help arrived.'

Mummy tells Ian he's quite the gentleman and wishes there were more like him in the world. She asks me to run back to the house, as fast as I can, to let Aunt Daphne know Ian and Fiona are safe, and that we need help to get Fiona home. Sarah will stay with Mummy and be a good nurse.

What a relief they are safe! Luckily I don't feel my stitch running back. My legs are strong again and they carry me back in no time. Aunt Daphne is by the door. No parents have arrived yet.

'Fiona twisted her ankle,' I pant. 'She can't walk but she's all right, just a bit upset. She's about fifteen minutes into the wood. From the end that is.'

Aunt Daphne is so relieved she claps both hands to her chest. Now that all the children are accounted for, she's happy to go ahead with the prizes. I follow her through the house into the garden. I don't know who actually won.

Aunt Daphne tells everyone that Ian and Fiona have been found, safe and well, apart from Fiona's ankle. Nanny Mae says she will save some chocolate cake for them.

'So, first prize goes to Robert,' says Aunt Daphne, handing over a big blue and orange kite to the dark-haired boy who overtook us. 'And full marks to you, Robert, because you started the race a good five minutes after everyone else!' Robert accepts his kite. He looks embarrassed but pleased.

'Second prize to Lorna!' I know Lorna cheated but it's her birthday after all. Lorna accepts her ping pong bats and ball.

'And third prize goes to Rachel.' I don't know Rachel, but she says something interesting when she accepts her jigsaw puzzle.

'Who was that woman in the wood?' Aunt Daphne frowns and says she has no idea. Perhaps a walker? Rachel shakes her head.

'She wore a long dress, and she stepped out in front of the runners. I thought she was there on purpose, trying to scare us. There was a little dog too.' Aunt Daphne looks blank.

'Nothing to do with us, no.' I stay very quiet. My legs feel like jelly now and I'm relieved when Nanny Mae says she'll do the walk back to Mummy to assure them that help is on its way.

'All's well that ends well!' says Mummy as we drive home. 'I rather enjoyed it. That Ian is a *very* nice boy. Perhaps we could have him over, do you think?'

I don't answer because I'm completely worn out. I'm tired of worrying about what Mercy might do next. Fiona didn't actually say a woman in a long dress jumped out at her, but Mercy *could* have easily done that. Perhaps Fiona will remember later.

I tell Mummy about the nightingale. Mummy says that sounds absolutely lovely, but I know she's thinking more about arranging for Ian to come over for tea.

I'm almost asleep as we turn into the driveway. I remember the nightingale's song. It's singing in my soul.

ANGELA

Well that was quite an adventure! I knew we had to get cracking with our search, and what a relief we found them. How would it be if people thought our woods were dangerous? Gerald would have a fit.

What a nice boy that Ian is. It was very grown up of him to stick with poor Fiona who was crying her eyes out. I had some sympathy for her, mind you. When I broke my ankle skiing, I remember what it was like to see my foot pointing in the wrong direction. I needed the blood wagon on that occasion, and we could have done with it yesterday, quite frankly.

Fiona's mother rang me this morning to report that the ankle isn't broken, just a nasty sprain. I suppose if you have children running around in the woods, then accidents are bound to happen. Fiona will learn she has to make sure she watches where she's going. I've made a decision about Camellia's birthday party in June. We'll stick to the garden for our games.

Camellia didn't say much about any of it. Her face wears a frown most of the time these days. She was exhausted when we got back, announcing that she was going to have a bath and then go straight to bed. She was asleep when I looked in on her, her face pale and peaky. I do hope she isn't coming down with something again, particularly as Nanny Jan is having the Easter weekend off, and we are off for a week's fishing in Scotland.

Thank heavens for Nanny who's coming to hold the fort. The children will go to lunch with Jack and Constance on Easter Sunday. So that's all good.

The piano's a *great* success. There are non-stop tunes coming from the nursery and, as long as Camellia is playing, she seems to be happy. On the subject of the piano, that nice Mr Impey said he'd call in tomorrow, something about Hansel and Gretel music for Camellia. He's got a lot to organise for Easter, as well a vicar might, and would four o'clock do? Annoyingly I might not be here.

Camellia was delighted when I told her; about Mr Impey, not Scotland! She tends to look glum whenever I tell her we're going away.

The house is calm and collected. Nanny Jan and Finn are happy, and the yellow nursery is a great success. Whenever Camellia's not playing her piano, she's busy drawing her bird pictures. She was surprised the nightingale is such a dull little bird, despite its charming song.

And talking of pictures I must find some dates for the Spanish artist to draw the children. Gerald wants him to draw me as well, but I'm not so sure. How on earth can I find the time to sit still? He's going to have his work cut out to make Finn sit still, but then that's his problem.

Now where's Mrs Betts to help me with my packing?

CAMELLIA

Lorna's party made me exhausted, and I knew it wasn't just the running. It was the worry! Finn wanted to hear all about it, but I didn't have the energy. I left it to Mummy.

Mercy was standing in her corner when I climbed into bed. I felt guilty for wishing she could go somewhere else. I was doing my best after all.

Now it's morning and I have a moment to think. How can I stop Mercy stealing my energy? I'm pretty sure she likes mine best, worst luck. Soon I'll have none left! Just like a car battery, I'll be completely drained. Daddy told me about that once.

I'm not going to tell Mummy about *any* of my worries. There's no point anyway because she won't believe me. I'm not sure who I am any more, and I know that sounds funny but it's true. It means I have to *pretend* to be all right and it's exhausting.

Mummy and Daddy are going away for a *whole* week to Scotland, so that means they're not here for Easter. This is pretty strange. Surely parents should be at home for Easter? Nanny Jan is off home, so Old Nanny's coming to look after us. I've been looking for the swallow who has to fly all the way from Africa, and Finn and I keep listening for the cuckoo. I haven't heard the nightingale again sadly.

Mummy cheered me up when she said Mr Impey was coming to tea. He's bringing his record player and then I'll be able to listen to the 'Evening Prayer' to my heart's content. I *never* have to put on an act for Mr Impey!

I need to talk to him without Finn around, and maybe we

could be brave enough to go down to the end of the garden. Then I can tell him about the hunter-horse. If we take the wheelbarrow down, we could bring the jackdaw cage back up.

I hope Gran is looking for Mercy's diary *right now*, and that reminds me, I must write in mine.

CAMELLIA

We are having our walk across the meadow this afternoon, and every two minutes I check my watch to make sure we're back in time for Mr Impey. What if he's early?

Even more trees are bursting into leaf and the grass under our feet is soft enough to sleep on. The spring grass is dangerous for ponies though, and poor Robin is stuck in his stable with laminitis. Henry says it makes his feet very sore, and I'm not allowed to ride him. We have to wait for it to go off.

I've never seen so many dandelions! Soon we will have lots of clocks and then we can make wishes. My wish will always be the same.

Where is Mercy today? Any minute she could appear from behind a tree. She's taken to appearing *right* in front of me, staring as I pass. I say bless you whenever this happens but *still* she does it. Finn knows I'm worried although he doesn't know how to help. Mercy is spoiling our walks and Finn complains I don't laugh any more.

'I'm so tired, Finn,' I say. 'I'm tired of worrying.' Finn's face is miserable. He doesn't like it when I'm like this. This new me isn't any fun. He catches up with Nanny Jan to chat with her instead.

Mercy appears in front of me, and I'm forced to stop. As usual she stands and stares. I want to shout *go away* but that wouldn't be kind. This time she raises her arm, pointing into the sky. I follow the direction and see a flash of blue swooping and diving. A swallow! It must be a swallow! Surely that's a good sign if Mercy has shown me a swallow.

'Nanny Jan!' I shout, catching up. 'I've seen my first swallow!'
'Hurrah!' says Finn.

'That means it's summer! Doesn't it, Nanny Jan?' Nanny Jan laughs.

'Nearly!' she says.

'Where is it?' Finn squints into the clouds. 'Perhaps it's gone back to Africa already?'

'One swallow does not a summer make,' Nanny Jan says in a serious voice.

'Says who?'

'I'm not sure, but I think they were Greek.'

'Bum to the Greek!' shouts Finn.

Nanny Jan says 'FINN!' and we burst out laughing. That's more like it. We have found our happiness again. We walk home with Finn saying 'There's a swallow, there's a swallow,' even when there isn't one.

We're almost home and there is Mr Impey's little blue car coming up the drive. He's on time. I run towards the house.

CAMELLIA

The record player

Mr Impey is already climbing out of his car as I run puffing across the driveway. He's dressed in his vicar's uniform.

'Mr Impey!' I cry happily, my feet crunching on the gravel. He's reaching into the back seat and out comes a blue and cream record player.

'For you,' he announces. 'It's yours for Easter. I won't get a spare minute to listen to music!' He peers into the distance behind me.

'Is she with you today?'

'Probably. She's always with me now. She's taken to standing right in front of me and staring.'

'No more books being thrown about?' I shake my head. He says that reminds him he's brought my Famous Five book back. He much enjoyed it, and it's on the front seat with the Hansel and Gretel record. I reach in for them both. Now Nanny Jan and Finn are coming over, and Finn tells Mr Impey we've been on a very long walk.

'We saw a swallow!' I tell him.

'Bravo!' says Mr Impey. 'They sleep on the wing, I believe. Can you imagine, sleeping and flying at the same time?'

'No,' says Finn.

'How much time have you got, Mr Impey?' I ask. I want to hear the 'Evening Prayer' and also show him the ha-ha. Mr Impey says he can spare at least an hour.

He follows me into the nursery. Meanwhile Mercy is on the terrace, watching us through the French windows. Nanny Jan says she will put the kettle on and, while she's getting the tea ready, Mr Impey wonders where he should set up the record player.

'On the chest near the piano I think,' I say, clearing the way. Mr Impey sets the record player up and opens the lid. Finn brings the record over and Mr Impey takes it out of its sleeve.

'Now we're very fortunate because the "Evening Prayer" is right at the beginning of side two, just after the Sandman's song which is very beautiful in itself. His song runs into the "Evening Prayer".' He pushes the lever, and the record drops down followed by the arm. Then the needle settles into its grooves. I hold my breath. Nanny Jan comes in with the tea trolley and I put my finger up to say 'shhhhhhh'.

The Sandman's song begins and I sit down to fully hear the music. It's very lovely and, as the music goes quiet, Mr Impey holds his arms up, as if conducting.

'Here we go,' he says. 'This is it.'

Mercy has stepped into the nursery. She's very close, and she's listening. The voices are singing in German, but it doesn't matter. The tune is soaring and heartbreaking, and I know it so well.

'You're crying, Melia,' Finn says, and I am not the only one. Mercy's face gleams with tears. Mr Impey notices but waits until the end of the song before he says:

'Your Mercy is a *very* musical ghost.' He lifts the needle from the record to play it again. I go to the piano to find the starting note. It is the note beside middle C.

'I've found the first note,' I say smiling.

'D,' Mr Impey says. 'The song is in D major. It has sharps and flats but you will soon find your way around.' He jumps up, saying he must fetch something from the car. Nanny Jan pours out the tea and cuts the cake.

'Isn't this exciting?' she says.

'Where's Mercy now?' Finn asks. 'I think I can feel her.'

'She's right beside you,' I tell him. Finn shudders.

'She won't hurt you,' I reassure him. At least I hope she won't.

Mr Impey bounds back into the nursery waving a violin in the air.

'Let's play this "Evening Prayer" on the violin!' I'm in heaven, sitting on the sofa, sipping my tea and listening to Mr Impey playing his violin at the same time as the record. He doesn't make a single mistake!

He takes a bow at the end. He suggests that I play the song over and over, feeling around for the notes while the record is actually playing. He says it's much easier that way. He shows me how to lift the needle very carefully. You have to be careful not to scratch the record, but he says he trusts me.

Mercy has disappeared. She has heard enough. It's time for Mr Impey to have some cake.

'Playing by ear can make a musician very hungry,' he says. 'Now Camellia, what else can I do?' He's read my mind as usual.

I ask if he would mind helping me bring the jackdaw cage up from the bottom of the garden. He says he would be delighted. He's never seen a jackdaw cage before.

'What's the witch's song like?' Finn asks. I don't know why he has to ask this, because I know she frightens him. Mr Impey says that, if we let the record carry on playing, we will hear the witch. Finn goes white.

'I'll pick up the needle after the "Evening Prayer", Finn. I promise.' Nanny Jan asks Mr Impey if he would like another slice of cake, and of course he says yes.

Mercy is back looking through the window. She didn't stay away for long.

NANNY JAN

As ever Mr Impey spread his magic over the house, the children and me. The record player is with us for the Easter weekend, and I'm only sorry I shan't be able to enjoy the music.

Camellia is not herself at all. It's as if she's not quite here. Her shoulders are rounded, her expression stern. It's only when she breaks into a smile that we're reminded of the old Camellia. Finn has picked up on her mood, no longer asking to join in as much. He knows she needs more time to herself, and I'm hoping this is just a phase. My mother is a great one for phases. They don't last, she says. Children grow up and move on.

We did enjoy our Hansel and Gretel concert this afternoon, and Mr Impey played his violin beautifully. During tea he told us how he passed his Grade 8 with distinction, but what he really likes to do is play any tune he fancies by ear.

Mrs Devon was away shopping in Horsham this afternoon and tomorrow she fetches Old Nanny first thing. Then I will be off. It will be a relief to get away from the night-time crying. I could ask Mr Impey about that, but not in front of the children. I will consult Mrs Betts on my return after Easter. She did say I could ask for help.

I fetched the big wheelbarrow for the jackdaw cage and Finn wanted to bring his wheelbarrow down to help, but I managed to persuade him that Mr Impey and Camellia needed to have a little chat by themselves.

'About Mercy, probably,' said Finn with a big sigh.

'I should think so, Finn,' I said. 'I'm sure Mr Impey's a very good listener.'

We watched them crossing the east lawn, Mr Impey pushing the wheelbarrow and Banger following at Camellia's heels. There were tall grey clouds in the east, building themselves up for a shower.

We were in April after all.

CAMELLIA
End of the garden

'This wheelbarrow seems to have a mind of its own,' Mr Impey says. 'Maybe it wants to go the other way.' He stops to wag his finger at it, ordering it to behave. I can't help laughing. Mr Impey always makes everything better.

'I don't really want to go this way either,' I tell him. 'But we have to.' We carry on walking, quite slowly now. We're leaving the light and entering the shadows. This part of the garden is always shady in the afternoon, but now there are other shadows.

Mr Impey asks me what's up, and I hardly know where to begin. I turn to look behind me and there she is, following us like Grandmother's Footsteps.

'She's with me nearly *all* the time now,' I tell him. 'It's exhausting because I don't know what she's going to do next.'

We reach the bottom of the garden, deep in the yew tree shade. In front of us are the fields towards the farm, lit up in spring sunshine. To my relief the jackdaw cage is exactly where we left it. Mr Impey thinks it a fine-looking cage and easily lifts it into the wheelbarrow. Then he paces about.

'This is a sad place,' he says. I explain to him how the hunter-horse's leg appeared in the ha-ha, kicking as if trying to escape. Mr Impey goes to the edge of the lawn to see for himself.

'There,' I say, pointing. 'Right there.' As soon as I say the words, the ground heaves again and this time, instead of a leg, a dark head appears with flattened ears and rolling eyes. I back away in horror. Where is Mercy now?

'Do you see it?!' I cry. My whole body has gone cold. 'What's the *matter* with the poor hunter-horse?'

Even more scary is that, while the poor horse struggles and struggles to free its shoulders from the mud, a blackbird sings above. Such a pretty song. It's all wrong! Banger stands shaking on Bo's grave, but at least she isn't howling.

The hunter-horse is forever stuck in its grave! It can't get out no matter how hard it tries. It's a terrible sight and I can't bear it. Mr Impey stretches out his arms as if to send the horse peace, and now Mercy is down in the ha-ha too. We watch as she strokes the horse's ears, bending her head close as if she's whispering.

'What are you looking at?'

It's Finn. He has followed us. He's standing behind me with his little wheelbarrow.

'A phenomenon,' Mr Impey says quickly, shaking his arms out. 'A supernatural phenomenon.'

Mercy and the hunter-horse have vanished. The ground has sealed over.

'What's a phenomenon?' Finn asks. 'Is it a sort of frog?'

'Not really,' says Mr Impey.

'Did you see Mercy?' Finn leans over, peering into the ha-ha.

'We did indeed.' Mr Impey takes a deep breath. 'I am going to bless this place. This part of the garden needs love because it's very sad.'

Mr Impey has taken charge! It's not all down to me for once. My knees are giving way and I force myself to straighten them. Before he does his blessing, I tell him about the other animals buried here, as well as the hunter-horse. Banger is fast asleep, curled up on Bo's grave. Mr Impey does his blessing which includes the Lord's Prayer. He blesses the horse, the little dogs, the big dogs and Mercy and the yew trees.

'What about the phenomenon?' Finn asks. How has he picked this word up so easily? Mr Impey gives the phenomenon a blessing too and we are finished.

As we get ready to walk back, we feel the first few drops of rain. An April shower is coming. Mr Impey pushes the wheelbarrow up the lawn, while I support the jackdaw cage, and Finn trots along behind with his. I make sure Banger is with us.

Finn runs into the house to find Nanny Jan which gives me time to have a few more words with Mr Impey. He says he'll find the time to call on Gran after Easter and he'll do his best to persuade her to search for the diary. He thinks the reason that part of the garden feels sad is because none of the animals have gone to the Light.

'Is that why they're waking up and trying to get out of their graves? Is Mercy waking them up?' I think I know the answer. More rain is falling.

Mercy is beside the car, listening. Mr Impey asks her to be kind. He says kindness is the key to everything.

'And music of course!' He starts up the engine and his little car roars into life. Its battery is strong.

'Courage, Camellia!' He reverses with a crunch of gravel. 'See! As good as my backwards skating.' I smile and remember to thank him again for the record player. He says he will see me next in church on Sunday. This is a big weekend for him and for Jesus.

I wave him off and watch the car go down the drive. I stand on the lawn in the rain and watch Mercy glide back down to her animal graveyard. I know she's on a mission to wake up the buried animals, but I'm tired. I'm going to let her get on with it.

I walk back across the gravel, scuffing my sandals on purpose and then I hear a familiar sound. It's the cuckoo! He's quite near so I stop to listen. Seven calls. He has arrived safely, all the way from Africa, just like the swallow.

I run into the house to find Finn.

ANGELA

Mr Impey had been and gone by the time I arrived back from Horsham, having driven through a cloudburst. I found the children in the nursery, enjoying a second lot of tea, and they were both keen to tell me their news.

Camellia jumped down from the table to show me Mr Impey's record player. She was all set to play her Hansel and Gretel, but I needed to get my stuff upstairs, ready for the last-minute packing.

'But it only lasts five minutes, Mummy,' she said, frowning. I know Camellia's sort of five minutes. They are often more like fifteen and, if I didn't get myself organised, I would be in trouble with Gerald.

'Perhaps later, darling.' Finn scowled at me for saying that. Now I was in trouble with both of them!

'Mr Impey blessed a phenomenon,' he announced. 'As well as other things.' I wasn't entirely sure what he was talking about. I heard Camellia mutter something under her breath.

'Sorry, Camellia. I didn't quite catch that?' She gave it to me then, with both barrels.

'*You wouldn't understand, Mummy!* You haven't got *time* to understand. You're so *busy*.' In the silence that followed Nanny Jan asked me if I wanted a cup of tea. She said there was plenty in the pot. I felt rather stunned. Finn sensed weakness, holding up the Hansel and Gretel record cover.

'Have a cup of tea, Mummy and listen. Camellia's right. Only five minutes and we don't have to listen to the witch's song.' He exchanged a glance with Camellia who took her cue. I was being ganged up on!

I decided to give in, and accepted Nanny Jan's cup of tea, collapsing on the sofa with my shopping bags around me.

I lit a cigarette and listened. I was glad I did because it was rather a pretty tune. I couldn't understand a word of it, mind you, being sung in German. It came to an end and Camellia lifted the needle carefully.

'Well?' she said. 'Isn't that just heavenly?'

'Heavenly,' said Finn. 'Not the witch's tune though!'

I was clever enough to tell her what she needed to hear.

'Just heavenly,' I said, putting my cigarette out. 'Thank you for playing it to me. Now I really must dash upstairs and sort these bags out.'

Finn offered to come and help pack, so I let him. I could hear Camellia play the first few notes of her 'Evening Prayer'. That will keep her happy for days.

I wonder if I need waterproof trousers for Scotland?

CAMELLIA
Good Friday

Nanny Jan has gone. Mummy and Daddy have gone. Old Nanny is here and the house feels peaceful. Cook is staying over Easter to help Old Nanny, staying in the flat next door.

Before Mummy left and while Old Nanny was settling in, she told us that Finn and I were to have our portraits drawn by a Spanish artist. Mummy says he's coming along at the end of April and the pictures shouldn't take longer than a week. I know I'm very good at sitting still, but Finn might have trouble. He often has ants in his pants. I tell Mummy I might show the Spanish artist some of my drawings, and she says only the nice ones. We know what that means!

I've been busy all day listening to the 'Evening Prayer' and finding the notes. It's completely in my head now, and Finn says it is in his as well. It's in my heart too. It starts quite easily, but I soon run into more difficult bits. I just have to keep going.

Old Nanny is sitting in the sun on the terrace, while Finn trundles his wheelbarrow around on the lawn below. I am at the piano, wishing I could do more to add to the tune with my left hand. Annabel will help me with that.

Mercy is nowhere to be seen. This happened before when Old Nanny came to stay. We are having hot cross buns for tea because it's Good Friday, but there's plenty of time for me to walk down to Gran's garden to say hello to the rowan tree. The leaves might be out now.

'Old Nanny,' I say, 'I'm going to run down into Gran's garden to see the rowan tree! I promise I'll be very quick.' Old Nanny says she thinks that sounds like a lovely idea.

If we ever ask Old Nanny's permission to do something, she mostly answers 'Yes, pet, I don't see why not.' It's as if we have all the time in the world to do whatever we want, and I love that. Finn loves her almost as much as I do.

I step into Gran's garden and all around me are tall camellias with their waxy leathery leaves. Some of them have flowers, white, pale pink and others a deeper pink. I put my nose into a pure white flower and it smells of nothing, just the afternoon. What a waste to be so beautiful and have no scent. There are buds on the azaleas and rhododendrons and below them are the bluebell flowers, not yet blue.

There is my rowan tree and it's in the sun. Its feathery leaves are bursting out and such a green! The palest yellowest green *ever.* I look up through the leaves to the sky above, and it's as if I'm in a cocoon. But unlike the poor hunter-horse, I can set myself free at any time. I'm not in a grave.

I search for the lily of the valley under the rhododendron and there are masses of flower bells, still green. In a week or so they will have turned white.

I set off back up the path and there ahead of me is a big black Labrador. I don't know why I call out *Bramble*, because I know it isn't her. This is one of Mercy's ghost dogs. She must have managed to set this one free. I watch as the Labrador walks slowly back up the hill. It's a weary dog and I can see the garden through it. I will follow it so far, but not as far as the graveyard. I'm not that brave!

I have a thought. I wonder if, with Mummy and Daddy away, I might search Daddy's study for Mercy's diary. Perhaps it isn't at Gran's house after all. Perhaps it was always here. I'll ask Old Nanny if that's all right.

We reach the top of the garden. The ghost Labrador wanders off to the left and I run up the drive to the right.

CAMELLIA

Of course, Old Nanny said yes! I've spent about an hour searching this morning. Because I'm not tall enough, I can only reach the lower shelves. Daddy has got some very boring books I must say! Hardly any of them are stories. Lots of big leather books about hunting and the history of hunting, not my sort of books at all. I still take each and every one out, in case there is anything hidden inside.

Daddy's study faces east with a view down to the animal graveyard. I take a breather from my work to climb on to Daddy's chair for a better look, and Mercy appears suddenly. She gives me a shock and I feel like telling her to go away.

Immediately she turns and glides back down the garden. She can read my thoughts! She may have gone away, but now the study doesn't feel friendly at all.

Mrs Betts is calling me through for elevenses. I tear off a piece of my pad to mark my place on the shelf. I don't feel like coming back today.

CAMELLIA
Easter Sunday church

It's Easter Sunday and thank goodness the service is over. If I have to sing one more *Alleluia*, I will go mad! Luckily Mercy didn't cause any trouble. She could have done with all the people here, but not today. I must say Old Nanny has quite a good voice for her age.

Mr Impey is dressed in his white Easter robes, looking like an advert for Fairy Snow. We're in a queue to shake his hand and, when it's my turn, I tell him how well I'm getting on with the 'Evening Prayer'.

'Do you know it by heart?' he asks. Then he mouths the word '*Mercy*' and I whisper 'all quiet.'

'Good,' says Mr Impey.

'But I know she's busy at the end of the garden.'

'So do I,' says Finn. Old Nanny gives us a gentle push.

'Come on, children. Out we go. Good morning, Mr Impey.'

We step out into the morning sun where Gran and Grandpop are waiting. I can't see any magpies about, only a robin on a gravestone, singing his thin song. I wonder how Mummy is enjoying her fishing? I'm very happy with my new Famous Five book, and I shall read it in between my piano playing and diary searching.

I *really* hope we don't have leeks for lunch. Surely Gran's cook will give us carrots and peas with the lamb? It's not the same having Easter lunch with Gran and Grandpop, and I know Finn feels the same.

I miss Mummy.

CAMELLIA

We have finished our lunch, luckily it wasn't leeks, and Gran has said we can get down. She gave us an Easter egg each, but sadly Gran doesn't know that plain chocolate is too dark and bitter for children. Finn made a face when he saw his egg, but I don't think Gran noticed. We politely carry them through to the little sitting room.

I find myself beside Gran's desk again and it gives me a chance to study the little photograph of Mercy. I don't dare take it off the desk, but instead I lean forward as close as possible to take in every detail. This Mercy is very solemn and the background looks as if it's been pencilled in. If only there was a great big colour portrait of her, but I suppose there wasn't time. In this photo, I can't tell whether her eyes are blue or green.

I wander out into the hall, pretending I want to go upstairs to Gran's bathroom. What I'm really interested in is Grandpop's library and, if I could just have a peek inside, I might understand how many books Gran has to search through.

'Looking for something, Camellia?' It's Grandpop's voice.

'Have you got a book about horses?' I think of that question on the spot. He offers to fetch it, and I hover in the hall and wait.

He carries a big green book through to the sitting room, telling me it's a family album of hunter-horses. He goes through them one by one, explaining how many of them once belonged to Gran's father. He shows me a picture of a dark horse called Nara. I know that face with a white star! It's the same hunter-horse who can't get out of its grave.

'What happened to Nara?' I ask Grandpop but it's Gran who answers.

'Nara was a favourite, a big dark brown mare.' I hold my breath waiting for what Gran will say next.

'Isn't she the one buried at the top of the garden?' Grandpop turns the page over, but I turn it back to Nara.

'She broke her leg out hunting and my father had to shoot her.' Gran's voice sounds matter of fact. I am shocked! I can't imagine having to shoot my favourite horse.

'Where did he shoot her?' My voice is quiet.

'In the head,' Gran replies.

'I hope I don't break my leg,' says Finn. He has heard every word.

'I know my father said he didn't want Nara to be fed to the hounds. That's why he buried her.'

Gran sits back down on the sofa. Fed to the hounds? This is getting worse and worse! I feel like marching straight to the top of the garden to scrabble with my bare hands so that poor Nara can be free.

'Would you like to eat a bit of your Easter egg?' Gran asks. I shake my head. I feel rather sick. No wonder Mercy wants to set her free.

Old Nanny notices I need some fresh air. She suggests Finn and I go and find some daisies for a daisy-chain. Once outside, I run down the lawn away from the pond and let out a great wail. The afternoon is *corrupted*! Nara can't get out of her grave. She isn't free. She can't walk into the Light.

Then I know I'm going to be sick. The afternoon spins and I heave into the grass. Old Nanny hurries down the lawn to ask if I'm all right, followed by Finn. Gran and Grandpop are standing on the terrace. I wipe my chin with my sleeve. There's some sick on my shoes. I feel awful but there's something else stirring within me.

It's anger.

CAMELLIA

I'm out of sorts, I know I am. I'm angry and sad at the same time, which leaves very little space for being happy.

Old Nanny was kind to me when I was sick. She said she understood it wasn't nice to hear about the poor horse being shot, that it was a shock to learn how these things were done. She said it was the quickest way when an animal was in pain. I put my hands over my ears. I didn't want to hear *any* more about it.

She said I could walk up the garden by myself, that she would thank Gran and Grandpop for me. Old Nanny knew I couldn't face them. I felt ashamed for being sick and only hoped they didn't think it was the treacle tart. I hadn't even touched my dark chocolate Easter egg.

I trudge very, very slowly up the hill. I try going through the long grass to clean the sick off my shoe, but it's no good. Some of it stays stuck in the holes of my sandals. This is the last straw. I allow myself to cry, letting the tears run down my face. Some of them drip onto my sandals, but not enough to wash away the sick. I cry for myself, even though Gran says self-pity is a sin, but mostly I cry for the poor hunter-horse, Nara. Did she know she was going to be shot? Could she have known what was going to happen?

Why do grown-ups have to be so *mean*? Well, not Old Nanny of course, but how could Gran talk about it so calmly? She might as well have been talking about what she had for breakfast! What about the fox whose tail blood was painted on my face? How *dare* they kill a fox and cut off its tail? I would never, ever cry for the huntsman who broke his arm. Instead I feel a surge of anger giving me power. All my tears dry up and I march on across the drive, heading for the west side of the garden. I don't want to see Gran when she brings Old Nanny and Finn back.

The dogs bark in the grass-run because they know I'm near. I let them out, glad to be able to set them free. I call for them to follow me to the great west oak tree above the ha-ha wall. Then I sit down, leaning back against the trunk and putting my head in my hands.

Mercy must care very much for Nara to want to set her free and, now that I know how Nara was killed, I wonder if I could be brave enough to help her. She has already managed to free one of the Labradors, as well as Bo, so perhaps it's just a question of time.

How much can I tell Old Nanny? Can I trust her about the diary? Can I trust Mrs Betts? Of course, I can trust Mr Impey, and perhaps he might be able to help me search when he comes back for his record player? Could Nanny Jan help search?

Why only me? I'm so weary. My eyes are closing and the next thing I know Finn is there, shaking my shoulder.

'Melia, we didn't know where you were.' I rub my eyes. They are sore from crying.

'Luckily Banger led us to you.' He points at Banger, wagging her tail and panting. He asks if I still feel sick. He pats my head when I say no.

'Don't Finn!' He stops.

'Don't be kind. I'll just start crying again.'

'Don't know what to do then.' His mouth goes down. 'Old Nanny says do you want a cup of tea?' I haul myself to my feet.

'I'll come back then.'

Finn is happy now. While we walk back to the house, he says he ate a bit of his plain chocolate egg, and it was disgusting.

Mercy walks behind us. I can feel her.

CAMELLIA

I sit at the piano practising the 'Evening Prayer'. I can now play it through without a single mistake, well almost. I've made a start on the Sandman's song as that is lovely too.

It's raining outside, a sharp shower as Old Nanny calls it, and the terrace has great big puddles. The cherry blossom tree is being blown to bits, but it's cosy in the nursery. Finn is busy on the carpet, sorting out the animals in his wooden farm.

I tried talking to Old Nanny last night while she was tucking me in. I told her I felt weary from being haunted. I told her about Mercy and the prayer books and magpies, as well as Lorna's birthday party and how I was worried she would make one of the children disappear. I told her about how frightened I was at the bottom of the garden because of the hunter-horse.

I didn't tell her about the diary, and I wasn't quite sure why not. All the time I was telling Old Nanny my worries, Mercy stood staring in her corner. I'm a bit disappointed Old Nanny can't see Mercy actually. It would really help if she could. All the time I was talking, Old Nanny listened patiently, as if she was taking in every word. In any case I was pleased to get things off my chest.

'Camellia,' she said, smoothing the eiderdown with her old hands, 'You are very special, my pet. I am sure there's a very good reason for all of this. Now sleep tight and know that your Old Nanny loves you very much.'

That was very nice to hear of course, but it wasn't enough. I wasn't sure she believed me. As soon as Old Nanny pulled the door shut, Mercy threw a doll off the shelf.

I knew how she felt!

The shower is finished and there are a pair of blackbirds hopping through the puddles. Finn is happy, talking to himself.

'Now where did I put that fat sheep? Ah, here he is.'

I hear the telephone ringing. It rings and rings and nobody answers because Mummy isn't here, or Nanny Jan. I run through to the little room and pick up the receiver.

'Hello?' I say.

'How about playing a duet this afternoon?' says a familiar voice.

It's Mr Impey!

CAMELLIA

We are having a little concert in the nursery! Old Nanny is our audience as well as Banger and Bramble, fast asleep on the carpet. Finn is *not* in the audience because he insists on playing his notes, standing beside me. I limit him to two notes, but every time he gets the second one wrong.

Mr Impey ends the 'Evening Prayer' on his violin with a flourish, and I turn to Old Nanny.

'What do you think?' I ask her.

'Lovely, pet. Really lovely to hear the piano and violin

together.' She gives Finn an encouraging smile as he stands with his finger poised over the D note. Then she goes through to the kitchen to make tea.

'So, do you think you know it by heart?' Mr Impey asks.

'It's in my soul. I know it that well.'

'And that's why you play it with feeling. If you *can't* feel the music, then it's no good at all.'

'I can feel my two notes,' Finn says. 'But I like the first note more than the second one.' He rubs his ear. 'Sometimes the second note hides.'

Mr Impey says practice makes perfect. I know I've been practising and practising! Mercy must have enjoyed hearing the 'Evening Prayer' over and over again, surely?

I want to talk to Mr Impey about the diary and Nara, the hunter-horse, so I tell him that there's a book in Daddy's study for him to see. How do I stop Finn following us? The dogs prick up their ears, sensing movement.

I have a brainwave. I tell Finn I will teach him how to dance the waltz after tea and, in the meantime, can he keep a special look-out for Mercy for me. Finn opens his mouth to say no, but I'm ready for this.

'You can *feel* her, Finn, just like last time, remember? It would be *such* a help. She might be out on the terrace?' That wins him over. He steps outside, putting his head on one side with his eyes shut.

Mr Impey follows me through to the study and I show him all the books I have to search through. The study feels cold.

'And I can't reach the top shelves because I'm not tall enough.'

Mr Impey sees my point. He reaches up for a book. It's a Swallows and Amazons one with a dark green cover.

'Not as good as the Famous Five,' he says, flicking through the pages. 'Ah *hello*.' Mercy has found us. She watches what we are doing from outside.

I tell Mr Impey that the hunter-horse in the ha-ha was called Nara. She broke her leg out hunting and had to be shot.

'Grim!' says Mr Impey, keeping his eyes on Mercy. 'Not

Nara's day.' Then he asks me if we have a step-ladder.

'Perhaps in the garage? What for?' Mr Impey mimes climbing stairs.

'For you, of course. Then you can reach the shelves. You can do a thorough search.' Mr Impey is right of course! A step-ladder is much more useful than a chair. We walk back through the kitchen and Old Nanny says she's made the tea.

'Just two minutes, Old Nanny,' I say. 'I've just got to check something in the garage.' The useful thing about Old Nanny is that she very rarely says *what are you up to*? Mr Impey and I go through.

Finn follows us. He says he couldn't feel Mercy on the terrace, and anyway what are we doing? We tell him we're on the hunt for something, and soon we find it, a paint spattered step-ladder in the far garage. Mr Impey says it will do the job nicely. While we admire the step-ladder, there's a swooping above our heads and a swallow flies up to the rafters. It must be building a nest because there are bits of mud stuck to the wood.

'Swallow,' Finn says. 'All the way from Africa.'

Mercy has appeared beside us. She looks angry.

'She's here, Finn,' I tell him, putting my arm round his shoulders. 'Can you feel her?' Finn goes pale.

'I feel a bit sick actually,' he says quietly.

'Let's go back to the nursery, Finn.'

Mr Impey says to go ahead. If Mercy's in a mood, he can deal with her. We have a quiet tea. I'm not sure what went on between Mr Impey and Mercy, but I don't want to ask.

Mr Impey's off now, taking the record player with him. He promises he will visit Gran on Thursday.

'Thank you, Mr Impey. I'm that weary, I really am.'

'Courage, Camellia! I am on your side.'

He drives away and I burst into tears.

CAMELLIA

I've been busy searching in Daddy's study for three days now. Mummy and Daddy come back from their holiday tomorrow, as does Nanny Jan, so the step-ladder will have to be put back. It hasn't been easy balancing and reaching for books as well as keeping Finn happy. His job is Mercy duty, standing on Daddy's chair to feel if she's outside. She's often there, staring in, but he doesn't see her.

We're on our last morning's search, and it's raining quite hard. I'm searching the second top shelf when I hear Old Nanny's voice calling us through. She says Gran's here to see us. Finn spins round on the chair and I give him a look, clattering down the step-ladder. We don't want Gran to find us here! We might get into trouble.

'Coming!' I shout, waving at Finn to get down off the chair. We run through to find Gran in the nursery. She's dressed in her raincoat and a gardening hat. The hat doesn't really suit her, and Finn is staring. I feel a bit shy going over to give Gran a kiss. The raindrops from her hat drip over my face as she bends forward. I feel her sadness.

'Heavy dew,' she says and I laugh. That's what Daddy always says! She says it's good for the garden.

'I brought this for you,' she says, reaching into a canvas bag. 'I know you were dreadfully upset about the horse, and I'm sorry if I gave you a shock.' My heart expands with love when Gran says this. She understands.

'What is it?' Finn asks.

'I wonder?' says Gran, watching me. 'It's for you to keep.'

I stare in wonder at the little painting. It's of a big, brown horse in a spring field. I know it's spring because the trees are in blossom, and the picture is full of sunshine.

'Is it Nara?' I know it is.

'It *is* Nara. I'm not sure who painted it, but this is Nara in happier times at home in her field.' I turn the picture over and read *Nara 1887*.

'Do you remember her?' I ask. Gran shakes her head.

'She died before I was born.'

'*SHOT*,' says Finn. I glare at him. Finn makes his '*what have I done wrong*?' face.

'Do you like it?' Gran asks.

'I *love* it! Thank you!' I give her another kiss. Then I take the painting over to show Old Nanny. Outside the rain is pelting down and Mercy stands tall on the terrace. She never feels the rain. Old Nanny admires Nara's picture and wonders where it should go, here in the nursery or in my bedroom?

'I think it needs to be in a sunny room because it's a sunny picture. So, what about here?' I point at a space above my new piano.

'I promise I'm still looking for the diary, Camellia,' Gran says. Finn opens his mouth to say something, and I quickly ask Gran if she would like to hear the 'Evening Prayer' on the piano. I wave at Finn to join me. Luckily, he forgets about searching in Daddy's study, if only for a moment. We play it through and Finn does quite well.

'Hansel and Gretel,' he announces to Gran. 'That's what you sing when you're lost in a wood.' He takes a bow.

'What musical children!' says Gran. Her face has a faraway expression. 'It reminds me, there was talk of my mother's being able to play the piano. However, there wasn't a piano in the house when I was growing up.'

'Can you play as well as me?' Finn asks Gran, and at that she really laughs, confessing she cannot. I'm very interested in what Gran says. Mercy could play the piano! I don't know why I didn't guess that before. Now I have proof, well almost.

Gran says she really must be getting home. When Finn says it's still raining, she says she never minds the rain, there's nothing we can do about it anyway. We wave her off and watch her walk across the driveway with Mercy following her.

Old Nanny and Finn go back into the nursery, and I'm left standing in the doorway. Gran disappears into the rain, and I have another thought. I wonder if Nara belonged to Mercy, not Gran's father? And that's why Mercy wants to set her free.

A song thrush begins his song in the copper beech above. He doesn't mind the rain. Mercy is back. She didn't want to follow Gran after all. Instead she glides down to the graveyard.

Nara is waiting for her.

CAMELLIA

I've had my bath and I'm reading my Famous Five book while Mercy is busy making the drawer open and shut. I am quite used to this now and can't believe how much it scared me on Christmas Eve, which seems *ages* ago. Mind you, if she keeps this up, the poor drawer is going to come off its runners!

'Where's your diary, Mercy?' I ask out loud, squinting into the corner, but she has gone. The drawer is quiet, and I return to my book. It's light outside. I never like going to bed while the birds are still singing. Mind you, Old Nanny lets me read for as long as I like, and it isn't term time.

I think about Nara. Who was riding her when she broke her leg? I remember how Mercy stroked the horse's ears, whispering words of comfort. Perhaps there's a proper gravestone there? Would I be brave enough to search for it? It wouldn't be that easy with all the spring grass and nettles, but it might give me the date when poor Nara was buried.

Banger might help. She was good at finding Bo's grave after all. I make up my mind to go down there tomorrow with Banger, and I will tell her to dig. If Mercy wants to help, then I will let her. With a bit of luck Finn will be busy helping Nanny Jan unpack.

I feel proud of myself, having made a proper plan, and take a last look out the window. It's becoming dark now, so the birds are quieter, and there's a strange milky light as if fog is forming. It's thickest at the end of the garden, and I can just make out the shape of a black Labrador running back and forth. I know it isn't Bramble.

I close my curtains. I'm too sleepy for anything now.

ANGELA

Well I only *quite* enjoyed that holiday. Oh, for a holiday when you don't have to be freezing bloody cold the whole time. Gerald had three fish so he was happy. I had one on for a few minutes, but Gerald shouted at me so much, how to keep the rod up and let the fish run, that it got off. I never heard the end of it.

Everything is wonderfully green back in Sussex. Scotland is months behind. Our Sussex oaks are fully out with only the ash to break. Gerald reminded me of the saying: *Oak before ash, we're in for a splash.* We drove through lots of puddles on the way home. It is April after all. How I long for a bit of proper sun.

The children gave me a terrific welcome. Camellia loves her Famous Five book, so at least I got that right. When I asked how Easter lunch went, Camellia stared at her shoes, and Finn told me she was sick. I decided to let that go and ask Nanny about it later.

Finn says he's become a very good piano player. Camellia has worked out the Hansel and Gretel tune, and they can now play a duet. I'm very, very pleased the piano has worked out so well. It should give them endless amusement.

I can hardly bear to think how many things are waiting for me on my desk. All that post and then non-stop telephone calls. And that's before I have to sort out the lunch and dinner menus. I haven't been home five minutes and I'm already feeling overwhelmed.

Nanny can go back to my parents after lunch and then Nanny Jan is due here at teatime. One of my first telephone calls will be to confirm the Spanish artist. He's meant to be starting on Monday. What on earth shall I give him for lunch? What do Spanish artists like to eat? I know Cook doesn't like doing foreign food.

It's all such a worry.

CAMELLIA

I'm on a mission this afternoon. Mummy has taken Old Nanny back in the car, with Finn on board. This means there's only Daddy and me at home. Nanny Jan is not due back until teatime, and Daddy is busy catching up with stuff in his study.

He has *no* idea how much time I have spent in there!

Of course, Daddy can see all the way down the garden from his study window. For this reason, I arm myself with a little blanket, a basket with a trowel, borrowed from Mr Gibbs's greenhouse, and an apple in case I get hungry. Dorothy Baby is under my arm because I want Daddy to think I'm off for a doll's picnic. I don't want him to know what I'm really going to do. I'm going to *dig*!

I call for Banger and she's at my heels at once, running ahead over the sunny lawn, happy as can be. When we reach the graveyard, it's shady and cold as usual. I peer into the ha-ha and worry it's quite a big jump down. I decide it would be a better idea to lead Banger round, over the cattle grid, under the fence and into the field. The grass is already pretty long, and I'm glad I'm wearing my long trousers and cardigan.

We reach the spot where the hoof and head came out and immediately a magpie starts chattering. The chattering is so loud it sounds like guns going off. Another magpie starts up, then another. There's no sign of Mercy. She's leaving this to me.

Banger is panting by my side, her eyes bright. I say *diggy-dig* to her and point at the ground. All around the magpie chattering is deafening, so much so I try to bat the sound away with my arm.

'Yes, I know. I know!'

Banger gets digging, her front paws scratching at the earth. I begin with my trowel, kneeling on the blanket. The ground is quite soft but it's hard work pressing the blade into the thick grass. I manage to cut a square of turf and I slide my trowel underneath, flipping it over like a trap door. I see some roots and two worms. This is going to be a long job!

After about fifteen minutes (I time it) I pause for a rest. We've made a fine old mess! Banger's nose is a pale brown, no longer black, and her claws are thick with mud. My hands are tired from digging and we're getting nowhere! I keep pushing the trowel down into the earth to feel for a big stone but there is nothing, just more mud.

I feel Mercy's presence and look up. There she is above us, leaning into the ha-ha. Banger sits and pants, looking from me to her, not sure whether to carry on digging. We watch as Mercy raises her arms.

All at once I feel a tremendous vibration beneath me and there is a roaring sound as if a train is coming. The earth is heaving yet again, and I throw myself out of the way. Nettles sting my right hand, holding the trowel. I let it go with a cry.

The head is emerging again. I reach out to grab Banger's collar. Luckily, she's worn one ever since she disappeared, and I pull her back. She barks and barks, trying to get at the head and I'm worried she'll get hurt or, worse still, disappear into the grave. The ground heaves and churns in a shimmering blur and I scrabble myself back, dragging Banger with me as best I can. I manage to pick her up and hold her close. She no longer barks. We can scarcely believe our eyes.

In front of us stands Nara, the hunter-horse. She is huge and dark with a white star on her face, and all four legs are strong. She gives a great big shake, the air spinning around her. Mercy joins us in the field, walking slowly. She brings her head close to Nara and strokes her ears just as she did before. I hold on tight to Banger who's wriggling to get free. She's quite a handful.

And then they are gone.

All that's left behind is our muddy mess. That has stayed the same. The heaving grave has completely disappeared, but it's only when I pick up my trowel from the nettles that I notice there *is* something different. At the very edge of our digging area I see a flat stone tipped upright. I lean in to pull it free and read the inscription. The letters are quite clear. They read:

Nara, 1896.

CAMELLIA

So now I know all three of them died in 1896. Mercy, Bo and Nara, the same year that Gran was born. And right now we need the diary. It's the missing piece of the puzzle.

Finn is happy to have Nanny Jan back, and so am I. Of course, he told her about the step-ladder, even when I told him not to. I heard Nanny Jan ask Finn what did he need a step-ladder for, and he told her it was a secret. A bit late in the day, Finn! She's bound to question me about it, but I'll worry about that when it happens.

I have no idea whether Mr Impey has talked to Gran yet, and I don't know what excuse he can use to call here again. I know he would be interested to know how Nara broke free of her grave, and I'm proud that I helped her.

Mummy has said the Spanish artist arrives tomorrow and that he'll draw me first. Mummy knows I can sit as still as a statue! I wonder what he'll be like and if he speaks any English. We need to be ready from ten o'clock and I'm to wear a pretty summer dress and make sure my hair is nicely brushed. Finn's turn will come on Tuesday.

I keep catching myself feeling angry and have to take deep breaths to make it go away. I force myself stop frowning by raising my eyebrows and painting on a fixed smile. Finn tells me I look odd these days. I daresay I do.

It helps if I sit on the lawn by myself. Sometimes I lie on my back, with the daisies all around, looking up at the clouds. Finn often joins me but complains about the ants in the grass. I tell him to go in then, they are not crawling over me.

I can play the 'Evening Prayer' with my eyes closed! I know it *that* well. The Nara painting looks very well above the piano. But why do I want to growl at everyone? It's not like me at all. I must remember to smile for the Spanish artist.

NANNY JAN

Camellia has closed herself off. Finn is just the same as ever and he gave me a lovely welcome back. Camellia smiled, but it's as if her smile is forced. Her hands were dreadfully muddy when she came in for tea. When I asked her what she'd been up to, she looked vague, saying she and Banger had been digging.

I didn't know what to make of that. Then Finn said the pair of them had been using the step-ladder in Mr Devon's study, but that it was a secret. Finn wouldn't make a very good spy!

Old Nanny was gone by the time I got back so I didn't get a chance to exchange news. How do I think the house feels? No better, if you ask me. If anything, it's worse. The atmosphere actually feels dangerous now, as if the whole house is tarnished. I wish my bedroom was more friendly. I can't help feeling that something is hovering, just out of sight. It's not very pleasant and I was glad of Finn's company, to be honest.

The children are to have their portraits drawn tomorrow. Camellia can sit still, but as for Finn! That child has permanent ants in his pants. He told me he actually had real ants in his pants, sitting on the lawn with Camellia. I didn't doubt it.

Although the days are getting longer and more summery, it's as if the house is trapped in winter. The children gave me a welcome, but not so the house. And I'm sure Camellia is thinner, but perhaps that's just because she has grown?

Why do I hear the words *wasting away* in my head? I quickly shrug them off and call the children in for tea.

CAMELLIA

I'm sitting for the Spanish artist! He's called Señor Ordinand and he's stern but quite friendly. I don't think his English is very good. I'm very interested in his easel, his large pieces of paper, his pencils and his artist's bag. I should like one of those!

He tells me to sit on my chair and relax. It's not that easy to relax when you know someone is staring at you, and I feel my frown coming on. We are set up in the dining room, with the big table pushed back. His wife is with us and she wears her black hair in a bun. She's there to entertain me, but I'm happy enough staring off into space. I look through the window at the hedge, and right at this very moment there's a magpie sitting on it.

Señor Ordinand begins his drawing with big sweeps of his arm. He squints at me, then points to himself. So, he wants me to look at him, not the magpie on the hedge. It's as if I'm staring into Nanny Jan's camera. My portrait is beginning!

Mummy comes into the dining room to ask Señor Ordinand
if everything is all right. She likes to check on things, always.

I know Mercy is behind me. That didn't take long for her
to join us. When Señor Ordinand asks his wife to pass over
his artist's bag, I quickly glance round. Mercy isn't behind
me, she's beside me and she's seated in mid-air, ready for her
portrait to be drawn. I think Señor Ordinand would struggle
to draw her though because she's a ghost! You can't make a
portrait of someone you can't see. This makes me smile and his
wife notices, saying *si bueno*.

I sit for a whole hour. At last Señor Ordinand puts his pencil
down and mimes drinking a cup of tea. I nod and run through
to the nursery to tell Nanny Jan to organise something for the
Spanish couple to drink.

'What's it like?' asks Finn in our break.

'You have to sit *very* still,' I tell him. He makes a face.

When I come back into the dining room, Mercy is in *my* seat.
In my head I ask her to move and she doesn't. Señor Ordinand
invites me to sit down and I hesitate.

'*Aqui*,' he says, pointing towards the chair. '*Por favor*.' Mercy
doesn't move, and I'm not sure what to do. I hardly like to sit
on her. Señor Ordinand now looks more stern than friendly, so
I close my eyes and climb into the chair. As I do so, I drop into
a deep sadness. I am immersed in icy cold, and it's terrifying.

Señor Ordinand is busy drawing again while I fight back
tears. I'm so cold that I'm shivering. His wife sees I'm in trouble
and produces a cat glove-puppet, waving it around. It's so ridiculous that I have to smile, in spite of sitting in Mercy's sorrow,
but it's lifting now and I take a deep breath.

I sit for another hour. It takes a lot of concentration to sit that
still. I have absolutely no idea how Finn will manage it.

Señor Ordinand invites me round to view the portrait. I'm
impressed! Already I can see it's me and he has got my eyes.
They are coloured with the lightest of greens. I put my nose
close to my green eyes and say '*Bueno!*' Señor Ordinand laughs.

We have a break for lunch. Mummy takes Señor Ordinand

and his wife out onto the terrace where she has set up lunch under the big umbrella. Nanny Jan, Finn and I are in the nursery of course.

Finn is longing to see the portrait, so we slip into the dining room while the grown-ups are outside. Mercy stands behind the easel and I wonder what she's up to now. I take Finn by the hand and walk over. She steps aside for us to view the portrait.

My eyes are changed to blue.

CAMELLIA

Of course, I get the blame! Señor Ordinand comes back into the dining room to find Finn and me staring at the portrait. Finn gives the game away.

'Blue,' he says, pointing at the eyes. Then he points at *my* eyes and says 'green'.

Señor Ordinand is furious. Anyone can see that. He glares at the picture, his eyes narrowed. He beckons his wife around with a finger, and Finn runs off to find Mummy. I have about a hundred and one butterflies flying around my tummy when Mummy comes in, smoking a cigarette. She too stares at the portrait.

'It's a phenomenon,' Finn says.

Señor Ordinand says something in Spanish. Then he throws his arms about in a temper and picks up his green coloured pencil, waving it in front of me.

'Aqui,' he says. '*Aqui.*' He is *not* amused.

'Camellia, did you do this?' I knew this was coming. I don't answer Mummy, so she turns to Finn. 'Someone must have done this?'

'We were having lunch all the time, Mummy,' says Finn. I don't bother to say anything. Señor Ordinand is busy, studying his pencils. He brings out a dull yellow one and waves it in front of me. I wonder what the Spanish word for sorry is, even though it's not my fault.

I know exactly who has done this and she's there in the corner. She's actually laughing. I turn my back. It's *not* fair.

Señor Ordinand shoos Mummy and Finn out of the room and sets about repairing my eyes with the dull yellow pencil. He beckons me round and shows me my eyes.

'*Aqui*,' he says. My eyes are green once more. I give him a weak smile, praying that Mercy does not play that trick twice. While sitting for my final session of the day, keeping my eyes fixed on the top of the easel, I remember it's not possible to change green into blue. Surely Señor Ordinand knows that? He's an artist after all.

I'm very tired by the time I'm allowed to climb down off my chair. Señor Ordinand is in a good mood again and says '*gracias*'. I'm free to go. I escape to the nursery and collapse on the sofa, telling Finn I desperately need tea and a banana sandwich. That was hard work!

'You wait, Finn. Your turn tomorrow.'

'You didn't change the eyes, Melia,' he says.

'Mercy did it.'

'Can she do that sort of thing?' He looks scared.

'She certainly can.'

'How?'

'Magic. Ghost magic.'

'Bad magic? Bad phenomenons?' Now Finn is panicky. 'Not like the witch in Hansel and Gretel?'

To calm Finn down, I play the 'Evening Prayer' until Nanny Jan comes in with tea and a banana sandwich.

I am so tired of keeping everyone happy.

NANNY JAN

Well yesterday was a day and a half! Today it was Finn's turn to be drawn and I put out his nice white shirt and shorts first thing. He made a fuss about having to wear smart clothes, complaining that the shorts were just the sort of pair ants like to run around in.

I let him wear his long trousers in the end because the Spanish artist is only drawing his top half. Camellia looked paler than ever at breakfast time. Her rosy cheeks have disappeared. It will do her the world of good to have a week by the sea at Middleton. There is nothing like sea air and June will soon come around.

Finn had to have many more breaks than Camellia. I put my head round the door to see how things were going, and Señor Ordinand's wife was putting on a puppet show for Finn, as best she could with that mangy old cat. If anything, she was making Finn wriggle round in his seat even more. I asked Finn how he was doing in the first break.

'Terrible ants,' was his reply. 'I can't sit still.' Camellia looked up from her drawing and made a very good suggestion.

'Why don't I read you a story, Finn? While you're sitting?' She's such a thoughtful child. We wondered if Señor Ordinand would agree to this or if it would put his wife's nose out of joint.

In the end it was agreed that Finn would be entertained by a combination of Camellia's reading and the mangy cat puppet show, while Señor Ordinand grimly carried on, determined to catch a moving likeness.

Mrs Devon left us to it. She drove off to Horsham to find more interesting food for lunch. She said Cook's efforts yesterday were not Mediterranean enough. I didn't know what they had to talk about on the terrace. Mrs Devon's Spanish is pretty non-existent.

After lunch I had a chance to talk to Camellia about how she was feeling and gently touched on the subject of the ghost.

'She's making me tired, Nanny Jan. I never know what she's going to do next.' She put her pencils away in the tin. '*She* changed my eyes to blue and laughed about it afterwards, can you imagine? And Mummy thought it was me.'

I assured her that I did *not*. She thanked me for that.

'She's getting too much for me, Nanny Jan, and I don't want her to hurt Finn. I couldn't bear that.' She paused for a breath.

'You can't see Mercy yet, can you Nanny Jan?' I shook my head. I told her I wished I could, if that would help.

'You can hear her though, can't you?' How could Camellia

know that? I certainly hadn't told her. What was the point of lying?

'I have,' I replied. 'I've heard her crying, mainly in my room. It's not easy to hear. Most nights I hear her crying.'

'She's crying for her baby.' Camellia's face crumpled. 'I know that much. I *have* to find her diary. That's why we were using the step-ladder in Daddy's study.'

'Ah.' It made sense now.

'The diary will tell us what really happened. Gran's looking for the diary too, and I hope Mr Impey will have talked to Gran by now. He said he would. Gran needs to *believe* to see Mercy.'

'Believing is seeing, you mean?' Camellia nodded.

'She's not believing enough. Well, she's believing in the wrong things.' Camellia glanced towards the piano. 'At least I have my Nara picture.' She brought the picture over to me.

'Look Nanny Jan. That's Nara! She was Mercy's horse and she was shot because she broke her leg. Isn't she beautiful? I have set her free. That's what I was doing with Banger at the end of the garden when I came back for tea all muddy.'

I wanted to believe Camellia when she told me this, but there was a part of me that wondered if it was her imagination. It was as if she read my mind because she scowled.

'You don't believe in that, do you Nanny Jan? Well, you can talk to Mr Impey about it. We *both* saw Nara's head. Luckily Finn didn't but he nearly did.' She cradled the picture in her hands and whispered. 'Nara is free and just needs to find her way to the Light.'

Camellia then jumped up off the sofa and went over to the window.

'Look, Nanny Jan!' she cried. 'Mercy and Nara are walking across the meadow, right there, with Mercy's little dog Bo and the ghost Labrador.' Camellia pointed to where she saw them. All I could see was green grass, oak trees and a beautiful sunny day. I shook my head and she smiled sadly.

'I'll talk to Mr Impey when he comes here, I promise,' I assured her. I needed someone to share this with, someone else who had witnessed these strange goings-on. This was out of my depth and experience. Camellia sank back in the sofa.

'Thank you, Nanny Jan.' Then I heard her say in a low voice, almost as much to herself as to me.

'*Because she's growing more powerful.*' She reached out for my arm. 'And I get scared.'

CAMELLIA

Nanny Jan was very kind this afternoon. I hadn't meant to tell her so much but actually it was a relief to own up to how tired and angry I'm feeling.

Nanny Jan can hear Mercy, but not see her. Finn can hear Mercy too because he heard her screaming that night after Christmas. I wish Mercy could actually speak, not just cry. Then she could tell me exactly where her diary is for a start. I make sure I keep writing in my own diary and I don't keep anything back from that. There's stuff in there that would make Mummy's hair stand on end!

I made Nanny Jan promise not to tell Mummy anything. She looked a bit uncomfortable, but she did promise. I know Mummy wouldn't understand and I have a big dread of being seen by another doctor. Even worse, she might send me away! I'm not mad. I'm doing very well, considering.

Señor Ordinand came back for the third day to finish Finn's portrait. Finn doesn't really like his picture and, although there is a *bit* of a likeness, I think his eyes are too big. At least they stayed green! Mercy didn't play any tricks on Finn, but she could have done.

Señor Ordinand has taken the portraits away with him to finish off. They will be returned after two weeks and then Mummy will see about framing them. I'm pleased the Spanish artist has gone. I don't think he understands children very well.

Where *is* Mercy's diary? It *has* to be somewhere! Nanny Jan said this morning that she would help search Daddy's study as soon as we have the house to ourselves again. We have to wait two weeks until Mummy and Daddy go to Spain. On holiday again! At least we are going to the sea in June. Nanny Jan says it can get quite hot then. She says that will bring the roses back to my cheeks. I haven't noticed that I'm pale, but my trousers are definitely looser.

Finn starts school for the very first time on Monday, so I'll have to keep an eye on him. Miss Wiggins won't be happy if he can't sit still at his desk. Mummy says she will take us for Finn's first day. My first day was pretty awful because Mummy was late. I will never forget how everyone stared at me.

I'm in bed writing up my diary. Outside the blackbird is singing and of course it's still light. The last thing I write in capitals is *WHERE IS MERCY'S DIARY*? As soon as I close it, picking up my book to read, Mercy appears in her corner. She points downwards, and I watch as she lowers herself through the floor. This is a new trick!

The kitchen is underneath my room. Is she telling me her diary's in the kitchen? I can't see how, but maybe it's hidden in a cookery book? Did Mercy like cooking? Surely, she would have had a cook?

I haven't brushed my teeth, so I run to the bathroom. When I see my reflection, I'm shocked. My face is almost white and the eyes looking back at me are not green. They are blue. How has Mercy done this? My hands shake, trying to put the cap back on the toothpaste.

I run downstairs in a panic to find Nanny Jan. She's watching television and is surprised to see me in such a state. I slam the door behind me.

'Nanny Jan! My eyes! What colour are they?' Oh, please let her not say blue! Nanny Jan calmly takes me over to the window and smiles.

'The usual green, Camellia.'

I'm so relieved I want to cry. I tell her they were blue in the bathroom. Now it sounds rather silly. Nanny Jan says she will come back upstairs with me, and I find myself whispering 'thank you, thank you' over and over again. She wonders if my blue and white nightdress might have made my eyes seem blue? That can sometimes happen.

When I open the nursery door, Mercy is waiting in the corridor. I hold my arm up to stop Nanny Jan.

'She's here.' Nanny Jan moves forward to peer over my shoulder. Of course, she doesn't see what I see. I watch as Mercy lowers herself through the floor again. In that moment I forget about my blue eyes, because now I know exactly where the diary is.

It's in the cellar.

CAMELLIA
The cellar
Mercy *could* have shown me earlier, but maybe this was always her plan. It's easier to search the cellar than Daddy's study, less likely to get into trouble. We can always make up an excuse about wanting to find something. I say *we* because I know Finn won't want to be left out. I'll tell him we have to find a special book, and that won't be telling a fib.

My biggest fear in the cellar is that the lights will suddenly go off. The light switch is right outside the door, and anyone passing by can flick the switch. Sometimes people turn the light off on purpose! I'll take my torch with me, just in case.

This is my first expedition to find out how much of a job it's going to be. When Banger asks to come with me, I have to carry her down the wooden steps because she doesn't like the gaps in between. She wriggles in my arms and I have to tell her off. My nose is the first to tell me we are below ground, and I pause for a minute, leaning against the wall. Why I feel I have to look between the steps I don't know, but there is someone there. I brace myself.

Mercy is underneath, watching. Why does she have to lurk there and give me a shock? It's not very nice of her. I tramp down the last few steps and put Banger down. She runs off ahead and around the corner, leaving me standing beside the boiler room. Luckily the boiler's quiet. The stone walls are grey and cobwebby, and I bet there are lots of spiders living here. We need Mrs Betts with her duster!

I look around for Mercy, but she has disappeared. I call for Banger and she doesn't come. All I hear is a faint whistling and we know Banger mustn't follow *that*. It's dangerous. I don't want her to disappear again.

'Banger!' I call again. More whistling in front and behind me. Where's she gone now? And do I dare tiptoe ahead?

The lights go out.

'Nanny Jan!' I shout. 'Finn!' I'm in pitch darkness and need to find my torch. Where is it? Which pocket? I have to scrabble to get it out, my hand shaking. It's hopeless to shout in the cellar because *nobody* can hear above ground. We've played this game before. I switch on my torch and find Banger at my feet, her hackles up.

I make myself walk slowly around the corner, shining my torch towards the end wall. I have *never* liked the end wall. It's a dead end with lots of shadows, but at least the whistling has stopped. Where is Mercy? This isn't the time to play tricks. It's *not* fair at all. I'm only trying to help.

I inch forward along the corridor, step by step, and it's then that I hear the coughing, a sort of retching as if someone is about to be sick. It's a dreadful sound and I turn back. No one wants to hear this. It's disgusting! Mercy appears then, gliding into yet another room and I follow. I have to.

We stand in the doorway and Banger goes forward sniffing. The room is jam-packed with stuff and my torch shows how much work we have ahead. There are suitcases and chairs and prams and cots and beds and sun umbrellas, everything in a jumble.

More coughing and then silence. What should I do now? I don't have much time to think because the next thing I know is that the lights are back on. Mercy fades away and there are footsteps clattering down the stairs.

It's Mummy.

ANGELA

I have no idea *what* Camellia thought she was doing in the cellar with Banger. She waved her torch and said she'd been scared when the lights went off.

She told me she was looking for a jigsaw puzzle which I didn't think very likely. She was pretty quick off the mark, asking why was *I* in the cellar? Did I think it was Christmas? Was I after my Christmas tree? Really that was a quite extraordinary question. As if I would be doing that in May! I told her I was looking for some deck chairs to put on the terrace.

'That's nice, Mummy,' Camellia said, giving me a funny look. 'I'll help you find them.' I knew exactly where they were and fortunately they weren't in the bloody jam-packed room. Half the stuff in there doesn't even belong to us. We carted the chairs back upstairs and Banger managed to scamper up by herself.

'Why go down to the cellar on such a beautiful day?'

She scowled and declared she'd been outside most of the morning. She just needed to find her jigsaw puzzle, that was all. I let it go. I had far too many things to do. Jigsaw puzzle, no jigsaw puzzle. I can never see the point of them in any case.

'Go and run around in the sun, why don't you? You really *are* looking pale and peaky. Get some air into your lungs!'

I watched her march out of the nursery door, but not before she had crashed her hand down on the piano.

'Temper!' I shouted, but she was gone.

CAMELLIA

Finn's first day

It's Finn's first day at school and Mummy is driving. At least we're on time and this is because I told Mummy it's very, very important not to be late for a first day.

Finn holds his new satchel on his lap. There's not much in it, just a pencil case with some pencils and colours. Nanny Jan added a handkerchief in case. I told her Finn would be fine with me there.

Miss Wiggins comes forward to greet us and shakes Finn

by the hand. She's wearing quite a summery dress, blue with apricot flowers. She shows Finn his desk which is right at the front. He sits down obediently, and I leave him for a moment to see my friends. It's wonderful to see them again! We're like a great fluttering of birds, all wanting to talk at once.

Miss Wiggins claps her hands and we hurry to our places. I settle down at my desk between Sarah and Annabel, feeling protective of Finn in front. He's got a *lot* of learning ahead of him. Please let Miss Wiggins be kind.

Miss Wiggins welcomes us all back to school and gives the older children half an hour to write in our composition books: *What we did in the holidays?* I wonder what on earth to write? The magpies in church, Nara coming out of her grave, the ghost Labrador, the Spanish artist, my eyes changing colour, Mercy lowering herself through the floor, playing the 'Evening Prayer'? I decide on the Easter magpies because at least other people saw them.

It's very hard sitting next to your friends when you can't talk, and you have so much to tell. I feel ready to burst! Sarah keeps nudging me and smiling and Melanie-Anne's right behind, humming *'Frere Jacques'* quietly under her breath.

I pause for a moment in my story. I'm at the place where the magpie disappeared in front of our very eyes. Will this be too much for Miss Wiggins? I wouldn't like her to think I was lying. Perhaps I'll leave that bit out. I certainly won't include Mercy throwing prayer books around. I'm having to hide a lot of stuff from people! I *hate* not being believed.

At break-time I make sure Finn knows where to get his milk and biscuit, happy to see him chatting to one of the new boys. Finn never finds it difficult to make friends. We run through to the main hall and at *last* I can talk to my three best friends. We sit on the stage as usual.

'You're looking a bit thin, Melia,' Sarah says. Annabel makes a face.

'If you grow as fast as me, you can look thin sometimes,' says Annabel who is very tall for her age. I say I hadn't really noticed. I fill them in with the latest news. Melanie-Anne loves hearing about Nara rising up from her grave.

'Gosh, that sounds super!' she says. 'I would have loved to have seen that.' Sarah gives my eyes a close inspection when I explain about the portrait. Annabel is especially interested in the 'Evening Prayer' of course. She says she'll try and help me with the left hand.

'The diary's in the cellar!' I cry, smacking my knees. 'I'm not going to tell Gran though, just in case I've got it wrong.' Everyone agrees that's sensible, and I don't want Gran telling Mummy I'm searching in the cellar.

I ask if any of them want to help search and Sarah's the first to say yes. She actually puts her hand up! Melanie-Anne confesses she finds dark cellars *unbelievably* frightening and Annabel has always hated going underground. So Sarah's the one!

Finn comes over to say hello. We've finished our meeting and Sarah kindly welcomes him up. Finn is over the moon. Annabel asks him if he has found any magpie feathers lately.

'No more magpie feathers,' says Finn. I ask how he's feeling on his first day at school.

'Exhausted!' he says with a great sigh. Sarah pats the top of his head gently.

'You wait till long divisional sums of money!'

Miss Wiggins rings the bell to call us back, and Finn yawns. I bet Nanny Jan picks us up, not Mummy. I bet Mummy's too busy trying on new clothes for her holiday in Spain.

Sure enough, Nanny Jan collects us and is the first to hear about Finn's morning.

NANNY JAN
The telephone call
When Mrs Devon was out this morning, I found Mr Impey's telephone number in her address book. I felt a bit guilty, going behind my employer's back as it were, but only momentarily. The children were at school and Mrs Betts was upstairs, so I took the opportunity there and then to pick up the telephone.

Mr Impey answered on the second ring!! I apologised for disturbing him but he said not to worry, he was only writing his next sermon, or at least thinking about it. He said the Sundays after Easter tend to be rather flat and uninspiring.

When asked, he said he did indeed witness a strange phenomenon. So, the horse's head episode was completely true. I explained that Camellia's latest quest was to find the ghost's diary, hidden somewhere in the cellar, and that she was determined to find it.

'And a good thing too,' said Mr Impey. 'Once this diary is found, wherever it is, it will encourage Camellia's grandmother to accept her ghost. I've tried having a conversation with her, but she's not budging in her belief that ghosts are sent from the Devil.' Mr Impey laughed, adding 'As if!!'

'Oh dear,' I said. 'Camellia will be disappointed when I tell her that. About her grandmother, that is ... not the Devil!'

I heard Mr Impey sigh down the telephone.

'What Camellia needs is as much fun and joy as possible to offset the worry. Of course, we are taking her situation seriously, but we must be careful not to be seen to take it *too* seriously, otherwise the poor child will be overwhelmed. Encourage her to talk to you as much as possible.' I said I would.

'Now has a day been set for the Great Diary Hunt?'

I told Mr Impey that the Saturday after next was the day. By good fortune that was the day after Mr and Mrs Devon were flying to Spain. We would have the house and cellar to ourselves.

'Capital!' Mr Impey said. 'I'm writing it in my diary right now. I can be over in the morning and spend all day helping if you like. We might have a few musical breaks and of course I wouldn't say no to nursery lunch.' I laughed.

'So that's Saturday, 18th May. I know we will find it and then all will be revealed.'

I'd forgotten to mention Camellia and the worry about her eyes changing colour, so I put this to Mr Impey at the end of our conversation.

'In that case,' he said, 'Time is of the essence. We don't want poor Camellia being taken over.'

'Taken over?' I wasn't sure what he meant.

'Possessed, Nanny Jan. Possessed. I am sending her a blessing even now.' With that he rang off.

I put the telephone down, feeling rather shaken. I was torn between keeping my promise to Camellia and my responsibilities to Mrs Devon. But it didn't take long to make up my mind. I was supporting the children.

I think we might give Mr Impey shepherd's pie for lunch when he comes. Everyone loves shepherd's pie.

CAMELLIA

Nanny Jan has told me that Mr Impey's going to help us search for the diary. That's the best news ever, because he'll make it fun. So, the hunting party will be Nanny Jan, Mr Impey, Sarah, Finn and me.

Nanny Jan gave me the good news while Finn was upstairs. We have agreed not to tell him until Saturday morning. This is because Finn can give the game away, more often than not actually, and I don't want Mummy to know about any of this. All Finn knows is that Sarah is coming over to play.

I haven't been down to the cellar again because I don't want to hear that dreadful coughing. Also, it's not much fun being down there on your own. It's a big relief to know Mr Impey and Nanny Jan are on my side.

As for Mummy, I don't know what to think. It's like I'm being judged for not being what she wants me to be. It's tiring and boring having to act the perfect daughter. Sometimes I feel she talks a different language, and I don't understand what she really means. What's important to her is not that important to me. I wish I could kick that blasted telephone right out of the house. Then perhaps she would notice the two children right under her nose.

Finn's getting on quite well at school. Miss Wiggins has just about got over the shock that he isn't like me at all. He doesn't want to learn all the time, not by any means. He's just himself.

I can tell Mercy is impatient. I think it annoys her that I'm not hunting in the cellar already. She lowers herself through my bedroom floor several times an evening, often when I'm reading my book. As soon as she's gone through the floor, she's back again. I've told her we will be searching next Saturday.

This evening I write her a message in my diary: *Go and play with your ghost dogs.* I hold the diary up with the page facing towards her, and she can't resist. I watch her glide down to the graveyard and wish her well, sending love for whatever she has to do. I hold Mr Fox close and we bless her together. He looks much more handsome these days and his yellow eyes have softened.

'Dear Mr Fox,' I say. 'You can come and read my book with me.'

Within minutes Mercy is back, beckoning me over to the window. I tiptoe over and she steps back to let me see.

On the lawn there are three Labradors, two black and one yellow, chasing each other in a great game. Bo runs to join in, and they welcome him, running round and round. We stand together, Mercy and I, and watch the four of them enjoying their freedom, their legs young and strong and tails wagging. We watch until one by one they fade away into the air.

There's nothing more to see, nothing more than the empty lawn. I rest my chin on my hands in case they appear again, but my feet are getting cold, so I go back to bed. Mercy is back in her corner when I put my book down. She will watch me fall asleep.

She's done well today.

CAMELLIA

I don't feel well this morning, as if I've got a sore throat hovering, prickling on one side. Nanny Jan feels my forehead at breakfast and tells me it isn't hot. We know this can't be chickenpox!

My battery's running flat, I just know it. I don't know why I'm getting thinner because I'm eating enough. Nanny Jan has noticed, always encouraging me to have second helpings. She measured us against the door in the larder yesterday and I've grown half an inch since Christmas. Finn hasn't.

There's a strange feeling in the middle of my chest, a sort of dull ache. It's not always there but, when it is, I want to cry. Big deep breaths help, the same as when I'm angry, but I'm getting funny looks at school when I do my sighing. I probably look like a fish on the bank. Sometimes I can't get enough air, even though there's lots around me. If I think about it too much, it makes it worse, so I try *not* to think about it.

I can't *wait* for Saturday. Time is ticking by so slowly. I wish it would hurry up, but then I remember Old Nanny warning us never to wish our days away. I'm trying not to. One day at a time.

After lunch I feel better and go outside. It's very warm with a gentle breeze. I lie on my back, studying the little clouds in the sky. I know they are fair-weather clouds because they're wider than they are tall and mostly white. Finn comes to find me and frowns at the grass. He's wearing shorts and doesn't dare risk sitting down. Nanny Jan comes to find us. What do we think about having our walk in Gran's garden today? We can collect azalea flowers on a stick. I love doing this, but Finn is never as keen.

'I can say hello to my rowan tree,' I say, rolling on to my tummy. 'It must have flowers now.' I remember how Gran said the lily of the valley scent was delicious. They must be out now, surely. I also remember how she said Mercy loved them.

'I shall look for very important things,' Finn says, and Nanny Jan thinks that's a very good idea.

'I must buy a colour film for my camera,' she says. 'Black and white doesn't do justice to the gorgeous colours.' I have an idea.

'I'll take my pad and colours. Then I can draw a beautiful picture.' Of course, Finn wants to do the same. I sigh because I am tired of giving Finn art lessons.

He runs back to the nursery to find some pencils. There's no getting out of it.

CAMELLIA
The garden

We make our expedition into Gran's garden, the dogs running ahead. Once over the drive and into the garden, we step into a world of colour and birdsong. Our feet are guided along little paths, between pink, white and purple rhododendrons and further along bright yellow azaleas which smell tangy and warm. The bluebells are at their very best, a shimmering mass of blue.

'Ooh, smell those bluebells!' Nanny Jan says, stopping in wonder. Finn takes a great sniff and says he can't smell a thing. I can't either. Nanny Jan must have a special bluebell nose.

I'm searching for something to draw. I turn right along the path that leads to the rowan tree and I find it, standing alone, its flowers a soft cream and alive with bees. I manage to find a flower without a bee and breathe in the scent. It does *not* smell as sweet as a rose, more like hawthorn which we all know smells of old socks. The bees obviously don't mind because they are as busy as can be.

'Melia!' It's Finn. 'Where are you?'

'I'm here,' I call back. 'Under my rowan tree.'

Finn appears in the clearing, carrying his blanket.

'Where *are* you?' he calls. He's looking straight at me.

'I'm *here*, right in front of you!' What on earth is Finn going on about?

'Where?' Finn looks from side to side.

Mercy has appeared, the other side of the rowan tree. I see her blue eyes quite clearly today, and they are focused on Finn.

'I'm *HERE*!' I shout. Mercy moves off towards the lily of the valley, flicking her skirts. Her dress has changed colour. It has become pink.

Banger scampers up and luckily she knows it's me. Her tail is wagging. I move towards Finn, afraid now. I don't think he can see me. Where have I gone? Have I become invisible? It's not another go of the Alice Syndrome, is it?

'Finn!' I cry again. 'I'm *here*!' He looks straight through me, and then he turns back.

'Nanny Jan! Nanny Jan!' His voice is full of fear.

Where am I? Surely, I am here.

'Where are you, Finn?' It's Nanny Jan now. She appears in the clearing with her basket. She says she'd been taking some photos.

'What's the matter, children?'

'I can't find Melia,' Finn is close to tears.

'Why here she is,' Nanny Jan replies, pointing at me. 'Here's your sister.' I feel rather faint, so I sit down right in the middle of the bluebells. Banger sits on my foot.

'Where were you?' Finn asks crossly.

'I was here all the time, Finn. I was here all the time.'

I hear laughing and it's not Nanny Jan or Finn. The laughing is coming from the lily of the valley.

'Stop laughing!' I shout over my shoulder. Nanny Jan and Finn stare at me as if I'm mad. My chest hurts so I have to do one of my big sighs. I gasp for air like a fish. Finn spreads his blanket out and sits beside me.

'Let's have our picnic now, Nanny Jan,' he says. 'Melia needs a jaffa cake, and so do I.'

So, we sit under the rowan tree with the bees buzzing over our heads. All the time Mercy stands in the shade of the rhododendrons watching us. I don't really feel like drawing now. I feel more like going to sleep.

'You were playing hide and seek, weren't you Melia,' says Finn. It's easier to say yes so that's what I do.

But Mercy and I know this wasn't hide and seek. This was another trick and it wasn't kind.

NANNY JAN

It's strange how one moment you can be having a perfectly happy time, enjoying a sunny afternoon in the garden and the next you are tipped into a whirl of fear, a fear that came from nowhere.

The fear was all around Camellia and the rowan tree. I could actually feel it. No wonder Finn was bewildered. Camellia by this time had collapsed in a heap, declaring that she wanted to sleep. Finn and I heard her shout *stop laughing* to no one in particular, we could hardly not as a matter of fact. But we let it go. Finn was keener on the jaffa cakes by this stage.

I tried my best to persuade Camellia to take up her pad and pencils. In the end she stayed put under the rowan tree, while I walked Finn down the garden. He complained he wanted Camellia to get him started, but I told him Camellia needed a bit of peace, anyone could see that.

After a short while, we made our way back and found her fast asleep, pad on knee, pencil in hand. I whispered to Finn to keep quiet, while we crept round to view Camellia's picture.

It was of her ghost. This Mercy had a smile but with angry blue eyes, eyebrows in a thick line. Around the figure she had drawn what looked like giant white bluebells. The background was as dark as plain chocolate, matching the pencil in her hand.

'Is it Mercy?' Finn asked in a loud, theatrical whisper. It was enough to wake Camellia up.

'It's Mercy,' she confirmed, yawning. 'It's always Mercy.'

'How come?' Finn asked.

'I can't get away from her these days.' She began to pack away her pad and pencils.

'Let's go back home,' I suggested, feeling the fear surround us yet again, and aware now of a faint ticking sound. I tried to keep calm as I chivvied the children along, but the afternoon air was becoming dense and claggy, as if it might suffocate us at any moment. I knew it wasn't healthy. We needed to get away, right away to the fresh air at the top of the hill. I grabbed Finn's hand.

'Not before I pick some lily of the valley,' Camellia said sleepily, and we had to watch her walk as if in a dream across the clearing. I managed to push Finn a little way uphill in the meantime where the air was clearer. I wished Camellia would hurry up, but no, she took her time.

We had to wait while she bent down beneath the shade of

the big red rhododendron. Come on, Camellia, come on! I was about to run and fetch her, not wanting to wait a moment longer, but then suddenly she was beside us. In her hand she held a pretty white posy, surrounded by smooth pale leaves. She buried her nose in the flowers, taking a deep breath.

'I know this so well, Nanny Jan!' she cried, offering it to us to sniff. I thought it was like a delicious soap and said so.

'Let's take them back and give them some water, and then we can decide where to put them.' The sooner we left the garden the better. I actually wanted to run!

At last we were on our way, walking briskly, back across the drive and into our garden. Camellia declared she wanted to put them on the piano beneath Nara's picture.

Once back home she did exactly that. Then she ran over to me, her eyes full of tears.

'Mercy loves them so, you see.'

She took a deep breath and put her hand on her chest.

'But their scent makes me cry.'

ANGELA

I think it's fair to say I *really* need this holiday. To be able to get away for two whole weeks in the sun, leaving everything behind, will be absolute bliss.

Mrs Day has made me some summer dresses in super colours, so I won't let the side down in Spain. I must remember to pack my hat, actually I'll wear it on the plane so as not to squash it.

Finn seems to have settled in well with Miss Wiggins, and of course we never have to worry about Camellia. She picks new subjects up very quickly and I'm pretty sure she's Miss Wiggins's favourite. I'm proud to have such a clever daughter. If only she wouldn't frown so!

I have to say I *am* worried about Camellia's general attitude and health, in spite of her intelligence at school. I'm pretty used to being ignored by her. Mind you I say that, but it would be nice if she could pay a bit more attention every once in a while, and if she could be a *little* less serious. If she's still as pale and peaky when we get back from our holiday, I'll ask Dr Byng to give her a check over.

No chance of my being pale and peaky once back from Spain, at least I had better not be. I absolutely love the sun and can't get enough of it. The wonderful thing about this holiday is that I'm not expected to ride a horse or shoot anything. Our plans are to sit in the sun, swim, visit bodegas in Jerez and have lunches and dinners with friends. And plenty of siestas, I hope!

Nanny Jan will hold the fort beautifully I know. She can drive very well and is therefore capable of ferrying the children wherever and whenever. Camellia has her little friend Sarah coming over on Saturday, so with a bit of luck that will cheer her up.

Then in June the children go to Middleton. The sea air should do wonders for Camellia. In fact, I will hold off ringing Dr Byng until after that. We do want Camellia to be well for her birthday party on 11th June. I'm going to order a tent for the lawn so that, even if it rains, we can have tea in the garden. That reminds me I must organise a trip to the art shop in London. I thought I would buy Camellia an oil painting set for her birthday. She's going to be seven after all. Then after Camellia's birthday, it's Ascot. Honestly, it's non-stop.

As long as I write things down in my diary, they get done. Heaven knows what I'd do if I lost it. It doesn't bear thinking about! Now where's Mrs Betts? She doesn't need to do the drawing room today because I need her to help with my packing.

I wonder if I need two pairs of sunglasses? Just in case?

CAMELLIA

What happened under the rowan tree? Why was I invisible to Finn? I hardly remember drawing Mercy in the lily of the valley. I certainly don't remember making her eyes as cross as that, even with a smiling mouth. Those two don't usually go together! But perhaps they do if you wear a *mask*. I practise smiling and frowning in the mirror and it's hard. In fact, I look more like a dog snarling. Mummy would have something to say about that I'm sure.

The lily of the valley sits on my piano and, whenever I play, I catch a trace of the soapy scent. Gran said how much Mercy loved them, and that's why I picked my posy. I keep on practising the 'Evening Prayer', with or without Finn's help, and I've managed to add single notes with the left hand.

Mercy has taken to walking up and down the corridor. I know this because Nanny Jan says she hears footsteps in the night. Finn hears nothing and nor do Mummy and Daddy. Now that Nanny Jan hears footsteps and crying, I told her she'd be seeing Mercy next. Poor Nanny Jan! She gave a great shiver.

'I tell you, Camellia,' she said yesterday, once we had waved Mummy and Daddy off. 'I'm scared about going down into the cellar.'

'I will look after you,' I said, feeling very grown-up.

'Will there be magpies?' I felt sorry for Nanny Jan then. She really doesn't like them.

'You never can tell. But we'll have Mr Impey, and he's always so funny! He can protect us with big magic if Mercy's naughty.'

Of course, Mercy heard me, appearing beside Nanny Jan. With a small flick of her hand, she made the piano lid slam down. When poor Nanny jumped, I could tell Mercy was very pleased with herself. Nanny Jan hadn't been expecting it, but I had.

'Like that!' I said.

'So, she's capricious,' Nanny Jan had just about recovered.

'Capricious?' I asked. 'I don't know what that means. No, don't tell me. I want to look it up in Daddy's dictionary right now.'

I ran through to the study and found the word.

CAPRICIOUS: someone who is capricious changes their mood unexpectedly. Mercurial, unpredictable, changeable, impulsive.

That's Mercy! She's all of those things. She's capricious which means you never know what she's going to do next.

No wonder I'm tired.

CAMELLIA

At last it's Saturday and we're all set to go down to the cellar. Nanny Jan has made sure we all have torches in case Cook, or more likely Mercy, switches off the lights.

Mr Impey is in his home clothes and I notice Finn admiring his lemon yellow shirt. Nanny Jan suggested we wear scruffy clothes today, as searching might be dusty work. Sarah never looks scruffy and is wearing a pink and white tee shirt with blue trousers. She's ready for business though and says as much.

I'm nervous about the day, but very proud to have my team with me. I haven't seen Mercy this morning, but I'm hoping she's busy at the bottom of the the garden, talking to her animals. It's raining but of course we know that she doesn't mind that one bit.

Mr Impey says he wants to bless our Great Diary Hunt. Immediately Finn's expression changes. He frowns.

'I thought you said we were looking for a book, Melia.'

'Yes, we are. A diary is a book.' As I say this, I know the diary is hidden *in* a book, a real book. Mr Impey raises his hands for quiet, shutting his eyes.

'I bless this happy team of five. May we be successful in the cellar, supporting one another, and may the house and spirits remain tranquil.' He opens his eyes. 'And may I make a request for second helpings of shepherd's pie at lunchtime!' Nanny Jan laughs, as do we all.

Then Mr Impey leads us down the stairs into the cellar.

CAMELLIA

Finding the chest

We follow Mr Impey along the corridor, round the corner and stop outside the jam-packed room.

'This is it,' I say and Mr Impey peers in.

'Is there a light in this room?' he asks. We look up at the ceiling and there's nothing.

'Fair enough,' says Mr Impey.

It's agreed that everything will need to be brought out of the room in order to check it properly. Mr Impey says he'll start in the right hand corner, and perhaps Nanny Jan could help him move the sides of an old cot. Big things will be carried by Mr Impey and Nanny Jan, medium things by Sarah and me and Finn will carry the really important small stuff. Any trunks, cases or boxes will be taken into the alcove opposite the boiler room. They will need to be gone through later.

I'm impressed with Mr Impey's organisation. We're soon trooping in and out of the room, carrying whatever needs to be stacked or sorted. Mr Impey is the conductor, telling us what to do. He does a lot of shining his torch around the room.

Sarah's loving this, I can tell. No sign of Mercy at this stage and I'm a bit surprised to be honest. We're doing exactly what she wants after all, and I thought she might have liked to watch us work. I feel very loved and supported by the hunting team. Who needs to hunt a fox when you can hunt a diary in the cellar? I say this to Sarah as we cart a small wooden casket through into the sorting area.

'I think foxes are lovely,' she says, puffing.

'Specially Mr Fox!' I laugh, putting the chest down carefully. 'It just shows. He got mean and mangy because he wasn't loved.'

Suddenly I'm freezing! It's as if I've stepped into an ice bath. I ask Sarah if she can feel it and she nods. Then the dreadful coughing starts.

'Ugh,' says Sarah. 'That's an awful cough!'

'I think it's got something to do with this wooden chest.' I try to brush the dust off. 'Let's see if I can open it.' I pull and pull at the lid, but it's locked.

'Where's the key?' Sarah asks. I have no idea. More coughing.

Mr Impey comes round the corner at that moment. He stops dead, putting his head on one side. He's heard something too. His yellow shirt is covered in dust and cobwebs.

'Who's coughing?' We both shake our heads, and it stops.

'We need a key for this,' I tell Mr Impey, showing him the wooden chest but, before he can say a word, Nanny Jan comes running round the corner, followed by Finn.

'I swear there's a magpie in there! Terrible fluttering!' She's panting with fear, making little gasps. Finn pats her hand.

'There, there, Nanny Jan,' he says. 'Not to worry.'

Mr Impey strides back into the room to investigate and returns with the news that all is quiet.

'I think this is *just* the right time to take a break from hunting,' he announces. 'We're over halfway in any case. Let's return to the daylight for coffee and biscuits.' He looks hopefully at Nanny Jan who collects herself with a deep breath. Then she leads us away from the past, back up the stairs.

I'm last in line, knowing full well that there's someone or something behind me. I turn to see Mercy bent over the little wooden casket. She knows what's in there.

The lights go off, and immediately the coughing starts. I don't want to hear that again, so I run blindly on, feeling for my torch. I'm lucky there's enough light on the stairs for me to pound up, away from the darkness. Who played a trick with the light switch this time? I find the switch and it's on. The switch is on, but the lights are off. Perhaps Mercy prefers to work in the dark.

When I walk into the nursery, Finn is showing Sarah his little farm and Mr Impey is playing the piano. I wait for Mr Impey to finish his piece and then I make my announcement.

'The diary's in the little wooden casket.' All eyes are on me. 'We just need the key.'

CAMELLIA
The laugh

Mr Impey offers to go straight back down to the cellar, there and then, that's if we want to see the wooden casket during our elevenses.

'The lights have gone off,' I say. 'That is, even though they're switched on, they're still off.' Mr Impey raises his eyebrows.

'Mercy made the lights go off, I'm sure of it,' I say. 'She's down there now. I saw her. It might be better to leave her to it, just for the moment.' I put my torch back in my pocket. 'Who knows, the lights may come back on again after our break.'

Mr Impey agrees and plays us another tune while Nanny Jan brings in the trolley. We have milky coffee, orange squash, milk and a tin of biscuits. We tuck in, and Mr Impey says the hard work has made him hungry.

I am quiet. Now I'm so close to finding the diary, I am full of dread rather than excitement. I must keep cheerful because Sarah's here. I mustn't run out of energy. I must keep going. Nanny Jan notices me lost in my thoughts.

'Penny for them, Camellia?' she asks. I decide to be honest.

'I'm scared of what I might find.'

'So am I,' says Finn. 'It's very worrying.'

'What if it's awful?' My voice is a whisper. I don't want to say it, but I do. 'What if there are really horrible things in it?'

'Then we will understand,' Mr Impey says. 'I'm sending Mercy love even as I eat this biscuit.' He munches. 'And lots of understanding of course. Often one of the best things you can say to anyone is *'I understand.'* He gets up from the sofa and asks which one of us will be the first to follow him back into the cellar. Of course, it has to be me.

'Lights are back on, I see,' he says, flicking the switch. 'Torches at the ready, everyone, in case Mercy chooses to plunge us into darkness.'

We troop down the stairs, back into the past, wondering what we will find. Will Mercy be there beside the wooden chest, or will she have gone? We find she has gone but the chest is tipped onto its side. Mr Impey sets it right. Then he tries to open it, but the lid remains shut.

The lights go out. We are in the dark. Here we go again.

Nanny Jan gives a scream, gasping that if she hears any flutter-ing right now, her legs will give way, she just knows it. Instead of fluttering, there's a distinct sound of loud whistling with a high-pitched cry, followed by a sort of scrabbling at our feet.

'I don't like it!' Finn is the first to react.

'If that's a *rat*...' Nanny Jan's voice rises in panic. Sarah's hand reaches for mine and Mr Impey snaps on his torch.

'Calm,' he says, shining his beam into the shadows. 'Calm, and even more calm.' He makes a sign of the cross. 'We understand,' he says. 'We have come to help.' We hold our breath. 'Don't be scared,' he adds.

'Who are you talking to?' Finn asks.

'Mercy, of course. She's as scared as you are. More so in fact. Her story is about to be discovered.' I hear Finn whispering.

'So what?'

How dare he?

'So a *lot*,' I shout angrily. 'So a bloody *LOT*!'

'Camellia!' cries Nanny Jan.

'Well, it's all too bloody much. Don't think I haven't heard that word. I hear it a lot out hunting.' Sarah lets go of my hand because my fists are in balls. I am about to explode. Here we are in the cellar with the lights not working, Mercy's wooden chest at our feet, no key, and I'm getting told off for saying the word bloody.

'*BLOODY, BLOODY, BLOODY!*' I shout out loud.

'And *BUM!*' That was from Finn.

'Children!' Nanny Jan now.

Mr Impey roars with laughter. He tells us to give it some welly. As long as we don't take the Lord's name in vain, we can swear till kingdom come.

'*DAMN!*' shouts Sarah joining in. Mr Impey says that's more like it. Let it all hang out. I feel laughter bubbling up inside me.

'*POO POO PANTS!*' yells Finn.

'Blast?' offers Nanny Jan. She doesn't want to feel left out. From far along the passage there's a peal of laughter. I know it's Mercy.

'Did everyone hear that?' Mr Impey shines his torch around. 'That goes to show. Ghosts find swearing funny. We've made Mercy laugh and we all heard it. We are getting somewhere.'

The lights come back on, and Mr Impey turns to Nanny Jan.

Does she want to carry on? She and Finn can be excused, if they like. Nanny Jan looks a bit flustered after all the swearing. I'm sure they didn't teach her that at Nanny School.

It's decided that Mr Impey, Sarah and I will carry on with the clearing. We stand together listening to Nanny Jan's and Finn's footsteps as they go back upstairs. Mr Impey claps his hands and tells us we are the famous *Three Key Hunters* and that we must seek intuitively. When I ask what that means, he replies: 'From the heart, Camellia. From the heart.' How we can expect to find a key in all this junk I have no idea, but Mr Impey is not downcast.

'Seek and ye shall find,' he says.

After an hour of seeking intuitively, we have not found the key. As Mr Impey carries the wooden chest up into the light, I can smell the shepherd's pie and am pleased to feel my tummy rumbling. I'm truly hungry.

Mr Impey puts the chest down, declaring it made of the finest oak. It's heavy enough. Nanny Jan asks Mr Impey if he would like a drink and he says he would *love* a glass of sherry, as dry as possible. He thinks he deserves it. I remember the Spanish artist drank sherry before lunch, so I run through to the drawing room to fetch it.

Once Mr Impey has sherry in his glass, he asks Nanny Jan if she will join him. She laughs, shaking her head.

Mr Impey raises his glass to me, takes a sip and says '*Olé!*'

'Is that a swear word?' asks Finn. Mr Impey laughs heartily.

'No Finn. It's Spanish for *Bravo!*' He opens his arms wide to include all of us and raises his glass again.

'*Olé* to Mercy! We shall not let you down.' He has said exactly the right thing. He always does. I allow myself to relax a little during lunch. The shepherd's pie is delicious as usual and Mr Impey has thirds. I'm going to ask Nanny Jan to carry the chest up to my room this evening, and somehow or other I will find a way to open it, key or no key.

Outside it has stopped raining and the sun shines brightly on the terrace puddles, reflecting dazzling spots of silver and gold.

I open the French windows and take a deep breath.

The magpies are back in the tree. They chatter as if to say *We know you are nearly there.*

NANNY JAN

We left the children playing in the nursery while Mr Impey and I put everything back into the jam-packed room. They were understandably tired and, honestly and truly, we got the job finished quicker without them. I only hope Mrs Devon doesn't spot that things have been moved. Luckily there is no light in that room.

Camellia asked for some of Mrs Betts's beeswax polish, together with a duster, and she and Sarah cleaned and polished the little chest until the wood shone. It's such a shame the key is missing. The brass lock is strong and one hardly likes to force it. The chest is quite heavy, so there's something in it for sure.

I promised Camellia I'd carry it upstairs for her, that she could store it in her bedroom cupboard. We have two weeks until Mrs Devon gets back, giving us plenty of time to worry about what we say. I asked Camellia if she wanted to tell her Gran she'd found the chest, but she said no. For now she wanted to keep it to herself.

Once Mr Impey and Sarah had gone home, we sat on the sofa and watched television. We were quite exhausted and I couldn't help feeling guilty. I'm now complicit in encouraging Camellia with the supernatural, having been expressly told by Mrs Devon to quash any such goings-on.

I'm holding on to the belief that Mr Impey, our own vicar, deems it important and indeed essential to help Camellia and her ghost. Goodness, he's funny. How he made us all laugh! And when the children shouted those swear words, well I didn't know what to think! He said I could telephone him any time, if anything untoward happened, or if I or the children were frightened. I must say that was a great comfort. Who would have thought I've now heard a ghost cry, walk and laugh.

I couldn't have said that before Christmas! I dread seeing her, if truth be told.

I can't wait to take the children to Middleton. Oh, for some sea air to blow the cobwebs away, and what Camellia needs is to play on the beach in the sun. I didn't say anything when I last saw her in the bath, but her ribs are showing, quite distinctly. It isn't as if she isn't eating.

Not so Finn who's as sturdy as anything!

CAMELLIA

Nanny Jan carries Mercy's wooden chest upstairs, because it's far too heavy for me. It weighs a ton! I actually think it's got heavier. This might be because of what's in it, but I suppose the actual wood might be very thick. We're not going to know until the key is found.

I'm near, and yet so far. The chest sits in front of my dressing table, newly polished and gleaming. Finn comes in after his bath and tries saying *Open Sesame* to it. He's mad about Ali Baba at the moment and thinks the Flower Pot Men stole their huge pots from Ali Baba. He says the Flower Pot Men are as bad as the Forty Thieves.

'How are you going to open it, Melia?' he asks. 'What about *Abracadabra?*'

'Try that, Finn.' He does, three times for luck. Then he tugs at the lid.

'No, it's stuck.' We both stare at the chest. There's no sign of Mercy and we are alone.

'What about *Olé?*' Finn is full of bright ideas. I let him shout *Olé* at the chest. He looks disappointed when it doesn't work.

'Perhaps the chest doesn't speak Spanish?'

I tell him I don't think it does, and Finn says he's bored of trying to open it. He likes chests which aren't difficult to open. He says this one's bloody difficult.

'Finn! Mind your language!' I say, but I can't help laughing when Finn goes off to bed, whispering loudly 'Well, it IS bloody difficult!'

Of course, he's right.

CAMELLIA

I wake to a sun-filled room, the light pouring in through my open window. I could have sworn I drew my curtains last night, but perhaps I didn't. I check my watch and it says quarter past six. The air feels summery and warm, as if we are already at our little house by the sea. I climb out of bed to say hello to the day.

Mercy is sitting on the lawn in the early morning sunshine, her pretty pink dress spread out about her feet. Nara stands behind her, her head low and occasionally swishing her tail. The ghost dogs lie in a circle around Mercy, fast asleep. Three magpies perch in the oak above.

In this light, Mercy and her animals appear clearer than ever, as if they have greater form. I stand and watch them, all the time listening to the blackbird singing and singing. It's a new day.

Mercy looks up as if to say *'Good morning'* and I wave. She rises to her feet and leads her horse and sleepy dogs across the lawn into the sun. They are off somewhere.

I lean back on my bed and stretch my toes out. The chest feels warm from the sunlight. Then I reach down to lift the lid.

It opens.

CAMELLIA

It's a miracle the lid opened just like that! I reach into the chest with my heart jumping. I pause for a moment, taking a few deep breaths. What am I going to find?

First, I bring out a shawl, very like the one Gran gave Dorothy Baby. It was probably once a pretty pink, but now it's covered in grey and brown blotches. I shake it out and it smells of wool and dust. It will definitely need a wash!

Next there's a little sketchbook, full of painted scenes of trees, flowers, horses and dogs. Between some of the pages there are pressed flowers, and the writing underneath says they are violets, although the petals are brown. Then a paint-box!

I open it to find little squares of paints, some more used than others. So, Mercy was an artist like me!

This is like a Christmas stocking! I don't know what I'm going to find next. The diary must be in here somewhere though, and sure enough there are some books at the bottom. Laid on the top is a theatre programme. I lift it up to read the title. It isn't a play, it's an opera. The programme reads: *Hansel and Gretel by Engelbert Humperdinck – Carl Rosa Opera Company, Daly's Theatre, Leicester Square.* Someone has written on the front *29th December 1894, birthday treat*! Was Mercy's birthday 29th December I wonder?

Now I feel even more sorry for her! Not only did she die on Christmas Eve, but she also missed out on her birthday five days later. I should hate that to happen to me. What did they do with her presents? Just leave them? I open the programme and my heart leaps. Mercy *must* have heard the 'Evening Prayer' at the opera. Now I understand why it's so important. She loved it as I do.

What else do we have? There are three books, one dark green and one red and underneath a big cream-coloured book. I place them carefully on my eiderdown. These books must have been special to Mercy.

I pick up the big cream book first. It's called *The Happy Prince and Other Tales* by Oscar Wilde. I've never heard of Oscar Wilde. I thought only Hans Christian Andersen and the Grimm Brothers wrote fairy tales for children. I open the book to find page after page of beautiful illustrations.

Next the dark green book, which is called *The Picture of Dorian Gray*, also by Oscar Wilde. This one hasn't got any pictures and the print is very small.

The red book must be the diary surely, but I see it's called *Jane Eyre* by Charlotte Brontë. Just as I am about to open it, Mercy appears, and either a cloud has covered the sun or Mercy has blocked out the light because my room has grown dark. The temperature drops. I take a deep breath.

When I open the book, I discover that the pages have been

cut out neatly, forming a rectangular space inside, and within the space there's a dark blue leather-bound diary. The initials on the front are 'A.M.P.G.'

I lift the diary out and hold it up to show Mercy. Is this truly her diary? I can't see her clearly for it's as if she's shimmering. She has become a figure of moving lights, the colours moving so fast that my eyes can't keep up. I feel dizzy and quickly put my head down, fearing I might faint.

'Melia!'

It's Finn. He's awake! I don't want him to see what's in the chest, and I've got about a minute to pack this stuff away before he comes through. I shake my head, trying to clear it.

I cram everything back in as quickly as I can, everything except *Jane Eyre*, and then I slam the lid down, pushing the chest against my dressing table with my shoulder. And this is how Finn finds me, on the floor, hiding *Jane Eyre* under my eiderdown. Luckily, he's half-asleep so I tell him I've lost my slipper, that's what I was looking for.

Within a minute, Finn's fully awake. So much so that he tells me he's thought of another word that might make the chest open. I don't want to hear the word and tell him it's far too early.

'But I want to help?' He looks hurt.

'OK, Finn, what's this word?' Finn's going to try and lift the lid, whatever word he says. Then I'll have to show him everything. Finn says it's four words actually. I tell him to go ahead. He takes a deep breath, staring crossly at the chest.

'Open up or else!'

'Is that it?' I can't help laughing.

'Right, let's see if that worked.' Finn bends down. The lid's stuck fast.

'Bum,' he says. 'Didn't work.' Then he puts his hands on his hips and goes back to his room.

I try the lid, but it's locked itself again. I reach under my eiderdown, feeling for *Jane Eyre*. It's there! I tuck the book behind my dressing table on the floor, trusting that Mrs Betts only hoovers there once a year. Mercy is nowhere to be seen and I climb back into bed, falling back upon the pillow. I've found the diary at last, and now I'm worn out.

Whatever's written in the diary will have to wait. Right now I have to keep it secret. I draw Dorothy Baby to me and hug her tight.

CAMELLIA

I'm so tired after lunch that I plead with Nanny Jan *not* to do a walk this afternoon. I can hardly keep my eyes open. She suggests we have a quiet time in the nursery, but I decide to lie on the lawn, looking up at the sky. Nanny Jan says in that case she might sit in a deck chair and read her *Woman's Own*. Finn is busy with his farm.

The grass is dry thanks to the sun and I stretch out my arms and legs like a starfish, warming up and balancing my sun hat over my face. The clouds can race by without me.

The ache in my chest is back. I wish I could bury my head in the grass and sob. Instead I concentrate on drawing in big breaths, remembering how funny it was when Finn swore. It isn't really working, so I think about what Mummy and Daddy might be up to in Spain. Has Mummy swum in the sea yet?

What's in Mercy's diary? That's what's the matter. I'm frightened of what might happen when I read it, what she might do because you never know with her. One minute she's in a good mood like this morning on the lawn, and the next she's become a scary, whirling force that makes me dizzy and faint.

And what do I do about Gran? I really don't want to own up to finding the diary quite yet, but is it fair to let her keep on searching? Mr Impey did tell me that, when he last spoke to her, she wasn't budging at all, refusing to even *slightly* believe in Mercy's ghost.

Mercy is her own mother, for heaven's sake! How can you *not* believe in your own mother? I have to believe as much as I can in Mummy and not mind too much when she doesn't listen to me. Gran must buck up and *BELIEVE*. Your mother

Mercy is doing her best to get your attention. I have to take notice of her and now it's your turn.

Banger comes to join me, pressing herself beside me, then resting her head on my tummy. I pat her head gently. Banger's a kind dog and knows when I need her.

We are nicely settled into the grass and daisies, and for a moment I can rest. The ache in my chest has lifted and I'm drifting off to sleep.

CAMELLIA

The next thing I hear is Nanny Jan's voice, calling from the terrace. She says Gran would like to come to tea with us. Banger lifts her head up.

'Can we have a picnic tea?' Finn shouts from the lower lawn. He's busy with his wheelbarrow. Nanny Jan says she doesn't see why not, she will look out a rug for us and some picnic plates. The weather is that summery.

Finn comes up beside me.

'Gosh my wheelbarrow is useful,' he says. 'Look what I have picked up.' He shows me his afternoon collection of a big stone, some feathers, a fir cone and what looks like a dead moth.

'Very good, Finn,' I say, hoping I don't sound too like Mummy. 'Now listen, with Gran coming for tea, it's very important we don't tell her about Mr Impey and the cellar.'

'And the chest which doesn't open?'

'Exactly that.'

'Why not?'

He pats his big stone as if it's Banger.

'Because we don't want to get Nanny Jan into trouble. Mummy and Daddy didn't give us permission to go hunting in the cellar. It's Mercy stuff remember, and Mummy doesn't approve.' Finn nods.

'So, if Gran asks us if we went into the cellar, I say no.'

I sigh.

'She won't,' I say. 'I'm sure she won't.'

'But what if she does?'

Why can't he get this?

'Oh Finn,' I say crossly. 'Just leave it to me, then.'

He pushes his wheelbarrow away in a huff. Mercy stands on the terrace, laughing.

'And you're not much help either!'

Finn thinks I'm talking to him and shouts 'Temper!' over his shoulder.

I want everyone to go away.

CAMELLIA
Gran comes to tea

Before Gran arrives, I talk to Nanny Jan and of course she agrees we mustn't talk about the cellar. We can talk about Sarah but *not* that we went into the cellar. It might be better not to talk about Mr Impey either, because what was he doing here? I wish Finn were more reliable, but I suppose he's only four and three quarters. What can you expect?

Gran arrives, as usual calling *coo-ee* through the French windows. She carries a little wicker basket, saying she has something special for me. I know what it is, even before she gives me the lily of the valley. What a relief my own posy has been thrown away after the flowers curled up. I wouldn't want Gran to think I picked them without her permission, and now I'm annoyed I feel guilty.

I thank her very much and give Finn a quick frown as if to say *'Don't say Camellia has already picked some of those'*. He presses his mouth into a tight line and then smiles, making for a very strange look. It doesn't help that he rolls his eyes as well.

'We're going to have a picnic outside, Gran,' he tells her, checking with me as if to say *'can I say that?'* I run to fetch a vase for the posy and, when I get back, Gran is seated on the sofa.

'Finn tells me you had Mr Impey over yesterday.' I glare at Finn. Honestly! I only left the nursery for two minutes.

'He tells me you *didn't* go down into the cellar.'

Gran looks puzzled and then says how nice the flowers look in the vase. Nanny Jan comes in with the picnic basket and gives Finn a small cake tin to carry.

'Mr Impey came over to practise more music,' I say firmly. 'He's awfully good at the violin.'

'Where shall we go for our picnic, children?' Nanny Jan takes the lead, stepping out onto the terrace. I pick up a cushion for Gran's back in case she wants to lean against the tree. I already know where we are going.

'Let's go west,' I say and Gran agrees that it's always best to go west in the afternoon. We are headed for the oak tree beyond the flat square lawn.

'This is where I used to play tennis as a girl,' Gran says as we cross the grass.

'This is where we play cricket,' says Finn. 'And I always win.' Finn is seriously annoying me. I have to speak up.

'Only because you have to be bowled out three times before you're really out. It's not actually fair, and it's definitely not in the rules.'

'It's my cricket bat,' says Finn. As if I didn't know.

'Now, now children,' Nanny Jan says. 'We need our tea.'

Mercy is waiting for us under the oak tree. Of course, she is. I trudge up the bank, wondering how to contain both her and Finn. Maybe I won't have to. Maybe, like Mr Impey says, I'll let it all hang out. That makes me smile and I catch Mercy's eye. She agrees with me.

We settle down for tea.

CAMELLIA
The row

Nanny Jan and Finn take the picnic basket back to the house, so Gran and I can have a quiet moment alone. I say alone but of course Mercy is with us. She sits behind Gran, her daughter, wearing a sorrowful expression. I stretch out my legs and ask after Gran's back, hoping the cushion is helping. She smiles and says I'm a kind girl to think of her old back.

We sit in silence for a while, listening to the breeze rustling the leaves and from far away the sound of cows mooing.

'They'll want milking soon, I should think,' I say. 'That can't be much fun, going in to be milked.'

'Twice a day,' Gran says. 'And very early in the morning. You have to get up early when you're a cowman.' We talk about milking and how it must be more difficult in the winter. I can't believe I'm talking about milking cows when I should be getting on with asking Gran important questions.

Mercy stares hard at me, as if saying *come on*. I'm not even sure what I'm meant to be saying. Bo appears from behind Mercy and settles down on Gran's lap. This is my cue to start. I must start with Bo. I shift position on the rug, sitting back on my knees. Then I lean forward towards Gran. She's not prepared for what I am about to say. It's now or never.

'Do you know you have a little ghost dog on your lap?' Gran's head turns sharply towards me. Here we go. I'm in trouble already.

'*What* did you say?' Her voice is unfriendly. I must be brave and tell her whose dog it is.

'It's Bo, Gran. It's your mother's little dog. He was buried at the end of the garden in 1896.' My tummy's churning but I press on. 'He's a little red terrier, and he's sitting on your lap. I can see him. He's right there, even if you can't see him.' I pause for a moment. 'I promise.'

Gran stares and I can't tell if her eyes are angry or sad. Mercy reaches out her arm towards Gran and now she rests her head on Gran's shoulder. Her face is full of love. I blink back tears.

'Your Mummy is right beside you,' I say. 'She's as close as close can be.' I have to take a deep breath because my chest is hurting. 'And she loves you very much.' Above us a pigeon calls. It's a sleepy sound.

'I don't believe you,' says Gran.

This is a *dreadful* thing to hear, so dreadful I don't know what to say next. I look for support from Mercy, but she's fading. This is down to me.

'Why don't you believe me, Gran? Do you think me an untruthful child?' I am clenching my fists and I force myself to relax my hands. Bo has disappeared from Gran's lap. He doesn't like this.

'You've obviously got a very vivid imagination, Camellia.' Gran brushes imaginary crumbs from her summer skirt.

'This is *real*, Gran!' I cry. 'How can I make you believe? What do I have to do? How can you not believe in your Mummy?'

Gran is shocked at my outburst. From the corner of my eye I see Mercy returning with Nara. They walk slowly across the flat lawn, followed by the ghost dogs.

'Do you believe in Jesus?' I shout. Now Gran's eyebrows are frowning and she's very angry. She manages to say 'Of *course*.'

'Have you seen him lately?' I scramble to my feet, so now I'm taller than Gran. 'Well, *have* you?' Gran says she thinks this conversation has gone far enough. I don't.

'I'm only just getting started, Gran!' I point at Mercy, Nara and the ghost dogs. 'Your Mummy's there, right *there*, with her hunter-horse and all the dogs who were buried at the end of the garden. I can see Nara right now and she's dark brown with a lovely star on her face, just like the picture. Your Mummy's dress is pink. There are, let me count, three Labradors and Bo.'

Gran thinks I've gone completely mad. But at least her attention is on the lawn.

'They are *THERE*!' I shout again. Gran shakes her head in disbelief. Of course, she can't see them. I suddenly think of a great question.

'Do you,' I ask, pausing for breath, 'believe in Jesus more than your Mummy?' Gran says nothing. 'So, do you love Jesus more than your *Mummy*?'

Mercy stands patiently. Bo sits down beside her. Nara tosses her head and swishes her tail.

'Do you *have* to love Jesus more than your Mummy? Did Jesus tell you that believing in ghosts is wicked. *Did* he? Did he actually say that?'

There's a part of me that feels sorry for Gran. She's looking battered and defeated. She struggles to her feet, reaching out for the tree to steady herself. I can't stop now though. It's too important. I have to get my message through.

'All your Mummy wants is for you to *see* her. Then she can go to the Light.' Gran fumbles in her pocket for a handkerchief, but it is not in that pocket. It must be in the other one. I am shaking.

'Have you been searching for her diary?'

I'm the one looking stern now. I know she hasn't. It would be so easy to confess I found it yesterday, but I'm not going to tell her. She doesn't deserve it. She hasn't budged on anything. Gran finds her handkerchief and blows her nose.

'Well Gran? Have you? Why does it always have to be me? Mr Impey jolly well believes in ghosts, so *there*. *He's* seen your Mummy lots of times now, including in church. Yes, so that's allowed! Mercy is allowed in church. And yes, I call your Mummy Mercy. It suits her. On Mothering Sunday she stood right in front of you, but you didn't notice. I gave her the other bunch of primroses.'

Gran closes her eyes, holding the handkerchief to her mouth.

'How could I remember her?' she whispers. 'I was just a baby.'

'How could you *not* remember her, Gran? Anyway, she remembers you and she *sees* you now! And she loves you!'

Gran sways on her feet and I'm worried she might collapse. Mercy walks forward and puts a finger to her mouth, as if to say '*enough*'.

'Over to you then, Mercy,' I say. I'm already crying as I run off back to the house. I reach the other side of the lawn and turn back towards Gran, shouting as loud as I can.

'You've got to TRY, Gran!' My voice breaks up through the tears. I want to say 'You've got to *TRY*' again but I can't. The words won't come out properly.

Gran stands under the tree. Mercy stands on the lawn with Nara and the dogs. I can do no more.

I run up the steps and Banger's there to greet me.

NANNY JAN

I was putting the tea things away in the kitchen when I heard

Camellia shout 'NO Finn, just leave me alone!' followed by the sound of her thundering up the stairs and finally the slam of her bedroom door. I asked Finn what had happened, and his face was a picture of bewilderment.

'I only asked her why she was crying,' he said, and I feared we were going to have tears from him in a minute.

'It's not your fault, Finn. Don't you worry about that. Your Gran and Camellia must have had words, and Camellia's got herself upset.'

I was in a bit of a quandary then because I wanted to go upstairs to see how Camellia was but, on the other hand, I needed to be on hand for Old Mrs Devon who would no doubt be walking back through the garden.

Indeed, not two minutes had passed before Old Mrs Devon appeared in the nursery doorway, and I could tell she was mightily upset. She had her handkerchief screwed up tight in her right hand which was shaking. Finn took one look and announced he needed to fetch something from his room.

So that left Old Mrs Devon and me in the nursery. I invited her to sit down and asked if she wanted a restorative cup of tea? She nodded, not saying a word, and I rushed to the kitchen to boil the kettle.

I had a pretty good idea what had caused the upset. It would have been Camellia's ghost, and now I thought to myself what *was* I going to do if Old Mrs Devon asked me about yesterday. Thank heavens Finn had fled upstairs because I knew I wouldn't like lying in front of him. I made up a little tray with a pot of tea (not Lapsang unfortunately), cup and saucer, jug of milk and some sugar lumps just in case.

She was as white as sheet as I poured out her tea.

'This will set you right, Mrs Devon,' I said, passing her the cup and saucer. Unfortunately, her hand was shaking so much I had to take the cup back and set it down on the little table.

'Oh dear!' she managed to say, wringing her hands and twisting her handkerchief. And then again 'Oh dear, oh dear!'

I put on my most sympathetic face and asked her what I

could do to help. At that she threw herself back into the chair, shaking her head violently from side to side. I have to say I was alarmed to witness such distress. It was difficult to watch, and I wondered if she could do with some brandy. I said as much, but she shook her head even more.

'Such a shock, that's all,' she gasped. 'What Camellia said. She has a point though.' I was none the wiser as to what the point was, and I hoped she would tell me more.

'My faith, Nanny Jan. My faith in God is preventing me from seeing what is right in front of my nose.' I didn't know what to say to this.

'The Bible tells us it's *forbidden* to believe in spirits, several times as a matter of fact, neither must we communicate with them. I remember my father was very particular about it. He couldn't be doing with superstition either.' She paused for a moment, staring into space. 'And I've forgotten what it's like to be a little girl, Nanny Jan.'

She managed to take a sip of tea, and then another. I find there's nothing like a cup of tea to soothe the nerves.

'Because I've forgotten how it feels to be a child, I'm unable to understand Camellia. Yes, that is probably so. And of course, I didn't have a mother.' I nodded sympathetically.

'I had to follow my father's example but goodness I missed my mother, growing up. He didn't like tears, you see, or silly childish fancies.' She smiled weakly. 'It wasn't his fault of course.' I said I didn't suppose it was.

'He did his best, I know.' Her eyes filled with tears and right then my heart went out to Old Mrs Devon. What she said made me think of my own parents. My father was the best father ever, but goodness knows where I would be without my mother.

'What shall I do?' Mrs Devon asked, dabbing her eyes. 'I will find it very difficult to go against my faith.' If truth be told I was astonished Old Mrs Devon was confiding in me like this, and I wondered if it was appropriate for me to give her advice. She was ever so upset though.

I was about to suggest a nice, cosy conversation with Mr

Impey when I stopped myself. I didn't want to bring his name up in case that led to the cellar, and what we'd been doing there. Instead I shared that I'd heard the ghost several times.

'I might not have *seen* the ghost, Mrs Devon, but I can assure you I've witnessed some very strange goings-on in this house.' The words had only just left my mouth when something very strange happened. To my surprise Old Mrs Devon took on the appearance of a young girl, a girl with a solemn face and light brown hair. Was it something I said? Was I seeing things? I stared and stared, wondering what on earth was happening. I shut my eyes and shook my head, half-afraid to open them again. But when I did, Old Mrs Devon had resumed her usual form.

I wasn't sure she'd noticed because she was trying to gather up her handkerchief, folding it over and over. I decided to continue.

'I've heard crying and footsteps and I know it's not the children.' I didn't tell her about the laugh in the cellar. 'Mr and Mrs Devon worry about Camellia because they don't understand what's happening. However, I can assure you that she's a brave, intelligent little girl who's doing her very best under the circumstances. And I will do everything I can to keep her safe.'

Old Mrs Devon listened quietly. She finished her cup of tea and I offered her another, but she declined. She said it had done the trick, even if it wasn't Lapsang. At that she smiled, and I thought she must be feeling better if she made a little joke.

'I will pray for guidance,' she said.

At that she rose from her chair, saying she'd better be getting home. She thanked me for the picnic tea and for being so kind. She complimented me on my caring personality, adding that she thought the children were in very safe hands.

I thanked her and assured her that I was very fond of them. They were very easy to look after.

'Please apologise to Camellia for me. Tell her I'm not cross.

I would hate her to think that. I'm going to begin by trying to remember what it was like to be her age.' She smiled. 'I'll have to go back sixty years!'

I saw her to the door and watched her plod slowly across the gravel. I thought to myself we are all children underneath and, just for a moment, I had caught a glimpse of the child within Old Mrs Devon, a child who misses her mother.

I shut the back door and almost immediately heard Finn call from the top of the stairs.

'Well, Nanny Jan, did we get away with it?'

'Just about, Finn. Just about.'

'I didn't want to tell a fib, Nanny Jan.' I met him on the stairs.

'Nor did I, Finn. And I didn't have to. Now let's see how we can help that sister of yours.'

CAMELLIA

I wake to find Nanny Jan and Finn at my bedside.

'It's not bedtime yet,' Finn says. 'Why are you in bed? Are you ill?' Nanny Jan steps forward to place her hand on my forehead.

'No Finn, Camellia isn't ill. She's just exhausted, aren't you?' I nod, my eyes stinging from the crying. Nanny Jan sits down on one side of the bed, so Finn does the same on the other.

'We didn't give the game away,' he says. 'Nanny Jan was brilliant.' He reaches for Heidi and sits her on his knee. 'NO fibbing. I ran up here when Gran came back. I didn't want to fib.' He looks at Nanny Jan who smiles as if to say well done Finn.

'What happened?' I dread to think what Gran said to Nanny Jan after I ran off. I shouldn't have been so rude to Gran, but I didn't know any other way.

'Your Gran says she's very sorry and you don't need to worry about her being cross. She says she's going to pray for guidance.' I roll my eyes and say I'm not sure how much that's going to help.

'It's your Gran's way, Camellia. I made her a nice cup of tea and listened to what she had to say. She says she's forgotten what it's like to be your age, but she's going to try and remember.'

At least that's something. I know I'm smarting because Mercy wanted me to stop shouting at Gran. I can't bear to be told off by Mercy as well. She isn't standing in her corner. Honestly, I can't please everyone.

'Also', Nanny Jan continues, 'Your Gran told me that her father was very strict about not believing in ghosts, and that she really missed her mother when she was growing up.' At least Gran has owned up to that.

'And ... I didn't have to fib about Mr Impey. I just told your Gran that I too had heard unexplained noises in this house, the crying and the footsteps.

'I tell you what I am going to do, Camellia,' says Nanny Jan, reaching out to take my hand. 'I'm going to telephone Mr Impey and tell him about this, and I'm absolutely certain he will call on your Gran again. If anyone can persuade her, surely Mr Impey can. Goodness your hands are cold, Camellia!'

I tell her *all* of me is cold, even though I am under the blankets and eiderdown. Nanny Jan says she'll fetch me a hot-water bottle, and would I like another slice of that Victoria sponge?

I say yes to both. As they go downstairs, I hear Finn ask Nanny Jan if he can have another slice of cake too. Do I dare read some of Mercy's diary later?

Not yet. I am so very tired. My eyes are closing.

CAMELLIA

I couldn't stop my teeth chattering, even when Nanny Jan brought me the hot-water bottle. Honestly, a hot-water bottle in June! I ate my cake and then lay back again on my pillow, hugging on tight to the bottle's warmth, clenching my teeth together.

I knew Mercy was back when the drawer started opening and shutting. Her corner was very dark, as if she was spreading a deep, dark sadness over the rest of the room. I switched on my bedside light, but it didn't stop. Even the thrush singing outside sounded sorrowful and he gave up after a bit.

I sit in the middle of Mercy's sad twilight, wondering whether to have my bath before reading the diary. I shall keep my head down when I brush my teeth. I don't want to know if I've become invisible or if my eyes have changed colour. Lucky Finn, not having these worries.

The air in my room feels charged with electricity, like before a thunderstorm. What if there is nothing in the diary? Surely Mercy wouldn't have said *'Find the diary'* if she hadn't written in it? She stands in her corner, hands clasped in front of her. I am sure she's sorry Gran wasn't able to see her.

'It isn't my fault, it isn't my fault,' I say to the dark corner. She doesn't look up.

Now I hear Finn splashing around in the bath. He's singing 'We're all going on a summer holiday' and he follows each line with a very loud '*NEXT WEEK!*' Mercy hears him and lifts her head. Then she smiles and I can't help smiling too. At least he isn't singing 'Little Donkey' any more!

We are indeed going on a summer holiday as soon as Mummy and Daddy get back from Spain. Nanny Jan will look after us and Nanny Mae will look after Lorna and Julia, so we'll be six in all. We will be by the sea for a week and perhaps I'll feel stronger there. I wonder if Mercy likes the seaside, as no doubt she'll be coming too. Then we will be seven.

'Right, your turn next, Camellia.' It's Nanny Jan. 'A nice hot bath will really warm you up. Heavens above, why's your room so dark?' I tell her I don't know, it just is.

And then to Finn, 'Goodness me, Finn, you sound just like Cliff Richard.'

'I know,' says Finn. 'I can't help it!'

I will have plenty of time for the diary after my bath. For some reason I want to light a candle, but I know that won't be allowed. I will pretend to light a candle.

Finn is settled. I am bathed and in bed with my book. *Jane Eyre* is under my pillow. I wait to hear Nanny Jan's footsteps go downstairs. I open *Jane Eyre* and there it is. This is the moment.

I look up at Mercy and she holds a candle for me, the white light shining into her face.

'Here goes,' I say to her and open the diary.

CAMELLIA

The diary

On the first page I read:

'*This is the Diary of Alathea Mary Philippa Goodridge*'

I turn the page, and this is where her diary starts. Her handwriting is very small and neat, but I'm not used to the old-fashioned style, especially her capital letters. This is going to take me some time to read. She begins in black ink.

'29 December 1894 – my 34th birthday

'*This day was such a joy for me, and I do not recollect ever having a happier birthday. My dear William arranged for us to go to London to see a most wonderful Opera written by the German composer, Engelbert Humperdinck, libretto written by his sister Adelheid; Hansel and Gretel, first performed on Boxing Day three days ago, and with only two weeks in London. It was most beautifully sung, especially when the poor, dear children were lost in the wood and night falling. The Song of the Sandman was enchanting enough but it was when Hansel and Gretel sang their Evening Prayer, with a melody both simple and soaring, that I thought my heart would break with the beauty of it. Fourteen angels appeared on stage, surrounding the children with love and protection, and I vowed to include the angels in my own prayers at night. It was so very kind of William to accompany me because I know he does not have a musical note in his body, only appreciating the 'music' of hounds giving voice. He missed his hunting to come to London with me, so I think he must love me very much indeed. I did enjoy the train journey! Of course, I was more than happy to miss the day's hunting as I find it most dreadfully tiresome, with my back aching from the sidesaddle. I was not entirely convinced as to how much William enjoyed the performance as he closed his eyes for much of the second half.'*

I pause because it has taken me quite a long time to get this far. Her writing is difficult to read, and I have to concentrate very hard. William sounds just like Daddy! I'm interested Mercy didn't like hunting either, and poor thing having to ride side-saddle. It's hard enough with an ordinary saddle, but to have to canter, worrying you could slide off at any minute, must be very tiresome indeed!

How wonderful that she actually saw the opera in London, and of course that was the programme in the chest. It was her birthday treat!

I flick the pages of the diary and see some of it is written in ink and some in pencil. I'm not sure which is more difficult to read. There are short entries and long entries and she doesn't write up every day like me. This is because her diary pages are undated and unlined. She's clever at not writing in wiggly lines!

Even though Mercy writes in straight lines, the black letters make my eyes dance. I will only be able to read in short bursts otherwise I will get a headache! Hopefully the more I read, the more I will get used to her handwriting.

What if I go straight to the end? No that wouldn't be right. I would never do that with a Famous Five book. *Ever.* However, I could just look to see if she gets right to the end through half-closed eyes. That wouldn't be cheating. Here the handwriting is different and, if anything, more difficult. Not yet, not yet. I turn back to the beginning again. Perhaps I could manage a page every night? Or maybe I could open the diary wherever I felt like.

I am overwhelmed. I put the diary back in *Jane Eyre* and switch off my light. My room is in near total darkness and Mercy and her candle have gone.

In the garden the thrush begins his evening song.

CAMELLIA

I read Mercy's diary every evening after my bath. Not only do I write in my diary, but then I read Mercy's for about half an hour. It is about as much as I can manage, but it's worth it. I'm learning about her life.

I have discovered that the winter of 1894/95 was extremely cold, just like our winter, that the rivers froze so people could skate. Mercy skated on the very same pond as us. I liked that. Her diary says that February 1895 was the coldest month of the winter, not so much snow as lots of frosts, so there was no hunting and she says, 'For my part, I was much relieved.'

By March they were hunting again. She writes in her diary on Tuesday, March 12th:

'William and Thomas persuaded me, against my better judgment for I was recovering from a head cold, to join them in the Field. They maintained all the other ladies were coming out and I would be much missed. It was a dank, dim sort of day, the cloud hanging like a lid over us, with a sort of creeping coldness. How the menfolk, let alone the ladies, derive any enjoyment from riding about chasing hounds who are them-selves chasing the poor fox, is quite beyond me. Nara behaved herself very nicely; she takes care of me as a kindly aunt might, never cantering too fast nor stopping too suddenly. I am so very happy to have her here with me, although I fear she must miss her stable companions, left behind in Fordingbridge. She is a large mare at 16.2, but then so am I, in stature at least; tall and not in the first flush of youth by any means. We suit each other and I am very fond of her.

I fear I was in trouble with William today; I was offered the brush, being as I had managed a good run across the fields, without disgracing myself by sliding off. I refused and told the huntsman what I thought of such an offering. I am afraid that William was much offended by my behaviour, being as I am the Master's wife. His silence this evening said as much. Really and truly the huntsmen are quite the Barbarians with their customs and rituals, and I think it most unfair for ladies and children (none today fortunately) to be awarded the brush or the pate. Horrors!

I am glad to say my dear papa doesn't hunt. He does not have much confidence with horses, if truth be told, and I know it embarrasses him.

Once I am with child, I will be able to forgo hunting forever.'

I am not exactly sure what 'with child' means, but I'm pretty sure it's something to do with having a baby. I know Mary was 'with child' before she gave birth to Jesus in a stable. You would have thought people would say 'with baby'. Anyway, Mercy must have been longing to have a baby so that she would never have to go hunting again.

I understand now why Mercy was angry with my huntsman, and I'm happy to have the proof that she's on my side. I carry on reading.

I discover that Mercy has a piano! I don't know what sort, but she talks about playing it whenever she can. She says William doesn't appreciate her playing one little bit but that doesn't stop her. She has carried on teaching herself to read music, although she complains she doesn't find it easy. Just like me!

During the summer she writes that she takes herself off into the garden to paint. Bo is always by her side. She calls him her little shadow. She loves the garden very much and takes lots of interest in the roses, one in particular.

'I am entranced by the Thornless Rose, growing on the far wall. Its name is Zéphirine Drouhin, a deep cerise pink with an intoxicating scent. There is no other rose in the garden that smells as sweet. If I were a rose, I would not be thornless. I have thorns!'

I am going to ask Gran if we have a Zéphrine Drouhin rose. That will be a perfectly safe thing to ask. It might be growing here still. The only person who knows I'm reading the diary is Sarah. I have sworn her to secrecy, and I know I can trust her. If Mr Impey came over, then I would tell him, but for the moment the fewer people who know about it, the better.

Mercy watches as I read her diary. She's going through a quiet time. Mummy and Daddy get back from Spain tomorrow and then on Saturday we are off to the Sea.

I will take the diary to the Sea. I can't stop reading it now.

CAMELLIA

Mummy and Daddy are back from Spain! Mummy gives me a little black donkey made out of basket stuff. He wears a hat with orange flowers, and she says he's a present from Spain. Finn has been given one too, except his donkey's grey. Already I know Finn wishes he had the black one, but it's too bad. I'm keeping him! I point out that Finn's grey donkey has longer ears than mine, but I know I don't fool him at all.

Mummy is as brown as a berry and in a very good mood. She tells us she and Daddy had the most tremendous fun and that the weather was boiling. She says she thinks I've grown and that Finn might have done too.

'I do most of my growing in the summer, Mummy,' Finn tells her. 'I really get going when it's hot.'

'Like a sunflower!' I laugh. Mummy laughs too and thinks this a very good joke.

She says she has lots to do, her desk must be overflowing with things to deal with. Even though she asks us questions about what we've been up to, I know she doesn't really want to hear the details. I can tell when Mummy isn't really listening and often catch her out. She hates this of course.

'Finn darling, that all sounds absolutely marvellous. How clever you are learning your sums!' Her face is brown and bright, but she wants to get on. I don't bother telling her what I have been doing.

'Camellia,' Now Mummy is asking me a question, 'Are you eating enough? You seem rather pale and peaky to me.'

'Growing is very tiring,' Finn says. 'Summer can be tiring for me.' Mummy gives him a playful cuff and says she really must ring some people up. I notice she didn't wait for my reply, not that I gave her one. There's no point.

Before she goes through, she tells us that our cottage by the sea is fixed up and Nanny Jan will be driving us there tomorrow. We're off school for a week because it's Whitsun. She tells us this will be our special holiday, just like hers and Daddy's in Spain.

'Why can't we be all together on holiday?' Finn's voice is whining. Mummy won't like this.

'Now then, Finn. You're a very lucky boy to be going to Middleton with Nanny Jan and Camellia. And the Cordleys are coming too, just think how much fun that will be.'

Finn isn't sure.

'And Spain is for grown-ups,' she says, going out the door.

'No boys and girls in Spain?' shouts Finn, but it's too late. Mummy has gone. We have lost her to the telephone.

'Bum,' says Finn. 'That's that then.'

ANGELA

I always feel rather peculiar coming back from a holiday abroad, as if part of me is not really home at all. That other part of me remains by the pool sunbathing, or swimming in the sea, or drifting from one delicious lunch, never before three o'clock, into a siesta and then dinner with friends not before eleven. I must say I consider eleven a bit late to start dinner, but when in Rome as they say.

We arrived back from the airport at lunchtime and of course the children were thrilled to see us. I hope they like their donkeys. I thought they were very charming and goodness there were donkeys enough in Spain, some of them not being treated too well I'm sorry to say.

Camellia is *far* too thin. I accept she might have grown in the week we've been away but not that much. It's almost as if she's *emaciated*, never a good look. I don't like it one bit, and it's too late now to fix an appointment with Dr Byng. They're off to the sea tomorrow after all, but I will assess the situation when they get back. Let's hope the weather will be kind to them so they can play on the beach, as well as the garden.

In the meantime, I'll organise the oil paints and tent for Camellia's party. June 11th will come round all too soon. Heavens, I haven't sent out the invitations! I could get Camellia to help me write them after tea. Her handwriting is very neat after all. She can do the invitations and I will address the envelopes. I should have thought about this before Spain. As if I hadn't got enough to do! And then there's Ascot after that with all the picnics to organise.

I wonder if I might make the Ascot picnics a little more *Spanish*? Cook could easily practise making gazpacho next week. I will need to find a recipe, and that reminds me I must collect the portraits from the framer.

Heavens. I had better get going!

NANNY JAN

If Mrs Devon thinks she has plenty to do, it's nothing compared with me!

The children were thoroughly over-excited to have their parents back. I find it rather sad to observe how much their parents' homecoming means to the two of them. Yes, there are kisses and laughter and presents, but all too soon Mr and Mrs Devon disappear off into their own worlds. Even Finn notices it now.

I'm not entirely sure why it's a 'Nannies and Children Only' holiday in Middleton. But of course we will have fun and I like what I've seen of Mae. It certainly helps that she's only a couple of years younger than me.

So, this afternoon found me madly packing the children's suitcases. I had to send Finn out because he was driving me mad. I assured him I would pack his shorts and both pairs of swimming trunks. I made sure I packed plenty of jerseys. You can never have too many jerseys in my opinion, especially on a seaside holiday in the south of England.

Mrs Devon found me packing and asked if I thought Camellia much thinner. I suppose she notices it more having been away for a week. I assured her that Camellia had been eating all her food, and perhaps she was putting on a growth spurt. I did share that she was more tired these days but, there again, that could be the growing. Mrs Devon didn't look that convinced and I'm certainly not going to tell Camellia that she might be getting another visit from Dr Byng.

I'm putting my faith in the sea air. Surely, we won't be having any crying or footsteps at Rosemary Cottage, and the only slamming of doors and loud knocking will be thanks to Lorna. That child really does have a temper. It will be interesting to note how Mae copes with it.

I was hugely relieved Mrs Devon didn't ask me directly about anything supernatural. I don't think *she* wants to accept any of it, so easier for her not to enquire. I did mention we had Old Mrs Devon to tea, but it's not my place to repeat what happened that day. If she wants to share that, then it's up to her.

I only hope I'm doing the right thing? To be honest I have no idea why Camellia is getting thinner. I'm worried about it actually. We can't have her wasting away entirely.

I must remember to pack my wireless because the children are loving the records at the moment. Finn particularly likes 'I Like It' by Gerry and the Pacemakers, as well as 'Blame it on the Bossa Nova', while Camellia loves 'Do You Want to Know a Secret', but I forget who that's by.

I'm a 'Summer Holiday' girl because there's no one quite like Cliff Richard.

PART IV

CAMELLIA
The sea

We're on our way to the sea at last, after a busy morning of trying to remember to pack everything. I'm in the back of the car with Finn, my satchel beside me. Inside is *Jane Eyre* and the diary, along with my pad and colours.

I'm not sure how much I'm looking forward to this holiday. Usually I'd be more excited about going to the beach and the thought of sleeping in bunk beds. Our cottage has high ceilings with a big thatched roof. Right now I feel as if a big heavy stone is squashing my heart. I do some big sighs like a fish gasping for air. Finn gives me a funny look.

'You all right, Melia?'

I wind down my window and tell him I feel a bit car sick, that's all. At least it's a sunny day and I watch the trees and sky fly by.

I helped write my party invitations yesterday, having to pretend I was really excited. Mummy's very good at organising, and she promised the tent would be up by the time we get back. As well as my friends, Mr Impey has been invited and Gran and Grandpop too, not forgetting Mummy's brother Peter with his wife and new baby. Mummy promises it will be quite a party, and she will do her very best to make sure everyone has a wonderful time. She said she has a super birthday present lined up for me.

I yawn and ask Nanny Jan for a travel sweet. She finds them and passes them back to Finn. He makes a great business of opening the tin and the icing sugar spills out in a cloud, along with about four sweets.

'Two each,' he says, dusting himself down.

I know what the best birthday present in the world would be. It would be for Gran to be able to see Mercy. Then Mercy would stop bothering me and I could go back to normal, back to the old me who used to be full of fun, as well as beans. I've lost my fun and my beans, and I want them back. Finn says his purple sweet is really disgusting and wonders if he can spit it out. He prefers the yellow ones.

'Into your hanky, Finn,' Nanny Jan says. 'Only about half an hour to go. And then we'll be able to see the sea.'

'See the sea! See the sea!' shouts Finn happily and I feel his joy. I know he won't mind if I borrow some of his.

Soon Nanny Jan drives the car along the bumpy seaside road, and I can smell the salty air. It's warm and tangy and I fill up my lungs with my head half out the window. Finn does a lot of big sniffs too.

'We're here!' announces Nanny Jan. 'Now let me find the key to the cottage. Children, you can get out of the car and take something with you.'

I carry my satchel along the side of the house, bumping against the fence which is covered in honeysuckle and roses. The lawn lies ahead with thousands of summer daisies. At the end of the garden there's a little fence and beyond that the sea.

I take off my socks and sandals and walk barefoot across the grass. It feels warm and gives strength to my legs which are wobbly after the car journey. I rest my arms on the little gate and take a deep breath, feeling the heaviness in my chest lift.

'I can see the sea!' I shout to no one in particular. The tide is way out and the sand is pale and dry. I hear gulls overhead and then from next door's garden the chatter of a magpie.

I turn to walk back to the cottage and see a figure in front of the house. There is no mistaking her. It is Mercy. She has come with us to the sea.

Of course she has.

CAMELLIA
Middleton first night
We have a funny first evening in the kitchen. Nanny Jan and
Nanny Mae aren't very good at finding pots and pans for
cooking our high tea. Nanny Jan says it can take quite a while
to get used to a new kitchen. In the end we have fish fingers and
baked beans with apples for pudding. Lorna moans that the
apples are fluffy, but I notice she eats two.

After tea we run around on the lawn while Nanny Jan and
Nanny Mae unpack. I make sure my satchel is fastened shut,
safe in our room. If Lorna finds the diary, she might cause all
sorts of trouble. She causes all sorts of trouble most of the time
anyway. When she falls flat on her face, trying to catch the
beach ball, she blames it on Julia who's nowhere near. I stand
up for Julia and that makes Lorna cross.

All the time we play on the lawn, Mercy watches us. She
stands quietly in the shadows of her overhanging tree. Some
people might say she's a shadow or a trick of the light, but I
know her form by heart. Even when Julia runs up to her feet,
fetching the ball, she can't see Mercy. She does see the magpie
though and runs back to us, screaming. He chatters as if he's
laughing at her.

'Only a magpie, Julia,' Finn says kindly. 'We love magpies.'

Nanny Jan calls us in for our baths, and I'm the last to leave the
garden, but not before seeing Mercy step out of the shadows.
She walks towards the little gate with Bo trotting behind her.
She's off to the beach, passing straight through the gate and
down on to the sand.

'Bless you, Mercy and Bo,' I whisper. 'Have fun on the beach.'

CAMELLIA
Reading the diary
I'm not going to get much chance to read Mercy's diary on this
holiday because I'm in bunk beds with Finn. He wanted to be
on the top bunk, but Nanny Jan said she can't have him falling
out of bed in the middle of the night. I hang my satchel over the

feet end of the top bunk, so that Finn doesn't knock himself out getting out of bed.

Our ceiling is very high and thatched and I hope there aren't bats living up there. It scares me when they swoop down, and Mummy says they can easily get caught in your hair.

'Bats be gone!' Finn says, wearing his blue and yellow striped pyjamas.

'Bats be gone,' I say. If only it was that easy with Mercy. Out of the corner of my eye I see her, only this time she's outside our window peering in. Perhaps she's enjoying the sea air. I need my torch so I scramble down to the foot of my bunk, reaching into my satchel. I bring out *Jane Eyre* and my normal reading book.

'Read me a story, Melia.' Finn's voice is already sleepy. Because I am a kind sister, I read him half a page of my book. After a few minutes I pause, leaning over the side of the bunk with my head hanging down. His eyes are closed. He's asleep, thank goodness. I hear Nanny Jan and Mae chatting and laughing in the kitchen, and there's no sound from Lorna and Julia. I have a moment to myself.

I open the diary and read about Mercy's magpie.

'29th July 1895

This afternoon I had a most extraordinary experience. I was taking my customary walk through and beyond the grounds, in the hope of finding some betony for my headache. Fortunately, it was quite cool after yesterday's oppressive weather, so all the more pleasant for meandering. Very soon I became aware of a bird following me.

The bird was a magpie and such a comical fellow, pursuing me with large hops. If I walked forwards three paces, he hopped three times. His tail was not so long as other magpies, a juvenile from this year's brood perhaps. I tested him by going this way and that and still he was my faithful companion.

I decided to pause awhile, settling down in the long dry grass. I called for Bo to sit on my lap. Now the magpie observed me

with his head on one side and for the best part of half an hour
we regarded each other.

'Why have you taken a fancy to me?' I asked as he hopped
ever closer, all the time fixing me with his bright eye. I told him
I hadn't anything for him to eat and rather wished I had. All
the while Bo sat as still as a stone.

My eventual return to the house was accompanied by the
magpie, who now, as well as hopping, flew from shrub to shrub.
I told him I must go in and wished him good afternoon. I am
sorry to say Bo took the opportunity to bark loudly. However,
the magpie was unperturbed.

At dinner I recounted to William what had happened, and my
heart sank when he teased me for being taken in by a magpie.
This was our sorry conversation as near as I remembered it.

'What next?' he said. 'Magpies are vermin. Need shooting.'
William succeeded in making me feel very foolish, and that
brought about a spark of anger.

'And foxes?'

'Vermin also, and we hunt those.'

I don't know how I found the courage, but I said it anyway.

'Don't you dare shoot my magpie.'

'Your magpie now, is it?' I couldn't guess if he was teasing me.
I smiled at him, taking a sip of my wine for courage.

'It might be. The Thieving Magpie. An opera by Rossini, you
know. He was Italian. Do you know any Italian composers by
any chance?'

William was silent after that.

A little victory for me and my magpie!'

I close the diary at this point. My eyes are aching from reading
with the torch. I'm very sleepy too. Nanny Jan would say that's
the sea air for you.

Mercy isn't outside the window or in our room. She must be
somewhere else.

She always is.

CAMELLIA

I wake and for a moment I'm not sure where I am. The room seems dark even though my watch says half past six. Outside is bright sunshine. We must have forgotten to draw the curtains, probably because it was light when we went to sleep. A blackbird sings in the seaside garden.

Finn's asleep so I'm going to use the time to read a few more pages of the diary. I want to know more about Mercy's magpie. I'm proud of her for standing up for herself. Perhaps Mr Impey knows about *The Thieving Magpie*, being as he's so musical, and now we know why Mercy is a musical ghost.

I open the diary and read on. I'm becoming used to the handwriting and the way Mercy says things. I find out that the magpie visited her the next day, and the next and the next. Then on the fourth day he perched on the windowsill of the dining room and on the fifth at her bedroom window. Mercy has even drawn a little sketch of him. Her magpie.

'Melia,' Finn's awake. 'Are you there?'

'I am.' I close the diary, put it safely in *Jane Eyre*, then back in my satchel.

'Bats be gone and bum,' says Finn. I laugh out loud.

'Honestly, Finn. You can't say bum any old time.'

'Who says?'

'No one really. Look, it's sunny outside! We'll be able to spend all day on the beach.' Finn climbs out of bed and peers out the window, through the rose leaves.

'*I LIKE it, I LIKE it!*' he sings. 'Red swimming trunks today.'

'The sea might be cold.'

'Cold as snow?'

'Nearly.'

'Don't mind, don't care,' says Finn, padding over to the door. 'I'm going to find Nanny Jan. She needs to wake up and make our breakfast!'

I'm going to wear my favourite swimming costume which is red, like Finn's trunks, with pretty ruffles. For now I dress in a tee shirt and shorts and slip out of the house, across the lawn to the little fence.

In front of me the tide is in, the sea a pale blue which exactly matches the sky. The sun is already high, warming my face and arms. There are no clouds to be seen and I already know it's going to be a beautiful day. My heart lifts.

All day on the beach.

CAMELLIA
Nina

We're on the beach and it's heaven! The tide has gone out far enough for the sand to be exactly right for building sandcastles, and already I've made a big town of them, with roads and bridges. Finn is struggling a bit. Either he doesn't pat the sand down enough in his bucket before turning over or, once he's whacked the bucket with his metal spade, he forgets to give it a little shake before tipping out.

Nanny Jan is helping him and Nanny Mae fills Julia's bucket for her. Lorna sets up her sandcastle building area far away. She says she doesn't want to be too near the babies. She's nine after all. I'm easily as good as her at building sandcastles and can keep going for much longer.

Nanny Jan smothers our shoulders in Nivea which she says will stop us from burning. Finn wears a hat with his seaside sunglasses and Nanny Mae says he looks like a film star.

Lorna wonders why am I so thin? Nanny Jan tells her it's none of her business and it's very rude to comment on someone else's appearance. I mouth '*thank you*' to Nanny Jan.

I've dug a trench around my castle and now all I need is some water to make it into a moat. I carry my bucket to the sea. The water is cold, not as cold as snow luckily, and my feet soon get used to it. I stand and watch the little waves break against my legs, but the ridges in the sand make my feet ache so I stand sideways, facing along the beach.

Mercy is with us this morning, and she walks along the sand with Bo scampering beside her. There are other children on the beach and one girl in particular catches my eye. She has short brown hair and she wears a green swimming costume. She must be about my age and, just as I'm wondering whether I could go up to her, she splashes over and asks if I would like to play catch.

'I'm Nina and I'm nearly eight.' She has a sunburnt face with hazel eyes. 'What's your name?'

'Camellia. Like the flower.'

'That's a good name. More exciting than Nina! How old are you?'

'Nearly seven. Seven next week actually.' Nina tells me that she's here with her mother who's Dutch.

'Where the windmills come from?' I ask.

'And cheese!' Nina has a beautiful smile.

We play catch and laugh when we drop the ball into the waves. I see Nanny Jan waving at me, so I wave back to let her know I'm all right. I've made a new friend.

'I wonder who that woman is?' Nina says, pointing at Mercy. 'Fancy wearing a long dress on the beach!'

'She's my ghost,' I say. Nina's eyes widen.

'She's your ghost? How come?' I can't believe Nina can see Mercy, and I can't believe I'm telling my new friend all about her. I've only just met her! Nina says she often sees ghosts and sometimes it can be a right pain.

'So, what's up with your great-grandmother then?'

'She can't go to the Light until my Gran sees her.' Nina throws the ball to me again.

'And why can't your Gran see her?' I catch the ball.

'Because she doesn't believe.'

Finn marches over to us, swinging his bucket.

'Hello, hello,' says Nina. 'Who's this then?' Finn's toes have met the sea. He makes a terrible face.

'This is my brother, Finn.'

'Bum!' Finn shouts, running back from the waves. Nina laughs out loud.

'I'm Nina,' she calls to him. 'Here, Finn. Catch!'

In that moment Finn falls in love. Kind Nina has included him in our game. He drops the ball more often than not, and Nina says better luck next time. We're having so much fun that Lorna and Julia come over to join us. Nina includes us all. She's clever at making Lorna feel welcome which means I can relax and enjoy the game.

Nanny Jan waves and calls us over for our elevenses. I beckon Nina to come too.

'This is my new friend, Nina.' I catch Finn's eye. '*Our* new friend.'

'She's half Dutch,' Finn says proudly.

'Well, you're very welcome,' Nanny Jan says. 'Would you like some orange and a biscuit? There's plenty for everyone.'

Nina says yes and becomes part of our family.

CAMELLIA

Nina has made all the difference! Sometimes with a new friend you have to be careful because they can get bossy or moody, especially if they don't want to play your games. Nina is just right! She's very clever at picking up our ways so quickly. She asks lots of interesting questions like 'What's your favourite colour?' and 'Does red or blue make you feel happy or cross?' I never imagined a colour could make you feel cross.

'I have trouble with mauve,' Finn says, and everyone laughs. I know he gets that from Mummy.

She joins us again after lunch. She says her mother's writing a book so needs peace and quiet to think. I say I know how her mother feels. I wish I could have more peace and quiet, especially from Mercy.

We walk away from the others, far out across the sand, set on collecting shells to decorate our sandcastles. This means we can talk without the others listening. I tell Nina how tired I'm feeling and how worried I am about getting thinner, in spite of eating normally.

'Do you think you've got a tapeworm?' Nina asks, dropping a yellow shell into her bucket. It makes a clang.

'What's that?' It sounds revolting. When Nina explains I feel sick. Goodness I hope I haven't got one of those, eating away inside me. 'How do you get a tapeworm?'

Nina knows because her mother was once in Africa. She says you get it mainly from eating meat that isn't cooked enough.

'Ugh!' I shake myself. Surely Cook is careful about that?

In that moment I have to give myself a talking to. I *was* worried about my canine teeth and being a vampire, and who might be sucked into a portal, even Mummy's Christmas tree and *none* of it was true. The tapeworm isn't true. It can't be. Mind you, my eyes changing colour was true and, for that matter, so was a lot of it.

'I'm sure you have to go to Africa to get a tapeworm,' Nina's voice is kind. Goodness I hope so.

We collect shells for a while, dropping them into our buckets. We don't collect crabs because I hate watching them scrabble round the bucket, searching for escape. I tell Nina it's mean, and she agrees, saying crabs should be left in peace.

'Where's your ghost now?' she asks. I scan the beach.

'Probably in the garden. Or else in the house. I never know where she'll be. She's never far away though.'

'Do you think your ghost is making you thin?' As soon as Nina says this, I know it's true. I just hadn't thought of it before. Is she eating away at me from the inside, like the tapeworm? It's a horrible thought!

'She might be. But surely ghosts can't eat people up?'

'I don't know,' Nina says. 'It doesn't seem very likely.'

We carry our buckets back across the sand to where the others are gathered. Nanny Jan says we've got a fine collection there. The sun is hot on my back but I'm cold inside. If I'm not careful I'll get eaten up and disappear. I whisper this to Nina and she links arms with me.

'Not if I've got anything to do with it you won't!' I try and smile. We're running out of time, I know it.

The thought of Mercy's feeding off me goes round and round in my head. I imagine her holding up a tiny knife and fork.

I'm doing everything to help her and she's eating me up. No wonder I'm so thin and tired.

I'm scared. How do I stop getting thinner? I have to protect myself, and that's when I remember what Sarah said. I imagine wrapping myself up in a beautiful lilac cloak, and carry on decorating my castles. Nanny Jan gives us all a paper union jack and we stand back, admiring our hard work. I can tell Finn is tired.

Later the sea will flatten our sandcastles. It always happens, and it makes me sad. We have to remember to take our little flags back to the house, otherwise they'll be lost too.

The sea always wins.

CAMELLIA

I keep my lilac cloak wrapped round me for the rest of the day, even when I'm reading Mercy's diary. I say sorry to her for needing protection, but she really shouldn't be feeding off me. It's not fair when I'm trying so hard.

It's eight o'clock and Finn's asleep. Outside the sunny evening grows cooler, cool enough for the thrush to sing merrily. I re-read the magpie entries, trying to feel kind and loving towards Mercy, not scared. I bless her over and over again and, when I look up from the diary, she's back in the room. Her face is sad and drawn, and I feel guilty for doubting her.

'I'm sorry, Mercy,' I whisper and her eyes close when she hears me. 'I shall stay true to you, I promise.' I say this in my head which aches. Too much sun. I will wear a hat tomorrow like Finn.

I read on and now Mercy is in October. She writes how sad she is that summer is gone with the nights drawing in fast. She says that summer belongs to the women and winter to the men, with their hunting and shooting. In October she enjoys riding out on Nara and Bo comes too.

Her magpie is with her still and she writes how she finds him a big cage, which she sets up in the conservatory, amongst all the growing plants. She says her magpie sometimes sits in it like a parrot. She puts food in the cage, making sure the door is *always* open. She says she would never ever lock him up. He chatters away as if he is talking. William has given up over the magpie and admits women have their fancies.

Mercy writes about the weather and which birds are singing. She says she finds the song of the robin particularly melancholy. This is a word I don't know, so I will ask Nanny Jan about it tomorrow. I will pretend it's come from my normal book of course.

I reach 4th November 1895 and know I've read enough for tonight. I put the diary away and settle down into my bunk. As I lie, staring up at the thatched ceiling, I take myself back to the nursery at home, and sit myself at the piano. Then I play the 'Evening Prayer' twice, bringing the fourteen angels in to watch over me.

I give a last glance to see if Mercy's there, but she's gone.

CAMELLIA

Finn is awake before me. He's in his swimming trunks already, marching around the room. Now he's trying to blow up his yellow rubber ring.

'Sunny, sunny,' he says. 'Another glorious day!' Where's he got that expression from?

'I'm going to swim today,' he gasps in between blowing. I stretch out my arms and legs, praying they haven't got any thinner in the night and, while Finn's busy puffing, I slide *Jane Eyre* into my satchel. No reading for me this morning.

It would be good to show Nina the diary. Can I risk taking my satchel down to the beach? I can always say I'm going to do some drawing. I might even draw Nina in her green swimming costume. That's a very good idea.

'This ring's got a hole in it.' Finn holds it up and I can see it's pretty saggy. 'It's bloody annoying.'

'You can borrow mine,' I tell him. 'I'm going to do some drawing on the beach.' Finn likes the sound of this idea and says he's going to show Nina how well he can swim. He can't wait. He's going to swim like a fish.

I test my headache by shaking my head gently. It's better. I wish I was more excited about being here, and I wish I *really* knew what's wrong with me. I try not to think of being eaten from the inside. That little knife and fork. The horrible thought has come back, even after a good night's sleep.

Maybe one day I will simply disappear.

Finn goes running down the passage to find Nanny Jan. I must remember to ask her what melancholy means.

I think it's how I'm feeling.

NANNY JAN

Camellia asked me what melancholy meant this morning at breakfast. I told her I thought it meant sad in a thoughtful sort of way. Finn picked the word up immediately, pronouncing it *melon-coley*, as if it were a combination of a melon and a fish.

'I can feel a bit melancholy some days, especially in the autumn,' said Mae. 'When you go for a walk by yourself and kick through the leaves.' The children crunched through their cereal, taking this in.

Lorna announced that she had never felt melancholy in her life, and as for feeling *melon-coley* (she used Finn's pronunciation), that was for sissies. Camellia ate her rice krispies and didn't comment, but I noticed she smiled at Mae. It's nice when people admit they aren't strong all the time.

We finished breakfast and I told the children we'd be off to the beach in half an hour, so they needed to look out their buckets and spades and, if anyone wanted a shrimping net, there were two in the shed. What a blessing it was to have another beautiful day. The sun was already hot when I fetched the towels off the washing line. I packed the basket with a thermos of coffee for Mae and me, orange squash and biscuits, together with extra sun hats and Nivea.

Camellia said she wanted to do some drawing on the beach. She's never ever a problem because she entertains herself. Finn and Julia get on very well, with only a year between them. The difficult one is Lorna and I can see Mae has her work cut out with her sulky moods.

The little Dutch girl Nina is such a pet, and Camellia has taken to her like anything. I too like her very much because she's kind and generous to the other children, and Mae and me come to that. It makes you feel good to be around her.

Mae took the car to the shops to buy extra provisions and we went to the beach. What a joy to have the beach right at the end of the garden!

Camellia is getting a bit of colour at last. I do wish she weren't so listless. Of course, she isn't like that all the time because she makes an effort, but I can tell from her eyes that she's drained.

I have shared some of our comings and goings with Mae. She told me her first job involved living in a house that was properly haunted. Doors banging, saucepans flying off the shelves, dogs disappearing and then reappearing and no end of carryings on. I thought it sounded awful and Mae said it was too. She said she was more than happy to move on to the Cordleys. I explained how I could hear the ghost, but not see it. Not yet anyway!

So far I've enjoyed Mae's company very much indeed. She has a great sense of humour and knows a considerable amount about nature. I'm encouraging Camellia to eat up everything on her plate and Mae plans to get some sausage rolls from the baker's for today's tea.

I'm certainly *not* losing weight and I know I won't be able to resist those sausage rolls. I never can!

CAMELLIA

It's hot on the beach. I'm wearing my sun hat because I don't want to get another headache. Nina sits on a towel in front of me, posing in her green swimming costume, and I am drawing her portrait. It's easy because Nina is very good at sitting still. Every now and then she bursts out laughing because Finn's prancing round behind me, pretending to be a film star with *melon-coley*.

'I'm doing this so Nina doesn't get bored,' he tells me when I order him to stop. He's putting my model off. Nanny Jan says why doesn't he go and find some nice green sea lettuce. He sets off to the nearest rock pool with Julia.

I'm at the colouring-in stage, needing to find just the right green and brown for Nina's eyes. She opens them very wide for me to see, reminding me of Heidi, and her face is so funny that I can't help laughing.

'Oh Nina, you do make me feel better.' She really does. She asks to see my picture and I show her.

'What do you think?' She says it's definitely her.

Nanny Jan is busy helping Lorna dig a trench to the sea, while Finn and Julia are fishing seaweed out of their rock pool so now's a good time to show Nina the diary, even if only for a moment.

'Have you got it?' Nina asks.

'I have.' I bring *Jane Eyre* out of my satchel and give it to her. Nina carefully lifts the diary out. I keep a look-out for the others.

'Wow! So old.' She strokes the dark blue leather. 'Your ghost wrote this?' I show her where I'm up to. My bookmark is an oak leaf. Nina smiles at this.

'The writing is hard to read! So black!'

I find Mercy's magpie sketch, which Nina loves. She wishes she could draw. She says she's better at making things.

'My mum loves sewing and she taught me. I also love building things like little boxes and houses, and then painting them.'

'What are you two looking at?'

Lorna's big shadow falls across us, blocking out the sun.

'Is that an old book? Why would you bring an old book to the beach?' She flings herself down on the sand, much too close. As calmly as I can, I put the diary and *Jane Eyre* back in my satchel. I don't want Lorna to see how the diary fits inside *Jane Eyre*.

'Carry on with my portrait,' Nina says cheerfully, arranging her pose.

'How's your trench to the sea?' I ask, picking up a tan brown pencil. It should do for Nina's legs.

'Brilliant,' says Lorna. When I dare to face her, I feel sick. Her eyes are on my satchel. I know she wants to steal the diary.

Finn runs back to us. He says he has got *mountains* of seaweed. Nanny Mae is also back from shopping. She holds up two kites.

'Look what I found in the shop!' We gather round, admiring them. One is blue and green, the other red and yellow. Finn dances up and down.

'I want the red one.' Lorna holds her hands out and Julia scowls.

'I want doesn't get, Lorna.' This from Nanny Jan.

'There isn't enough wind yet,' Nanny Mae says. 'But there may be this afternoon. The wind usually gets up later.' She scans the horizon, as if sensing the right sort of wind for our kites. 'Goodness, who's that by the sea? Right there. Tall, wearing a long dress.' She points and everyone looks.

'I can't see anyone,' Julia says. Finn says he can't either and neither can Nanny Jan. Lorna hasn't bothered to look because she can't take her eyes off my satchel. Nina and I watch her, exchanging glances. Nanny Mae drops her arm, shrugs her shoulders and says never mind. There are some funny people about. But I find this interesting.

For some reason Nanny Mae can see Mercy.

CAMELLIA
Kite flying

Nanny Mae's right. The wind does get up after lunch, sending little clouds racing along the blue sky.

Finn tried swimming like a fish this morning but said it was *far* too cold. He preferred to sit, wearing my yellow rubber ring, in his own little pool of sea warmed up by the sun. He leaned back in his hat and sunglasses, saying this was the life.

But now is the time for kites. The wind is buffeting us, making little backward ripples on the sea, and gulls wheel around in the sky. We have enough sand to run along, and all the time the tide is racing in.

Nanny Mae is trying to launch the red kite and Nanny Jan

the green. We children are to take it in turns to hold the kites up while the two Nannies walk backwards, using jerking movements so that the kites soar up.

Lorna has got her own way with the red kite and she and Nanny Mae are a team. I hold up the green kite, with Nina encouraging me while Nanny Jan tries to run backwards. We laugh and laugh because she keeps tripping. But all at once our green kite is up and away. Nanny Jan lets out the string and it soars higher and higher.

'Can I have a go?' I'm beside her and she passes me the wooden handle. She tells me to hang on tight, really tight. The kite is a live thing, pulling and tugging. I'm not sure how much I like it. It feels as if the kite might cart me up into the sky, and I would be lost forever.

'Here, Nina,' I say. 'You have a go.' Nina knows all about kites, probably because of all the wind and windmills in Holland. She's an expert, tugging back on the kite when it needs it and letting out more string. Our green kite is alive in the sky!

I can hear Nanny Mae shouting instructions at Lorna. They are not airborne yet.

'Let *go*, Lorna, for *heaven's sake!*'

'I *am* letting go!' Lorna actually stamps her foot.

'Come on, we can do it!' Nanny Mae shouts, running backwards again. One last try! Meanwhile Finn watches our kite with his hands on his hips. Already there are quite a few people on the beach looking our way. I bet they wish they had kites.

The last try has worked and Nanny Mae's red kite is up and away. She has to run towards the sea, pulling her kite away from ours. We don't want them to get tangled up. But Nina knows exactly what she's doing and calmly steers ours out of trouble. She lets Finn have a go but has to snatch it back when our kite tries to dive bomb.

Mercy has joined us, standing very close. Her eyes dance and she's laughing, as if cheering us on. I nudge Nina and she smiles.

'Of course, your ghost loves a kite. Who doesn't?' She hands the kite back to me and I try and get used to the tugging. Mercy claps her hands together. She's full of joy. Nina watches her carefully and says she knows what she's going to do.

'I'm going to build a kite for your ghost.'

'Wow,' I say. Clever Nina.

Everyone has had a turn, including some of the other children on the beach. There's no more string to let out, and seeing the kite flying so small in the sky makes me feel a bit strange. It can't go any higher or further away, can it? Surely, we ought to wind them back in now, bring them home.

Nanny Jan says that's enough kite flying for now because it's time for tea. She says she doesn't much like the look of those clouds in the south-east. She reckons they're coming over from France.

Nanny Mae suggests Finn bring all his seaweed back to the house and then we can use it to forecast the weather. She says you can do it with fir cones too.

The clouds are grey with brown edges, merging with the sea on the horizon. As we pack our stuff up, I tell Nanny Jan that Mrs Betts would say those clouds were full of snow. She laughs and says not in June surely?

'Thunder more like,' says Nanny Mae. 'June thunder clouds. They can grow big and tall, miles high.'

We're all packed up and walking back up the little path. I carry my satchel over my shoulder. Nina says she'll see me tomorrow and wishes me good luck if there's a storm.

'I love a storm actually,' I tell her.

'I think your ghost does too.' She points at Mercy.

Mercy stands at the water's edge with her back to us, looking out to sea. I know she's not happy for some reason. She's capricious.

'Is she bringing on the storm?' Nina's voice is low. The wind has completely dropped. All is still.

'Yes. I think she can do that. Something has made her angry. I never know what or why.'

'I'll see you tomorrow, dear friend. No matter what.'

'No matter what.'

And she runs off down the beach.

CAMELLIA

We are *so* covered in sand from the wind and kite flying that Nanny Jan suggests we have our baths before tea rather than afterwards. I go in with Finn first and then Julia, then Lorna.

There is a delicious smell coming from the kitchen. It's the sausage rolls warming in the oven, and it makes me feel properly hungry. I change into a clean pair of shorts and tee shirt and my skin feels tight and scratchy from the sun and wind. Finn has got sunglasses marks and looks a bit like a panda.

'Panda this, panda that,' he says when I tell him.

It's very dark outside, but my watch says it's only half past five. I climb on to the windowsill to look up at the clouds. The sky doesn't look friendly at all, as if a great bruise is spreading, and the air feels yellow and still. Finn doesn't notice any of this. He says he's hungry and sets off to the kitchen. It gives me a chance to check Mercy's diary is safe.

I open my satchel and take out my pad and colours, then my ordinary book and *Jane Eyre*. No diary. I open *Jane Eyre* and it isn't in there either. Mercy's diary is *missing*. Perhaps I left it on the beach but even as I think that, I know it isn't true. Lorna has stolen it! My heart hammers and jolts, and I have to gasp because I'm running out of air. I must think.

Do I ask her about it now or do I run down to the beach? It *might* have fallen out? The blood in my legs is slowing and cooling, and it takes all my strength to cross the lawn to the little gate.

Ahead of me is the sea and sky. The bruised-plum clouds have spread right across the sky and the sea gleams a sickly green. All the way from France I hear the first rumble of thunder. There isn't a breath of wind.

I find our picnic spot and the diary isn't there. I trace our path back and still no diary. Another rumble of thunder and another. I stand and wonder what to do. If I accuse Lorna, then everyone will know about the diary. I make another search along the path, but it's hopeless.

There's a flash of lightning and I count until I hear the thunder. Seven. The storm is seven miles away. Time to go back to the house because I know lightning is very dangerous if it hasn't started raining. Henry told me that.

Nanny Jan is calling. I trudge slowly back across the lawn with the thunder behind me. I call on Mercy for help.

She is the storm. And she's coming.

CAMELLIA

The sausage rolls sit in the middle of the table. The pastry is toasted and crispy, but I don't feel like eating anything because I'm angry. It's burning a hole through my chest, at least that's what it feels like. The kitchen light is on because it's so dark outside. It's as if we're in the middle of the night.

'Sit here, Melia,' Finn says, patting the chair beside him. Lorna is opposite me and I watch her help herself to a sausage roll. Then I *stare*. Perhaps she will give the diary back if I stare at her for long enough. Nanny Jan tells us to tuck in. There are sausage rolls, bread and butter, cake as well as fruit and Penguin biscuits. She says she can warm up some baked beans if we're really hungry.

'What's up with you?' Lorna voice is sneering.

'You know,' I say.

'I don't!' She sticks her tongue out. Mercy won't like that.

Nanny Mae remembers she left the car windows open. She'd better shut them if we're in for a storm. When she comes back, she says it's ever so close out there and now the wind's picking up. I nibble on the edge of a sausage roll and carry on staring at Lorna. Finn has joined in and says he's easily the best at not blinking.

'You jolly well *do* know!' I shout.

'Shut up!' She sticks her tongue out again.

Three things happen then. There's a flash of lightning, an

almighty crash of thunder (one mile away) and the wooden fruit bowl comes flying off the sideboard, scattering apples. Julia screams and puts her hands over her ears. Nanny Jan bends down to pick up the apples and Finn helps gather those that have rolled under the table.

'It's only a storm, children,' Nanny Mae says when we have another flash, followed by a thunderclap (overhead). 'It's God moving his furniture about, that's all.'

Our overhead light goes out.

'Bum,' shouts Finn.

Two mugs come flying off the dresser. They smash on the floor. Another crash of thunder.

'How on earth did that happen?' Nanny Jan shouts. 'Careful children! Mind your feet. You don't want to step on broken china.'

All the time I stare at Lorna. She's given up, her head down. It's as if we're in the dark but underwater, every second or so being lit up. Nanny Mae takes Julia onto her knee. Finn shouts at the top of his voice that he's quite all right, thank you. He can look after us.

Outside the rain is hissing down. From the corner of my eye I see a plate lift up off the table and throw itself down onto the floor. Then another mug from the dresser.

'Heavens,' Nanny Jan shouts. 'We shall have to pay for this!'

I feel powerful, as if Mercy and the storm are surging through me. I don't care how many mugs or plates have to break and if the others are frightened. I want the diary back.

'You *stole* it!' Lorna looks up and in between the flashes of lightning I can tell she's scared.

'*GIVE IT BACK!*' I yell.

'What's going on between you two?' Nanny Jan has found the dustpan and brush and asks Finn to hold the torch while she tries to sweep up.

'Lorna has stolen something of mine!' I shout. 'And I want her to *GIVE IT BACK*.'

Another crash of thunder. This is a big storm, a Mercy storm. I push back my chair and it falls over with a crash. Julia's sobbing on Nanny Mae's knee and Finn's eyes are wide.

'DAMN YOU!' My voice is strong. Lorna turns her face away. The whole table is shaking now and it's not from the thunder.

I know I've got to escape. I run to the front door and open it, and this is what I see.

Mercy stands in the middle of the lawn, quite dry in the strange half-light of the dark afternoon, while the rain pours down. It pours through her and around her, and the flashes light her up, so that her pretty dress glows pink. The thunder cracks and booms above, and she beckons me with her hand.

I don't hesitate. I step out into the storm and am instantly drenched. I welcome the rain! Let it run down over my face and down my back. I step towards her and she holds out her arms to greet me. Then she curtseys, inviting me to dance.

We dance together and I'm not a bit frightened. I could dance like this forever.

Nanny Jan and Finn are in the doorway watching, and I can just about see Nanny Mae's face behind. It must be odd for them to see me dancing by myself in the rain, but I don't care. Nanny Jan waves as if she's calling me in, but I can't hear her. Why should I want to stop dancing? I am at home in the storm.

Mercy fades away and now I really am dancing alone. It's then that Nanny Mae runs across to rescue me. She ducks her head as the thunder crashes overhead.

'Come in, Camellia!' she shouts with her arms over her head. 'It's dangerous out here!' The spell is broken. She puts an arm around me and leads me back to the house. My teeth are chattering. The party's over, and I'm cold.

Once inside she shines her torch into my face, and her head jerks back.

'What? What's the matter?' I search her face as best I can. What's she seen? She says nothing's the matter, just a trick of the light, that's all. She has a beach towel ready for me and she wraps me up, rubbing my back. I want to cry. She's not my nanny, yet she's showing me such kindness.

'By the way, I've found what you were looking for. It was in Lorna's room, under her bed.' I sag into her arms with relief. 'And who you were dancing with? Is that your ghost?'

'It is.'

Nanny Mae dries my hair with the towel, saying the sooner I get into my pyjamas the better, and very soon we're going to gather in the sitting room where she'll read us a story. I climb up my bunk bed and find the diary on my pillow. It is safe. I hug it to my chest and take a deep breath. Outside the rain has stopped, and the room is growing lighter. The storm is over.

I smile to myself. I did love dancing with Mercy in the rain. I'm always helping her, but this time she helped me.

And that feels right.

NANNY JAN

Mae had more trouble settling her two down than I did. I suppose we're more accustomed to the supernatural. Mind you what happened this evening took things to a whole new level.

We had such a lovely time flying the kites, a welcome change from buckets and spades. All was well at bath time, in spite of the threatening storm, a storm in more ways than one as it turned out. I could tell Camellia was in a terrific sulk about something, having quite the long face. However, at that stage, I had no idea what it was about.

It was *that* frightening to witness china and plates flying about the kitchen, what with the storm raging overhead as well. Mae and I did our best to keep things as normal as possible, but I was terribly afraid our thatched roof might be struck. The storm was right over us, and for that matter we had a right old storm going on in the kitchen. I couldn't get over the table shaking like that. I think the children thought it was caused by the thunder, but I knew it wasn't, and I didn't like it one bit.

The next thing we knew was Camellia yelling at Lorna to give something back, and then she was out of the house. We lost a bit of time then because I had to fetch shoes for the children so that they didn't cut themselves on the broken china. I found it hard to think straight with the flashing and crashing, all the time praying that the lightning didn't hit us. Julia was in a dreadful state, really scared, poor little mite. Finn was amazingly calm considering.

But it was Camellia I was most concerned about. I stood in the doorway with Finn, shouting for her to come back into the house but she heard nothing. Such a strange sight watching her dance by herself, nightmarish if truth be told. Then Mae told me she had 'found *it* under Lorna's bed' and replaced '*it*' on Camellia's pillow.

As we stood in the doorway, scarcely believing our eyes at what was happening, Mae asked who Camellia was dancing with.

'No one.' I couldn't see anyone else.

'Melia's gone mad again,' said Finn, not very helpfully.

'She's dancing with a woman in a pink dress,' said Mae. 'It looks like they are doing a sort of waltz.'

'How come you can see ghosts and I can't?' I wondered what was wrong with me. 'We must bring her in. What if she's struck?!'

Mae offered to rescue her. She said the ghost had gone, so now was the time. She ran out into the rain there and then. At the same time Julia began to scream for Mae, so I had to run and comfort her. That meant I wasn't there to dry Camellia when she came in, and didn't see what Mae saw.

She told me later, once she had read the children a story. They were that shaken up to need three quarters of an hour's story-telling, but by then the storm was over. I hoped it was *properly* over, without another one developing in the night. I told my two the storm in the kitchen was over in any case. I washed up and by eight all four of them were tucked up in bed. We were back to daylight by then. During the storm it was as dark as night.

At last Mae and I were able to have a moment to ourselves. I told her I was that relieved to have her company during the storm. Surely mugs and plates flying across the room weren't normal? Mae reminded me again about her other job. She'd seen all sorts of things fly around. You just had to duck if a saucepan came your way.

'Camellia is at the centre of it, I'm sure,' she said, pressing her fingertips together. 'The ghost is working through her. Poor love, it's not her fault. She can't help any of it.' I poured boiling water into a teapot and set the kettle down. Mae went on.

'You weren't there when we first got back into the house, but I shone the torch into Camellia's face, and it was very pale, white as her ghost in fact.'

'That's not very surprising though, is it, after dancing in the rain?' I stirred the tea leaves in the pot.

'It wasn't just her face, Jan, it was her eyes. They'd changed colour. They were blue.'

My heart sank. This was what Mr Impey was afraid of. *Soon the ghost will take Camellia over.*

'It's happened before, you know. Camellia was in a panic about her eyes changing colour, not to mention the portrait.' I poured out the tea. 'How on earth can that happen?'

Mae shrugged her shoulders and took a sip of tea.

'What had Lorna taken?' I asked.

'A navy-blue book with initials on it, *A.M.* or something. Goodness only knows why Lorna does these things. It's a very odd way to get attention. It isn't as if she even likes books!'

I understood now, able to offer an explanation.

'It must be the ghost's diary, the one Camellia's been looking for all this time. We thought it was in the chest we brought up from the cellar, but no one could open it. She must have managed somehow. I wonder why she didn't tell me?'

Mae smiled and said that children have their ways.

'Doesn't a cup of tea set everything to rights?' she said, putting her feet up on a kitchen chair. I did the same. It had been quite a day.

'Now the diary is back with Camellia, do you think things will settle down?' My voice sounded doubtful. 'And are we going to mention any of this to the parents?' I suddenly felt very tired. I knew Mrs Devon would go right off the deep end if I told her any of this. She'd be bound to ask me all sorts of questions which I wouldn't know how to answer, having kept things quiet. And what about my promise to Camellia? Did promises to children not count?

Mae poured out a second cup. She said she reckoned Lorna wouldn't want to share much of it with anybody, seeing as she had stolen Camellia's book, and Julia hadn't actually seen Camellia dancing in the rain. Finn might tell his mother, but I would deal with that when it came up. More important was to get hold of Mr Impey and ask his advice. In the meantime, I would have a gentle word with Camellia about the diary and reassure her she was not in any trouble. I'm intrigued to discover what's in it in any case. That Nina will cheer us all up tomorrow I'm sure. And we go home on Friday, so only one more day.

I looked in on the children before turning in. Finn was on his back with the bedclothes kicked off, sound asleep. Camellia had wrapped herself in a ball, a frown on her face even while sleeping. She didn't eat any tea with all the upset, and that worried me because she can't afford to lose any more weight. Hopefully she would be hungry tomorrow. I might do boiled eggs for breakfast with white toast soldiers. She loves that.

I'm so relieved I don't have to deal with Lorna. She's obviously craving attention, but it's very tiresome. Give me my two every time, even if one of them comes with a ghost. We can sort this out. At least I hope we can.

Fingers crossed.

CAMELLIA

I wake to hear Finn muttering something about seaweed.

'Melia, my seaweed says it's going to rain today, and look my fir cone's gone all tight.' He holds it up for me to see. I don't answer because I feel very odd, as if I'm not really here at all. I hope I haven't become invisible again! I call out his name.

'Finn!' He's busy draping his seaweed on the windowsill. 'Am I here?' He climbs up the bunk and pats my arm.

'Poor Melia,' he says kindly. 'You are here.' Then he climbs down the ladder and trots off to find Nanny Jan.

I stare up at the ceiling, remembering the storm and dancing with Mercy. Why did I do it? I know I couldn't *not* do it. But now there's a part of me worrying I caused all the trouble last night. I was furious with Lorna for stealing the diary and I can't bear to think how much she might have read. How dare she? It's *private*. And of course she stole the snowman's scarf. That was very mean of her. I don't know how I am going to face her at breakfast. If she sticks her tongue out at me again, I will be sick. I don't want to have to see her again. Ever.

But now I remember Mr Impey's advice about helping people who scare you. Dear Mr Impey! I wish he had been here last night for the storm. He would have known what to do. I know I must try and bless Lorna so that she becomes kinder, just like with Mr Fox, but how do I do it without snowflakes? There aren't any by the sea in June! I must do it another way.

I hold Mercy's diary to my heart and then I think of all the people and things I love, concentrating very hard. I think of my birthday party on Tuesday and all my friends. Then I imagine Lorna in her room with Julia and send her as much love and blessings as I can. It's pretty hard to begin with, but soon I feel a whole stream of love pouring out of me. I actually laugh out loud because I'm so very pleased with myself. It is much better than feeling angry! Poor Lorna not having many friends, when I have lots! That must be hard for her.

Mercy's in the corner smiling. She is peaceful.

I close my eyes. Just a bit more sleep.

CAMELLIA

Lorna said she was sorry at breakfast. Her actual words, while we were eating our boiled eggs and soldiers, were: 'Camellia, I'm really sorry.' My blessing worked!

'Thank you for saying that,' I say, and I mean it. Nanny Mae puts her arm round Lorna, giving her a squeeze as if to say well done.

'The weather's going to be very bad today,' Finn says, munching his toast. 'My seaweed and fir cone say so.'

'Can they talk?' Lorna asks, laughing. You can tell she is trying to be nice. Finn laughs too and says of course they can.

Nanny Jan comes in from outside. She says it is a bit grey and muggy. The storm hasn't cleared the air properly. She certainly couldn't see enough blue sky to make a sailor's trousers. In fact, she couldn't see any blue sky at all. Perhaps not a morning for the beach. We carry on eating our breakfast. I have a huge longing for oranges and tell Nanny Jan so.

'Not sure we will find any in the shop, Camellia. They are not really in season. Oranges are at their best at Christmas.'

'Carrots?' suggests Finn. 'They're orange.'

'Carrots for breakfast?' Lorna nearly falls off her chair laughing. I know she's trying her best, and her voice isn't mocking.

'Maybe some oranges when we get home,' I say. 'I feel like I need lots of orange things. Perhaps people will bring me orange presents for my birthday?'

Nina is tapping on the window. We welcome her in and tell her we're talking about orange presents.

'Well I'm Orange,' she says. We stare at her, not understanding what she means. 'I'm Dutch. We Dutch are Orange. Something to do with our Royal Family.' Nina says yes to a piece of toast and jam. She says she will find me an orange birthday present today. Her mum is taking her to the shops. They are going to Littlehampton.

'How did you get on in the storm?' she asks me. 'Were you afraid?' I tell her what happened in the kitchen and how I went out in the rain. I will share more about the diary later. Now Lorna and I are friends, I don't want to make her feel guilty.

'When are you coming back here?' Nina asks, looking round at all of us, seated at the table. I'm not sure and I nod towards Nanny Jan, hoping she might know.

'We are back the third week of August, with your parents, so it will be a real family holiday.' I hope Lorna and Julia don't feel left out hearing this. There won't be room for everyone in the little cottage.

'Mum and I are here for August,' Nina says. 'Right next door, and I will have made your kite by then.' She gives the sweetest smile. I wish I didn't have to say goodbye to Nina tomorrow, and wonder if Mercy can wait until August for her kite.

Nina says she has to go now because her mum is waiting. I walk out with her across the lawn and tell her about Lorna, the diary and dancing with Mercy.

'Wow,' she says. 'Dancing with your ghost. I should have liked to have seen that.' I take her hand.

'I'll miss you, dear friend.' A magpie chatters in Nina's garden. 'Mercy's visiting you now!'

Nina laughs and says she'll see me tomorrow before we go. She promises she will have something orange for me, and not just herself.

Finn runs towards us, waving his seaweed.

'Goldfish?' he gasps. We stare at him, shaking our heads.

'Well goldfish are orange.'

CAMELLIA

I am exhausted after lunch, so Nanny Mae takes the others to the beach and Nanny Jan stays with me here. I tuck myself into a chair in our sitting room close to the window. I have Mercy's diary on my lap. The secret is out now. It has to be, since Nanny Mae rescued the diary from Lorna. It doesn't really matter if people see me reading it.

Nanny Jan comes in with a cup of tea and sits herself down. I know she wants to talk about the diary. So, I make it easier for her.

'The chest opened, Nanny Jan. Only for about ten minutes but then Finn woke up and came in, and after that it wouldn't open again.

'I didn't put the diary back in. I hid it under my eiderdown, and then behind my dressing table.' Nanny Jan listens.

'It's really interesting. She had a pet magpie, can you believe it? It used to sit in the jackdaw cage sometimes. So, I think that's why we see magpies all over the place. It means she's near.'

'Is she near us now?' Nanny Jan's voice is gentle.

'Yes.' I look behind me. 'She's here.'

'Are you going to tell your Gran you've found the diary?' I think about this and tell Nanny Jan it would be better to wait until after my birthday. I wonder where *praying for guidance* has got her.

'You won't tell Mummy, will you? You promised.'

'I won't tell your Mummy unless I really have to.'

'And not about dancing in the rain with Mercy?' Nanny Jan presses her lips together and says 'No.' She tells me that Nanny Mae saw Mercy with me on the lawn, how we were dancing a waltz.

'She's *real*, Nanny Jan. Nanny Mae saw Mercy on the beach, you know.'

I open the diary and Nanny Jan asks if she can have a look. I pass it over to her and she admires how neat the handwriting is.

'Written all that time ago, with a fountain pen of course. Her thoughts and feelings. This is very valuable, Camellia.'

'You're telling me. I have learned so much about her. She hates hunting, just like me and she went to the Hansel and Gretel opera on her birthday. She loves the "Evening Prayer"! I'm nearly up to 1896.'

It's such a relief to share Mercy's diary with Nanny Jan, so much so that I ask her if she would like to read some of it herself. More than anything I would like to curl up in this chair and fall asleep. They won't be back from the beach for quite a while.

Nanny Jan says she would love to read the diary. I feel her cool hand smooth my forehead as I settle into the chair. The wireless is on very quietly and the sound makes me sleepy.

I can rest.

NANNY JAN

My heart went out to Camellia fast asleep in the chair. Her face and hair were lit up by the dappled light from the window, and for once she wasn't frowning!

Her high cheekbones are even more pronounced, either because her face is growing or because she's so much thinner. Her arms and legs are like pieces of spaghetti! Normally she goes as brown as a berry in the sun but not this time. Finn has more colour! He's fair, and it's not as if I haven't slathered him in Nivea.

I suppose I put too much faith in the sea air, and I certainly didn't imagine her ghost would follow her here. The ghost is indeed real. I have the honour of holding her diary in my hands and I've read on past Camellia's oak leaf bookmark. I've read right to the end.

I know how her great-grandmother died. It's all here in the diary, and the last entry wasn't written by her. It was written by her nurse after her death.

Camellia stirs in the chair, rearranging her limbs and I am thankful she carries on sleeping.

I now understand why her ghost cannot let go. The December entries are dreadfully sad because she knew she was dying, that there was no hope. The doctors forbade her to have any contact with her baby due to fear of infection. She was isolated in her bedroom with the nurse, waiting for Christmas and death. That poor, unfortunate woman and a new mother too! She writes of being able to hear her baby crying and not able to go to her. I find the page again and see what she writes:

'*I hear the cries of Constance and I can do nothing but lie here in bed. It is surely too cruel to endure. My little Bo does what he can to bring comfort, curling up beside me, ever faithful, and my brave magpie visits me often through the open window. It is believed that fresh air has the power to cleanse the contagion from the room, yet not from me. Constance is crying again…*'

Then more: '*Constance cries and I cough.*'

I am so moved by her words. How is Camellia, a little girl of nearly seven, expected to bear this? And a little adopted girl for that matter. I don't believe for one moment her mother died. There must have been a reason for giving her baby up and that must have been a very difficult decision. I can't imagine giving away a baby of my own!

Camellia wakes, complaining that her legs are stiff. She stretches and asks how much I have read. She notices my red eyes.

'Nanny Jan! What's the matter?' She's over to my side in an instant. 'What have you read?' She leans into me on the chair.

'It's so very sad,' I say, searching for my handkerchief. She nods.

'I know, Nanny Jan. Poor Mercy.'

'I've read to the end. I couldn't stop reading actually.' I find my handkerchief.

'And?' Camellia's eyes widen. Thank goodness they're green at the moment.

'She died on Christmas Eve.'

'I know that, Nanny Jan. The window in church says that.'

'She asked for some of the villagers to come and sing "Silent Night" outside her window.'

'When?'

'Christmas Eve morning.'

I open the diary and find the last pages.

'The last entry is written by her nurse, saying she became very peaceful after the carol. She said it was her favourite.'

'And mine,' Camellia says. 'Even though the last two lines are too high for my voice!'

'She had her little dog Bo with her and, believe it or not, her pet magpie visited her often, hopping right into her room.'

'I'm glad,' Camellia says. 'What about Nara?' I make a face then because I know what happened to the horse. There lies even more sadness.

'Come on Nanny Jan, please! Honestly, it's easier that you tell me. I find Mercy's handwriting difficult to read. What happened?' I take a deep breath and begin.

'The ghost's husband...'

'Call her Mercy, Nanny Jan. She won't mind.'

So, I tell her how Mercy's husband took the horse out, against her wishes. He said the horse needed exercise. This was because Mercy was expecting and couldn't ride.

'With child?' Camellia asks. I nod.

'By the January she knew she was going to have a baby. She was very happy, and said it gave her an excuse not to hunt. But she didn't want her husband riding her horse because, as Master, he would expect Nara to jump too high and go too fast.'

I find the page and read it out.

'*Tuesday, 29th January*

My poor Nara is dead. She broke a leg today and had to be shot. I know I have to forgive William, for he says these unfortunate things happen, and he is very sorry. I cannot believe I shall never see my Nara again. I fear I broke into a storm of weeping when he gave me the news and took to my room.'

And later on: '*William says he is preparing to dig a grave for Nara at the end of the garden to make amends. How does "digging a grave" make amends I would like to know?*'

And later: '*My emotions overspill at the slightest recollection of Nara. I have visited her poor frozen grave, where all that is left of her is a huge mound of earth. Bo howled, as if he knew. I cannot bear to think her in the mud, soon to be eaten by worms. William is impatient with my weeping.*'

And later:

'*She was my beloved horse.*'

Camellia's eyes fill with tears.

'Oh, Nanny Jan! It's too, too sad!' I find my handkerchief again and blow my nose. Camellia seems happy to let the tears run down her face. She smiles through them.

'But now Mercy has rescued Nara from her grave and she is free. I've seen them together, Nanny Jan. Nara hasn't come to the sea, mind you. I think she prefers it at home.'

I put the diary down and give Camellia a hug. She is composed. Then she asks me the question I've been dreading.

'What did she die of, Nanny Jan?' I play for time.

'Is Mercy here right now?' I want to be able to see her. Camellia points to the chair in the window, her chair.

'She's sitting in my chair, Nanny Jan, and she's watching us.' I fix my eyes on the chair and fancy I see a shimmer of pink and silver, but that may be my tears.

'What did she die of, Nanny Jan?'

'TB. Your Mercy died of tuberculosis.' Camellia asks what that is, and I tell her as best I can. 'Disease of the lungs. Very infectious. You cough up blood. The doctors wouldn't have wanted the baby, your Gran, to catch it.'

Camellia's face grows even paler.

'Do you think I've got TB? That's why I am getting so thin?' She lifts up her tee shirt to feel her ribs. I can pretty much count them all. There's no flesh around her middle, poor child.

'I do *not*,' I tell her firmly. 'And you aren't coughing in any case!'

'I might start coughing soon though. I might.'

'These days they know how to cure it.' She looks doubtful.

We hear voices in the garden and I'm relieved the beach party has returned. I hand the diary back to Camellia and tell her how honoured I was to read it, that we were in this together.

Finn bursts into the room, saying he did have a crab in his bucket but then he put it back. Instead he has collected more seaweed to take home, so he can be a weather man.

Lorna is the one who surprises us. She reaches into her pocket and pulls out a pretty coiled shell with orange and white swirls. She holds it out towards Camellia.

'For you,' she says. 'It's a bit orange, so I thought it would do. I missed you on the beach.' Camellia politely says thank you. We are both astonished at Lorna's kindness.

'I missed you more!' says Finn and Julia joins in too.

Mae staggers in, weighed down by towels, rubber rings and the like. Her curly hair has obviously had an afternoon of being blown about. She shakes her head and laughs. She says sea air is good for lungs, but not so good for hair. She reckons it's full of sand.

'Time for tea, children! Last tea here and then home tomorrow.'

Lorna, Julia and Finn shout 'Oh *NO!*' in unison. I bend down to give Camellia a kiss on the top of her head.

'Brave girl,' I whisper. She smiles and thanks me. Then she takes the diary and Lorna's pretty shell back to her room.

It will be good to discuss the diary with Mae once the children are in bed. Goodness knows what I will say to Mrs Devon when we get home, or *not* say more like. She's bound to ask questions. What to leave in, what to leave out? I won't get a chance to telephone Mr Impey before next week, not unless Mr and Mrs Devon both go out. In the meantime, I have Mae. She may be only twenty-two but she's full of wisdom.

Tea, then sorting and packing up. The children can play in the garden while we're busy doing that. I must remember the kites. Having read the diary, I wish I could see Mercy properly. I don't think I would be frightened any more.

Not really.

CAMELLIA

It's our last morning and we're all set to leave. The weather is dull and clammy, and Nanny Mae says we have a sea fret coming in. She says she's glad she took the towels off the washing line last night.

I look at my watch. Nina said she would be here by ten, and I'm worried she might be late. Then she'll miss us, and I couldn't bear that. I *must* say goodbye, even though it's hard. Since yesterday I've been overcome with everyone's kindness, and it makes me feel as if I might burst into tears at any minute. I'm brimming like an over-full glass. Nanny Jan has been so kind and helpful with the diary, breaking the news as gently as possible, and now she's trying hard to see Mercy.

I am believed by my Nanny! That's a wonderful thing. I haven't seen Mercy anywhere this morning so Nanny Jan can stop looking here, not that she has much time with the packing and tidying up. I helped her make a list of the things broken in the storm, and I hope it doesn't get us into too much trouble.

The diary is safely packed in my satchel along with Lorna's

shell. My kind magic has worked very well with Lorna. She's kinder to me, so I am kinder to her and that makes her kinder to Julia and Nanny Mae and so on. Nanny Mae told Nanny Jan that Lorna even offered to strip her bunk bed. That's a miracle indeed!

I look at my watch again. Please Nina, don't let me down. The mist is damp and cold, and I can't see any people on the beach this morning. It's deserted.

But suddenly it's not! Here comes Nina flying up the path, calling my name. Her hair and eyelashes are dewy from the sea fret, and she stands before me holding out her present. It's a soft, flat parcel wrapped up in blue and white paper.

'Open it,' she says. 'Seriously, don't wait for your birthday. Open it now!' Nanny Jan calls from the house. She says we really have to be off. There are people coming in after us.

'Coming!' I shout. 'A couple of minutes, that's all.' I tear open the paper to find what's inside. It is an orange sunhat with a bird on the front. I'm not sure what bird.

'I tried to sew a magpie on to the front,' Nina explains. 'That's my best magpie, and that's why I'm a bit late. I was still sewing.' I stroke the bird and tell her it's perfect.

'I promise it's a magpie!' she says, laughing. 'Lucky they're black and white, and my mum had those colours in her sewing basket.' Nina has sewn a magpie on to an orange sunhat, especially for me. I am brimming. I am overflowing. I take a deep breath. I have to tell her.

'I know my ghost died of TB.'

'Tuberculosis?' Nina knows what that is. She says it's very bad. 'Poor ghost.' Nina says why don't I put the hat on, and then she can see how pretty I look. Tears spill out of my eyes and I let them fall. I can't do it myself, so Nina places the hat on my head for me.

'There,' she says. 'Don't cry, my friend. We shall see each other in August and then you'll have a fine kite for your ghost.' She presses an envelope into my hand and says she wrote her address on the inside.

'Happy Birthday, Camellia.' I brush the tears off my face. 'Don't you go opening your card until Tuesday. I shall know if you do, you know!'

'I hate goodbyes,' I say.

'Don't let's say goodbye then.' She pats me on the head. 'Write to me. And tell me what colour ribbons and things you want on the kite.'

It's all too much. All this kindness is breaking me up. Nina knows and pulls my hat down over my eyes, her face close to mine.

'I'll be seeing you, dear friend,' she says.

'No goodbyes?'

'No goodbyes.'

And she runs off into the fret. I stand for a moment in Nina's orange hat, holding my birthday card. My new friend. Then a voice calls up from the beach.

'Give my love to your ghost!'

CAMELLIA

We are home! We tumble out of the car in a sticky, sandy muddle, and my orange hat already feels part of me. Finn runs to the back door carrying his bucket of seaweed. He wants to find Mummy first. Nanny Jan and I hang back and I help her unpack a few things. We have secrets we want to hide from Mummy. Lots of secrets.

There's a white tent up on the lawn! This is all thanks to Mummy, the best party organiser in the world. I run over for a closer look. It's quite a big tent, big enough to block the view to the end of the garden. I open the flap door, and my nose immediately picks up on the familiar tent smell, that smell which means a party! I skip around on the grass carpet. *My* birthday party and I shall be seven, no longer young because seven is surely very grown up.

I hear Finn's voice shouting my name.

'Mummy's here!' and again 'Mummy's here!'

Why do I feel so worried about seeing Mummy? I know why.

She's going to find something wrong with me, I just know it. I step out of the tent, and there's Mummy with Finn standing beside her, bucket in hand. Mummy's wearing a pretty blue shirt and white skirt, and she puts her head on one side when she sees me.

'Hello darling,' she says, and I walk forward to kiss her hello. She smells delicious, *Madame Rochas* I think. 'What do you think of the tent?'

'It's super,' I say truthfully. 'And so big! When did they put it up?' Mummy says the men came yesterday, and she's ordered tables and chairs as well so, whatever the weather, I shall have a garden birthday party. She puts her hand out to pat my head.

'New hat?' I tell her it's an early birthday present.

'Rather a frightful colour.' I know Mummy doesn't like orange, just as Daddy doesn't like mauve. But they're only colours, aren't they?

'Nina gave it to her,' Finn says. He has noticed my face. 'She sewed the magpie on herself.'

'A magpie on an orange hat!' says Mummy. 'Not sure I'd wear that to Ascot.'

'Nina was fun,' says Finn.

'A new friend?' Mummy's smile is bright.

'Yes,' I tell her. 'She's Dutch and that means she's Orange.'

I'm feeling so hurt I have to walk off. I can't bear to be with Mummy. I'm not going to tell her about the kites. Finn can do that. I look around for Mercy. She would understand. Why do I have to have a Mummy who doesn't like orange?

I run upstairs to find my satchel on my bed. Kind Nanny Jan. My dolls stare down at me from the shelves. Dorothy Baby is fast asleep on my bed and Heidi has dust on her hair. I brush it off. But I know who I want more than anyone. I reach up to Mr Fox and hug him to my chest.

'Oh Mr Fox,' I say, loving him. 'You are orange, you are kind and I've missed you.'

His yellow eyes glow. I know he loves me back.

NANNY JAN

The drive home was easy, and the children were as good as gold in the back. We sang along a bit, not Cliff Richard this time but one of Finn's favourites. It's called 'Blame it on the Bossa Nova', whatever a Bossa Nova is. Finn calls it the *Bossa Bova*.

We left the sea fret behind, but the skies remained grey for the journey, the air sticky. I hoped we weren't in for another storm. At least this house has a lightning conductor and no thatched roof to worry about.

I didn't know how I was going to explain all the breakages to Mrs Devon. I could hardly say they flew off the shelves by themselves. How about we couldn't see in the dark and we knocked them off the table by mistake? I couldn't expect Finn to lie, so we would have to wait and see what he said to his mother.

We hadn't been home five minutes before Camellia and her mother had fallen out. Finn told me it was something to do with her orange hat. He likes Camellia's orange hat and I do too. It suits her. I must say the tent looked good on the lawn. That is one thing I can say about Mrs Devon. She knows how to organise a party.

I was bracing myself for the inevitable 'wanting to have a word with me', and I wondered if it would come before or after lunch. As it happened it was neither. Mrs Devon helped me unload a few things from the car, while telling me that she and Mr Devon had been asked to go fishing for the weekend in Hampshire. Not only that but they had two friends invited for lunch today, and they were arriving any minute.

I knew the children would be disappointed. We've only just got back and now their parents are away again. On the other hand, maybe that suited me? Let a bit of time go by. Let the dust settle.

I found Camellia in her room staring into space. Banger was sat on her bed, panting. That dog does a lot of panting, I must say. I gave her a hug and told her I understood. She didn't seem to mind about her parents going off fishing. She just said '*typical*'. I noticed Mercy's diary in full view on her bedside table. She told me with a sigh that her ghost was back '*in her corner*'. I squinted but couldn't make her out. 'You will soon,' she said. I went back down to the nursery where I found Finn draping seaweed over the terrace. He told me his mother liked the seaweed, so I suppose that was something.

Why did I feel so flat? Our welcome home was not as warm as it could have been. However, the fishing trip would give me an opportunity to telephone Mr Impey. I would try this evening.

There wasn't a breath of wind about, so not much good for the washing line.

ANGELA

I can never get it right with Camellia! I thought she would have been more pleased about her birthday tent but no, she just looked sulky beneath that awful hat. It did nothing for her complexion which was a strange colour anyway. I would have thought her face would be browner after a week by the sea.

At least Finn seemed happy and he was really very funny showing me his different bits of seaweed. He's now an absolute expert in forecasting the weather. If the seaweed is dry, it will be sunny and if damp, it will rain.

His face fell when I told him about our fishing trip. I do feel rather guilty about going away just when the children are back. However, Gerald was terribly pleased to get a last-minute invitation to fish on the Test, that the mayfly would be just so. I feel a bit like a mayfly myself, gadding about trying to organise everything.

I have organised the tent, the tables and chairs, what flowers are needed to decorate the tables, Camellia's present (oil paints), the party invitation replies (who is coming, who is not), organised for Constance and John to come, organised for Peter and Rosemary to come, with their new baby, organised for Mr Impey to come, organised the party food with Cook, organised what party games to play, etc etc. What else?

I've also organised for the children's portraits to go up in the corridor. I've just about packed for Hampshire. I have kept Gerald happy. I've found my fishing rod. I haven't found my polaroids annoyingly. I can't think about the Ascot picnics yet, but at least I know what I'm wearing. Certainly not orange!

Finn gave me a bit of seaweed when we were setting off in the car. He posted it through the car window. Camellia stood sulking by the back door in that hat.

'Then you'll know what the weather will be like tomorrow, Mummy.'

I kept it on my lap for the journey, even when Gerald said it smelt bloody awful and why didn't I throw it away.

What would I say to Finn? Sometimes Gerald is very stupid.

CAMELLIA

I'm having a bit of peace in my room when I hear voices in the corridor. I edge along the wall to listen properly.

'Such a good likeness of Camellia!' says Mummy. 'We love it. Not so good of Finn, but then he wouldn't sit still. I couldn't blame Señor Ordinand for that!'

Laughter. Then Mummy's friend talks, something about wanting the Spanish artist to draw her children.

'He's very busy, I know that.' Mummy again. I know something about Mummy. She won't want lots of children being drawn by the Spanish artist. They go back downstairs and it's safe for me to creep along to view the portraits for myself. Mercy stands right at the far end, waiting.

I look at Finn's portrait first and it isn't really Finn. His eyes are too big, but at least they are the right colour. It's a three-quarters view and his face is strangely doll-like.

Next I look at myself. This face is rounder than mine now, and the fringe shorter. I peer closely at the eyes which are green, as well as the faintest traces of blue in the dress, the lace in white chalk. He has signed the picture Ordinand 63 in pencil.

Who is that person in the picture? Am I the same Camellia? I am thinner surely. Is my *soul* thinner? Am I wasting away like poor Mercy? Nanny Jan told me that TB was called the wasting disease. I take a deep breath and cough, but the cough sounds normal, not an ill cough.

Mercy is behind me. She's breathing on me, making me cold. I tell her to leave me alone. Please, just for once.

We watch television after tea, and it feels good to lie on the sofa doing absolutely nothing. Outside the clouds are building up, piling one on top of the other, growing tall and thundery. Finn feels his seaweed, saying it's definitely damper than it was.

There are two ghost dogs on the terrace. They pad slowly up to the nursery window and stare in, wagging their tails. I tell Finn and he says they had better not steal his seaweed. It's amazing how normal it feels to talk about ghost dogs, on or off the terrace.

One of them, the pale Labrador, is new. That makes four Labradors rescued by Mercy. I wonder if they're all out of their graves now.

I close my eyes. *Wagon Train* is sending me to sleep.

CAMELLIA
Mercy dead

The most enormous crash of thunder wakes me up! I tell myself it's only God moving his furniture about, that's all, but this is like he's *throwing* it about, just like Mercy with the mugs and plates. There's no point counting from flash to thunder because there's non-stop flashing and non-stop crashing. The storm must be right overhead, and the windows are rattling like mad. They might break! I pull back the curtains, noticing that Mercy is missing from her corner. Outside the garden is silver-white from the lightning and the rain hammers down on the roof.

'Melia!!' Finn is in my doorway. 'Don't like it!' There's another crash and I have to put my hands over my ears.

'Let's go to Nanny Jan!' I shout. 'Then we can get into her bed.'

'Argggghhh!' cries Finn, ducking down from the noise.

'Follow me!' I yell. 'Stay close behind!' We walk carefully down the flashing corridor, past our new portraits, lit up in silver and white.

I push Nanny Jan's bedroom door open. If anything, the storm is worse in here because the windows face out over the whole sky. Nanny Jan's curtains aren't stopping the lightning coming in at all. How *is* she sleeping through this? She must look after us! Why isn't she awake? I go over to the bed, reaching out to pull back the covers. She *has* to wake up.

'Nanny Jan, wake up *please!*' Again. 'Please wake up!' Nothing happens, so I pull back the covers even more. Where has she gone? She isn't there! She isn't here!

But someone else is.

NO, NO, NO! How can this be? I jump back from the bed, my head buzzing with the horror of it. I know exactly why Nanny Jan doesn't hear me and why she can't wake up. It's because she has turned into Mercy. Mercy now lies in Nanny Jan's bed with her eyes closed, her face like chalk. Mercy has died. Mercy is *dead.* She has died in the middle of a thunderstorm and if she opens her eyes...

I scream. It's too much. Behind me I hear Finn shout 'What is it? What is it?' I can't tell him. He mustn't see this. I back away from the bed, screaming and screaming.

Nanny Jan sits up in bed and everything goes black.

NANNY JAN

I sat bolt upright in bed to find both children in my room, Camellia on the floor and Finn dancing about her in distress. We were in the middle of yet another thunderstorm, this one even more violent than Middleton.

'She's dead, Nanny Jan! She's dead!' I could just about hear Finn above the thunder, but it was enough to put me into a flat panic.

'What on earth happened?' Finn said he didn't know. Camellia was motionless on her back, arms outstretched. I shook her shoulder gently, calling her name. Nothing.

'Fetch me my flannel from the basin, Finn. Just over there, look. Turn the tap on first and run it under the cold.' Finn was very quick for his age. I wiped the dripping flannel around

Camellia's face. She stirred and tried to sit up, her eyes staring.

'The face, the face!' she cried. 'It wasn't you!' I didn't understand. 'You turned into Mercy. She was lying there. Dead!'

Finn very bravely trotted over to my bed.

'Not there now, Melia,' he shouted. 'All gone now.'

'It was Mercy, Nanny Jan. It was awful.' She put her hands over her eyes.

'She died in this room, Nanny Jan. I know it.'

'But this is a new house, Camellia. Only a couple of years old.'

'Well her room must have been here, in the same place, in the old house.'

'Not here now!' shouted Finn again, patting the bed.

The windows were rattling in their frames that much, and the thunder shaking the very foundations of the house. Thank goodness for the lightning conductor! I asked the children if they wanted to climb into bed. Finn was happy to, but Camellia was reluctant. She didn't want me to turn into Mercy again. I assured her that I would stay awake and, once the storm had finished, she could go back to her own room.

As I sat there, with the children either side, taking it in turns to count to ten after each and every flash, I worried about what in heaven's name I should tell Mrs Devon.

It was a real shame Mr Impey wasn't at home when I tried him earlier. It's Sunday today, and no doubt he will be extremely busy. However, busy or not, I must try and get hold of him. Who knows what really happened in this room but, whatever it was, it was an escalation. I'm out of my depth. I simply don't understand why I didn't wake up earlier with the storm. If I had, none of this would have happened.

I tucked the children back into their own beds at 4.15am. We hadn't heard any thunder for over half an hour and the birds were singing. Dawn was breaking as I walked back along the corridor, light enough anyway to see how the eyes had changed in Camellia's portrait. They were almost black, as if she were Chinese.

I smoothed my finger over the glass but they didn't change.

I shook my head, weary now from lack of sleep. I would think about this in the morning, except that we were morning already. Once back in bed, I closed my eyes. What a night!

I was sleeping in Mercy's bedroom, a poor dead woman whose spirit wouldn't let go. I mustn't worry about that now.

There would be a magpie at the window next...

CAMELLIA

When I wake, Mercy is standing in her corner as if she's asleep. Oh, to have my bedroom to myself! As soon as I have the thought, she opens her eyes.

Every bone in my body feels weary, and no wonder after that storm. I try not to remember the chalkiness of Mercy's face, sharp yet sunken in, the storm raging around us, a horrible storm this time. I certainly didn't feel like dancing. Where had Nanny Jan gone in any case? Did Mercy hide her in the portal, while she took her place in bed?

Only I saw Mercy like that. Luckily Finn was behind me. I wouldn't have wanted him to see her dead. But I'm forgetting Finn can't see Mercy! Perhaps Mercy jumped into Nanny Jan? I wish she could settle on being nice and stop being capricious. I don't think it's fair.

I open the curtains and outside all is mist. Not a November fog or a sea fret. This is a summer mist full of birdsong. I should feel full of joy because it's nearly my birthday but instead I feel a sense of dread. I know I'm ill.

Finn calls my name and the next thing I know he has joined me at the windowsill to look at the day. He has to stand on my little chair to see out. We both lean on our elbows, Finn in his summer pyjamas and me in my white nightdress with tiny blue flowers.

'There's the tent,' Finn says.

I watch as Mercy walks straight through it. She will be off down to the end of the garden I'm sure, so she can rescue the last of the dogs. At least that will keep her busy.

'What shall we do today?' Finn asks. When I don't answer, he stares at me. 'You've got red spots on your cheeks.'

'What?' Not chickenpox again?

'Bit like Heidi,' he says. 'Big spots.'

I rush to the bathroom mirror. I have spots, the size of half crowns, on both cheeks, not like a doll, more like a clown. I press my fingers to the spots, and they turn white but then, when I take my fingers away, they become red again. I splash cold water on to my face, hoping to make them go away, but it just makes them more red.

'Oh NO!' I cry, holding the towel up to my poor clown face. Finn comes into the bathroom and asks to see my face again. I lower the towel.

'Blame it on the *Bossa Bova*,' he says.

'I'm not sure we can do that, Finn.' I know he's trying to cheer me up.

'I'll get Nanny Jan,' he says. 'She'll know what to do.' He runs off down the passage, while I look in the mirror once more. I look a fright.

I'm back in my room when Finn comes in with Nanny Jan. She looks very tired, as well she might, having spent time in the portal.

'Now Camellia. Finn says you look like a clown.' I glare at Finn. He takes no notice.

'I can't see anything wrong with your face,' Nanny Jan says, peering at me.

'They were there,' Finn says, hands on hips. 'Promise.'

I rush over to my dressing-table mirror. The spots have disappeared.

CAMELLIA

Finn and I spend a quiet morning together. Instead of sunning themselves on the terrace, the dogs lie on the nursery carpet. It's too hot outside. I play the piano a bit, trying out some new tunes. I've brought a little mirror down with me so I can check my face every five minutes. The spots haven't come back yet.

After breakfast Nanny Jan weighed us on Mummy's scales.

She didn't say anything as she wrote down the amounts. She said she didn't dare weigh herself, not after all those sausage rolls. We laughed at that.

She tells us we need to amuse ourselves this morning, seeing as she's got lots of chores to do, washing and sorting. We're lucky it's a good hot day for clothes on the line. And of course we are back to school tomorrow. I wonder how Mummy and Daddy are enjoying their fishing? I only hope Mummy's in a good mood when she gets back.

I step out on to the sunny terrace, wearing my orange hat. I feel like wandering around the garden a bit and promise Nanny Jan I will keep in the shade as much as possible. Mercy is nowhere to be seen.

A soft breeze is rustling the leaves of the copper beech, and the lawn looks parched, even after all that rain. Banger follows me and pants, her tongue very pink. I want to just drift about, not to have to think about anything at all. When I hear the bees buzzing, I am glad I don't have to be a bee today.

I sit in the shade letting my eyes wander around the flower-bed, watching the bees, and it's then that I glimpse a rose at the very back, hidden away. It's a deep, clear pink and I know at once it's Mercy's rose. How do I know? Well, if it's thornless, then it's the same rose. Getting up wearily, I push through the scratchy plants and bushes, keeping my elbows tucked in.

When I bury my nose into a half-open rose, my heart leaps for joy. Never have I come across a scent as sweet as this, and it's as if I cannot get enough of it. I run my fingers along the stems for thorns and of course there are none. This must be Zéphirine Drouhin, the thornless rose.

It's already my favourite, and surely it would be safe to ask Gran about this rose? She might be able to tell me how old it is. It could be the *very* same rose. She might even have a rose book.

Finn asks what I'm doing. Am I looking for magpie feathers?

'This rose, Finn! It's just brilliant. No thorns and it smells heaven.'

'Will you pick one?'

I say I will need some scissors, so Finn runs off to fetch some and, because he knows scissors are dangerous, he puts them safely in his wheelbarrow, bumping it down the steps. I snip off one rose and carry my treasure back to the nursery. I shall draw and paint this rose. I have enough energy to do that.

There's a ghost terrier lying beside Banger in the shade. She doesn't seem to mind.

NANNY JAN

I had no idea what the children were going on about this morning. Finn insisted Camellia looked like a clown but, by the time I arrived in her bedroom, she was fine.

I must say I felt dead beat. What with the thunderstorm, the scare with Camellia, lack of sea air, so many chores to do, the prospect of Mrs Devon's *having a word with me,* keeping the children calm, preparing the stuff for school, needing to telephone Mr Impey, cooking lunch (no Cook on a Sunday), it was rather a lot to manage.

I weighed the children after breakfast. I didn't dare weigh myself! Finn's the same as last time but Camellia has lost five pounds. No wonder she looks thin! And it's not as if she isn't eating. She's tired though, most of the time. Mind you, I should think being haunted is pretty tiring.

I tried telephoning Mr Impey before lunch, giving him enough time to recover from church, but he didn't answer.

Camellia has found herself a beautiful pink rose, thornless and the very one her ghost was fond of. She settled down and painted a lovely picture. She included a little bee and, when I asked her why, she said every rose needs a bee.

I tried Mr Impey at teatime, and then again after my small supper. He must have gone away for the weekend. Still, he's invited to Camellia's birthday party and we can make a plan then, not that I will have much spare time. I had a chance to view the party list. I believe we shall be over thirty in the tent.

I was just about dropping off on the sofa when I heard Mr

Devon's car drawing up outside. They told me they had a most productive day, twelve trout between them! Finn will be pleased.

Mrs Devon suggested I get off to bed immediately, so that was kind of her. She said she would like a word with me in the morning, but after I had taken the children to school.

I will need to have my wits about me!

ANGELA

After a long and sticky drive, it was a relief to be home. A successful day's fishing though, with so many mayfly about you could barely see your hand in front of your face. There was a fair bit of rain in the night which freshened up the river no end, or so Gerald said.

I'm never very sure about mixing alcohol with fishing, even if the sherry was icy cold. All I wanted to do after lunch was fall asleep quite frankly.

At least I slept well back in my own bed. I popped in on the children during breakfast and was horrified by Camellia's appearance. She seems so dreadfully pale and droopy. While fending off Finn and his questions about how many fish we'd caught, I asked Nanny Jan how the children had been over the weekend. She gave me a funny look.

'Never mind now,' I said in my brightest voice. Camellia was sitting slumped at the breakfast table, stirring her bowl of cornflakes. She had two red patches on her cheeks which I didn't like the look of. Not scarlet fever surely?

'Melia's birthday tomorrow,' said Finn. I said it most certainly was, trying not to think about scarlet fever.

'All ready for school?' Why did my voice sound false? 'I've got lots to organise for the party, Camellia.' For a moment I had her attention.

'Thank you, Mummy.' And then she went back to her cornflakes.

I need to find out what's been going on, but I will have to wait until Nanny Jan gets back from the school run. It's obvious Camellia is ill and will need to see Dr Byng. Perhaps an appointment for this afternoon?

In the meantime, Mrs Betts can help me unpack.

NANNY JAN

Camellia was very dispirited this morning, as if all the joy was drained out of her. Finn jumped up and down, singing 'Blame it on the Bossa Nova'. It's his way of cheering her up, but it didn't work. She sat at the breakfast table, most subdued.

She pointed at her clown spots, her eyes full of tears. They were unusual, I had to say. I took her temperature to be on the safe side, but she was normal.

So, Camellia had no temperature, just clown spots. I suggested how seeing her friends might cheer her up, and she gave me a half-smile. She told me she'd hidden the diary in the drawer of her dressing table. Of course, the chest is in her cupboard. So many things I promised I wouldn't tell Mrs Devon!

We were safe at breakfast when Mrs Devon popped in to say hello, but I won't be when I get back from school. I really needed to consult with Mae before my interrogation.

As it happened Mae was dropping Julia off, and I waved at her among the parked cars. I was able to tell her what had happened on Saturday night, about the clown spots and how I was going to handle Mrs Devon.

'They sound to me like hectic spots,' Mae said. 'I've heard they come up when a child is overwrought. They come and go. My brother had them once and my mother didn't take much notice. She just tucked him tighter at bedtime!' I had to smile at this. She asked if I'd been able to talk to Mr Impey and I shook my head.

'I think he must have been away.'

'Your poor Camellia is weighed down with it all,' said Mae kindly. 'Good luck with Mrs Devon and I'll be there at the party tomorrow to help.'

She closed her car door and wound down the window.

'You wouldn't believe how nice and kind Lorna is being. She actually asked her mother yesterday if she could help clear the table.' Mae laughed out loud. 'You see, miracles do happen!'

I laughed too. I gave a last glance across the road towards the school. I hoped Camellia would survive the morning.

I wasn't sure I was going to!

NANNY JAN

Mrs Devon was waiting for me on my return. *Here we go* I thought. She suggested we have our talk in the nursery which suited me fine, and we sat down at the table as if we were having a business meeting. Mrs Devon had her diary out and I could see Monday 10th was covered in blue writing.

'I've made an appointment for Camellia to see Dr Byng.' Her eyes fixed mine. So this was already organised. I nodded politely and asked her when for.

'This afternoon. He had a space at 5.30pm. Now if you could take her, I would be so grateful. I will need to be here, waiting for the tables and chairs to arrive. They are coming in the horse box.'

Ah, I thought. So, it has to be me. I will have to sit in that waiting room with a nervous Camellia, waiting for the red buzzer to go off.

'I have requested a blood test.'

'Camellia won't like that,' was all I could say. Mrs Devon pressed on.

'I'm worried she might be very ill. Why has she lost so much weight? And now those funny spots on her face. Something must be causing it and a blood test will no doubt reveal what's going on.' Mrs Devon used her biro to tick something off in her diary.

'I'm relying on you, Nanny Jan. Better to get the blood test over and done with today, then Camellia can really enjoy her birthday tomorrow.' She shut her diary with a snap.

'So ... how was the holiday? You had some lovely weather, didn't you? At least it was scorching here. All well?'

I told her we had a wonderful time, that the children had fun with a pair of kites, that they all got on like a house on fire. All this was true. I told her how much I liked Nanny Mae, that we were a good team.

I confessed to the breakages, putting it down to a terrific thunderstorm. Mrs Devon looked puzzled, so I explained that the kitchen light had gone out and we couldn't see what we were doing. No feet cut on the broken china luckily. Mrs Devon opened her diary again and scanned Monday, 10th June.

'Lots to do, Nanny Jan. We will be about thirty tomorrow, remembering my brother and his wife are coming. They are bringing their dear little baby, Martha, so that will be popular with the children. She's not yet two weeks old!' Mrs Devon's face softened. She loves a newborn baby, as do we all.

'Camellia wondered if she might have some oranges?' I congratulated myself on remembering this. 'I know they're not very good at this time of year but even June oranges must have *some* vitamin C.'

Mrs Devon liked the sound of vitamin C and said she would add oranges to the fruiterers' order. She wondered if strawberries were full of vitamin C too. She had ordered lots of those.

She then gave me various tasks connected with the party, including helping with a table plan. I could hear Mrs Betts's voice outside. She was wondering if she could come in and give the nursery a good hoover. I knew it was an excuse to have a chat about the holiday, but Mrs Devon rose from her chair and opened the nursery door. She'd heard what Mrs Betts had said, and firmly informed her that she would prefer Mrs Betts to come upstairs and help with the unpacking.

How can a woman not unpack for herself? It's not that difficult surely. We all have to dance to Mrs Devon's tune but *she's* the employer. In the meantime, I needed to get busy, all the while remembering I had the unhappy task of explaining to Camellia why she had a doctor's appointment this afternoon. I wouldn't tell her about the blood test. We would cross that bridge when we came to it. I saw no reason to confess any more to Mrs Devon, especially as she did not once ask if Camellia was happy.

I tidied up the children's rooms first. I made Camellia's bed and carefully arranged Mr Fox and Dorothy Baby on her pillow. They do make a funny pair, I must say. I caught the faintest trace of rose scent in the corner by the cupboard, and then, coming out of my bedroom with my wireless, I distinctly heard crying at the end of the corridor.

She was crying in the daytime now! I might get Mrs Betts up here later to listen.

CAMELLIA

Now I know I'm *really* ill. Nanny Jan tells me in the car that Mummy has booked me to see Dr Byng at 5.30 this afternoon. She says it's just for a *check-up* and everything in me screams NO.

I can scream NO as much as I like but it won't make any difference. If Mummy says I have to go to the doctor, then I have to. I'm glad Nanny Jan is taking me because, if Mummy did, then I might say something mean.

I just have to get through it, a bit like hunting. The dread sits over and around me right through lunch. It has spoilt the day before my birthday, after the morning had been all right.

My friends at school were very kind, gathering round and asking about the latest news. Finn was allowed to join our meeting on the stage and loved all the attention. Julia hovered halfway through and we welcomed her up. Anyone who can survive a Mercy thunderstorm deserves to join our meetings. I could tell she was thrilled because the tips of her ears went pink. No Lorna as she goes to another school. She is nine after all.

My clown spots had faded by the time we got to school, but they came back at break. No one said I was thinner, but I bet they noticed. I drank my milk at break and it made me feel sick. Sarah offered me some of her orange juice and that reminded me.

'I can't get enough orange,' I said. 'It's odd.'

'I love orange,' said Melanie-Anne. 'My best colour.'

'I prefer green,' said Finn. 'Like seaweed.'

'Your birthday tomorrow, Melia,' Sarah said. 'Can't wait for your party!' Her eyes sparkled. 'Just wait till you see *my* present.'

Miss Wiggins rang the bell for us to return to class. This was all before I knew I was going to the doctor.

I hate doctors.

CAMELLIA
Dr Byng

Nanny Jan and I sit in the waiting room. I watch the second hand crawl round the clock. It's 5.27pm. There's one other person waiting, a fat woman in a brown dress with brown shoes. She has a brown handbag perched on her lap. She could do with a bit of orange!

Dr Byng's buzzer is red so that's our one. The green buzzer goes off and the fat woman rises to her feet, shuffling slowly through to the other doctor. Nanny Jan squeezes my hand.

'Soon be over, Camellia,' she says. 'Then we'll be counting down till your birthday.' The words *counting down* fill me with fear. Counting down to what?

I close my eyes and call on Mercy for help. When I open them, I stare at my sandals. There's a trace of sand in one of the holes, precious Middleton sand. We wait for ten whole minutes. Dr Byng is running late! Then the red buzzer goes. This is it.

Nanny Jan keeps hold of my hand as she pushes the doctor's door open. She wonders if I want to sit on her lap, but I shake my head. Mercy is already standing behind Dr Byng. She's with me. I whisper to Nanny Jan 'She's here.'

'Eh?' says Dr Byng. He didn't quite catch what I said.

Dr Byng's moustache is as neat as ever, less like Samuel Whiskers today, more like a sandy Charlie Chaplin. His eyes are beady and sharp. He asks how I'm getting on with my drawing. I sit up very straight, knowing he's trying to get around me by being nice. I lift my chin.

'Very well thank you, Dr Byng. I painted a beautiful pink rose yesterday, a thornless rose. It's the Zéphirine Drouhin. Perhaps you know it?'

Dr Byng says he doesn't and puts a thermometer in my mouth. We sit quietly for a minute while I watch Mercy lift a book from Dr Byng's desk. She puts a finger to her lips and then deliberately drops it. Dr Byng jumps and turns around. It's given him a shock and I smile.

Dr Byng reads the thermometer and says my temperature is perfectly normal. He examines my face when Nanny Jan mentions the spots but, as they are not there at the moment, Dr Byng says it's difficult to judge. Then he feels my neck, looks in my ears, makes me say *aah* with a lolly stick and finally asks me to raise my shirt, so he can listen to my heart and lungs. He puts the cold stethoscope on my back first and then, when I turn for him to listen to my heart, I see Mercy lift something else off the desk. We then *combine* to frighten Dr Byng.

She drops a metal dish on the floor at the exact moment I breathe out into Dr Byng's face with a loud '*HAH!*' Now his eyes are darting about in fear and I say one word to him.

'*CONTAGION!*'

'Are you all right, Dr Byng?' Nanny Jan's voice is concerned, but she's on my side. Dr Byng is trying to write his notes and I notice his hand is shaking and his moustache twitching. He finishes writing.

'Well I can find nothing wrong. But perhaps just to be absolutely sure I would like to do a blood test.'

I swing round to Nanny Jan. Surely not? She gives me a weak smile and promises to hold my hand. It will be over in a jiffy. Mercy doesn't interfere while Dr Byng prepares the needle and draws the blood out of my arm.

'All done,' Dr Byng says, placing a piece of cotton wool on the puncture wound. 'You press down on that hard, Camellia, like a good girl.' It aches in a horrible way. Dr Byng suddenly remembers he hasn't put my weight down in his notes. He asks me to stand on his set of scales but not before he sellotapes the cotton wool to my arm. He says I can take it off in the bath.

'*DAMN YOU,*' I shout. His head jerks up. Then there's an almighty crash behind Dr Byng. Three books have come flying off his bookcase. They lie scattered and broken on the lino. Dr Byng bends to pick them up while Mercy leaves us, walking straight through the door. She has done *well*. I stand on the scales and Dr Byng records my weight. I notice his hand is shaking again. I'm *glad* he's scared.

'The results of the blood test should be through in less than a week.' He peers at one of the books, its spine badly damaged. 'I'll telephone your mother when they're in.'

'Thank you, Dr Byng,' I say politely. 'I'm sorry about your books.' Then I give him one of my stares. 'Perhaps your room is haunted?'

'We thought oranges and vitamin C might help,' Nanny Jan says, picking up her handbag, getting ready to leave. Dr Byng says that vitamin C is always useful and recommends Haliborange tablets. He glances at his damaged books again, then back at the bookcase, shaking his head.

Nanny Jan follows me as we leave the surgery.

'Crikey,' she says. 'That was some show.'

It was. I felt powerful in the surgery, but now I'm tired.

NANNY JAN

I've never known a doctor's appointment like it! That poor Dr Byng didn't stand a chance against Camellia and Mercy. I reckon Mr Impey will soon be getting a call to bless his consulting room.

Nevertheless, there *is* a serious side to this. I didn't like the words coming out of Camellia's mouth as I'm pretty sure they weren't hers. I don't believe she would ever say *CONTAGION* or *DAMN YOU*. That was shocking actually. I fear Mr Impey's warning is coming true.

Camellia was exhausted by the time we got back home. The tables and chairs had indeed arrived and Mr and Mrs Devon were setting them up in the tent. Finn was dancing around making helicopter noises, along with singing his *Bossa Bova*. Anyone could see he was thoroughly overexcited.

'All done?' Mrs Devon asked. Camellia frowned and showed Finn her arm with cotton wool and sellotape.

'He stole my *blood*!' she said, scowling. 'But I showed him.' Then she whispered into Finn's ear and he jumped up and down laughing.

'What's all this?' Mrs Devon didn't want to be left out. I noticed she had a dirty smudge on her front, probably from one of the tables. Camellia didn't answer. Instead she trailed round the tables and chairs counting.

'Twenty-eight, Mummy,' she said. 'We don't need one for Baby Martha because she'll be in her pram, but we do need one for my *GHOST*!!!'

'*What* did you say, Camellia?' Mrs Devon had frozen, halfway through wiping down a table.

'Ghosty Goo Goos!' cried Finn, saving the day. 'Ghosty Goo Goos.' Then he doubled up laughing before yelling 'Ghosty Poo Poos.' I knew he was overexcited and dreaded anything worse. Of course, it came.

'Bum! Bum! Bum!' he shouted, waving his arms. His parents laughed. That meant I could laugh and even Camellia's frown lifted. Finn was loving the attention. He opened his mouth again, but I got there just in time.

'Bath time, you two. The sooner you bath and get to bed, the sooner it will be Camellia's birthday.' By lucky chance they both accepted it *was* bath time, and Finn took my hand to walk back but not before he burst out with 'Helicopter Bum.'

The children laughed all the way up the stairs. That cheered me up. Mrs Devon can get on with arranging the tables and chairs and I will care for Camellia and Finn. That's my job after all.

PART V

CAMELLIA

June 11ᵗʰ

It's my birthday and I'm seven years old! I draw back the curtains to find three magpies perched on my windowsill. They turn around to face me, their clear eyes blinking, so I bow my head and smile. They are wishing me Happy Birthday, and I wonder why three of them?

Their tails are not very long, so perhaps they are magpie children. Mercy isn't in her corner, so I share a moment with the the magpies while my birthday morning shimmers beyond. Mercy loves this sort of morning. I bet she's out and about, walking through the garden and breathing in the fresh air, although I'm not sure she breathes like me.

I test my arms and legs for strength and they're not too bad. They feel stronger than yesterday, but my arm is still sore from where the blood was taken. The sellotape came off in the bath, leaving a dark purple bruise. I do a cough and my cough sounds normal. Then I check my eyes in my dressing-table mirror and they are green. I take a deep breath. All is well on my birthday.

Nina's card sits on my bedside table and when I open it, I find she has drawn it herself. It's a picture of us on the beach. I am in my red swimsuit, wearing Nina's orange hat and she's in her green swimsuit, holding a yellow bucket. Behind is the sea and above us blue sky with a big, shining sun. Inside she has written *'To my dear new friend Camellia, Happy Birthday, love from Orange Nina xoxox.'* On the back she has written her address.

It's a beautiful card, the first card of the day. It's only seven o'clock on my seventh birthday, so I have time to read a little of Mercy's diary. I shall shut my eyes and read wherever it falls open.

'*Thursday, 27ᵗʰ August.*

Oh, how ravenous my baby Constance is! And how proud I am for feeding her myself. I have insisted on her sleeping in my room since the birth, and William doesn't seem to mind much, having been banished to his dressing room. Who would have thought a baby could bring so much joy? I confess I am mightily tired, and Constance and I exist in a sort of milky, twilight dream of feeding and soothing, and feeding and sleeping. I have never been happier. My magpie comes often to my window, and he loves to perch on the sill, quietly observing, while I feed Constance in the nursing chair. The blackbird and thrush have ceased their summer singing. Instead we have the melancholy robin and occasional shrill wren.

Constance much enjoyed her bath this sunny morning. The nurse wanted to bath her, and chided me for not resting, but how could I forfeit the joy of observing my baby's firm limbs, gently splashing in warm water. And then to wrap Constance in a fresh, white cloth, the scent of her quite perfect and familiar.'

I put the diary down. So, Mercy was good at bathing her baby! She didn't need the nurse to do that. Nor would I, if it were my baby.

'Happy Birthday, Melia!' Finn puts his head round the door. 'Is it too early?' He waves at the trio of magpies. 'Morning magpies!'

'No, Finn. Not too early at all.'

'This is for you,' he says, giving me an orange piece of paper. He has coloured in every bit of it with one of my orange pencils. Nanny Jan had to sharpen it several times.

'Do you like it?' I see he's even signed it in the corner.

'It is perfect,' I tell him. 'Quite perfect.' I show him Nina's card. He's delighted it has some orange in it. Then he walks over to the window and the magpies fly off, one by one.

'Off they go,' he says. 'One, two, three.'

'One for sorrow, two for joy,' I chant. 'Three for a *girl*.'

'And four for a *boy!*' shouts Finn. I laugh and wave his orange picture.

'But we don't believe in that old rubbish, do we Finn?'

'NO!' he shouts. 'NO, NO, NO!'

CAMELLIA
Birthday breakfast

I'm having my birthday breakfast in the nursery and it's special because Mummy and Daddy have joined us. There's a glass of real orange juice at my place and Finn tells me how he helped Nanny Jan squeeze the oranges. I take a sip and it's delicious, if a bit warm. Mummy and Daddy are drinking their coffee, poured from a grand coffee pot on the side. It's usually in the dining room.

'Go on then,' Mummy says. 'You can open your presents.'

'Lots of time, Camellia,' says Nanny Jan, noticing me glance at my watch. 'A good fifteen minutes before we need to set off for school.'

There are two presents from Mummy and Daddy. I open Mummy's first and it's a beautiful wooden box about the size of one of Finn's big books. There are two golden hooks on the side, and I flick them up.

'What's inside, Melia?' Finn jumps off his chair, pressing against me. I open the box. It's an oil painting set, complete with a palette, three brushes and ten tubes in bright colours. Also tucked into the box are two little bottles, one of linseed oil and one of turpentine.

'Wow!' I'm so pleased Mummy has actually thought about this present. Something I love, not what she wants me to love. I go over to kiss her and say thank you. She smiles her pretty smile and pours herself another cup of coffee.

'Now you're a *real* painter,' Finn says, running his fingers over the coloured tubes. Mummy says she thought I would like them, and that someone else is giving me a book on how to paint with oils. Then I'll be like Picasso.

I open Daddy's present and find a small pair of binoculars, just like the ones he takes to the races.

'They are for watching birds when you're out for walks,' he says. 'It's amazing how much more you can see with a pair of binoculars.' Daddy shows me how they work, and we take it in turns to look through the window towards the cows, trees and Downs beyond. The day is sunny and warm with a little morning mist. The binoculars are *very* powerful. I would be able to see Mercy all the way to the primrose wood with these.

Nanny Jan says she will save her present for after school as we had better be getting on. Finn tells me he has a very special after-lunch birthday surprise for me. Goodness knows what that will be! I smile and smile because it's so special to have Mummy and Daddy here, as well as Nanny Jan and Finn. They are both in a good mood because I love my presents.

I go upstairs to fetch my orange hat because I want to show it to my friends. There, on my pillow are three Zéphirine Drouhin roses. They are a surprise present from someone, and I know who that someone is.

Nanny Jan calls for me to hurry up. I fill my tooth mug with water and quickly arrange the roses. That will have to do for now. I put them on my dressing table.

On the way downstairs I begin to cough.

CAMELLIA

We're all set for the party! I wish I didn't have this annoying cough though. It's spoiling things. It's come out of *nowhere*. I haven't even had a sore throat and cold. I knew we shouldn't have gone to the doctor yesterday because everyone knows that's where you catch things.

Even as I say this to myself, there's another voice saying 'This isn't your cough. It belongs to Mercy. She has given you her cough.'

I told people at school that I'd swallowed a fly, you know how it is, and that seemed to keep them quiet. This morning was all right except I found it hard to concentrate. My friends loved my orange hat and sang Happy Birthday to me at break-time. Miss Wiggins even gave me a card! She doesn't do that for everyone. I felt a bit guilty I hadn't asked her to the party.

I step into my birthday tent and it's as pretty as a picture and very welcoming. Actually, it looks a bit like a French cafe, at least that's what Mummy says. The tablecloths are red and white check and on every table there are jam jars of sweet peas. The plates are white and the glasses are different colours. Of course, my glass is orange.

There are balloons everywhere, tied up with string. Mummy said she nearly went mad with Mrs Betts, trying to blow them up. Everyone has a place name. I have Sarah and Melanie-Anne either side of me, and then opposite me are Annabel and Lorna. I thought Lorna would like that. Mummy and Nanny Jan arranged the other name places and Finn asked to be next to Julia and Mummy.

I cough and cough and try taking a deep breath to stop it. Nanny Jan has found me a tin of Allen and Hanburys Blackcurrant Pastilles and, because it's my birthday, I'm allowed to keep the whole tin in my pocket. I take one now and it helps.

I'm in my blue and lilac smocked dress with a bow at the back. Mummy bought it in London and, although it's the right length, it hangs off me. I wonder if I wore my orange hat, people would look at that and not my figure? Mummy would have a fit, even on my birthday. No hat until later.

Uncle Peter and Aunt Rosemary are first to arrive, and I run over to the baby. Nanny Jan has brushed up our pram for Baby Martha, and it stands clean and smart by the back door. The baby is small and smells delicious. She's wrapped up in a delicate white shawl and is the prettiest little thing ever. I stroke her tiny hand and Aunt Rosemary gives me a tired smile.

'Happy Birthday, Camellia,' she says. 'Just wait till you have one of these. Sleep goes right out the window.' Finn comes around the side of the house and makes a bee line for Baby

Martha. He's wearing red shorts and a navy shirt. Finn loves babies.

'Baby Boo Boo,' he says, breathing heavily. He looks up at Aunt Rosemary and tells her it's my birthday.

'It was Martha's on 27th May,' Aunt Rosemary says. 'Her actual birth day that is. She's fifteen days old.'

When Aunt Rosemary says '*fifteen days old*' I know something dreadful is going to happen. I stand frozen. How can I stop it, whatever it is? I'm only seven years old after all and it's my birthday party. I have enough to do! I shake my head to make the feeling go away and that sets me off coughing. I walk off back to the tent and leave Nanny Jan and Finn cooing over the baby.

Where is Mercy? I haven't seen her today. What's she planning? I pray she isn't thinking of playing any tricks with the baby. I have just enough time to run down the garden to see if she's there, but she's not. Instead I see the first of the cars bringing the guests to my party.

I shall make them all welcome.

CAMELLIA
The treasure hunt

Our first game is a treasure hunt but not in the woods this time. Mummy didn't want any children going missing, so ours is limited to around the garden with the furthest point up at the stables. Sarah and Melanie-Anne stick with me, followed by Annabel who complains she's hopeless at this sort of thing. We are a foursome, and we have a little bag for our treasure.

I'm boiling hot, my party dress sticking to my back. It's my birthday and already I'm running out of energy. I cough and cough.

'Wait a minute!' I gasp. I reach into my pocket for my blackcurrant sweets. Melanie-Anne pats me on the back and says '*choke up chicken*', and Annabel wonders how many chickens actually have coughing fits. Suddenly, Ian comes flying past, followed by the boy Robert. I didn't know Mummy had asked him.

'He'll win,' Sarah says, leaning against my oak tree. 'Just look at him go!' We stand and admire the boys' speed and determination. Then we set off again, wondering whether we are on clue seven or eight. All of a sudden Sarah stops dead and points.

'There she is,' she says. 'There's your Mercy.'

'I can see her!' shouts Melanie-Anne. 'I can see a ghost!' Annabel moves forward to join us, brushing her hair out of her eyes. She squints into the near distance.

'There? By the ditch or ha-ha or whatever it's called?'

'Yes, there she is.'

In my mind I invite Mercy to come towards us. All three of my friends believe, and all three of them can see her. I'm *very* proud of them! Of course, Mercy draws near, so near that the air grows frosty, and close enough for her necklace to shine and her dress to glow the palest pink. Annabel shivers and takes a step back while Melanie-Anne stares with her mouth open. Sarah seems calm.

'This is my great-grandmother,' I say, giving a curtsey. 'She misses her baby very much.'

'Is that a ghost magpie on her shoulder?' Melanie-Anne asks.

'It is, and sometimes she has her hunter-horse with her and all her ghost dogs too.'

I know Mercy wants to leave, that she has something to do, that she can't stay. We watch as she turns gracefully, then glides back across the lawn, away to the other side of the garden, all the time fading, becoming fainter, until she has gone.

'Pity we can't put her in our treasure bag,' says Melanie-Anne. 'Then people might believe us.' Annabel lets out a huge sigh, as if she's been holding her breath for ages.

'I can't believe I've seen a real *live* ghost.'

'A real *dead* ghost,' says Melanie-Anne. 'Except she's alive, so yes, I suppose you're right.'

'She's so very sad,' Sarah says, picking up our treasure bag. 'It hurts in here.' She points at her heart. Tears are pouring down my face, making it sting and smart.

'Just look what she does to me!'

Then I start to cough and cough. Sarah, Melanie-Anne and Annabel say they will take care of the clues for the rest of the treasure hunt. All I have to do is follow them. They are on a mission to help me and my ghost.

But I know Mercy is waiting. She's waiting for a chance to upset the party. It's just a question of how.

CAMELLIA
Teatime

It's teatime and we're all tucking in. On the tables are mountains of delicious food, hot sausages on sticks as well as sausage rolls, egg sandwiches in tiny triangles, ham sandwiches, tomato sandwiches, iced gem biscuits, jellies in pleated cases, strawberries and chocolate biscuits which are melting. We have orange and lemon squash to drink, real pieces of orange and lemon in the tall glass jugs.

Mummy has organised it all beautifully and my friends are smiling and laughing because this is the best birthday party ever. Gran and Granpop are here with Mr Impey, sitting at the same table. On another table are Uncle Peter and Aunt Rosemary, while Baby Martha sleeps in her pram outside the tent on the shady side.

Lorna is opposite me and she's grinning from ear to ear. She actually said thank you for putting her in such a special place. I'm surrounded by my best friends and, as I look around the tent and listen to everyone chattering, I know I'm a very lucky girl.

Nanny Jan brings in my cake. She has to walk slowly so the seven candles don't blow out. It's a chocolate birthday cake with CAMELLIA written in orange smarties. Just for me! Everyone sings Happy Birthday. The candles flutter and there's a big shout of BLOW! Finn stands beside me. So, I blow and every candle but one goes out.

'Bum!' shouts Finn and everyone laughs. He has a big audience here. I make a wish as I cut the cake. I only have one birthday wish, for Gran to believe in Mercy. Mummy comes in with vanilla ice cream to go with the chocolate cake, and Nanny Jan helps me slice it up.

This is what we're doing when Rosemary screams.

Mummy throws down the bowl of ice cream and runs out the tent. Seconds later she rushes back in, arms waving.

'The pram has disappeared!'

People goggle at her. They can't believe it.

'Baby Martha has gone!'

There's an awful silence, but I'm out of the tent in a flash. I know exactly where Baby Martha has gone and who has taken her. I run as fast as I can down to the end of the garden, hearing Sarah call my name behind me. I've got to get to Mercy before she takes Martha into the portal. Baby Martha was too tempting for Mercy. She's desperate for a baby to love. Please, please let me not be too late.

I come crashing round the side of the yew trees to find Mercy with her hands on the pram.

'NO, MERCY NO!' I cry. 'She isn't yours!'

'Oh Camellia!' Sarah's behind me now. 'What shall we do?'

Mercy doesn't move. I hear screaming and commotion coming from further up the garden. They don't know we're here.

'She's someone else's baby,' I plead. 'You *CAN'T* take her.'

Mr Impey appears just as Mercy fades. He catches a glimpse of her though, moving off across the field. I grab the pram handle and peer in.

'Oh, thank heavens Martha is here. She's here, Mr Impey. She's here.'

Mr Impey puts his arm around me and I burst into tears. I sob into his smart pink shirt, as if I'm sobbing for all the lost babies in the world. It makes me cough, and I cough and cough until I'm nearly sick. Not near Baby Martha though. I cough into a nettle patch.

'We need to let them know the baby is found,' Mr Impey says. 'Sarah, be a good girl and run back to the tent to give them the happy news.' Sarah is off, her yellow hair flying behind her.

I struggle to reach my tin of blackcurrant sweets. I must stop coughing or I will die! I can't catch my breath. At last I put one in my mouth, offering the tin to Mr Impey. He says yes please, they look lovely.

'What a to-do,' he says, sucking his sweet. 'Now let's get this dear baby back to her mother.'

I am sniffing and snorting like Robin. It's hard to stop coughing and crying while sucking a cough sweet. I still can't get enough air, but I manage to say thank you. Mr Impey pushes the pram back round the yew trees, noticing he has to let the brake off first. Mercy had managed to push the pram down the lawn with the brake on.

There's a crowd of people hurrying down the lawn to meet us. Aunt Rosemary is out in front, her face white and pinched.

'Is she all right? Oh, for God's sake, what can have happened?' She rushes over and scoops out a sleeping Martha.

Thank *goodness* I have Mr Impey by my side.

'A bit of a mystery,' he says to Rosemary. 'But Camellia is our heroine. She rescued the pram.'

I know I'm being stared at, and I can't stop the hot tears pouring down my cheeks. I'm making a scene and Mummy will hate it.

I try to say '*It wasn't me, it was Mercy*', but I can't get the words out. I know I will be blamed. I hold onto Mr Impey's pink shirt, holding on for dear life. Mummy's face is stern. I know she thinks I did this. I would like to know how, but grown-ups never work things out properly.

'Where was the pram, Mr Impey?'

'At the bottom of the garden.'

'How did Camellia know it was there?'

Now it would all have to come out. Mr Impey hesitates before answering. Baby Martha cries while Aunt Rosemary rocks her. Mummy is waiting. I know I'm in big trouble.

'I just knew the pram would be there, Mummy,' I manage to say, deciding to tell the truth. 'Mercy wanted to take the baby.' Mummy says she's never heard such nonsense. Finn pushes through to make an announcement.

'Mr Impey and Melia saw a phenomenon at the end of the garden.' There's a hush and Finn pulls his ear, staring at the ground.

'WHAT did you say?' Mummy has heard it all now. I know she's upset that something so awful should have happened, but it's not as if Baby Martha disappeared completely. We rescued her. Mr Impey then makes his own announcement, and everyone hears it.

'The end of your garden is a graveyard, Mrs Devon, and it's haunted.' My legs are giving way beneath me. Now the cat's out of the bag.

'I can vouch for it.' Mr Impey's voice is calm and matter of fact. By now some of the children are running around screaming, but on purpose. They are full of tea and cake and that is making them go mad.

The rest of the party was a blur. Uncle Peter and Aunt Rosemary left with Baby Martha very soon afterwards. Nobody felt like playing games after tea. Instead there were little parties of children daring each other to go down the garden. Then they would come back, screaming their heads off.

Nanny Mae found me and said she was ever so sorry. Nanny Jan gave me a kind look, as if to say let's talk about it later. Sarah, Melanie-Anne and Annabel stuck to me like glue. My presents were all piled up on a side table, but I didn't feel like opening them. I felt that miserable. Sarah insisted I open hers. It was a beautiful crystal which she said was rose quartz which would keep my heart safe. That made me cry again.

Mr Impey found us sitting on the lawn and said he had to go. He would be back tomorrow afternoon for a chat with me and Mummy and Daddy. I was so overcome, all I could do was nod and blink.

Everyone has gone home now and I'm alone in the tent. Gran

finds me amongst the wrapping-up paper, having opened all my presents. I sat and opened them alone. I have been given seven new Famous Five Books and someone must have arranged this, because every one of them is different. I have enough to last me till Christmas.

Gran holds out her present.

'For you, darling.'

It's a book called *Beginning to Paint in Oils*. I thank her and she invites me to open the first page. I find a small photograph.

'It's my mother. I thought you should like to have it.' This is a different picture of Mercy. In this one she wears a hat.

'Thank you, Gran. It's a lovely picture and book.' She asks me quietly what happened. I'm so tired by now I give her the truth.

'It was your Mummy. She took Baby Martha but it's you she really wants.' Gran's eyebrows go up. Honestly, she should understand this by now.

'So, this is my fault?'

'In a way, yes. Sorry.'

Now would be a good time to tell Gran about the diary, but again I don't. I want Mr Impey to read it first.

'Have you been praying for guidance?' I ask her.

'Always.'

'Has it worked?' Gran says she's not sure it has.

I find it hard to believe that Gran was ever a baby as tiny as Martha, but I suppose she must have been, that very same baby Mercy bathed on a sunny morning in 1896.

'It was a lovely party, Camellia,' Gran says. 'And at least Baby Martha is safe.'

'She is.'

I remember to ask Gran about the Zéphirine Drouhin. She says she knows exactly where it is, it's on the lower wall. Then it's true, it's the very same rose. I always knew that.

I want some peace now because I feel cold and shivery, and rather sick. Gran walks me back over to the house. She kisses me goodbye and says she'll keep praying. The nursery is quiet and I collapse on the sofa. I need some time to myself.

Mummy comes through to find me, and her eyes are blazing. She then gives me the biggest ticking off of my life *on my birthday*. It doesn't seem fair. I cough and cough and it's only when Nanny Jan calls me for my bath that I'm able to escape.

'Mummy's just being silly,' Finn says to me later when I'm tucked up in bed. 'It wasn't your fault.'

He pats the painted fir cone on my bedside table, asking if I really like it. This was my surprise present, an orange fir cone which he painted himself.

'I know who we can blame,' he says with a grin. Already he's laughing, holding his sides.

'Who?'

'The *Bossa Bova* of course.' I smile.

'If only, Finn.'

'I'm here next door, Melia, if you need me.'

I thank him very much.

'Always here!' he shouts from his bedroom.

Mercy is in her corner. I put on my orange hat and glare at her. How could she get me into so much trouble?

And now she's given me her cough.

NANNY JAN

What a pity Camellia's seventh birthday party will be remembered for all the wrong reasons. I won't forget that scream in a hurry, so loud we could hear it over the noise of the children.

In all the hullabaloo I noticed Camellia was missing and I was pretty sure I knew where she had gone. That poor mother was circling the tent outside calling for her baby, 'Martha, Martha.' As if the baby could answer! Mr and Mrs Devon rushed out too, leaving the children sitting in their chairs open-mouthed.

I found Mr Impey as soon as I could, beckoning him over with my chocolate-covered knife. Of course, he knew exactly what to do. Mae was more than helpful keeping the children calm. A couple of the younger girls were most upset, and I was ever so grateful to Mae hurrying over to reassure them. 'There, there...' she said. 'Baby Martha will soon be found, you mark my words.' Finn stood on a chair to announce he was pretty sure Mercy did it. I told him to get down.

The next thing we knew Sarah was back, shouting: 'The baby's safe, the baby's safe!' There was no stopping the children crowding out of the tent by then. They wanted to see what was happening.

I will never forget the sight of Mr Impey and Camellia making their way slowly up the lawn. It was hard to see them at first, deep in the shadows, but I could tell Mr Impey was pushing the pram. They emerged into the sunlight and one look at Camellia's face told me she was dreadfully upset. She knew what was coming as did I.

When Mrs Devon interrogated Mr Impey about the pram, I made up my mind there and then I was going to support Camellia through thick and thin. Mr Impey stood up for himself I'm glad to say, and it was just a pity that the children all heard him declare that the bottom of the garden was a graveyard and haunted. That set them off and no mistake.

I knew Finn meant to help when he made his announcement about the 'phenomenon', but all it did was make Mrs Devon even more angry. I think, if you ask me, she was more upset that the party hadn't gone to plan. Then all the distress caused poor Camellia to cough and cough. That cough does worry me. Where on earth has it come from? Surely, it's not possible to catch TB from a *ghost*? Dr Byng said her chest was clear only yesterday. Could it come on that suddenly?

I longed to go give Camellia a hug, but I knew Mrs Devon wouldn't approve. There would be time for that later. I caught Mae's eye and she nodded her understanding. Then we herded the children back into the tent where they finished their cake and ice cream. It gave me an opportunity to speak to Mr Impey and he listened carefully while I gave him the latest. The thunderstorm, Camellia fainting, as well as the ghost's diary and the fact that I had read it. He asked if he could read it and I said I would ask Camellia.

'We must make sure everything is as normal as possible

around the poor child,' he said. 'I'll come over tomorrow and try to explain the situation to her parents.'

I raised my eyes to heaven.

'Leave it to me,' he said with a smile. 'I shall be very discreet and not give anything away that I shouldn't.' He tapped the side of his nose and I laughed at that. He reached over to the pile of presents and extracted one.

'This is my present for Camellia. Give it to her later, perhaps at bedtime.'

'I fear Camellia will be told off by her mother for this,' I sighed, keeping my eye on Ian who was on to his third helping of cake and ice cream. 'As will I,' I added.

'Sometimes we have to make a stand,' said Mr Impey. 'Like Custer.' I looked blank.

'Battle of Little Bighorn,' Mr Impey explained. 'Although come to think of it, it didn't end well for General Custer.' He laughed. 'The Indians won, and quite rightly so actually.' Mr Impey gave his merry smile and patted me on the back.

'*We* shall be the Indians!'

Then he went off to find Camellia.

CAMELLIA

Mummy hasn't come in to say goodnight.

I'm in disgrace. Finn might say it wasn't my fault, but it was really. I should have sorted everything out by now. And today was my birthday. How can I be in such disgrace on my *birthday*.

I am wound up like a spring, yet exhausted at the same time. It's not a nice feeling. Not one bit. I know I've been given super presents and a lovely party, and I should be happy. But how can I be, when Mummy is *cross* with me. If I could have stopped Mercy taking the baby, I would have done, so it does seem unfair.

While Mummy was telling me off, I tried to explain that I couldn't possibly have taken the pram away. I was in the tent all the time, but she wouldn't listen.

She never listens. Well, she does listen to grown-ups, but

never to me. How can I make her listen? As I think that, I see Mercy raise her head as if she has an idea. I wave Mr Fox at her as if to say 'No, no, Mercy, not tonight.'

Nanny Jan pops her head round my door with a lovely smile, saying she's got a surprise for me. She sits on my bed and gives me two presents. The first one is from her, and I open it to find two blocks of paper.

'They're canvasses, Camellia. I know they seem a bit boring, but you can't do your oil painting on ordinary paper. You need canvasses. So here they are, just waiting for you to start painting.' I thank her very much. I hadn't known about canvasses.

'This one's from Mr Impey,' she says, handing me the second parcel. 'He specially said he wanted you to have it when everything was quiet.'

When I unwrap the parcel, I discover Mr Impey has given me a picture of a little girl with short brown hair. She's in a meadow with a smart fox sitting beside her, amongst the flowers and butterflies. It's perfect!

Nanny Jan admires it. She tells me that Mr Impey is coming over tomorrow and he is going to do everything he can to help. I know that already. I'm so relieved. I flop back on the pillow and Nanny Jan feels my forehead.

'Any more coughing?' she asks.

'Not for a bit.' I rattle the last few sweets left in my tin. 'Do you think it will go away soon?'

'I'm sure it will.' Nanny Jan kisses me goodnight and asks whether I'm going to sleep in my orange hat.

'I wish Mummy hadn't told me off like that.'

Nanny Jan doesn't know what to say. She tucks me in tight and blows another kiss from the door.

My *heart* hurts.

ANGELA

I did everything I could, and more quite frankly, to make sure Camellia's birthday party was as happy and fun as possible, and then we had a disaster. Thank God Martha was safely rescued, but it wasn't easy explaining what the hell had happened to the mothers and nannies collecting. Gerald went to his study so that was helpful. It was left to me as usual.

I simply cannot understand how a pram gets itself down the garden all by itself. Camellia, either with or without her friends, must have been involved because surely it was a prank? A nasty prank at that. I suppose it could have been one of the other children?

I felt simply dreadful that Peter and Rosemary should be put through such an ordeal, and at our house too! They scuttled off pretty smartish and who could blame them? I fear it was me who reassured Rosemary that the baby would be more comfortable and perfectly safe *outside* the tent. More fool me! I completely forgot Rosemary doesn't have a nanny.

All this talk of a ghost pushing the pram and deliberately doing so is absolute nonsense. Mr Impey was *completely* out of order saying what he did in front of everyone. I will need to have a word with him tomorrow. He thinks he's coming to have a word with me, but I will give him a piece of my mind. It doesn't matter how well I organise a party, something always goes wrong. Mind you, at least no one died, not like Teresa's party last year when Frank collapsed of a heart attack. That was inconvenient, I must say.

Was I too harsh on Camellia? I admit I saw red when she and our vicar emerged from the gloom, the heroes of the day or so it seemed. They were a little too cosy for my liking, as if in cahoots. God only knows what Finn was going on about with his 'phenomenon', or whatever he called it. Probably one of Camellia's dolls falling off a branch or Banger barking at a wasp. How does he even remember the word 'phenomenon' in any case?

No, I need to clamp down on all of this. I thought it was over and done with after Christmas, but I shouldn't have lowered my guard. I can't have Camellia upsetting the family. And I will never live down hosting a children's birthday party where babies in prams are not safe.

The tables and chairs need to go back tomorrow, and then there's the tent. If truth be told, I'll be glad when it's gone, because it's a horrid reminder of the day. I couldn't face saying goodnight to Camellia. Instead I had two whiskies in the drawing room. I thought I deserved them.

If Camellia is ill and disturbed, what do I do then?

CAMELLIA

Mercy strikes back

I wake all hot and sweaty. I feel my own forehead and it's as hot as my hand. My watch says 7.25am, and Mercy isn't in her corner. She must be on the prowl. I remember what happened yesterday and groan. Everyone will want to talk about it at school and I don't feel strong enough. In fact, I think I've got a temperature. Perhaps I won't have to go to school. I reach for my hat. Orange, orange... I feel myself drifting off to sleep.

Nanny Jan takes my temperature when she finds me in bed, half-asleep. She says it's over 99 so I can have a morning off school. It looks like rain anyway, so I'm not missing much. I close my eyes, listening to her explain to Finn that I need to be left in peace. Of course, he comes in.

'Don't worry, Melia. I will give everyone the news.' I picture him at break-time on the stage, centre of attention.

I hear the car drive off, taking Finn to school and then Mrs Betts's voice. Far, far off there is a rumble of thunder. Not another storm! I close my eyes again. I need more sleep.

Suddenly Mrs Betts is shouting. It's something about 'Everything everywhere!' Her footsteps bang down the stairs, then more footsteps coming back up with Mummy's voice saying 'What do you mean?' I am glad I can stay out of it. I'm safe in my room, or so I think.

Mummy flings my bedroom door open. Her eyes are flashing like green stones, and she stamps her foot. She's lost her temper! I duck my head.

'Are you responsible for my room?' she shouts, glaring at my orange hat. 'Why the hell are you wearing that in bed?'

'It's my hat and my room.' I'm quite pleased with my reply. Mrs Betts peers over Mummy's shoulder, waving her duster.

'Good morning, Mrs Betts,' I say politely. 'I'm ill.'

Mummy grabs my arm to get me out of bed. She pulls my hat off, but I manage to catch it, jamming it back on. Then she marches me into her bedroom.

Mummy shows me the mess. Everything *is* everywhere! Clothes have been pulled out of the chest of drawers and thrown on to the floor. There are shoes scattered round the room, all jumbled up. I can see scarves and socks and pants, and the bars of soap Mummy keeps in her underwear drawer are in a pile on the bed. One of Mummy's skirts is halfway out the window.

'Well?'

'Well what?'

'Did you do this?'

I start to laugh. What else can I do? But laughing makes me cough, and kind Mrs Betts has to fetch me a drink of water from Mummy's bathroom.

'Why would I want to do this, Mummy?' I gasp, gulping down water.

'I really don't know,' she says frowning. 'You tell me.'

Mrs Betts says it's going to take a bit of tidying up before she can hoover, but she'll get there in the end. Mercy suddenly appears in the middle of the room, and I watch her fling Daddy's pyjama bottoms out of the window. I suppose they go sailing down to the grass below. Of course, Mummy and Mrs Betts do not see her do this because their attention is on me.

But they *do* see what she does next and I'm glad. She sends Mummy's early morning tea cup flying across the room and it smashes against the dressing-table mirror. It makes the most tremendous crash, and Mummy screams. Serves her right! Now she knows it isn't me. Mrs Betts sits down on the bed in shock. Not only is the cup broken into tiny pieces, but the mirror is badly cracked. Mrs Betts is very superstitious, as is Mummy.

'Thank you, Mercy,' I say out loud.

Outside the rain is falling, the thunder rumbling. Daddy's pyjama bottoms will be getting wet.

'Do you believe me now, Mummy? I wasn't anywhere near your tea cup. I *couldn't* have thrown it. And now I need to go back to bed. I feel awful.'

Mummy is shaking her head in disbelief, and Mrs Betts is as white as a Mummy's sheets. The only thing I hear Mummy say as I walk out of her room is 'I can't believe it.'

They both saw it. That's a start.

CAMELLIA

Nanny Jan wakes me up when she comes in, followed by Finn.

'Lazy bones,' says Finn. 'It's lunchtime!' I've been asleep all morning, in my room full of light.

'Big storm at school,' Finn says. 'I looked after everyone.' He goes over to my chair and pats Heidi on the head, then forces her eye open.

'Don't, Finn! She doesn't like it when you do that.'

Nanny Jan wants to take my temperature again. The sleep might have brought it down. While I sit with the thermometer in my mouth, Finn tells me about school. He says Sarah, Melanie-Anne and Annabel have already written their thank-you letters, how much they enjoyed meeting Mercy.

I roll my eyes. Mummy won't like that! She's probably still in shock, drinking sherry for her nerves. Nanny Jan says my temperature's back down to normal and do I want any lunch? I need fattening up. It's chops and mashed potatoes. I'm not that keen on chops.

'Did you hear what happened after you went to school?' I ask. Finn says he didn't.

Nanny Jan says Mrs Betts had to have a brandy to calm down and Mummy spent all morning in the drawing room on the telephone, complaining about the lightning. She couldn't hear what people were saying. And I slept right through!

'*WHAT HAPPENED?*' Finn bounces on the bed, while

Nanny Jan straightens my pillow. I tell him.

'Mercy threw a tea cup at Mummy's mirror, and it smashed!'

'You'll be in trouble now, Melia,' Finn says, screwing his eyes up. 'Oh dear, oh dear.'

'I don't think so, actually. Mummy and Mrs Betts saw it happen and they knew it wasn't me this time.'

'That's a mercy,' says Finn.

CAMELLIA

I have my lunch brought up on a tray and kind Nanny Jan has cut all the fat from the chops. I force myself to eat everything on the plate and then feel sick.

I am listening to Nanny Jan's wireless, a song by the Beatles called *If there's anything that you want*, at least I think that's what it's called. There are a lot of things I want, the day after my birthday.

I want Gran to believe in Mercy, I want Mummy to believe in me, I want Mercy to go to the Light, I want to stop feeling ill and get well, I want Robin to stop having laminitis, I want to stop worrying that Mercy is eating me up from inside, I want this cough to go, I want to stop looking like a clown, I want to get fatter, I want to have some peace.

My eyes sting and all I want to do is sleep! I wait for Nanny Jan to collect my tray and then I lie down. I could sleep for a hundred years like Sleeping Beauty. I'm that tired.

Nanny Jan has told Finn that he can't come up and see me until teatime, which is when Mr Impey is expected. I'm putting all my faith in Mr Impey to sort out *anything that I want*.

I lie very still, listening to the sounds of the house downstairs, Cook clattering pans as she washes up, and outside, everyday sounds that you wouldn't notice if you weren't ill in bed upstairs. The fat pigeon cooing on my roof is sending me to sleep. I let go.

CAMELLIA

I dream of not being able to wake up. It's as if my eyes won't open because the daylight is too bright. So, I give up and lie down in the darkness again. I hear knocking on my door. This isn't a dream because Finn marches into the room, carrying two of my new Famous Five books.

'Teatime, Melia,' he says, throwing the books down on my bed. He peers at Heidi, checking her eye. He wonders if she needs a patch. 'Mr Impey's here.'

When I sit up, my head feels swimmy.

'He's talking to Mummy *and* Daddy in the drawing room. I know because I took my wheelbarrow round there on purpose.'

'Good work, Finn,' I say, rubbing the top of my head.

'But I couldn't hear what they were saying.'

'Never mind.'

He says he found Daddy's pyjama bottoms hanging from a bush. He says they were soaked and wonders how they ended up there. When I tell him Mercy threw them out, he doesn't look at all surprised.

Nanny Jan comes in to ask if I would like a cup of tea and some left-over birthday cake. I know the chocolate will make me feel sick. Instead I ask for a banana sandwich. Nanny Jan says Mr Impey will soon be up to talk to me, so I ask her if she would hang his picture up.

Nanny Jan and Finn go downstairs while I change into a clean nightdress, then into my summer dressing gown because I feel shivery again. Then I put on my orange hat. My clown spots are there but only very faint thank goodness.

Mercy is nowhere to be seen.

CAMELLIA

Mr Impey arrives at my door, carrying the tea tray. There are two cups and my banana sandwich sits on a plate, cut into quarters.

'Yum yum,' he says. Then he pours out our tea and settles himself down on Heidi's chair, but not before asking about her hangover. I smile. Mummy has a hangover sometimes, if she's been to a party.

I point at his picture on the wall and tell him how much I love it. He says he thought it could have been me, that little girl, and it's why he bought it.

'Nice hat,' he says, nodding at me. 'I've always loved orange.' Then he takes a big slurp of tea.

'Now,' Mr Impey says. 'To business. We need to make a plan.' I tell him about the tea cup and of course he knows already.

'Your mother may never need to backcomb her hair again.' He laughs and so do I. 'I understand your Mercy hurled it at the mirror.' I tell him she certainly did and Mr Impey says that at least Mummy now believes there's something funny going on. She saw it with her own eyes, as did Mrs Betts.

'That's to our advantage.' Mr Impey is dressed in his black today, saying it gives him distinction, as well as a bit of power when he wants to get his point across.

'Your parents, Camellia, have now accepted that the house is haunted. Fact. They know the strange goings-on are not down to you, but your great-grandmother's ghost. Fact. They do not know about the search in the cellar or the chest or the diary. But we do. That gives us another advantage.'

Mr Impey pours himself another cup of tea.

'Although they have accepted it's your ghost doing the haunting, I don't think they are ready to understand what needs to happen next. I've told them I shall bless the whole house, going into various rooms ... I can do that later ... I have some holy water in my car.'

'Gosh.' I am impressed!

Apparently Mummy wanted a Bishop to bless the house. That's typical of Mummy. Luckily Mr Impey told her he could do the job perfectly well.

'I managed to have a word with Nanny Jan, and she said you would like me to read the diary. I am more than happy to do that for you.' He smiles.

'Thank you, Mr Impey.' I reach under my pillow and bring the diary out. He takes it, then raises it to his lips to kiss. He knows it's very, very precious, and he'll take good care of it. He thanks me again.

'Now what about the chest?' he asks. I explain about the other things in it, but that it's stuck fast again.

'If you like, I could take it home and break into it.' He tells me not to look so shocked. He won't take it today but perhaps after he has read the diary.

'Then, I believe your grandmother must read it. She is the child after all.' He pours out the last drop of tea. It's rather strong.

'Once she has read the diary, then we will make a final push to encourage your grandmother to open her eyes, literally that is, into believing. Perhaps we could put on a little concert at the end of the garden? I could help of course, play the violin? Entice Mercy and your grandmother to get together. "Silent Night"? "Evening Prayer"? I know we could do it.'

At last I am not on my own. I'm so grateful to Mr Impey for thinking this through. I ask him to bless me for not getting the Big Smalls again. I'm worried about that. He stands to make the blessing and I am comforted.

'We did well, rescuing the baby, did we not?' he says, smiling down at me. His face is so very kind.

'She's desperate.' I close my eyes. 'She's rescued all the dogs now, as well as Nara. She's ready to go to the Light.'

'I shall be back tomorrow, never fear. First, I will stow the diary safely in my car. Then I will fetch the holy water and then I will bless the house.' He holds the diary up. 'You rest, dearest girl. You will find your strength again and, whatever happens, I am your friend.'

He leaves me, blinking back tears.

CAMELLIA

Mummy comes in to see me after my bath. She chats to Finn in his room first and my heart is thudding by the time she wishes him goodnight. I haven't seen her since Mercy smashed her tea cup.

She puts her head round the door and asks how I'm feeling. I know my clown spots are red again because I saw them in the mirror, brushing my teeth. I think she must be feeling calmer now because her hair is rather flat.

'I am rather tired,' I say. Mummy makes a sad face at that, and then I tell her I'm always tired these days.

Poor Mummy doesn't know how to be with me, and I feel a bit sorry for her. I pat the bed and ask her to sit down, but *already* Mummy isn't concentrating, she's looking around the room. I don't know what she's looking for to be honest. She hasn't even noticed my new picture. How can she miss it? She asks me if I had a nice chat with Mr Impey.

I nod. I'm actually wearing my orange hat, but I don't think Mummy will dare say anything rude about it. Not now. We stare at each other for a moment. Then Mummy says something surprising.

'I'm sorry.' She takes a deep breath. 'I'm sorry for blaming you for taking the pram down the garden.'

'It was Mercy, you see,' I say, sitting up straight. I stroke Mr Fox's ears and he loves the attention. I hold him out to Mummy. 'See how kind he is now!' Mummy isn't sure I can tell. She says she's not sure she can trust anyone with eyes that close together. We laugh at that.

'He's been blessed,' I explain. 'And now he's *loved* and that makes all the difference. Even if you can't quite trust him, you can still love him. Anyway, I trust him now.' Mummy spots Heidi on the chair and reaches out for her. Of course, Heidi gives her the one-eyed look. Mummy puts her back.

'We want to get you well, Camellia,' says Mummy. 'So tomorrow, if your temperature is still up, we'll move you into the pink room, and then you'll have the sun coming in all day. You'll also be right next door to Nanny Jan. And Mr Impey says he'll lend you his record player again so you can listen to music. Won't that be fun? And there's nothing stopping you having a go with your new oil paints. After all there's a lovely view from the pink room.'

I listen quietly to Mummy's kind words.

She asks if I've been coughing today and I tell her not so much. Nanny Jan says the cough will soon be gone. Mummy says Dr Byng will ring in the next couple of days to let us know about the blood test, but she's sure it will be all right.

Mummy hasn't said anything about the tea cup.

'Mr Impey was very kind and blessed the whole house. With a bit of luck that will settle everything down.' I don't say anything to that.

She kisses me goodnight and I sink back into my pillow. My hat tips over my eyes and I push it back. In the corner stands Mercy. She was listening to every word.

'We have a plan,' I tell her. 'We have a *plan*.'

ANGELA

Well, I managed to say that I was sorry to Camellia yesterday evening. I have never found saying sorry easy, particularly when I know I'm in the wrong. She sat in bed, the spots on her cheeks very apparent and wearing that ridiculous hat. She was both gracious and kind and I felt we understood each other better.

I couldn't talk about what happened because I'm still terrified by it. How on earth does a cup fling itself against a mirror? It isn't natural and now I'll have seven years bad luck. Mrs Betts was quick to remind me about that!

Has Camellia come to us with darkness in her? My mind keeps going round and round and I realised something yesterday. I love her, but I'm also frightened by her. So, it took quite a bit of courage to go and say goodnight.

I feel inferior to my daughter and that's not a comfortable feeling. She's far more talented than me and, let's face it, braver. Mr Impey was very clear in his explanation as to what we are dealing with in the house. So much for my thinking I was going to be the one ticking *him* off!

Gerald was so obviously out of his depth during the conversation. This is way beyond his understanding and, if I'm honest, mine. However, I want to learn how we can best help Camellia and return the household to its previous happy state. That's my job, to keep things on an even keel.

So now I shall be more involved in caring for Camellia. I will have to go to Ascot for two days next week and organise the picnics, but there are a few days before that to get her well again.

We moved Camellia into the pink room this morning, and I helped Nanny Jan carry her things through. She wanted her Nara picture, as well as Mr Impey's present. What a dear little picture that is! We brought her binoculars too, so she can look for birds from the window and whatever else she chooses. I lined up the new Famous Five books on the chest of drawers and Gerald lent her his wireless, so Nanny Jan can carry on listening to hers downstairs.

There were some wilting pink roses in Camellia's tooth mug, and I asked her if she wanted me to pick her some more. That made her very happy indeed. Afterwards I wandered round the garden looking for roses, for once feeling as if I was doing something really useful.

Camellia says she's going to have a go with the oil paints tomorrow, that's if she feels up to it. Her temperature was nearly 100 this morning so she might just want to sleep. She's still coughing but she says her lungs don't hurt, only her heart. I found that unbearably sad. A seven-year-old girl's heart shouldn't hurt, surely it shouldn't.

I'm afraid I haven't been much of a mother to her, and now I've been told off by our vicar! He understands her better than me, and it's my fault I know. My daughter is ill, and I don't know what's wrong with her. I'm worried about what the blood test might say.

I confess to being terrified of her ghost. I know I would scream if I saw her. Poor Camellia sees her all the time. Mr Impey is coming back this afternoon. We must put our faith in him. Mind you, I shall ring Nanny this evening. I need to hear her voice.

And I will buy some Lucozade for Camellia. It's filthy stuff but it's stuffed full of vitamins I believe.

CAMELLIA

I feel rotten but my heart is singing because Mummy's being so kind to me. I'm in the pink room now and it's full of sun. Nanny Jan opened all four windows to let the day in as well as the morning breeze.

Mummy helped move all my things in here, and what made me happiest of all was when she picked some roses from the garden and brought them up to me, arranged in the prettiest vase. I gave her a great big smile for that.

My temperature was up this morning, so Nanny Jan gave me a junior aspirin. I love them because they taste of orange. Mummy has also bought me some Haliborange and they are really delicious. I'm allowed one a day to suck.

Mrs Betts comes in, rolling her eyes as if to say no flying tea cups in here, I hope.

'Poor Mrs Betts,' I say, putting down my Famous Five book. 'Did you get the most frightful shock?'

'My heart's still hammering!' she says pushing her carpet sweeper around the other spare bed. 'I've covered the broken mirror up with one of your mother's scarves. Nobody wants to see a mirror in that state.' Mrs Betts doesn't realise Mercy is sitting in the button-backed chair and she's hoovering straight through her.

'She can be a bit naughty,' I tell her. 'She's quiet at the moment.' Mrs Betts says she's very relieved to hear that. She asks me if I feel very bad?

'Bad. Not very bad.' The word *yet* drops into my mind and I don't like it. I want to get better, not worse. She flicks her duster along the windowsill and says it's going to be another hot day.

My head aches now and my eyes sting. It's horrible being ill when there's a beautiful day outside. I put my book down and close my eyes.

NANNY JAN

What a relief Camellia and her mother have made things up. That's how it should be. It makes my life easier too, and Mrs Devon was most helpful moving Camellia into the pink room.

I'll be happier once we get the results of the blood test, although I'm not sure what Dr Byng was testing for. Children do get funny bugs sometimes, and let's hope it's one of those which goes away by itself. In the meantime, we are all doing everything we can to make Camellia as comfortable as possible, surrounding her with her favourite things, in a room full of sunshine. Mr Fox has pride of place in her bed! Dorothy Baby sits on the chair and Heidi has been left behind of course.

Finn feels very important going to school by himself as if he's the most grown-up boy in the world. He loves being a messenger and brings Camellia the news. He says her friends miss her terribly.

It was lovely when Mrs Devon brought up some of the children's thank-you letters to show Camellia. Instead of getting cross, Mrs Devon actually laughed out loud when she read Melanie-Anne's letter. Camellia's face was a picture when her mother said: 'After all you don't get the opportunity to be introduced to a ghost at *every* party.'

By the time Mr Impey comes along this afternoon, allowing enough time for Camellia to have a sleep, he will have read the diary. Finn and I can go for a walk while Camellia sleeps.

If we could just get Camellia's temperature to stay normal for 24 hours. Her eyes were blue at lunchtime.

CAMELLIA

I know Mummy would like me to try out the oil paints, but it will take a big effort. I have looked through Gran's book and it seems painting with oils is quite complicated, too complicated for how I'm feeling right now. My bones ache. I haven't told Nanny Jan or Mummy this. I lie in bed and count my ribs by feeling them.

Mercy's new place is sitting in the button-backed chair. It's as if she's my constant nurse, watching me. I wonder if she will move for Mr Impey, otherwise he'll have to sit on the other bed.

Lunch makes me feel sick. I can only manage the strawberries. I say sorry to Nanny Jan. Mummy brings me the Lucozade and unwraps the cellophane. She pours some out and I take a sip. It's pretty disgusting so I hold my nose while I drink. Mummy says well done.

I miss Finn. I know Nanny Jan is doing her best to keep him downstairs because he wears me out with his chattering.

It's time for my afternoon rest. Nanny Jan draws my curtains but not completely as I need to feel a breeze.

Mercy stares.

CAMELLIA

When I wake from my rest, I'm hot and sweaty. Do I feel better? I'm not sure. I feel a sort of hunger grumbling in my tummy but perhaps that's what is eating me up from the inside. How can I feel hungry and sick at the same time?

I walk along the passage to the loo and I can't help staggering. My legs are jelly. I sit on the cold loo seat and cry. What's the matter with me? I am wasting away. I meet Banger in the corridor. Her dark eyes are very bright, and she wags her tail. She follows me back to my room.

'Come on, Banger. Jump up!' She can't so I lift her and she settles down on the eiderdown. Now I'm cold and sweaty. I bravely take a sip of warm Lucozade and then I draw my curtains back.

On my windowsill are eleven magpies. I know there are eleven because I count them. They are all magpie children.

In that moment I know I am a magpie child too.

CAMELLIA

Finn brings Mr Impey up the stairs. I can hear them chatting about fir cones. Mr Impey stands in the doorway with the record player. Finn carries some records.

'I thought you could listen to some music,' he says, looking round the skirting board for a plug. 'What we need is a little table to set this up. Finn, be a good boy and ask Nanny Jan for a table.' Finn rushes off. Mr Impey sits down in the chair, not on Mercy because she has gone off somewhere. He gets the diary out of his pocket.

'Fascinating!' he says. 'And, of course, very sad.'

My head hurts and my back aches so, but I don't tell him.

'I found a scrap of paper within the diary,' Mr Impey says, searching for the page. 'Here.' He holds up a little piece of cof-fee-coloured paper. 'You and Nanny Jan must have missed it. It was well tucked in.' He leans forward.

'This is very important, Camellia. It tells of a letter written by your great-grandmother to her daughter.'

'Oh,' I say.

'Shall I read what's written on this scrap of paper?' I nod. I wish I didn't feel so dreadful.

'*Mrs Goodridge died at 5.30pm on the 24th December 1896. I never heard an animal howl like that little dog. He remained beside her body throughout the night. I have hidden this diary within* Jane Eyre, *as promised. I am not entirely sure what to do with the letter, so I have tucked it into* The Happy Prince *for now. Baby Constance is yet too young to read, and Mrs Goodridge did not want her husband to see it. Rest in Peace. Eunice Fowler.*'

Mr Impey stares at me. I take a deep breath.

'I know where the Happy Prince book is. I saw it in the chest. It's in the chest in my other room. It's in the cupboard.'

'If we thought the diary was the key, then the letter is the *ultimate* magical key,' Mr Impey says. 'We must get into that chest. Shall I fetch it now?'

At that moment Nanny Jan comes in with a little table, followed by Finn who is carrying two apples. He says they're for me.

'We must fetch the chest, Nanny Jan,' says Mr Impey. 'There is more to this than meets the eye.'

Finn pats Banger while Mr Impey and Nanny Jan go off to find the chest. I wonder where Mummy is? Finn says she's gone shopping. I tell Finn I feel sick and I wish I hadn't because he looks frantic. He rushes out of the room shouting 'Nanny Jan! Sick bowl!'

It's not that I'm going to *be* sick. It's more that I'm sick in my *soul*, but how can I tell Finn that? It wouldn't be fair.

I just need more sleep.

NANNY JAN

Poor Camellia was nearly asleep once we came back with the chest. Finn had rushed to find me, dancing up and down, shouting that she was about to be sick. I grabbed the sick bowl out of the bathroom just in case. Luckily, we didn't need it.

I took her temperature again with Mr Impey there. It had sunk to 96. I reassured her that she didn't need an aspirin. What worried me more than anything was that she didn't seem that interested in the chest. It was if all the vitality had gone out of her.

Mr Impey said it was most important we find a certain letter, written by Mrs Goodridge, and he would take the chest away in order to break into it. Camellia managed a 'Thank you' and then turned over on her side. Finn was upset because he wanted to talk to his sister, having been with me for most of the afternoon.

Mr Impey set the record player up and put his records on the spare bed. I called for Banger to come out, but she didn't want to jump down off the bed. I heard Camellia say 'Leave her', so I did. It's too hot outside in any case.

'I'll be back in about an hour to see how you're getting on,' I assured her, leaving the door slightly ajar. She said she wanted the curtains left open.

Mr Impey sped off in his car with the chest on board. He promised he would be back tomorrow with news. He would find a tool in his garage to break into the chest. He did make me laugh when he asked if I had any spare axes hanging around. He gave the diary back to me, and I will keep it safe

in my room. He said the next person to read it should be Old
Mrs Devon.

I didn't doubt it. We are running out of time.

CAMELLIA

I think I am going to die. It's the middle of the night, and I'm
shivery. That means my temperature is going up *again*. I don't
remember much after Mr Impey brought the record player. I
don't think I had any supper, or did I?

I switch on my light to see Mercy in her chair, watchful as
ever. I know I need to listen to some music, so I climb out of
bed and go through Mr Impey's records. My legs and arms are
like cotton wool. There is the Hansel and Gretel record. Right
now I need fourteen angels to take care of me.

I lie back while the Sandman's song fills the room. I feel the
tears slide down the side of my face, and I try and concentrate
hard on the music. I am the Sandman, I am Hansel, I am Gretel,
I am each and every angel. Then, because I am too tired to lift
the needle, I have to listen to the witch's tune.

I am ill and can never get better.

CAMELLIA

I am wrong! I do feel better in the morning and I'm sure it was
the music that helped me. It's Friday and I can hear Nanny
Jan getting up next door. I wonder what sort of day it is, so I
open my curtains to see Mercy taking Nara for a walk across
the meadow. There are lots of dogs running after her, and this
time there's a new figure right at the back. I can't see the person
properly, so I pick up my new binoculars. This is what they are
for!

I feel sick when I see who it is. It is *me*. I know it's me because
the figure is wearing the same dress I wore for my birthday.
She's following Mercy and Nara and the ghost dogs. Shadows
from the big oak trees fall across the field and for a moment I
lose sight of her.

Nanny Jan comes in. She says she's pleased to see me awake and out of bed. I hold the binoculars out in front of me. I am shaking.

'I've seen myself out there.' I point, leaning out of the open window. 'I am with Mercy and the ghost dogs!' Nanny Jan doesn't understand how this is possible.

'She's taking me to the Light, Nanny Jan. But I don't *want* to go to the Light. I want to stay with you and Finn and Mummy and Daddy and Mr Impey.' I force myself to look through the binoculars again, afraid of what I will see.

They have gone. The meadow is deserted, apart from some rooks hopping about. That's all. No magpies.

'I've got to buck up,' I say. 'I've got to try and stay here.'

Nanny Jan smiles and says of course I will. She will bring me up some breakfast, with extra fresh orange juice.

I pick up my new oil painting book.

CAMELLIA

I eat my breakfast, as much as I can anyway, with a temperature of 99. Mummy comes in to see me and tells me that Dr Byng is going to look in on me this morning, probably after eleven.

I ask her about the blood test, and she tells me it was as clear as a bell. She says she knew it would be, but I don't think she did. I'm very relieved, as much as I can be after seeing myself in the meadow with Mercy. I decide not to tell Mummy that.

Instead I open my oil painting set and squeeze some big, fat juicy worms of colour onto the palette. I have no idea how to mix them and I stare at the colours for a bit. I pick up one of the brushes and dip it into the red, then I carefully scoop up a tiny blob of yellow. I mix the two together and there is my beloved orange. I paint an orange ball onto the new canvass. That could be an orange or the setting sun.

Already I'm tired of painting so I put the palette and canvas on the windowsill, just out of the sun. They should be all right there.

I pick up the binoculars again, searching the meadow. Mercy isn't with me, and neither is she out there. She's somewhere though. She's always somewhere.

I climb back into bed and stare at Mercy's chair.

CAMELLIA
Dr Byng and the oil paints

I hear Dr Byng's voice coming up the stairs. I wonder if he's as nervous of me as I am of him. Mummy shows him in. Why is he carrying that horrible black bag? I hate it.

'Good morning, Camellia,' he says in a cheerful voice. 'I've just come to see how you're getting on.' He's wearing a tweed jacket in summer! Mummy says what good news it is about the blood test.

'All clear.' He peers at me with his beady eyes. 'Probably some sort of summer virus.'

'Not TB?' I smile sweetly at him. 'You said it was TB before, remember?'

Both Dr Byng and Mummy are shocked. Dr Byng feels my forehead and says I might be a bit feverish.

'Am I going to die?' The words fall out of my mouth.

'Heavens no,' says Dr Byng. 'We'll have you right as rain in no time.'

He takes my temperature, listens to my heart, my lungs and checks my eyes, ears and throat again. All is clear.

'Coughing?' he asks.

'Better thank you, Dr Byng.'

He puts the stethoscope back into his horrible black bag. Then he notices my binoculars on the bedside table. He asks if I'd mind if he had a look through them. Then he goes to the window and sits on the sill. What he doesn't know is that he has sat on my palette.

'These are a fine pair of binoculars, Camellia,' he says. 'I can see the Downs very clearly, even the monastery clock!'

He hands them back to me with a smile, then turns around for Mummy to show him out. His bottom is covered in red, yellow and blue with a touch of orange. Mummy hasn't noticed yet, but she will soon.

'Plenty of fluids and rest,' Dr Byng says. 'Goodbye.'

I raise my arm. I don't tell him his trousers are covered in oil paints. He will need a lot of turpentine to get that out.

Mercy appears and rocks with laughter.

CAMELLIA

I'm drifting off to sleep when Mummy says I have another visitor. This time it's Gran. She's downstairs and wants to come up and see me. Mummy tells me she saw the paint on Dr Byng's trousers but that she couldn't bring herself to warn him. Those colours will be all over his car seat by now. She laughs and laughs, saying she knows she shouldn't. Poor Dr Byng.

I'm feeling funny which means my temperature has gone up again. I get the shivers when it's on the rise. I ask Mummy to call Nanny Jan to come and take it, then perhaps Gran can come up in five minutes? Nanny Jan takes my temperature and sure enough I'm over 100 again. I ask her to bring Mercy's diary because I'm going to give it to Gran.

'Are you sure you feel strong enough for this, Camellia?'

'No, but I've got to do it.'

'Mr Impey's coming later, remember. He might have got into the chest.'

When she gives me the diary, I ask her to wish me luck. I hold it tight and right now my heart feels like it's going to burst. How will Gran take the news? Will she be cross with me for not telling her before? My temperature's going up and I'm feeling worse and worse. I sip some water. I can't face Lucozade any more.

Gran comes in and sits at the end of my bed. She's wearing a pretty green and violet dress, even if a bit old fashioned. Mummy says she'll leave us to have a nice chat. She has *no* idea. Gran smiles at me, asking me how I'm feeling.

'Pretty awful actually, Gran. No one knows what's the matter with me.'

Gran admires my vase of roses. She doesn't know what to say. I have to get it over and done with. I hold out Mercy's diary.

'This is what we were looking for. This is your Mummy's diary. We found it. Here it is.'

Gran doesn't know what to do. Her face is blank.

'You *must* read it, Gran. I have.' I don't tell her that Nanny Jan and Mr Impey have read it as well. That wouldn't be kind. 'Her writing is quite small. You might need your glasses to read it.'

Gran hasn't said one single word. She sits there on the bed, the diary in her lap. Perhaps she's turned to stone.

'It will make you understand your Mummy more,' I say. 'I'm sorry we didn't tell you that we'd found it.' Now Gran speaks.

'Where was it?'

'In the cellar. In a chest.' I hope Gran doesn't ask to see the chest because it isn't here.

'Ah,' says Gran. She smoothes a finger over the initials.

'Will you read it?' I ask her.

'Of course.'

'Then you might believe in her ghost.' Gran gives me her stony face. We are not there yet. 'Please read it soon,' I say to her. 'I feel so ill.'

Gran's face crumples. She's going to cry.

'I'm afraid,' she whispers. 'I'm afraid it will hurt too much.'

That's *not* an excuse.

'You've got to be *brave*, Gran,' I cry, beating my fists on the eiderdown. 'I have to be brave, *all* the time. It's exhausting. Your Mummy is lovely, even if a bit capricious. And she's very sad because you don't believe in her.'

Gran staggers to her feet, clutching the diary. She makes her way to the door.

'Just *try*, Gran,' I plead.

I must be over 101 by now.

'Jesus won't mind!'

CAMELLIA

I'm too uncomfortable to sleep. I'm so very hot, and I wish someone could come in and see me. My watch says 12.30, the time Nanny Jan should be collecting Finn. Where's Mummy got to now? Mrs Betts must be downstairs and I never know where Daddy is.

I'm worried my temperature will go up and up and then I'll burn up like a bonfire. I won't be able to stop it! I take a deep breath to calm myself down and my lungs hurt. My heart hurts. My head hurts. My bones hurt and I'm terribly hot. I kick the bedclothes away and fall back on my pillows.

Gran will be reading the diary soon. She might need a glass of sherry to help her. I know it helps Mummy. That and a cigarette, but Gran doesn't smoke of course. Only her fire does that.

Where *are* you Mercy?

NANNY JAN

Camellia's temperature had jumped to 103 by the time I got back with Finn. Her eyes were glassy, and she was coughing again. I can't say I wasn't worried, but it's no good letting children know you are worried. Instead I reassured her that her temperature would come down very soon, and we could help it along with another junior aspirin.

Finn tried to hide his concern, offering to sing the *Bossa Bova*. He was so sure that would cheer her up. He said he could sing any tune she wanted. He was so disappointed when Camellia waved him away. Instead I put on one of Mr Impey's records. Finn chose it. It was a selection of slow movements from piano concertos.

'You'll like these, Melia,' he said, studying the record cover. 'These will make you better.'

Camellia told me in a low voice that she had given her grandmother the diary. It had made both of them upset. I thought as much and told her she was very brave. As we went downstairs Finn said he was scared. Why wasn't his sister getting better? He hoped she wasn't going to go mad again with the Alice Syndrome.

'Mr Impey's going to make her better, Finn. Just you wait and see.'

As it happened, Mr Impey found me in the car park waiting for the children to come out of school. He said he had broken into the chest (he felt rather bad about that because the lid was now damaged) and found the letter in a fairy tale book. He was going to read it to Camellia this afternoon and then the plan would be hatched.

'What's going to happen to that poor child?'

'We are going to help her, Nanny Jan. I have thought of a plan. We are going to stage a little concert at the end of the garden for Mercy and her daughter. Sunday is the day!'

'How will she be strong enough to walk down there? She's worse today you know.'

'I will carry her,' Mr Impey said. Then he smiled. 'Either that or we'll have to put her in the wheelbarrow!' You have to laugh at Mr Impey.

I left Finn eating his strawberries in the nursery, carrying a little bowl of them up for Camellia. I thought she might be able to face them. The piano music filling her room was very beautiful. She said it was the second tune on side one. I glanced at the cover.

'Shostakovich Piano Concerto No. 2 in F major.'

'It's making me cry,' she said, wiping her eyes. I offered to switch it off, but she said no.

'Try a strawberry, there's a good girl.' She took a bite of one and said it tasted sour.

'Mr Impey has found the letter!' At least her eyes lit up at that. 'He's bringing it over this afternoon and then we are going to make a fine plan, and that will make you well again.'

'I hope so, Nanny Jan. I hope so. I don't want to go to the Light, even if Mercy wants me to. Look, the magpie children are back!'

There were five magpies perched on the sill outside. I wanted to shoo them away. I can't help but think they're unlucky.

'They are just babies,' she said. 'Mercy loves them, you see.'

She brushed her hands down her nightdress. 'Do you think I could have a new nightie, Nanny Jan? This one's all wet.'

Sunday can't come soon enough for me.

CAMELLIA

I lie in bed listening to the beautiful piano music, waiting for Mr Impey to arrive. I have listened to side one three times over and the Shostakovich is my favourite. I must be feeling a little better because I'm strong enough to put the record on again. The junior aspirin is working.

I watch as a magpie child hops in through the window.

'Hello,' I say. 'Would you like a strawberry? They're a bit sour for me, but they might be all right for you.'

The magpie puts his head on one side. Then he flies right onto my bed to peck at a strawberry in the bowl. He goes back for more and more. Soon there are strawberry bits all over my bed and I worry they look like blood. I move the bowl to the windowsill so the magpie can make a mess there. Even doing that is exhausting! The magpie flies off with half a strawberry in his beak.

Nanny Jan brings Mr Impey in. He's carrying a cardboard box which he says is full of Mercy stuff. My heart lifts at his merry smile, and the first thing I tell him is that I've given Gran the diary.

'Bravo,' Mr Impey says. 'That had to come first.'

'She was awfully upset though. I felt sick giving it to her.' Mr Impey looks round for somewhere to put the box. 'And she asked where we found it,' I add. 'Luckily I didn't have to fib.'

'We are nearly there, Camellia! That I promise you.' He looks down at the bed, asking whether I've cut my toe by any chance? Nanny Jan hurries over, her face worried.

'A magpie had some of my strawberries, that's all. Sorry about the mess.' Poor Nanny Jan doesn't like the idea of a magpie eating my strawberries.

Finn appears in the doorway. He doesn't want to be left out. Nanny Jan says that Mr Impey and I need to be left alone for five minutes or so, and then Finn can join in. She says he can help her find some more strawberries for Camellia.

'We don't have to pick them, do we?' I hear Finn asking as they leave, and Nanny Jan says no, there are some in the larder.

Mr Impey spreads out the contents of the box on to my bed. There are the books, the Hansel and Gretel programme and then Mr Impey waves a magpie feather at me.

'This was right at the bottom of the chest,' he says. 'You can fix it to your orange hat!'

'Then it would be good enough for Ascot!' I say. 'Well almost.'

'Quite so, quite so. Now…' Mr Impey opens *The Happy Prince and Other Tales* at page 11, 'The Nightingale and the Rose'. 'Here is the letter!'

'Mercy's letter to her baby?'

Mr Impey nods.

'The very same. The *ultimate* magical key. Now I have already read the letter, and I warn you it's very, very sad. Do you feel brave enough for me to read it?'

My heart hurts, as do my bones, but I am brave enough.

'Please read it to me, Mr Impey.'

This is what Mr Impey reads…

ALATHEA

'*9th December 1896*

To my dear darling daughter,

Remember me on your birthday each year, the 18th of August, and be reassured that as much as you are thinking of me, I am thinking of you and loving you always.

The doctor told me yesterday that there is no hope of my recovery. That can't have been easy for him. I am growing so very weak and if only I could stop this relentless coughing, then I might be able to sleep. My body may be weak, yet my soul is strong, and I love you, my darling daughter, with all the strength I have left.

You were the dearest newborn baby and your birth was both easy and joyful. I stood my ground upon feeding you myself, in spite of the nurse provided from the village. How could William entertain that idea? I suppose he thought I would regain my strength more quickly, and indeed that was a kindly notion, but what do men know of these things?

It was while I was feeding you one late September afternoon that you gave me your first smile. How happy we were, smiling at one another. We were in our own enchanted world.

October brought the first sharp frosts and it was in the second week that I began to cough. That same cough has brought me to where I am now, isolated and alone, but for my dear nurse and faithful Bo. The windows are permanently open because it is thought the bitter winter wind has the power to purge the contagion. For this is tuberculosis, and I am constantly cold.

I am forcibly separated from you, my dearest child. I hear you crying for me and I can do nothing. I am forbidden to see you by my husband and the doctors. They inform me it is too dangerous and, God knows, I should not want you to become infected.

I am to die soon, I know it. I do not fear death, but I fear leaving you without a mother. My own mother died when I was but six years old and I grieved for her.

So, remember me on your birthday, my darling child, for I was never so happy as the day I brought you into this world. I promise I shall never be far away.

You have my love forever
Your mother
Alathea'

CAMELLIA

Mr Impey finishes reading the letter with tears in his eyes! He finds his handkerchief.

'Gran will be very sad when she reads this letter,' I say.

Mr Impey blows his nose, and says he's sure she will. Anyone would find the letter sad. However, it shows that her mother loved her very much indeed.

'Poor Mercy,' I say. 'Not to be able to go to your little baby, especially when you can hear her crying so.'

'Grim,' says Mr Impey. 'And to feel that isolated.'

We sit for a moment in silence.

'How are you feeling today?' Mr Impey folds the letter up.

'*GRIM!*' I tell him. I rather like that word.

'Mercy wants to take me to the Light. I saw myself out in the meadow yesterday with her and the ghost dogs.' Mr Impey frowns when I tell him this.

'That's very naughty of her. You go to the Light when you are *dead*, and not before. You, Camellia, are most certainly alive.'

'At the moment. Just about.'

'So, this is why I have thought of a proper plan. If this doesn't help your grandmother to see Mercy, I don't know what will.'

'What if your plan doesn't work, Mr Impey? What if Gran won't believe?' Mr Impey waves the letter at me.

'Of *course,* it will work. Now here's what will happen.'

Finn arrives with the strawberries and Mr Impey says they look rather good. He helps himself.

Nanny Jan, Finn and I listen while Mr Impey sets out his plan for Sunday. We will hold a little concert at the end of the garden. He asks me which songs I would like played on the violin, and of course it has to be 'Silent Night' and the 'Evening Prayer'. Finn wonders if Mercy would like the *Bossa Bova*?

'She *might*, Finn,' Mr Impey says, 'But perhaps at the very end, once your Gran has seen Mercy properly.' He writes 'Silent Night' and the 'Evening Prayer' on his list. Then he looks at me.

'It would help if you could sing yourself, Camellia.' I shake my head. It would be too much. So Mr Impey asks which one of my friends has a good voice and I think of Sarah. She can sing high.

So, it's decided that Sarah will be invited over for Sunday morning. Mr Impey will do his church service and after that he will drive over to see Gran and give her the letter. Then he will bring her up through the garden to join us. In the meantime, we will be ready, and he suggests midday. He will deliver his violin tomorrow, if we could be so kind as to carry it down.

'I would like lots of roses,' I say. 'And Banger with me.'

'You shall have plenty of roses,' says Mr Impey. 'Finn, that can be your job to carry them down in your wheelbarrow.'

'Jaffa cakes?' Finn's voice is hopeful.

'Mr Fox and Dorothy Baby,' I say.

Mr Impey says he will leave me to think of all the things I would like taken down to the end of the garden. He will come over again tomorrow to explain the plan to Mummy and Daddy. He will wear his black uniform, so he looks important. Nanny Jan smiles at Mr Impey as he sets out his plan. I think she likes him very much! She says she will make sure Sarah is invited over for Sunday morning. That can be one of her jobs. Mr Impey says he will practise 'Silent Night' and the 'Evening Prayer' on his violin, although of course he knows them by heart.

My temperature is going up again. I am shivery. I'm going to let everyone else take care of the plan. Nanny Jan draws the bedclothes up around me and suggests a little sleep.

Mr Impey waves goodbye. He takes the letter with him and leaves me with the books. I had forgotten about Mercy's little sketchbook and paints. I'm too tired to look at them now.

I hope I wake up from my little sleep. I'm not sure now.

CAMELLIA

I have to stay alive for two more nights. Just two more nights. Surely, I can do that?

Finn says goodnight to me after his bath and I can tell he's worried because he keeps rubbing his ear. He brings one of his favourite books *Harry the Dirty Dog*, just in case I feel like reading it during the night. He tells me that Nanny Jan says Sarah's definitely coming over on Sunday and that she's practising her singing. I smile at that. I hope she knows the words! Perhaps her Mummy will have them written down somewhere.

'Is Mercy here now?' Finn asks. I shake my head.

'She comes and goes. But she knows about the plan.'

'Do you want an apple?' Finn offers to get me one from

downstairs. I don't really want one, but I don't want to disappoint him.

'That's a very good idea, Finn. An apple a day keeps the doctor away.' I hear him running down the corridor and calling.

'Nanny Jan! Melia wants an apple.'

While I wait for Finn to come back, I pick up the binoculars to see if anyone is in the meadow. My temperature must be down because my legs feel stronger. I look out into the early evening light.

Mercy is leading Nara and the dogs across the field again. They are having their evening walk. I move the binoculars towards the back and see myself, wearing the same party dress but this time Banger is at my heels. *No, no, no!*

I shout for Nanny Jan. Finn comes running in with the apple. He knows something is wrong. I'm frantic.

'WHERE'S BANGER?' Finn stares at me. *'WHERE IS SHE?'*

Finn doesn't know. Maybe she's in the nursery? He runs off again to find Nanny Jan and Banger. He's still carrying the apple. I don't want to look through the binoculars again. How *dare* Mercy think she can take Banger away as well? Finn returns with Nanny Jan.

'Here's Banger,' she says, calling her name. Banger trots in, wagging her tail, her eyes bright.

'Mercy wants her!' I cry. 'Please can Banger stay with me tonight, Nanny Jan?' Nanny Jan says of course she can. Banger will love sleeping on the other bed, much more comfortable than her basket downstairs.

'I knew Melia wanted Banger,' Finn says to Nanny Jan. 'That's why I brought her *Harry the Dirty Dog*.' He puts the apple on my bedside table.

I'm so full of fear that all I can do is pick up Banger and hold her tight. Of course, I know that Mercy will be with me tonight and she could take Banger at any time, especially when I'm asleep.

'Eat your apple, Melia,' says Finn.

I burst into tears.

CAMELLIA

Nanny Jan and Finn were very kind to me when I cried. Banger was kind too, allowing me to hug her tight and have my tears drip into her coat. Nanny Jan took my temperature after I'd calmed down and it was nearly 100. I thought I was normal, but I was 100. Finn had run out of things to make me better and his face was miserable.

'Maybe some rowan, Finn?'

'All better tomorrow, Melia,' he said as Nanny Jan led him off to his own bed, and then 'She needs rowan, Nanny Jan.'

Mummy came up to see me after that, and she brought Daddy in as well. Instead of making me feel better, it made me even more worried. I know from books and films that fathers only come to see you when you are really ill and about to die. I hardly heard what Daddy said about Banger and the binoculars. I was moving further and further away.

Mummy said that she was looking forward to Mr Impey's visit tomorrow and hearing about the plan. She would do everything she could to make it all go beautifully.

There were tears in Mummy's eyes when she kissed me goodnight, and that terrified me. Then Daddy kissed me goodnight. Luckily, *he* didn't have tears in his eyes. I kept saying to myself *'Once I'm through this night, I only have one more night to go.'*

Mercy was back in her chair. I told her Banger didn't belong to her. She was mine.

I try to settle. I try to keep calm. I try to make my temperature go down. I try to get better. But there's only one thought going around in my mind and in my heart.

I want my Mummy.

I don't want Mercy because she's Gran's Mummy. Nanny Jan and Finn are not enough. I want my Mummy.

The tears are sliding down the side of my face. This is the way tears flow when you're lying down.

I let them flow.

FINN
I'm scared.
I don't want Melia to die.
She needs rowan.
I will find some rowan tomorrow.
She needs rowan.
I don't want Melia to die.
I'm scared.

CAMELLIA
I'm lying on my back and I must be alive because I can see, even though it's pretty dark in my room. There's no moon but my curtains are drawn back, giving enough starlight to reveal who's kneeling beside my bed.

It's Mummy! She's wearing her nightdress and her head is bent over her hands as if in prayer. I cannot speak in this moment. But there is someone else praying beside Mummy. It's Mercy. Her head is also bent over her hands, and I stare in wonder at these two figures at my bedside. Are they praying for me?

Mercy raises her head. Her face is beautiful and her expression kind. How can I doubt her?

Now I hear the song of the nightingale and it's as if he's singing right outside my window, the song just as I remembered from the primrose wood. His song is bubbling and clear and very loud! Perhaps he has flown out of the fairy tale 'The Nightingale and the Rose'? I certainly have roses in my room. I look over to the other bed where Banger is snoring peacefully. She is safe.

I'm not sure if I'm hot or cold. Perhaps this is what dying is like? I feel no fear in any case.

Mummy has gone now, as has Mercy. Instead the room is filled with angels, and the light from them is golden and pink, reflecting off their faces and wings. They are Hansel and Gretel's angels, all fourteen of them, and now the 'Evening Prayer' floats towards me on a musical wave. The nightingale sings his song outside, making a perfect duet. I can let go of everything.

But this is *dying*! I clench my fists and straighten my arms. I want to live!

I reach out for Mr Fox, feeling his hard, bumpy face and the velvet of his coat. He knows what to do. The angels melt away and the song of the nightingale fades.

I am back, but that was close.

My Mummy's prayers must have worked.

ANGELA

I had the strangest dream last night. I dreamt I was kneeling beside Camellia's bed, praying my very hardest for her recovery and then I became aware of someone else beside me, also kneeling in prayer.

That someone was a woman, about the same age as me, dressed in clothes from another era. Her hair was drawn up in a bun and I especially noticed her unusual necklace.

It was as if we were competing for Camellia. *She's mine. No, she's mine.* All this was said with thoughts.

By the time I heard the nightingale sing, the words in my head were:

She's ours.

When I woke, my pillow was wet from tears.

NANNY JAN

Finn came running into my room this morning with news, and I expected the worst, but it was only to say he'd already been in to see Camellia and that she was all right.

I hurried along to her room and found her reading *Harry the Dirty Dog*, with Mr Fox in her lap.

'See!' said Finn, laughing.

'I nearly died last night.' She sounded very matter of fact about it.

'The angels came, and then I heard the nightingale. Mummy

was praying by my bed as well as Mercy. And then Mr Fox saved me.' She waved Mr Fox to illustrate the point.

Finn shouted *hurrah* and ran off to give his mother the good news. I couldn't stop him and anyway why should I? I took her temperature and it was down to 99. Mind you, we've seen this before and then the fever comes back. What we wanted was 24 hours of normal.

Finn came running back in and flung himself against Camellia's bed. He told her he was going to find her some rowan from his Gran's garden to make extra sure she was going to live. He asked her to read him a page or two from the Harry book and Camellia must have been feeling better because she did, and the two of them laughed. It was then that Finn noticed something amiss.

'Melia, why are your eyes blue?'

At that very moment Mrs Devon appeared in the doorway.

CAMELLIA

Mummy appears wearing exactly the same nightdress as last night, only now with her floaty dressing gown. I wish I had one like that.

Mummy is really here! Finn says I'm all better now, apart from my blue eyes. He says the rowan will fix that, he just knows it. Then they will be green again. Mummy turns my face to the window and frowns.

'They are a bit blue.'

'It's happened before, Mummy,' I say. 'It used to frighten me, but it doesn't now. It's Mercy.'

Nanny Jan gives Mummy a look, as if to say she knows what I'm talking about. Mummy asks her to help get Finn dressed because she'd like to talk to me. I notice she doesn't say 'have a word', so perhaps this is going to be a nice talk. Finn complains as Nanny Jan leads him out. He doesn't want to miss anything. Banger jumps down off the bed, following them.

'*Mummy!*' I cry and I can't help smiling. I feel *completely* at

ease with her. I'm excited too because I know Mummy is going
to share something important.

I help her by telling I saw her by my bed in the night, saying
her prayers, *and* that her prayers worked! Mummy's face lights
up.

'And Mercy was praying beside you, Mummy.'

Mummy stares off into space. I hope she's listening.

'I saw your ghost in my dream, Camellia. She was wearing a
very unusual necklace.'

'That's her!' At *last* Mummy is listening to me. I find my diary
and show Mummy my very first drawing of Mercy. I don't say
I've already shown it to her. She's probably forgotten. Mummy
takes the picture and nods.

'That's her,' she says.

'This was her home, Mummy, and she died here. We found
her diary and now Gran's reading it. Mercy loved her diary, just
as we love ours.' I smile at this. 'We are diary girls!' Mummy
says she doesn't know where she would be without her diary.

'But Mercy's diary is where she writes her thoughts and
feelings, so it's very useful.' Mummy's face falls when I say this.
'Not that your diary isn't useful of course!'

I tell her Mr Impey has made a very fine plan and he will
explain everything later. Mummy says she will do everything
she possibly can to make the plan go with a bang. That makes
me laugh because it nearly rhymes and, when Nanny Jan comes
back asking what I want for breakfast, she finds Mummy and
me helpless with laughter.

Nanny Jan says the laughter has made my eyes green again,
and Mummy agrees.

I am back and my Mummy's back.

Now for the plan.

CAMELLIA

As promised, Mr Impey arrives soon after lunch. I hear his
voice downstairs talking to Mummy and Daddy by the front

door, and soon Finn runs in to tell me that Mr Impey has asked him to look after his violin.

He gives me a scrappy piece of rowan. It's a piece that's neither one thing nor the other, which is how I feel. There are a few battered flowers attached at the end of the twig, and the beginnings of green berries.

'Just what I need,' I say, and he beams. He wonders if I would like a piece of seaweed as well?

'It's all right, Finn. I can tell it's sunny outside.'

'But my seaweed's gone soggy.'

'All of it?'

'No,' he admits.

'That means it *might* rain, and it *might* be sunny.' He gives a big sigh. Finn likes to be sure, one way or the other. I feel tired again and say so. Finn peers into my eyes.

'It's OK, Melia. They're green.'

'Thank the Lord for that,' I say, and Finn looks startled.

'What?'

'Your voice, Melia. It didn't sound like you.' I lean back on my pillows. What's he talking about?

'It's me. It's Saturday afternoon, June 15th and this is me.'

'Now it is.' But he doesn't sound that sure. We wonder how long Mr Impey will be talking to Mummy and Daddy.

'Bloody ages probably,' says Finn and I have to smile.

CAMELLIA
Thunderclouds

Finn was right. Mr Impey *has* been bloody ages talking to Mummy and Daddy. My eyelids want to close, and I have to force myself to stay awake. Finn puts his head through the bannisters before creeping down the front stairs to listen. The breeze outside has dropped and the air feels sticky. I'm not sure I could bear another storm.

'Still talking,' he says, scrambling on to the spare bed. Two minutes later he's off again to listen. Luckily the spaces between the bannisters are quite wide. All we need is for his head to get stuck.

'Look out! They're coming up!' he shouts, running round in circles. Outside the sky is yellow and I hear the faintest rumble of thunder. Mercy must be out and about because she isn't here. She too is preparing for the Plan.

Mr Impey stands in the doorway again and Finn jumps up and down. We have come a long way from Finn's thinking Mr Impey was a jelly baby thief.

'Some of my bits of seaweed are soggy,' Finn announces with a long face. Mr Impey isn't at all surprised. He heard a rumble or two of thunder, leaving the Vicarage. He knows a bit about thunderclouds though.

'You have to be a King Thundercloud to make thunder and lightning and you need to be at least eight miles high. If you are a mere Prince Thundercloud, then you can't conduct a proper storm.' Finn scowls. He knows he isn't tall enough to conduct a proper storm.

'You can if you're a Queen,' I say.

Mr Impey picks up the binoculars to scan the sky.

'Mere Princely clouds,' he says. 'They will not come to anything, you mark my words. And now...' He sits down in Mercy's chair. He has a notepad and pen. 'The *Plan*!'

Finn bounces up and down on the bed. He's keen to get started. Mr Impey says he will need *plenty* of sweets to discuss the Plan, and perhaps Finn could go downstairs and fetch them. Finn's out of the door in a flash.

Mr Impey uses the time to explain how Mummy and Daddy are now fully up to date on everything. He says they were a bit bewildered at first but it helps hugely that he, Mr Impey, is a Man of the Cloth. His eyes dance when he says a Cloth, not a dishcloth. I burst out laughing.

'Temperature?' he asks me.

'Better today, thank you. But I nearly died last night.'

I tell him about Mummy and Mercy and the angels, as well as the nightingale. His face is serious. He congratulates me for holding on. He says Mummy told him about her dream and in front of Daddy too! He calls that corroborative evidence and, before I ask him to explain, he says it's when a story is backed up by another person. It helps us very much, and he will give that evidence to Gran tomorrow.

'And talking of your Gran, I visited her this morning. She has read the diary from start to finish, but of course she doesn't yet know about the letter. That will be left for tomorrow. She knows I am to visit her again after church. She's ready for that.'

'Is she ready to see her Mummy?' My voice is a whisper.

'Very, very nearly.' I give a sigh of relief, and Mr Impey fans himself with the notebook.

'Finn says my voice changed while we were waiting for you. I didn't notice it, but Finn didn't like it.'

If Mr Impey's worried by this, he doesn't show it.

'This time tomorrow we will be through and out the other side. It will all be over,' he says. 'Now where's that Finn? We need jelly babies to draw up our plan.'

As if by magic, Finn and Nanny Jan appear. Finn has the whole tin in his arms. He can't believe his luck. Nanny Jan has a notebook and pen, as well as a tray with a teapot and four cups.

We mean business. Just one more night.

NANNY JAN

Mr Impey outlined his own thoughts on the plan, while we enjoyed our tea and sweets, and then he invited both Camellia and Finn to put forward any suggestions. It made the children feel ever so important! We were having a proper meeting.

Every one of us has our duties for tomorrow and I have made a list. Who would have thought a plan to help a ghost and her daughter would be such fun?

While I was making a second pot of tea in the kitchen, Mrs Devon found me and asked if she could join our meeting. I had to stop myself from hugging her there and then. I didn't think hugging my employer appropriate, but I was that happy. She found herself an extra cup and saucer and carried the teapot upstairs for me.

'*Mummy!*' Camellia's face was a picture when her mother came in.

'Sit here, Mummy,' Finn said, patting the space on the bed beside him. 'Move up, Banger.'

'We're on to Any Other Business,' said Mr Impey. 'All bright ideas welcome!'

'One of my jobs is to keep Prince Thundercloud in order,' said Finn. 'And to bring seaweed down in my wheelbarrow.' Mrs Devon laughed and Mr Impey confirmed that seaweed was essential for the Plan to work.

'What can I do to help?' Mrs Devon sipped her tea. Then to Camellia she said 'Daddy wants to help too. He really does.'

'Isn't he too busy?' Camellia asked, and I wondered if her mother had noticed her eyes had turned blue again.

'He says he could go and talk to Gran. Try to help explain.'

You could have heard a pin drop in that moment. Camellia closed her blue eyes and scrunched up her face. I feared we were in for some tears. I held my breath, as did we all.

'Thank you, Mummy,' she said. And then again very quietly '*Thank you.*'

'Let's put that on the list then,' said Mr Impey. 'Nanny Jan, put that down and Mrs Devon, I see you are already writing.'

'Daddy's very good with timings,' Mrs Devon said to Camellia. 'He could help there too.'

'So am I,' said Finn.

'I'm not!' We all laughed when Mr Impey said that.

'Nor am I,' said Mrs Devon. 'I'm dreadful. Always late!'

I could tell Camellia was getting tired. She would need all her strength for tomorrow. It was agreed that Mr Devon would walk down the garden to see his mother for an evening drink at about six, and the rest of us would start collecting up what we needed for tomorrow.

Camellia said she wanted to have a bath and, before that, she went back to her room to choose a dress to wear for the Mercy

Concert, as we are calling it. Her eyes were changing colour constantly, but her temperature hadn't climbed above 99 all day. Her cough has gone.

If Finn isn't sick from eating all those sweets, I'll eat my hat. His little face kept breaking out in smiles in the bath, and indeed he laughed out loud, splashing his sponge. I remember well when he was a baby of eighteen months and Camellia had her tonsils out. She came out of hospital in the afternoon and that night Finn kept waking himself up and, whenever I went to check on him, he was laughing! He was that happy to see his sister again. That's how he was in the bath this evening.

All we have to do is get through tonight and tomorrow.

ANGELA

I must say I feel as if my world's been turned upside down. Mr Impey was very kind, clearly explaining to us how and why the ghost has been haunting Camellia and this house. Gerald was about as bewildered as I've ever seen him. I felt quite sorry for him actually, but not as sorry as I felt for myself. We are having to accept that we have failed as parents. We have failed to understand what has been going on right under our noses.

I didn't want to see it of course. I have deliberately refused to accept what's been causing such distress to our poor child. It was shocking, too shocking for me at least. But let's face it, most people *are* frightened of the unknown. They just don't want to look. Much easier to carry on with normal, everyday life.

I don't know how I will ever make up for not believing in Camellia, for not being there when she most needed me. I will try my best to find things to do with her. Perhaps we could both have a go with the oil paints? That would be fun. I'm going to tell Gerald he can stuff his hunting. That's no way to treat our daughter, or me come to that.

I have to accept that Nanny Jan knows Camellia better than I do. That's a bitter pill and entirely my own fault. It has taken a dream to show me how very much I love my daughter. She's the way she is, and we can both learn from each other. I'm not frightened of her any more. Gerald's going to Ascot next week, but I will play it by ear. I might do some oil painting with Camellia instead! I don't always have to do what Gerald says.

He was exhausted after returning from visiting Constance, mopping his head with a handkerchief. He dropped his walking staff with a clatter and the dogs stood behind him, wagging their tails and panting. I wasn't sure he had fed them.

'I can't believe I have spent the past hour and a half trying to persuade my mother to accept my grandmother's ghost. It was bloody hard work I'm telling you.'

'We have to. That's what tomorrow's all about.'

'Mother is convinced that if she "sees" the ghost, then she's betraying her father and will probably go to Hell.'

'Oh honestly!'

'That was before I told her about your dream. That helped.' My dream has certainly helped change our perspective. Thank goodness for my dream!

'More things in heaven and earth,' he muttered, pouring himself a drink. Then he collapsed on the sofa, kicking off his shoes. He sipped his whisky.

'I might buy a new pony for Camellia,' he said. I needed to stop him in his tracks there and then.

'She doesn't need a new pony, Gerald,' I said. 'She needs *us*.'

CAMELLIA
The last night

This is my last night. I didn't want to tell Nanny Jan or Mummy, when she came to say goodnight to me, that I felt swimmy and far away. They think I'm getting better but I'm not so sure.

At least I've chosen my dress for tomorrow. It's white with tiny pink and violet flowers. It's one of last year's dresses and it fits because I'm so thin. I tried it on and it's a bit short but at least I won't look like a rag bag. If I wore my birthday dress, it would *hang* off me.

I watched my eyes change colour as I was brushing my teeth. They went from blue to green, then green to blue over and over again. I tried singing the first two lines of the 'Evening Prayer' and my voice didn't sound like mine at all. Thank heavens the cough has gone.

Mummy and Daddy were helping with the plan. They must care. That made me feel very important!

Mercy isn't in her chair this evening. She's probably busy with *her* last-minute preparations. I have to trust her. I *think* I trust her.

We know what we have to do tomorrow.

One more night.

CAMELLIA
The stars

I am stepping between the stars, following golden trails of light and all around me are the songs of angels. Little ships make journeys between galaxies, their sails glowing in different colours, all bound for different destinations.

I am holding Jupiter and Mercy holds Saturn. She throws the planet up into the darkness and it floats free, its icy rings spinning. I let Jupiter go and his red eye blinks back at me, growing all the while. The red eye is kind and I'm not afraid at all.

Before me now are giant pillars of colour, and Mercy tells me these are star nurseries. Little stars are being born all the time, glowing with every colour of the rainbow.

All this she shows me, and more.

I wake to the song of the thrush, not the nightingale. The thrush means I'm *alive*. I see Banger on the bed, curled up in a ball, her back rising and falling with each breath. She's alive.

Sunday has arrived! *This is it.* The big day and it's bigger than my birthday.

A sunny day for Mercy's Concert.

I am *alive*.

CAMELLIA

I am weak and wobbly, but I want to come down for breakfast. Nanny Jan says my temperature is normal and, if I have breakfast downstairs, then I can always go back up afterwards to rest, before changing for the Concert.

I sit in the nursery and it feels strange to be here. How long have I been ill upstairs? How many days? I really can't remember.

There are lists for everyone spread out on the little table, so we all know what we are doing. Finn's list is long! He will need to make several trips with his wheelbarrow. He promises to cart Mr Fox, Dorothy Baby, cushions, Mr Impey's violin and his seaweed safely down to the bottom of the garden.

Mummy's list has *Pick roses* on it, amongst other things. Daddy's list has *Bring down magpie cage*. Nanny Jan's list has things like chairs and rugs and drinks and biscuits.

I don't have a list. But that doesn't really matter because my list is in my heart.

I sit at the piano, slowly picking out the tune of the 'Evening Prayer'. Again, I test my voice and *again* it sounds different, as if it were more grown up. I might be able to sing. Now I feel nervous.

I step out on to the terrace, thinking back to when it was covered with snow and how excited we were when the snow first came tumbling down. Today the air is warm, the copper beech leaves shining and waving in the morning breeze. I lean over the edge of the terrace to see Mercy's rose. A bee is rolling around in the very centre of the petals, happy as can be. Mummy has yet to pick them. I wander down the steps on to the lawn.

A chatter from overhead means only one thing. A magpie child is wishing me good morning.

Nanny Jan calls me in for breakfast. Finn is at the table already. There is a great pile of stuff in the nursery and I see Mr Fox sits on the top. He is ready.

We all are.

CAMELLIA

I sit in the nursery waiting. It's nearly eleven o'clock, and Sarah's about to arrive. Mr Impey must be finishing his ten o'clock service, and that means very soon he will be showing Gran the letter. There's one hour to go and I try very hard to keep calm. I haven't seen Mercy this morning.

Finn has carted most of his stuff down. Daddy gave him a hand with the big wheelbarrow, and Finn told me he felt proud, trundling his own wheelbarrow, side by side with Daddy. Mummy has picked armfuls of roses. She found an enormous glass bowl and is going to arrange them in that. I leave it to her.

I keep Mr Fox with me, and Nanny Jan tells Finn it's safer for her to carry Mr Impey's violin. We don't want it getting mixed up with seaweed. There's no need for any music for the Concert, but we do need some words. I copy out the 'Evening Prayer' from Mr Impey's music book in my best handwriting.

Sarah arrives wearing the prettiest dress of yellow and green. I tell her she looks like a primrose and she laughs. She has a dark pink hairband which she says is new.

'I'm so nervous about singing!' she says, nodding yes to a glass of orange squash from Nanny Jan.

'Do you want to practise now?' I ask. She gives a great big shudder, saying no, she has practised it enough.

'We can ask Mr Impey to play the violin quite loud, if you like.'

Sarah thinks that's a very good idea. I tell her I'm not sure I'm going to be able to sing, and she says why don't I wear my orange hat. That might do the trick.

I have about a hundred and one butterflies in my tummy when I look at my watch. It is 11.30 already. Soon we will be walking down the garden. So much depends on this Mercy Concert with two songs.

Finn comes puffing through the door. The last thing he took down was a big tin of biscuits. He says my rug is on the other side of the yew trees, and there's a rug for Sarah too. The roses are there already. Mummy has made them look lovely. The magpie cage is all set.

Nanny Jan comes in, bringing me a cardigan in case I get cold in the shade. Sarah says she will be all right. I play the 'Evening Prayer' through one more time. Nanny Jan takes Finn upstairs to change his shorts. He is going to wear his smart navy-blue party ones.

Mummy comes into the nursery and I have never seen her look prettier. Her dress is lime green with a pale pink belt. She comes forward and kisses me.

'This is *your* day, Camellia,' she says. 'Your roses are waiting for you. We are all waiting for you.' Then she smiles. 'And we mustn't be late!'

I pick up Mr Fox and hold him tight. If Mr Impey has done his job, then he and Gran will be walking up the garden right now.

We walk down the lawn, ready to meet them. Sarah and I are in the lead, with Banger running through the sun and shadows. I look round to see Mummy, Daddy and Finn, all in a row. Nanny Jan waves at me from behind. She's carrying Mr Impey's violin.

This is it.

CAMELLIA

Sarah and I find our rugs and sit down. I sit in the middle of all the things Finn has put on mine. Dorothy Baby lies fast asleep on the rug and Heidi sits up beside her, both eyes closed. I give her face a tap and one eye opens. The *Harry the Dirty Dog* book is here, along with a very small piece of seaweed, and three fir cones. There are two oranges and an apple and to my surprise quite a large branch of rowan. Banger settles down beside me.

Nanny Jan comes around the corner to give me the violin, still in its case. Mummy, Daddy and Finn are on the other side of the yew trees, because Mr Impey felt it would be too much for Gran if she had to face a big audience. Nanny Jan wishes me all the luck in the world and disappears.

Sarah peers over the ha-ha. She says she doesn't want to see another hoof coming out of the ground. A magpie chatters overhead.

'She must be near,' I say.

'Good luck Melia!' It is Finn calling. I hear Mummy telling him to be quiet.

'Look!' cries Sarah. She points into the field.

There in front of us is a great shimmering of light, growing ever bigger and brighter with every second, and out of it steps Mercy and Nara. They are coming through the portal. It's as if Mercy is a queen with little Bo at her heels.

I climb to my feet and step forward to greet her.

'I'm scared,' Sarah says.

'Don't be.' I make a curtsey to Mercy. 'I'm going to do my very best.'

I turn towards the voices coming up the garden path.

They are here.

CAMELLIA

Mr Impey leads Gran forward into our part of the garden. Her face is pale and she has red spots on her cheeks, just like mine. She's wearing a summer dress, the sort she wears for church and her hair is flat. She holds the letter in one hand, and a white handkerchief in the other. Poor Gran, she doesn't look very well. Sarah doesn't really know how to greet her, so she curtseys. Mr Impey bows. I go forward to give Gran a kiss.

'I don't know what I'm doing,' she whispers, glancing about her. I think she needs a chair, so Sarah runs round to the others. She returns, dragging a green chair behind her, and Mr Impey helps set it up for Gran. We hadn't thought of this in our plan. Poor Gran is ready to collapse, and we are just in time as she sinks into the chair.

'I read the letter.' She waves it at me. Then she brings the handkerchief up to her mouth. 'So very sad. I can hardly bear it.' Her face crumples.

Mr Impey is busy getting his violin out of the case. He tests the strings with his bow. A thrush begins to sing in the tree behind us. It's his midsummer song.

We are ready.

Mercy rises up out of the ha-ha and on to the lawn. Nara tosses her head in the field. She is good at waiting. Bo scrambles up the wall and wags his tail beside Mercy's skirts.

'She's here, Gran,' I say. 'Your Mummy is here.' Gran's face is a mask of misery.

'But I can't see her. It's as if I'm blind! Where is she?'

'I see her,' Mr Impey says, nodding at Sarah.

'I see her too,' Sarah says. 'And her hunter-horse and little dog.'

'She's here, Gran,' I say gently. 'You have to believe in her to see her. *Believing is seeing.*' I raise my arms to the sky.

Mr Impey is all set to play 'Silent Night' and Sarah takes a deep breath. I can tell she's very nervous. I wave my hand to stop them for a moment. I need to say something else to Gran.

'Gran?' She turns wearily towards me. 'I want you to think of all the people and things and places you love. Put your hand on your heart like this, and then fill your heart. Close your eyes, Gran. You can do it. *Please!*'

Gran closes her eyes and I give the nod for Mr Impey to begin 'Silent Night'.

He plays beautifully and Sarah sings beautifully. She sings like an angel and it's strange, yet wonderful to hear 'Silent Night' in June. After Mr Impey does his last sweep of the violin, I very gently ask Gran to open her eyes.

She says she can see a little red dog, she really can. Mr Impey catches my eye, holding the violin high above his head.

'*It is happening,*' he says.

'Who is that little red dog?' Gran asks, leaning forward in her chair. 'He seems so familiar.'

I breathe out and tell her it's Bo, her Mummy's beloved dog. Gran stares in wonder and Bo wags his tail.

Mr Impey catches my eye and I nod for him to start the 'Evening Prayer'. I am wearing my orange hat, and I am ready to sing. He plays the opening bars and I know I shall sing my heart out, just like the thrush singing above. My voice is different but it's strong. This song is in my soul and I reach the high notes with ease. I could sing forever! The fourteen angels are surely with us now.

Gran stands up and takes a step forward towards Mercy.

'I see her!' she cries. We hold our breath as Mercy throws open her arms for joy. Then she brings them together again with a rocking motion, as if she's holding a baby. I have never seen her with a baby before.

'There's my mother,' Gran's hands are held in prayer.

'Can you see the baby, Gran?' Gran says she can.

'That's YOU!' I cry. 'The baby is you. You are with your Mummy. You are with Mercy.'

I step forward to take Gran's hand in mine. A magpie appears, perching on the cage in front of us. His eye is kind.

We stand together and Mercy smiles at us. It's a beautiful smile full of love. We watch as she rocks her baby and I know that Gran is crying. I don't have to look at her to know, but I know they are good tears. I am crying too, and I let the tears run down my face.

From the corner of my eye I see Finn and Mummy, peering round the yew tree. I wave and Finn waves back. Sarah stands with Mr Impey, quietly witnessing the phenomenon.

Mercy gently rocks her baby, kissing the tiny head over and over again. But already she's becoming fainter and I know she will soon be gone, as will Bo. Nara has already disappeared.

'Goodbye Mercy,' I say.

In that moment I feel the blood coursing through my body, giving me strength. I know I am completely well again. The magpie flashes his wings and is away. I take Gran's hand again and squeeze it.

'See?' I say.

Her eyes are full of tears and she says just two words:

'My mother.'

PART VI

CAMELLIA
Middleton-on-Sea

We arrive at our seaside cottage on the afternoon of Friday, 16th August, two days before Gran's birthday. Nina finds me while Finn and I are running around the garden and she's pleased I'm wearing the orange hat.

'I'm so excited to see you again!' she cries. 'And Finn too!' Finn runs round in circles to show how pleased he is. Nina hugs me and asks if I'm well. I nod happily. I hope she received my letter, telling her about Gran and Mercy?

'I sure did,' she says. 'And I've made you the most beautiful kite, with pink, green and violet ribbons, just as you asked.'

Finn jumps up and down, saying he wants Nina to show it to him right *now*. He will burst if she doesn't. Nina laughs and tells him he will have to wait.

'All it needs is for you and your Gran to draw or paint on the material. My mum found some cream-coloured silk and we've stretched it nice and tight so it's easy to draw on.'

'Oh Nina! You are so kind to do this.' Nina gives a big smile and her hazel eyes shine.

'How could I not, dear friend?' She looks around the garden. 'Is your ghost here?'

I tell Nina that Mercy stays with Gran now. I miss her a bit but it's right she spends time with her daughter. Whenever Gran goes for a walk in her garden, Mercy is with her, and Gran says she finds it a great comfort. She also tells me how the rowan berries have turned orange, and Nina's pleased to hear this.

'And look at you!' Nina says. 'Not thin any more and nearly as brown as me!'

'I am *completely* well,' I say. 'And full of beans and fun.'

Finn brings Mummy out to meet Nina. They say hello and smile at one another. Mummy's quite different now because she doesn't spend all day on the telephone, and she laughs a lot. We have practised our oil painting together and last week Mummy even asked if she could learn how to play the 'Bossa Nova'. She wasn't very good, but at least she tried.

Finn runs back into the house, saying he wants Daddy to meet Nina. Poor Nanny Jan is still sorting stuff out.

Now Finn pulls Daddy across the lawn and Daddy pretends to fall over, laughing and joking. Daddy has changed a lot too. He has more time for us. I've even been riding with him through the woods now Robin is better. We ride and chat and there isn't a fox to be seen. We go early in the morning when it's cool, and then we come back and eat breakfast together in the nursery.

Nina tells Daddy she has made a fine kite and he claps his hands. He says he absolutely loves kites.

'This one's specially for Mercy though,' I say. 'Gran and I are going to fly it together and set Mercy free.'

Daddy thinks that's a fine idea and, because Gran is coming over tomorrow, we'll have plenty of time to draw our pictures on it. He says he'll check the tide-table, so we know when conditions are best for kite flying. Nina gives me a look. She knows that already!

At last Nanny Jan joins us. She's delighted to see Nina again and admires her new blue swimsuit. Finn has found his yellow bucket and produces his last piece of seaweed.

'Bone dry!' he says, and we all laugh.

'That means the weekend is set fair,' Daddy says happily. 'We're going to have a grand time.'

The sky is blue and the garden is golden.

We are happy. We are a family.

CAMELLIA
Sunday, 18th August
Gran and I step out across the sand. We walk side by side with

Gran holding the kite close to her chest. I'm wearing my new turquoise swimsuit and Gran wears a pretty silk dress. We have bare feet and the sand feels warm. The tide is out but it's turning, and we walk out as far as we can. There's quite a breeze blowing from the east, and Nina says the conditions couldn't be more perfect for flying Mercy's kite. She wished us luck, calling from the end of her garden as we passed. I know she'll be watching.

Gran and I spent yesterday drawing pictures on the kite. I had to help Gran quite a lot because she isn't much of an artist. On the kite's four quarters there are violets and lily of the valley, a fox, a Christmas tree, the rowan with orange berries, Nara (Gran coloured her in), Bo (Gran coloured him in), a beautiful magpie and lots and lots of pink roses. Then I drew a sun and moon and some stars.

Nanny Jan took some photos with her camera, this time with a colour film. She took one of the kite lying flat on the lawn, as if it were flying in a green sky, then another of Gran and me holding it up between us.

Gran is very pleased with the kite because it's in the shape of the Cross. She feels that, as well as setting Mercy free to go to the Light, she's also going to Jesus.

We find a space away from the other bathers on the beach. It's a good strip of damp sand, just right for us to launch the kite into the air. Gran holds the little wooden handle, and in her pocket she has a tiny pair of embroidery scissors. They are for when we snip the string.

I hold the kite up and the ribbons flutter into my face, making me laugh. I shut my eyes, feeling a surge of pure joy. I could fly myself! The breeze is strong and the kite pulls and wants to lift. I shout for Gran to start walking backwards.

'Come ON, Gran!' I yell. 'You can do it!' Gran isn't sure. I dance up and down holding the kite high. The pink, violet and green ribbons are dancing with me.

Gran takes one more step backwards, the string grows taut and I let go. Mercy's kite takes off into the air and I run to Gran to show her how to let out more string. The kite soars up with a life of its own. It tugs and tugs and Gran lets the kite fly higher and higher.

'You're doing really well, Gran.' I pat her arm. 'What a wonderful kite. Aren't you proud?' Gran says she is. Her hair is blowing all over the place, but she doesn't care. We watch as the kite sails up into the August sky, becoming ever smaller.

'I've reached the end of the string,' she cries, turning the handle over. 'What do we do now? I've forgotten in all the excitement.' I reach into her pocket and bring out the scissors. Gran's eyes are watering, but it could be the wind.

'She wants to be free, Gran. She's ready. We can let her go.' We can see the kite is very small, pulling away. Gran's fingers have turned white from holding onto the handle.

I open the scissors to snip and Gran closes her eyes. The moment has come.

The kite is free. Gran holds the handle out, as if it's still attached, and we watch as Mercy's kite soars into the sunlight. We have to look away as the sun is too bright.

'She has gone to the Light,' I say.

'And Jesus,' says Gran.

CAMELLIA
The procession
('Shostakovich Piano Concerto No. 2 in F major', Andante.)

The sun is so bright that Gran and I have to shade our eyes. Anyone would think we were scanning the horizon for a ship, but instead we search the sky, hoping to see the kite for one last time. We squint into the sun, but it has gone from our sight. It has flown away, and we have set Mercy free.

Yet there is more from her.

We turn, ready to walk back across the sand and I see something in the distance. From the eastern side of the beach, a Procession is making its way towards us, growing ever closer.

It is Mercy, riding her hunter-horse Nara, while around

her and behind her are the ghost dogs. They walk just within the incoming tide and the sun makes patterns on the little wavelets. There is Bo wagging his tail, running beside Nara, and the others follow, trotting along with strong legs. I count four Labradors and five terriers.

As Mercy passes us, she dips her head and blows us a kiss. I give a little wave. I know she's at peace and she's guiding her animals to the Light. Gran recognises one of the dogs and gives a sharp intake of breath, more like a sort of sob. I take her hand and squeeze it.

The little waves run in through Nara's legs and Bo runs ahead. Mercy is walking on, away from us and taking her little party with her. This is goodbye.

We watch the Procession as it moves further and further up the beach and away. The sea splashes around our feet and we step back over the ribbed sand.

All we can see now is what looks like a mirage against the sunlight.

They are gone.

CAMELLIA

We walk back up the path to the house, feeling rather windswept. Gran says she will have to make her hair tidy before her birthday tea. I tell her that her eyes have never been bluer or prettier, and her cheeks are rosy. The sea air is doing us both good.

'I feel like a girl again,' she says, her bare feet covered in sand. 'I can remember what that feels like!'

We stand together in the little gateway to the garden and pause. There before us is the happiest scene. Two big umbrellas have been set out on the lawn with tables and chairs. This is specially for Gran's birthday tea. Finn is waving and there is Nina too. Mummy looks pretty in her blue and white dress, while Daddy and Grandpop are putting more chairs around the table. Nanny Jan is behind with a big teapot.

Mummy is clapping her hands and now everyone joins in.

As Gran and I step into the garden, a magpie swerves past to land on the grass right in front of us. We stop and watch him as he hops three times, before flying off with a flash of violet and green.

I take Gran's hand and smile up at her. I wonder if she knows what I'm going to say. I say it anyway.

'One for Joy, Gran. *One for Joy.*'

Epilogue

MERCY

Thank you my little one for everything. You were brave and true, and you never gave up. Indeed, while you were helping me, I was helping you.

For so many years I longed to be reunited with my beloved baby. In you I saw the way, and you did not let me down.

I am home now. I am loved. I am free.

I am the wave light.

I am the shine on the magpie's wing.

I am the radiance of the Camellia flower.

I am within 'Silent Night' and the 'Evening Prayer'.

For I am you, and you are me.

We are one and the same, you and I,

For now, my love,

and always,

Alathea

Acknowledgements

Heavens … where do I start? Well, first and foremost I will start with my husband, Johnny, for supporting me while writing the book, always encouraging me and dropping in the occasional very good suggestion. Thank you, Johnny, for reading each episode as it came hot off the press, as it were. To Sarah Impey for being my other episode reader, thank you. Indeed Sarah Impey is the same Sarah in the story. Before I started writing, she asked if she could be included in a minor way and I ran with it, not realising what a key character she would turn out to be! To Stephanie Franz with whom I discussed *The Magpie Winter*'s genesis and what sort of book it would be. I remember saying it would be a UNIVERSAL book to be read by any person of any age. Stephanie took me into the future when the book was already completed and huge thanks for that. To Debra Kilby for giving me the confidence and inspiration to get going, and for also advising me to read Dickens's *A Christmas Carol*, which I did.

To all my early readers for giving me such useful feedback, you know who you are, and thank you for letting me know which parts you found most scary. That always interests me. In fact I often ask people to think about the Hansel and Gretel story; which bit gets to them the most? Is it being abandoned in the woods? Is it being tricked by the witch? Is it Hansel in the cage? Try it yourself and see…

To my brother Shane, and his wife Katie, for listening to me while I rambled away on a long car journey to Gloucestershire, giving ideas for the plot. And thank you, Shane, for reminding me about having to climb on big books to reach the bolt on your chicken wire door!